Abigail knew her cheeks were bright red.

"Thank you for being so nice about this, Ethan. The gossip must be embarrassing for you."

Ethan knitted his brows. "Are you kidding? These ladies just made my day. Apparently, I'm the most eligible Amish bachelor in Kent County."

He leaned forward. "And speaking of such things, a pretty, smart woman like yourself—it will only be a matter of time before someone asks to court you." He held her gaze. "Almost makes me think I ought to—" He cut himself off.

Abigail hesitated. He'd been about to say something, but what? She thought to press him, but then her mother took off and she had to hurry after her. "See you tomorrow," she said.

"Tomorrow," Ethan answered. "Hey, Abby. What kind of cake are you making?"

"Lemon icebox," she responded. She didn't look back, but she could feel him watching her. Had he been about to ask if he could court her? Abigail's heart gave a little pitter-patter...

Emma Miller lives quietly in her old farmhouse in rural Delaware. Fortunate enough to have been born into a family of strong faith, she grew up on a dairy farm, surrounded by loving parents, siblings, grandparents, aunts, uncles and cousins. Emma was educated in local schools and once taught in an Amish schoolhouse. When she's not caring for her large family, reading and writing are her favorite pastimes.

Growing up on a farm, **Jocelyn McClay** enjoyed livestock and pursued a degree in agriculture. She met her husband while weight lifting in a small town—he "spotted" her. After thirty years in business management, they moved to an acreage in southeastern Missouri to be closer to family when their eldest of three daughters made them grandparents. When not writing, she keeps busy hiking, bike riding, gardening, knitting and substitute teaching.

EMMA MILLER

A Summer Amish Courtship

&

JOCELYN McCLAY

Amish Reckoning

LOVE INSPIRED
INSPIRATIONAL ROMANCE

LOVE INSPIRED®
INSPIRATIONAL ROMANCE

Recycling programs
for this product may
not exist in your area.

ISBN-13: 978-1-335-50995-6

A Summer Amish Courtship and Amish Reckoning

Copyright © 2021 by Harlequin Books S.A.

A Summer Amish Courtship
First published in 2020. This edition published in 2021.
Copyright © 2020 by Emma Miller

Amish Reckoning
First published in 2020. This edition published in 2021.
Copyright © 2020 by Jocelyn Ord

This edition published by arrangement with Harlequin Books S.A.

For questions and comments about the quality of this book, please contact us at CustomerService@Harlequin.com.

Harlequin Enterprises ULC
22 Adelaide St. West, 40th Floor
Toronto, Ontario M5H 4E3, Canada
www.Harlequin.com

Printed in U.S.A.

CONTENTS

A SUMMER
AMISH COURTSHIP

Emma Miller

Two are better than one.
—*Ecclesiastes* 4:9

Chapter One

"Tietscher!" eight-year-old Mary Fisher cried. She ran up the steps, her prayer *kapp* strings bouncing, and through the open doorway into the cloakroom of the schoolhouse. In the cold months, coats, cloaks and hats were hung on hooks on the wall. In the warmer months, it became a clutter catchall for lunch pails, fishing poles, overlooked homework and muddy boots. "Teacher, come quick!"

Ethan Miller was busy lining up his students' lunch boxes on two shelves he'd built and just hung on the back wall. Without the shelves, the lunch boxes, bags and pails were all over the floor and constantly being knocked over. That morning, a peanut butter and raisin bread sandwich wrapped in wax paper had ended up on the bottom of someone's shoe and John B. had enjoyed Ethan's egg salad for lunch. Ethan had had an apple.

"Tietscher!" Mary exclaimed, waving both hands in the air. "It's him again!"

"English, please," Ethan instructed. He slid a wrinkled brown paper sack with the name Jacob S. scrawled across it onto the lower shelf. He'd painted the shelving a dark navy blue and he had to admit, for having made it from pine scraps from his father's woodpile, it had turned out nicely. "What's going on?"

The petite third grader huffed, peering at him through tiny wire-framed eyeglasses. She switched to English. "He's going to knock it over and she's inside!"

Ethan liked Mary Fisher. She was a good student and was kind to the younger children, but she could also be a tattletale. Which was probably expected from a girl who was the youngest of a family of fifteen children. The Fishers ran the youth group in Hickory Grove and everyone joked that it made sense considering the fact that they had enough children to have a youth group of their own.

Ethan looked down at Mary, trying not to be perturbed by the interruption. Not only did Mary Fisher like to tattle, but she tended to add drama to any event. A scratch on an arm became a broken bone. A boy tossing a stone could become a gang of teens throwing rocks and sticks.

Ethan took a moment to calm his irritation. His students had been outside only ten minutes without his supervision. All he wanted to do was finish installing the shelves. How much trouble could anyone get into in ten minutes? And he'd left two fifteen-year-old girls in charge, girls who could certainly be counted on to keep an eye on younger children for a few minutes.

Apparently they *couldn't* be trusted today.

Ethan didn't usually have recess this late in the day. In an hour he would dismiss his students, but it was so pretty outside, and spring had been late in coming that year. The students were all eager to get out into the sunshine after such a long, cold winter. That was why he'd given them half an hour, time enough for him to hang the new shelves. His plan was to then bring his students in and have a spelling bee. It was one of the events he had planned for their end-of-the-year program, which was to include a fund-raiser, the exact nature of which had yet to be decided.

Ethan added a tin lunch bucket to one of the shelves. "Who are we talking about, Mary?"

"Jamie Stolz!"

Ethan exhaled impatiently. He should have known.

Jamie was his new student. He'd been with them only six weeks. And in those six weeks the boy had caused more turmoil than the other twenty-six students put together in his one-room schoolhouse. Ethan squinted. "*What's* he going to do?"

"That's what I'm trying to tell you. He's rocking the girls' outhouse," Mary wailed, pushing her glasses up the bridge of her nose. "He's going to knock it over and Elsie Yoder is inside!"

"What?" Ethan looked down at the little girl, certain he'd misheard.

Mary's head bobbed, hands flapping. "Jamie is rocking the outhouse and he says he's going to knock it over! With Elsie inside!"

Ethan strode past his student. "Jamie Stolz!" he bellowed taking the schoolhouse steps two at a time. Behind the one-room building, he spotted a group of children gathered around the two outhouses that stood side by side, one for boys, one for girls. Both had small privacy fences in front of them.

"What's going on here?" Ethan asked, walking across the grass. Off to the left he saw several boys involved in a game of softball. To the far right, a group of teen girls huddled in a tight circle, their heads together, oblivious to the outhouse drama. His two appointed guardians were among them.

"Jamie, Teacher," Alfie, a third grader answered morosely. He hooked his thumbs through his suspenders. "He's being bad again."

Just then, a squeal arose from behind the girls' privacy fence. "Help!"

Ethan could see the top of the outhouse above the fence. It didn't appear to be rocking. But then he'd dug the foundations for the new outhouses the previous summer so he knew they were pretty stable.

"Elsie?" Ethan called.

"Teacher!" she shrieked.

Ethan halted at the little fence and peered under it. He didn't see Jamie.

Ethan hesitated, not sure what to do. It wouldn't be proper of him to go to the outhouse door with the little girl inside. "Elsie, just come out here!"

"I can't get out!" Elsie shrieked. "Door's stuck!"

"Jamie? Where are you?" Ethan called sternly. Then he heard a loud rapping on the rear wall of the outhouse.

Elsie began to cry.

"Mary Judith!" Ethan called in the direction of the cluster of teen girls who were still unaware of what was going on. "Could you come get your sister?"

The blonde teen with a blue scarf tied on her head looked up in surprise to hear her name and then hurried toward him.

"Go see if you can get your sister out," Ethan instructed. He turned around to the other students gathered in a semicircle. They were all talking at once. One of his first graders was crying. "Recess is over," he declared, pointing toward the schoolhouse. "Inside. Peter, get the boys off the ball field," he told one of his more responsible students.

Then, as Mary Judith walked behind the privacy fence, Ethan headed for the rear of the outhouses, which were on the edge of a small copse of trees. The woods were just beginning to spring to life and everywhere were shoots of new green leaves. "Jamie!" he called. "Jamie Stolz!"

Ethan came around the corner to see blond-haired Jamie shoving a thick branch between the girls' outhouse and its foundation. "Jamie," he barked just as the boy prepared to leap on the branch. And rock the outhouse again.

"Yes?" the little boy asked, taking a stumbling step back.

"I have her, Teacher," Mary Judith called from the other side of the outhouse. "Someone put a stick through the latch!"

"Everyone inside!" Ethan ordered again to the stragglers who'd not heard or obeyed his first command, trying not to transfer his displeasure with Jamie to the other children. He imagined they were as frustrated with the boy as he was. He was a constant disruption in the classroom: talking, throwing bits of paper, rocking loudly in his chair. And on the playground, he spent most of his time teasing younger children. "Everyone in the schoolhouse. Now, please." He turned back to his errant student. "Jamie, why would you do this?"

The boy tucked his hands behind his back. He was wearing denim pants, a pale blue shirt, suspenders and a straw hat. He looked like the other male students, yet he didn't. Most boys in Hickory Grove wore hand-me-downs. The clothes Jamie wore, though homemade like everyone else's, were all brand-spanking-new.

Ethan grabbed the stick Jamie had shoved under the outhouse and tossed it into the woods. "How did Elsie get locked inside?"

"I don't know."

Ethan pressed his lips together and glanced away, trying to calm the anger rising from his chest. If there was one thing he couldn't abide, it was a liar. He returned his gaze to his new student. "Did you lock Elsie in the outhouse?"

The boy stared at the ground.

"Why were you trying to tip it over?" Ethan pressed. "Jamie, if the outhouse had tipped over with her inside, Elsie could have been seriously hurt."

Jamie kicked at a pile of acorns on the ground. "I wasn't going to knock it over. Too heavy. I was just rocking it."

Ethan exhaled, looking away again. He was momentarily unsure what to do. He'd certainly encountered mischief since he'd accepted the job of the Hickory Grove schoolmaster two years ago, but it always had been the same sort of innocent naughtiness: frogs in lunch pails, the snapping of suspenders, the tugging of *kapp* strings. Until Jamie's arrival, the biggest problem he'd had was little boys arriving at school late because they stopped along the way to throw rocks in a pond.

Ethan looked at Jamie. "Have you something to say for yourself?" He opened his arms wide. "Anything?"

The boy concentrated on his new leather boots that looked as if they'd never been in a barn.

Ethan thought for a moment. He'd already talked with Jamie's widowed mother three times in the last six weeks. Three times! That was more than he'd spoken to other parents *since September*.

Abigail Stolz seemed like a nice enough woman. Though each time he approached her she was defensive, suggesting it was he who was responsible for her son's misbehavior. As if a schoolmaster was solely in charge of his students' discipline. And she was forward for an Amish woman, which had annoyed him the first time he met her, then amused him the second time. Truth was, she reminded him a lot of his stepsister Lovey, a woman who wasn't shy about speaking her mind. And he adored Lovey.

Ethan glanced down at Jamie. He didn't see any way out of this. He knew what he needed to do. "Get in my buggy," he ordered. With the warmer weather, he'd started walking to school again. It was less than a mile's walk if he cut across the fields, less than two if he took the road home. He'd only brought the buggy this morning because he'd intended to run into Byler's store after school and order a piece of stovepipe. He and his father were installing a woodstove to keep their shop warm where they were making a buggy.

Jamie looked up at Ethan. *"What?"*

"I said get in my buggy. I'll send one of the big boys out to hitch up Butter." Butter was his horse. Her name was Butterscotch. His dead wife had named her that after they bought the dun at an auction. She had said the mare was the color of her homemade butterscotch pudding. His Mary had teased him that the mare wasn't the proper color for an Amish man's buggy, but Ethan had bought her anyway. Because his Mary had liked her. He'd been razzed for years about the color of his driving horse and her name. He didn't care. She was one of the few things he had left of his wife.

"I don't understand," Jamie said. His English was excellent. Often children started school with no knowledge of the English language. In Kent County, Delaware, children usually strictly spoke Pennsylvania *Deitsch*—a form of German, not Dutch, as many Englishers mistakenly thought they used—in their homes, so it was up to the schoolmaster to teach them English. Ethan had been concerned when Jamie had arrived from out of state that he would have come from a school where the children were taught in Pennsylvania *Deitsch*. It happened in some places. But his concerns had been quickly dispelled; Jamie spoke English as well as Ethan did. And his diction might have been better.

"What do you not understand?" Ethan asked, beginning to lose his patience again. He was exasperated that the boy wasn't better behaved and exasperated with himself that he wasn't able to get him to act better. He was also annoyed with the child's mother. It was evident that she wasn't disciplining him. "I want you to get in my buggy and wait for me. I'm dismissing everyone early. And I'm taking you home." He pointed at the boy. "So I can speak to your mother. *Again*."

Jamie met Ethan's gaze and he thrust out his lower lip. "You're being mean to me. Everyone here is mean to me. I don't like this school."

"Jamie, no one is—" Ethan halted midsentence. There was no sense arguing with a nine-year-old. He knew better. And at this point, this was a matter for his mother to deal with. And if she couldn't, then…then he'd just expel the boy. Maybe that would get Abigail Stolz's attention.

* * *

"Buggy!" Abigail's mother announced from the back door. "Babby! Buggy coming!"

"Are you expecting someone?" Abigail asked, walking away from the kitchen sink as she dried her hands on a towel, a red-and-white one with a rooster on it. It wasn't a Plain towel; it wasn't the kind most Amish women had in their homes. But her mother had spotted it at Spence's Bazaar the previous week and had made such a fuss about wanting it that Abigail's father had bought it for her.

"It's not Plain," Abigail had argued under her breath as they'd gotten into line to pay for it. "We're new to Hickory Grove still, *Dat*. What will our bishop think?"

"What will he think?" he had asked as he peeled off dollar bills from a wad in his pocket that he kept together with a rubber band from a bunch of bananas. "He'll think I'm a husband who indulges his wife once in a while. That's what he'll think."

"But it's red, *Daddi*," Abigail had murmured.

"That's why she likes it," he had whispered back with a smile.

Abigail walked to the back door and peered out the window. There actually *was* a buggy approaching. It was not one of her mother's false alarms. Abigail didn't recognize the horse, though. It was a pretty light brown, almost caramel shade. Not the color horse one often saw pulling an Amish buggy. "Cover your head, *Mam*," she instructed absently, still watching out the window.

June's hands flew to the tight bun of thin hair that had grayed long ago. "Where's my *kapp*, Babby? Someone's taken my *kapp*."

"No one's taken your *kapp*. You've put it somewhere and I can't find it. It's been missing since morning."

Abigail walked into the mudroom that was off the kitchen and grabbed a dark blue scarf from a rusty nail in the wall. Her father had finished a lot of work in the last eight months since he and Abigail's mother had bought the property, but there was still a lot to be done. One item on Abigail's lengthy to-do list was to add pegs to the walls in the mudroom that also served as a laundry room. It just seemed uncivilized to her, to be hanging coats and cloaks and hats on nails.

"I don't like that scarf," June fussed, trying to push her daughter's hands away as Abigail wrapped it neatly around her mother's head, covering her hair. For modesty's sake, no one but a woman's husband was supposed to see her bare head.

"I want the pink one," June fussed.

"We don't wear pink scarves, *Mam*." Abigail deftly tied the scarf at the nape of her mother's neck. "There you go." She smiled as she smoothed the fabric at her mother's forehead. "All done."

June King was a small woman, frail in appearance. But even though she was seventy years old, she was as strong as an ox, especially when she took a notion to put up a fight. Which was happening with more frequency, in Abigail's opinion. Her father, however, disagreed. He either downplayed his wife's inappropriate behavior and speech or denied it altogether. Abigail knew that deep in her father's heart, he must know his wife of fifty years was showing signs of dementia, but she suspected he wasn't yet ready to face the truth.

"Who's here, Babby?" June asked, as excited as a

young girl going to her first singing. "Do you think it's the bishop?"

"I don't know who it is. Maybe a neighbor," Abigail responded.

"I think it's the bishop."

"*Ne*, I think not." Abigail walked back across the kitchen to turn down the apple butter simmering on the stove. She'd found some apples no longer in their prime in the cellar and decided to do something with them before they spoiled. "Bishop Simon's driving horse is black."

Outside, Abigail's father's dog, Boots, began to bark. He was an old border collie, mostly deaf and suffering from arthritis, but he still managed to stand watch over the farm. When her parents had moved to Delaware the previous fall and taken the dog with them, Abigail's son had missed him dearly. When she and Jamie had arrived in Delaware, Jamie had been as excited to see the dog as his grandparents.

"Oh, my! It's that handsome schoolmaster!" June declared, clapping her hands. She pushed open the screen door and walked out onto the back porch, leaving the door wide open.

"The schoolmaster?" Immediately concerned, Abigail dropped the wooden spoon she'd been using to stir the apple butter onto the counter. It fell so hard that it bounced. "What's he doing here?" She glanced at the round, black-and-white battery-powered clock on the kitchen wall. It was only two forty-five. School wasn't out for another fifteen minutes.

Abigail hustled to the open back door, her heart fluttering in her chest. It had to be Jamie. Was he ill? Had he been injured? She fought the panic rising in her chest as she went down the porch steps and into the driveway, walking past her mother.

"Schoolteacher!" June greeted, waving eagerly. "So glad you could stop by. Come in for coffee and apple streusel! My daughter makes a fine streusel!"

"*Mam*, shush," Abigail murmured. "It's not proper calling out to a man like that."

Now that the buggy was closer, Abigail could see that it was indeed the schoolmaster. And her Jamie. She could see her little boy through the buggy's windshield. He didn't look ill, or injured, but why else would the teacher be bringing him home in his buggy? And early, no less.

Abigail hurried out into the middle of the driveway, catching the pretty mare's halter as the buggy rolled to a stop. Boots barked and ran in circles around the conveyance.

Abigail went straightaway to the passenger's side and slid open the door. "Jamie? Are you all right?" she asked, trying as best she could to hide her alarm. "What's wrong, *sohn*?" She reached out to him to take him in her arms. He was really too big for her to carry anymore, or even hold in her lap. And he didn't like it. But Jamie was her baby boy, her only child. A mother couldn't be criticized for caring about her child, could she?

"I'm all right," Jamie said, pushing his mother away. "I'm fine. I can get down myself."

Abigail clasped his cheeks between her hands, looking into his brown eyes. He *looked* fine. Not sick at all. "Not hurt?" she asked.

"Not hurt or sick," the schoolmaster said dryly, pulling the brake on the buggy.

His name was Ethan Miller. Abigail had met him
several times. They were part of the same church district. The schoolmaster had also stopped by the house
a couple of times as he walked home from school—
to complain about her son's behavior. She didn't care
for Ethan Miller. He was grumpy and he expected too
much of Jamie too soon. The poor boy had just moved
halfway across the country. His life had been turned
upside down like an apple cart: leaving his friends in
Wisconsin, living with his grandparents, joining a new
community. Who could expect there wouldn't be a few
bumps in the road?

The schoolmaster got out of the buggy and walked
around to Abigail. He was a tall man, slender, with
blond hair, brown eyes and a carefully trimmed beard.
Some might have thought him handsome, and maybe
in other circumstances, she might have, too.

The border collie sniffed at the schoolmaster's heels
and then wandered away.

"I brought Jamie home because we had a problem at
school today," the schoolmaster said. *"Again."*

Abigail looked down at her son who was now standing beside her. "Go into the house with your *grossmami*," she told him, stroking his shoulder. "She'll find
you a snack."

Jamie smiled up at her. *"Ya, Mam."*

"I'm not making him a snack, Babby," her mother
put in. She was standing on the far side of the driveway,
but she had heard every word. Abigail's father was losing his hearing but her mother's was as good as her own
and it seemed as if she never missed a thing. "Jamie's
been naughty. I don't make snacks for naughty boys."

The schoolmaster glanced June's way and then returned his gaze to Abigail. "Actually, I'd like Jamie to stay here. And tell you for himself what he did."

Abigail looked at her son, then at the schoolmaster. "I don't understand."

When the teacher didn't say anything, she turned her stare back to Jamie. "What did you do?"

"I didn't mean to, *Mam*," Jamie said, pouting. "I'm very hungry. Could I have my snack?"

"Tell her," the schoolmaster said, using a tone of voice that Abigail didn't much care for. Who did he think he was, speaking to a young boy so harshly?

"Please, *Mam*?" Jamie whined. "I'm so hungry." He touched his forehead. "I'm feeling dizzy."

"Tell her," the schoolmaster repeated, lowering his voice until it was little more than a rumble.

"Tell her, you naughty boy!" June called from the other side of the driveway.

Jamie's eyes filled with tears. "I tried to tip over the girls' outhouse. I just wanted to see if I could do it." The words tumbled out of his mouth. "I was trying to use a lever. Like *Grossdadi* taught me. I didn't know Elsie was inside! I didn't want to hurt anyone."

Abigail's eyes widened. "You tried to tip over an outhouse? With someone inside?"

He grabbed the hem of her apron. "I didn't mean to, *Mam*!"

"There, there," Abigail soothed, stroking his blond curly head. "It's all right."

"It's *not* all right," the schoolmaster said. Now he was taking on a tone with *her*. "It was dangerous, what he did. Then he lied to me and when he finally *did* admit what he'd done, he wasn't even apologetic."

"I am sorry, *Mam*! I am," her son cried into her apron.

"He says he sorry," Abigail returned stiffly, meeting the schoolmaster's gaze.

"He's not sorry he did it. He's sorry he got caught." The schoolmaster brought his hand to his neatly trimmed beard and stroked it. "And that's not good enough, Abigail."

"Oh it isn't, *Ethan*? For whom?" She let go of Jamie to take a step closer to the schoolmaster. Her irritation was rising by the second. Her father had always said her quick temper was her worst trait, but sometimes she thought maybe it was her best. Life had been hard as a single woman since her husband's death and it had been her experience that sometimes standing up to men got things done when nothing else would.

"That's bad, tipping over outhouses," June put in from the far side of the driveway.

Ethan stood there in front of Abigail for a moment. He glanced away, then back at her. Maybe he had realized that she wasn't a weak-minded woman who could be pushed around by any man who wanted to give her advice on how to raise her son.

"This is the *fourth* time I've had to speak with you about Jamie's behavior at school," Ethan intoned, "and I'm ready to just ex—" He took a breath and glanced at her son. "Go with your grandmother," he said quietly.

Jamie took off for the house and Ethan met Abigail's gaze.

For some reason, his soft tone made her angrier than if he had just raised his voice to her. And who did he think he was to be ordering her son around after school hours? "You're ready to just what?" she demanded.

"Expel him," he answered flatly.

"Expel? *Expel* him?" Abigail sputtered.

"In my day, boys were paddled," June called. "That's what my *dat* did when my brothers were bad. A good switching is what this boy needs, Babby."

Abigail whipped around to her mother. "*Mam*, please see to your grandson. *Inside.*" She turned back to the schoolmaster.

"You've left me with little other choice. If Jamie's behavior doesn't improve, he's out," Ethan said. "I've asked you *repeatedly* to rein your son in and so far, I've seen no improvement. He doesn't turn in his school-work, or when he does it's not complete. He doesn't listen," Ethan said, ticking off on his fingers. "He's disruptive, disrespectful and out of control."

"*Out of control?* He's nine years old!" Abigail pointed toward the house in the direction Jamie had just gone. "And what does that say of you, Ethan?" She placed her hands on her hips. "A teacher who can't control one little mischievous boy?"

"*Mischievous?*" Ethan flared. "*Ne*, his behavior is beyond mischievous. What about last week when he cut the strings off Martha's prayer *kapp* with scissors? What of the cow pie he put in Johnny Fisher's bologna sandwich? What about—"

"You know what I have a mind to do, Ethan Miller," Abigail interrupted, gritting her teeth.

Ethan rested his hands on his hips. "What?" he demanded.

"I have a mind to go to the school board and have you dismissed."

He laughed, which made her even angrier. If that was possible.

"Dismissed under what grounds?" Ethan scoffed.

"On your lack of control in the classroom," she told him. She folded her arms over her chest. "What kind of teacher are you that little boys can get away with such things? It's clear to me that you are unable to control your students and that…that you should be replaced immediately because you—" she pointed at him "—are obviously not doing your job."

"*My job* is not to teach your child how to behave." He pointed back at her. "That is *your* job. It's obvious the boy needs discipline at home."

Abigail drew back, dropping her arms to her sides. Somewhere in the very back of her mind, she knew he had a point, but he had made her so angry that she couldn't think straight.

Ethan walked away. "Get your son under control or I'm expelling him," he warned.

"I certainly hope you don't speak to your wife with that tone," she flung back at him.

Without another word, the schoolmaster got into his buggy, turned around in the driveway and headed out the way he'd come. Abigail watched him until he was halfway down the lane and then marched toward the house. Who did Ethan Miller think he was? How dare he threaten to expel her son! She passed her mother who was still standing there beside the driveway.

June watched her daughter walk by. "What do you think of the schoolteacher, Babby?" she asked brightly. "Me?" She broke into a broad smile, not giving Abigail a chance to respond. "I *like* him."

Chapter Two

Ethan took his time seeing to Butterscotch, leading her to the water trough and then giving her a good brushing until her coat gleamed. Afterward, he fed her a scoop of oats and set her loose in the pasture to graze until sunset when he'd put her up in the barn for the night. He knew it was foolish, but the time he spent with the mare made him feel closer to his wife, more than five years gone now. Closer to her in memory at least. How she'd loved the mare, their little farm in upstate New York, their quiet life. How she had loved him.

He'd been so lost after her unexpected death that he thought he might die of his grief. He didn't, of course, just as his wise father had predicted. And as the days turned into months, then years, though he hadn't stopped loving her, the pain was no longer so sharp. Now, after so much time had passed, more often than not, he smiled when he thought her, rather than cried.

Ethan stood beside the gate and watched Butterscotch wander off to graze in a bed of fresh, flowering clover. Then, his hands deep in his pockets, he walked down the lane toward the harness shop in search of his father. He was still mulling over his conversation with Abigail Stolz. He was hoping to talk with his father about Jamie and the boy's mother. Maybe he could offer a different perspective.

Ethan took his time walking, taking in the two-hundred-acre farm, its fields that were now turning green, white fencing, barns and outbuildings. In the two years since the family had moved to Hickory Grove from New York, Millers' shop had flourished. Despite the local competition of Troyer's just three miles away, his father had found ways to provide goods and services to both Amish and Englisher customers. Not only did he repair and make nearly any kind of leatherwork, but he also sold the type of supplies a man with livestock needed: liniments, wormers, fly and pest control traps and sprays, you name it. And that wasn't all he was selling these days.

A year ago, Ethan's stepsister Bay Laurel, who they called Bay, had started selling jams and jellies, fresh eggs, preserves, and baked goods. Her single shelf had turned into an entire aisle and his father was considering expanding the size of the store to keep up with the women's side of the business. Then there was Ethan's brother Joshua, newly wed, who had built a greenhouse over the winter and was about to open a business selling seedlings, flowers and vegetable plants.

All that, and Benjamin, his father, was still dreaming of expanding his business inside the huge dairy barn he'd remodeled. He wanted to go into buggy making. Ethan wasn't much for working in the harness shop. That was why he had taken the job of schoolmaster when the position had become vacant. But buggy making was quickly becoming a passion of his. He still had a lot to learn, but he liked using his hands to make a wheel, a door, a padded seat. Alone in the shop, or even working beside his father, he loved the peacefulness of it. No little girls squirming in their seats, no little boys bringing toads into the schoolhouse. No Jamie Stoltz trying to tip over an outhouse.

Ethan's annoyance with the boy came back in a single breath. Which turned to near anger toward the mother. He felt sorry for Abigail, a widow alone trying to raise a boy without a father, but surely she understood that it was her duty to control the boy's behavior. Ethan couldn't help thinking that if Jamie was bad at school, it was likely he wasn't all that well behaved at home either. He got that impression from the grandmother. He couldn't remember her name, though they'd been introduced at church. Daniel King, Abigail's father, and his wife had been in the harness shop a couple of times and they'd bumped into each other at a dinner celebrating Epiphany back in January. That was just before Abigail and her son had arrived in Hickory Grove. He had heard from his stepsister Ginger that she was widowed three or four years ago, though Ginger hadn't known any of the details. That fact alone gave him good reason not to judge the woman so quickly, but—

"Ethan? You okay?"

He looked up. He'd been so lost in his thoughts that he hadn't seen or even heard his sister-in-law, Phoebe, approaching.

"I thought you were going to walk right by me." She met his gaze with a smile. She was wearing a blue scarf tied around her head and the denim coat one of his stepsisters had commandeered. Ordinarily, Amish women didn't wear men's denim barn coats, even around their house, but there was nothing ordinary about his step-mother's girls. Or his brother Joshua's new wife.

"Uh, sorry, just thinking. *Ya*, I'm fine," he said. He liked Phoebe. She'd come from a hard life, bringing a little boy with her, but she'd managed to make a new life there in Hickory Grove. She was sweet and kind and fun, but the thing Ethan liked most about her was her resilience. He admired her ability to see beyond her troubles and find the goodness in the world God provided. He was beginning to think maybe he needed to take a page from her book. As much as he hated to admit that his father and stepmother, Rosemary, were right, it *was* time to move on with his life. He knew it was what his Mary would want. But he just… So far, he just hadn't been able to get there.

"Been down to the mailbox," Phoebe said. She held up a bundle of flyers and envelopes. "Something here for you. A bank statement, I think." She stopped in front of him, sifting through the pile in her arms. With a family their size—his father and stepmother, his stepsisters, stepbrothers, and brothers still living at home, as well as Phoebe and her son—they numbered fifteen at the supper table. And that was if his stepsister Lovey and her family didn't join them. They received a lot of mail.

"It's here somewhere," she said, still thumbing through the stack.

"Just leave it on the counter," he told her, turning so he was still facing her, backing down the driveway, hands deep in his pants pockets. "Have you seen my *dat*?"

"In the shop. In the back, I think. I stopped to see Ginger on the way to the mailbox. She's working the register."

He nodded, turned and continued on his way.

"See you for supper," Phoebe called after him.

His back now to her, he raised his hand in response.

Ethan found Ginger occupied at the register ringing up an English woman. "My *dat*?"

She nodded over her shoulder as she dropped fly paper into a brown paper bag. "Back in the buggy shop, I think. UPS delivered leather for seat covers."

Ethan went through the swinging half door to get behind the counter, then through the next door and into the leather workshop. He nodded to his brother Jacob who was busy with an awl punching holes in what looked to be a new bridle he was making. Beside him, seated on a stool, was their eleven-year-old stepbrother, Jesse, who was talking a mile a minute about a bass in their pond he was set on catching.

Ethan walked through the shop and into a hall where the newly constructed walls had drywall but no paint yet. Doorway cuts in the walls led to empty space now that could be turned into additional workrooms or an office if his father wanted to expand later. At the end of the hall, he found the door to the buggy shop open.

Benjamin Miller's door was always open, figuratively and literally, and not just to his wife and children and stepchildren, but to his community, as well. He was a good listener, but he also didn't hesitate to give his opinion if it was asked. His father was the wisest man Ethan knew and even though he had just had his thirty-third birthday, he was still young enough to need his father's guidance occasionally. Old enough to know it.

Benjamin turned on the stool where he sat at his workbench and peered over the glasses he wore for up close work. "Get that stovepipe?"

Ethan shook his head. "Didn't make it to Byler's. Had a problem with one of my students. Had to take him home. I'll go get the stovepipe tomorrow."

"Whenever you get to it will be fine." Benjamin looked up at his eldest son, reading glasses perched on his nose. In his fifties, he was a heavyset man with a reddish beard that was going gray, a square chin and a broad nose. Ethan had his father's brown eyes, but his mother's tall, slender frame.

"I'm hoping this break in the weather means we won't be needing to light that old woodstove 'til fall," his father went on, nodding in the direction of the stove they'd recently installed. His father had traded a new full harness for the stove with a man from over in Rose Valley. Benjamin liked bartering and did it whenever he could. He said it reminded him of his childhood back in Canada where he'd grown up. In those days, he said, paper money was rarely exchanged; a checking account was unheard of. The sizable Amish community relied mostly on themselves and traded for everything.

Benjamin turned back to the piece of paper he was studying on his workbench: a sketch of the buggy he and Ethan were building together. It was a small, open buggy, referred to sometimes as a courting buggy. "You said you had a problem with a student. Get it worked out?"

Ethan took a deep breath. He sighed, removed his wide-brimmed straw hat and ran his fingers through his blond hair. His gaze settled on the box on the cement floor that had been opened to reveal yards of leather they would use to upholster the new buggy's seat. "*Ne...* Well, maybe. I don't know."

Benjamin removed his glasses. "Want to talk about it?"

Ethan sighed again, and then the whole story just came out. It wasn't the first time he'd talked to his father about Jamie. He knew the boy had been a problem since he'd arrived at school, but still, he listened patiently, commenting or urging Ethan on as he relayed the most recent incident.

When Ethan was done, he dropped down on a stool near the door. "I've just had it, *Dat*. I've half a mind to—" He halted and then started again. "I've half a mind to resign, effective the end of the school year. If I give the school board notice now, they'll have time to find another teacher by September."

"That what you want to do? Quit teaching?"

Ethan set his hat on his knee, studying the courting buggy that was nearly complete. The project was so close to being done that Benjamin was already working on the plans for a more traditional family-sized buggy. "I don't know, *Dat*. I'm thinking maybe there's some truth to what Abigail said. Maybe I'm not cut from the cloth of a schoolmaster."

"Not sure I agree with that. Other folks in Hickory Grove would say you're the best teacher they've had for their children. Last Saturday over at the mill, John Fisher was talking about inviting some other Amish teachers—men and women—to our schoolhouse for a day for you to run some kind of training. To get teachers together to talk about ways to teach our children about the world we live in these days. It's not like in my day when we were isolated from Englishers. Insulated. No denying that as the world has changed, we've been forced to change. But that doesn't mean we have to give up who we are. That means we've got to deal with the changes not just in our homes and our church, but our schools, too. Men like you, you understand that. You understand how hard it can be for our children. To hear the music, see the behavior and not covet it."

Ethan worried his lower lip, thinking. Everything his father said was true. Teaching school wasn't easy, not with Amish kids being exposed to Englishers: the clothes, the cars, the behavior. You couldn't keep young folks on the farm all the time so they had to know how to deal with the world they were supposed to stand apart from. He knew they needed to be guided in how to stay on the path their ancestors had set out for them and school was one of the places they could find that guidance.

What Ethan didn't know was if he was really the one to be doing it.

"That said," his father went on, "if you do decide teaching isn't your calling, you know you can join me here." He gestured to the workshop they were both proud of. "Before you know it, Levi will be home and we'll be getting serious about production."

Over the winter they'd added an overhead door in the shop big enough to accommodate a buggy, and they purchased quite a few tools. A buggy maker had to be a welder, an upholsterer, a carpenter, mechanic and painter all rolled into one and he needed different tools for each aspect of the construction. Ethan's brother Levi was staying with friends in Lancaster, Pennsylvania, apprenticing as a buggy maker. His plan was to learn what he could over the next year or so and then return to Hickory Grove. At least that's why he said he'd moved to Lancaster, though Ethan suspected it was the larger population of single women that had attracted him to accept the position.

Ethan eyed his father. "You think we're ready to go into business, do you? So far, we've just made that new family buggy for ourselves and the one for Lovey and Marshall."

"And your courting buggy is nearly done." Benjamin smiled, pointing at the sleek black buggy that took up the center of the shop.

Ethan shook his head. "Not mine. Will and Levi would get more use of it. Jacob. Before you know, Jesse will be taking girls home from singings."

Benjamin hesitated. "I know you don't want to hear this—"

Ethan held up his hand. *"Dat—"*

"I know you don't want to hear it but I'm going to say it anyway." He got off his stool and walked toward Ethan. "Because it's my duty as your father to say things you don't want to hear."

Ethan rose, clamping his hat down on his head.

"It's time for you to marry again, *sohn.*"

Ethan shook his head, surprised by the emotion that rose up in his throat, threatening to prevent him from speaking. He took a moment. *"Dat,"* he said when he found his voice. "We've been over this a hundred times. I don't know that I'll marry again." He stared at a spot on the floor, embarrassed by the feelings welling up in him. His father was never one to tell his sons it was wrong to show emotion. Benjamin Miller was an emotional man, Ethan's brother Joshua, too. But Ethan wasn't like them. He didn't know what to do with his sadness, his loneliness, except tamp it down, close it off, stay one step ahead of it.

"You need to find yourself a nice young woman, marry, have children."

Ethan stood there, unable to meet his father's gaze.

Benjamin smoothed the straps of his suspenders and then went on. "You join me in the shop and we'll start making buggies not just for family and neighbors but we'll take orders from Pennsylvania, Ohio, Kentucky, even. Rosemary's cousin in Kentucky says that when we're ready, he'll be the first one to put cash on our workbench. He's running a buggy that was his grandfather's because there's no one making them down there."

Benjamin took a step toward Ethan. "I'm not getting any younger, you know. Rosemary and I, we've talked about building a smaller house here on the property. Once you older boys are married, and Rosemary's girls, we'll have no need for such a big house. You marry and start having little ones and the big house is yours. Someday I'll be gone and this farm, this family, will be yours. Now, you know I've got things worked out so you and all your brothers will have a piece of it, but you'll be the head of this family someday—you'll be here to father your little brothers should I pass before they're full grown men."

"Dat," Ethan murmured.

"Sohn, it's what God means us to do. A man is to marry. And to marry, you have to get out there and meet a woman, court a woman."

Ethan closed his eyes, beginning to regret having come to his father. After the day he'd had, he didn't need a lecture. *"Dat*, even if I did have a notion to court a woman, who would that be?"

"Plenty of single young women in Hickory Grove," Benjamin declared, gesturing with his hands.

"Young. Exactly. Can you imagine me with one of

Ginger's or Nettie's friends?" Ethan lifted his gaze to meet his father's.

Benjamin shrugged. "So you want a more mature woman. A little harder to find, but they're around. There's that niece of Eunice's who stays with them sometimes. Dottie? She's not much to look at, but she's a woman of faith."

Ethan almost smiled. He knew Eunice Gruber's niece Dottie, one of the many nieces the woman paraded in front of the single men of Hickory Grove and he knew her well enough to know Dottie wasn't the kind he would court. It wasn't her looks that he cared about. He truly believed that beauty was in the eye of the be-holder. It was Dottie's incessant giggling that bothered him. She might have been a woman over thirty, but she acted more like she was fourteen.

"I don't think Dottie is my type, *Dat*."

"Fine." He threw up his hands. "What about Abigail Stoltz? Nice-looking woman. She lost her husband. She understands what it's like to be alone, to—"

"Abigail?" Ethan demanded, almost laughing out loud. "*Dat*, did you not hear anything I said? She accused me of doing my job poorly. She threatened to have me *fired*." He shook his head adamantly. "I can guarantee you that if I took a mind to court a woman, she'd be the last one I'd pursue." He turned toward the door. "I need to move hay before supper. We're short in the barn."

"Just think on what I said," Benjamin called after him.

I'll think on it all right, Ethan said to himself as he walked out the door. Now he was as frustrated with his father as he was with Abigail.

* * *

"Amen," Daniel King announced heartily as he drew silent grace to an end. He clasped his calloused hands together, looking across the kitchen table at Abigail. He was plump to his wife's slenderness, his gray hair cut short in a bowl cut, his beard long and gray. His gray eyes twinkled with kindness when he spoke. "Looks good, *dochder*. Let's eat. I did a little plowing in the garden this afternoon and I'm hungry enough to eat this table."

Jamie giggled. "You can't eat a table, *Grossdadi*. You'd get splinters in your mouth. Knock out some teeth."

"Only if the teeth were loose." Daniel tousled his grandson's blond hair. "Like yours."

"Just this one." Jamie wiggled one of his front teeth with his fingers.

"Not at the table," Abigail chastised as she put a pork chop smothered in gravy and onions on her mother's plate and then her son's. She passed the serving dish to her father.

"I knew a boy who once ate a table," June said, heaping cinnamon applesauce onto her plate. "A big supper table we used to use for church dinners. Ten feet, I suspect. Chewed the boards to sawdust and had nary a splinter to swallow."

Jamie cut his eyes at his mother but didn't contradict his grandmother. Instead, he began scooping the gravy and onions off his pork chop and dumping them on his mother's empty plate.

Abigail gave her mother and her son a serving of mashed potatoes, then passed the bowl to her father. "More gravy on the stove if anyone wants some." She

glanced at her mother who was now spooning applesauce onto her pork chop. She rested her hand on her
mother's for a moment. "You won't like that, *Mam*,"
she said quietly.

"I like it," June declared loudly. "They're dry." She
dumped another spoonful on her pork chop.

"They're not dry, wife," Daniel put in, adding pats
of fresh homemade butter to his potatoes. "Abby makes
a fine pork chop."

"Dry as the boards in that table that boy Israel ate."
June began putting applesauce on top of her mashed
potatoes.

Abigail gently took the Ball jar of applesauce from
her mother and served her son.

"Not near the potatoes!" Jamie complained, laying
his hand across his plate.

"My day," Daniel said good-naturedly as he took
the quart of applesauce from his daughter, "a boy ate
what his mother put on his plate. That or he put his own
food on his plate. You're old enough to get your own
pork chop, boy."

Abigail tried to spoon green beans onto Jamie's plate,
but he held out his hand to her.

"I don't like green beans. No green beans."

"I'm only giving you three. You can well eat three
measly green beans," she said, irritation creeping into
her voice. She wasn't upset with Jamie, of course. It was
his teacher. It was Ethan Miller who had her struggling
to control her exasperation and think of him with kindness in her heart. She'd been stewing over him since
he'd brought Jamie home. She still couldn't believe the
nerve he had to come there and try to tell her how she
should raise her son.

"You don't like green beans with bacon?" Daniel scoffed. He took the serving bowl from Abigail. "Suits me just fine. More for me." He put a healthy portion on his plate and then a smaller one on his wife's. "Saw that the teacher brought Jamie home. Spotted that dun of his from the garden," he remarked, directing his comment to Abigail. "My grandson in trouble again?"

Abigail took a moment to gather her thoughts before she responded. She and her father got along well, but like all parents and adult children, especially those living together, they had their disagreements.

He had a lot to say about how she was raising her son, and much of it critical. He thought she coddled Jamie, that he was immature and that she expected too little of her boy. He'd actually used the word *discipline* the other day, the same word Ethan had used, which had annoyed her all the more. Men didn't understand the relationship between a woman and her only son. And neither knew what it was like to lose a spouse, to be raising a child alone.

Abigail stalled, using the time to cut up Jamie's pork chop for him as she chose her words carefully. "There was an incident at school today. Ethan wanted to talk with me about it."

"Naughty boy," June chastised, shaking her fork at her grandson.

Abigail pushed Jamie's plate back to him and began to serve herself helpings of the green beans, pork chops and potatoes. Then, suddenly remembering that she had buttermilk biscuits in the oven, she rose from her chair. "Oh, goodness. The biscuits. I don't think that pesky timer is working." She hurried for the stove, grabbing a hot mitt off the counter.

"What'd you do, Jamie?" Abigail's father asked.

As Abigail opened the oven, she glanced over her shoulder, waiting to hear what her son would say.

Jamie stared at his supper plate, his hands clasping it. "The kids are mean to me. They don't want to play with me at recess." He stuck out his lower lip. "I want to go home to Maple Shade."

"Oh, Jamie, you know that's not possible." Abigail pulled the pan of biscuits from the oven. Luckily, she'd caught them before they began to burn. "We sold our farm, remember? We live with your grandmother and grandfather now. We came to help them with the farm."

"What did you do?" her father repeated, putting a forkful of mashed potatoes into his mouth. "Mmm. Just like I like them. Lots of pepper." He eyed his grandson as he chewed and waited.

After a long moment of silence, Abigail said, "The schoolmaster said—"

"Daughter, let my grandson tell me. He can speak. He has a mouth."

"Oh, you're in trouble now," June said quietly. She reached for the jar of applesauce again.

Abigail dumped the pan of biscuits onto a plate and carried them to the table. "You have to eat something besides applesauce, *Mam*." She set the biscuits in the middle of the table and put one on her plate.

"He's in trouble," June responded, pointing at Jamie with a serving spoon that was heaped with applesauce. "That handsome schoolteacher brought him home because he tipped over the outhouse, girl inside." She plopped more applesauce on top of her potatoes.

"He didn't knock it over." Abigail gently took the spoon and the jar from her mother's hands and then slid into her chair. "Go on," she encouraged. "Tell your granddad what you did."

The boy pressed his lips together, slowly looking up. "I was trying to make a lever. Like you showed me at the barn the other day when you were trying to get the cardboard under the rain barrel. I wanted to see if it would work."

Abigail's father met her gaze but he held his tongue, though only until supper was over and Jamie had been excused. The boy took no time at all to race from the kitchen and out the back door, headed for the barn he said, to feed the cats.

"So the schoolteacher had to bring him home this time?" Daniel intoned as he carried a stack of dirty dishes to the sink. "Because of his behavior?"

June had taken her position at the sink to wash. It was a chore she could still do well, and she liked it. Abigail had taken over most of the cooking, but she let her mother wash dishes, understanding that it was important that she still contribute to the household.

"Wasn't there a problem last week?" Abigail's father pressed when she didn't respond.

Abigail carried the leftover biscuits, covered in a clean dishtowel, to the pie safe. "Jamie told me he didn't know Elsie was inside when he started rocking the outhouse."

Daniel left the stack of dirty dishes on the counter and went back to gather more. "You believe him?"

Abigail hesitated as she tried to puzzle out her thoughts. She had caught Jamie in a few fibs from time to time, but she didn't want to believe he'd intentionally risk injuring someone and then lie to cover it up. Ethan belicved Jamie *had* known the little girl was inside, which would mean Jamie had lied. Abigail didn't think Ethan would make up such a thing...which meant her son had told them an untruth. She had to face it.

"He's having a hard time, *Dat*. He misses his home, his friends. He still misses his *dat*."

"But didn't you tell me he was having trouble in school *before* you moved here? Not getting along with the other children, not doing his lessons. Wasn't that one of the reasons why you decided not to stay in Wisconsin until the end of the school year?"

Abigail closed the pie safe and just stood there for a moment. Her stomach was in knots. She'd barely eaten. She didn't know what to say to her father. She didn't know what to do to help her son. She turned slowly to face him. "It's a hard age."

"He could have hurt that girl."

Abigail took a handful of dirty eating utensils from her father's hand. "I understand that. And I'm going to talk to him."

Her father stood there looking down at her. She knew he had more to say on the matter, but thankfully, he didn't. Instead, he said quietly, "I want to help you, daughter. I want to help Jamie. He's the only grandson I have."

"I know you do." She squeezed his arm. "Why don't you go out and finish up your chores. *Mam* and I can take care of the dishes." She shrugged. "Maybe take Jamie fishing in the pond for a little while? He loves fishing with you."

Daniel nodded. "I can do that." He turned to go, then back to her. "But you know this isn't just going to right itself on its own, don't you? It's only going to get worse. Something has to change. You keep doing the same thing and it doesn't work, you have to change your approach."

"I'll talk to him, *Dat*." Abigail bit down on her lower lip. "And I'll think on it. Figure out what I need to do differently." Her thoughts immediately returned to her conversation with Ethan. He'd threatened to expel Jamie. She couldn't let that happen. Schooling was too necessary, and she knew she couldn't teach him at home, not with the house and her mother to deal with.

She closed her eyes for a moment, listening to her father's footsteps as he left the kitchen. She had been feeling overwhelmed for weeks. She had hoped that being here would make things easier for her and Jamie. She'd thought a change of scenery might help Jamie at school, but obviously, she'd been wrong. Her first impulse had been to blame the schoolteacher, but now she felt bad. He was just doing his job. And she'd lashed out at him. She'd raised her voice.

And now she owed him an apology. She just wasn't sure how to go about it.

Chapter Three

It turned out that the opportunity to speak to Ethan presented itself quickly enough. The following afternoon, Abigail was visited by Karl Lapp whose property adjoined her father's. He'd caught Jamie, who'd been on his way home from school, trying to "ride" one of his cows. One about to give birth. She'd made Jamie apologize to Karl and then as punishment, she told her son she would be walking him to and from school for the rest of the week.

"You can't walk me to the door," Jamie whined the next morning as he and Abigail turned into the driveway to the white clapboard schoolhouse. "The kids will see you. They'll make fun of me."

Abigail drew her heavy cloak closer. Even though the grass was beginning to turn green and the trees to blossom, it was still chilly in the mornings. She lifted her face to feel the morning sun, enjoying its heat and the promise of a new day. The sunshine brought her hope, hope that her mother would have a good day mentally, that Jamie's behavior would improve and that she wouldn't feel quite so lonely in the world. Certainly, she had her mother and father and son, and she was thankful for them. But there was an ache in her heart where her husband, Egan, had once been. She still missed him every day. Mourned him every day.

"Mam?" Jamie tugged at his mother's cloak, getting her attention. "Did you hear what I said? Someone's going to see you."

"We're early enough that I doubt it. Unless I *want* them to see me," she added looking at him sternly, hoping he would read it as a warning. She shifted the basket she carried on her arm. Inside was a peace offering of sorts for the schoolmaster. "Unless Karl catches you on one of his cows again. Then I might decide to come to school with you every day. I'll sit beside you and help you with your lessons."

"Please, no," Jamie groaned. "I won't do it again." He kicked a piece of gravel in the driveway. "I was just bored is all. It's a long walk home. That's why I went to look at the cows."

"It wasn't the looking that got you into trouble." When he didn't say anything, she went on. "You know how I feel about saying you're bored. There's always work you can do around the house. And it's a mile from here home so I don't want to hear it. When I was your age, I walked four miles to school each day. Then four miles home." She hooked her thumb over her back.

"No one here walks. All the kids have a push scooter," he complained.

"Not *everyone* has a scooter," she countered. The gravel crunched under her sneakers. "I see boys and girls walking past our place on the way to school every morning."

He bounced up and down on the toes of his boots.

He was growing so fast that she'd had to buy them new just before they left Wisconsin. Being her only child, and having no family nearby, there were no hand-me-downs. Everything had to be made or bought new.

"But I *want* a scooter."

"Don't whine, *sohn*. You're not a *boppli* anymore. And maybe you *can* have one. When your behavior is better." She walked up the steps to open the door to the schoolhouse. "When you're doing better with your lessons."

He stood at the bottom of the stairs to the schoolhouse and looked up at her. "You're not coming inside, are you?" he groaned.

"I am." She walked through the doorway and into the small coatroom. One long wall was lined with hooks for coats and bonnets and such, the other with windows. "I need to talk to your teacher for a minute." She handed Jamie his lunch pail.

"It goes up there." He pointed at shelves built on the wall across from the entrance.

"Then you should probably put it there." She eyed him in a way that she hoped would be reprimanding, and he scuffed his feet across the floor toward the shelving. She tapped on the inner door that led into the one-room schoolhouse and opened it.

Ethan didn't glance up from a large wooden desk at the far end of the room. The schoolhouse looked little different than the one she'd attended as a girl back in Wisconsin. The single room was square with plenty of windows on the opposite walls so they would get a good breeze in the warmer months. A large woodstove with a stovepipe going up through the roof in the center of the room was cold but would put out plenty of heat in the winter. There was the teacher's desk at the head of the room with a green chalkboard behind it. The remainder of the space was filled with wooden desks and chairs. The only difference she saw from her school days was that instead of lining the desks and chairs in rows facing the blackboard, the desks were pushed together to form groups. Some had as many as eight desks together, some had as few as two.

Abigail halted a few steps inside the door. The schoolmaster still hadn't looked up at her so she could study him unnoticed. Her mother kept calling him the handsome schoolteacher, which annoyed her because... well, because *he* annoyed her. But also because she did find him handsome in a married schoolteacher way.

She cleared her throat.

He looked up. "Abigail." He didn't smile.

She pressed her lips together having second thoughts about coming there. About preparing the lunch for him she carried in her basket. She'd made it because Jamie had told her, in passing, that most days his teacher didn't get to eat his lunch. He was always giving it to a student for one reason or another. Jamie told her that the previous day, Mary Fisher had left hers at home on her kitchen table. Mary had eaten the teacher's pork chop sandwich, his potato chips and peach cobbler. He'd had water from the pump outside.

"Ethan." She nodded, forcing a quick smile that came as fast as it went.

He rose from his chair, setting a red ink pen on his desk. Her son disliked his red pen and the marks in the form of an X Ethan made on his math papers. "Where's Jamie?" he asked.

"Hiding, I think." She nodded in the direction of the cloakroom.

"From me?" He came around the big red oak desk that had to be fifty years old if not older.

"From both of us, I think."

"You walked him to school. Because of the incident yesterday with Karl's cows?" He leaned against the desk, crossing his arms over his chest. He had on the same clothes every Amish man in Kent County wore, denim trousers, suspenders and a long-sleeved colored shirt. His was a pale green, faded with years of laundering, but unblemished by rips or tears. On his feet, he wore a pair of black athletic sneakers.

She glanced down at her own sneakers that were similar to his though hers were blue. "How did you hear? It was just yesterday." She looked up at him.

"Amish telegraph." The corners of his mouth turned up ever so slightly. "That's what my stepmother likes to call it. Let's see…" He raised his thumb, counting. "Karl's wife, Bitty, told Mary Fisher's mother, Edna." He held up his forefinger. "Who told my stepsister Lovey's grandmother Lynita, who told Eunice Gruber." He added two more fingers. "Who then told all of the women at the less-than-ten-items checkout register at Byler's store." He started counting on his other hand. "Who included my stepmother, Rosemary, and her friend Hannah Hartman." He dropped both hands. "And Eunice, I have to warn you, has probably told every Amish woman in Hickory Grove by this morning. By tonight, I suspect the entire county will know. I give it a week to reach my great-aunt in Michigan."

Abigail, unable to help herself, chuckled. It had been the same way in Maple Shade, Wisconsin, where she'd come from. The women didn't have telephones of course, but there was always gossip to be had. And it traveled fast. Sometimes the subject was the antics of a naughty boy or the details of someone's cousin coming to visit after a betrothal breakup. But the good thing about the Amish telegraph was that the moment a member of the community was hurt or injured, or just needed a kind word, that was also shared, allowing the women to always be there for each other. And truth be told, the men gossiped, too; they were just less open about it.

"Jamie won't be riding anyone else's cows," Abigail told Ethan. "He's promised. And as punishment, I'll be walking him to and from school the rest of the week."

"Good thinking." Ethan lifted an eyebrow, nodding in approval. "Nothing a boy his age hates more than having his *mammi* walk him to school."

They were both quiet for a moment. Awkwardly quiet. Then Abigail spoke up, her gaze fixed on the old floorboards. "I… I wanted to apologize for the other day. What I said about going to the school board about you. It's only that… I was upset." When Ethan didn't respond, she glanced up at him.

He was watching her. After another stretch of silence that seemed to go on for days rather than seconds, he said, "I understand. Parents. Children. It's complicated."

The sound of children's voices came from the cloakroom. Students were beginning to arrive, which was a relief because now that Abigail had made her apology, she didn't have to stand here and talk to Ethan any longer. Just because she'd apologized didn't mean she approved of the way he was handling Jamie. And she didn't have time to dawdle anyway. She had chores waiting for her. It was Wednesday, which meant she had piles of dirty laundry to be washed and hung to dry on the line. She'd already hung a load of sheets and left the washer running. She had wet trousers and shirts waiting for her. "I… I packed a lunch for you."

"Lunch?" He looked at her questioningly. "I brought a lunch."

"I know, but… But Jamie said you don't always get to eat it." She handed him the basket, then, feeling embarrassed, took a step back. Who took lunch to their child's teacher? "Chicken salad sandwich, a banana and a whoopie pie." She took another step back. "I made the whoopie pies last night."

"Whoopie pie?" He peeked beneath the cloth napkin that covered the basket. "I do love a homemade whoopie pie. My mother used to make a great one. She passed a few years ago."

"I'm sorry," Abigail said softly. Mention of his mother immediately made her think of her own. She couldn't imagine losing her. She knew it would happen someday, in God's good time, but not when Abigail was still so young. Even with her mother's memory issues and strange behavior, Abigail still learned from her every day. June King still had plenty to offer not just to her daughter, but to her husband, grandson and community.

"My mother always said I had a sweet tooth." Ethan grimaced. "I've had whoopie pies store-bought, but they're just not the same as made from scratch."

"Well, I hope you enjoy it. The whoopie pie. The lunch. I'll be back to walk Jamie home after school."

He held up the basket. "Thank you. I'll return the basket."

She nodded, walking backward. "No hurry." She pressed her lips together and then said, "I guess I'll be seeing you every day this week. Twice a day." Then, feeling more like one of the teen girls in the coatroom than a widowed mother, she turned and hurried out of the schoolroom. That afternoon, she promised herself, she'd wait for her son at the end of the driveway. She wouldn't come inside. That way she wouldn't have to talk to Ethan again. In fact, if her son would behave himself, she'd never have to speak to him again.

Ethan approached four girls seated together at their desks near the rear of the classroom. The students were talking quietly, but there was clearly a disagreement going on. The third and fourth graders were working together on identifying all of the states on a US map. It was their second day on the project. The previous day, the girls had done pretty well on the East and West Coast, but they had struggled in the Midwest.

"Questions?" Ethan asked, leaning over to address ten-year-old Liz Fisher who had been the self-appointed leader of the group since school had begun in September.

Because he was trying to teach so many students of different ages and abilities, Ethan had found it helpful to divide them by approximate grades and then by boys and girls. There were some activities where girls and boys worked together, but often there was more hair pulling and squealing than concentration on lessons, so he didn't do it often. Usually this group of girls, as with most of the girls in the school, were self-sufficient once given an assignment. That gave him more time to work with the boys or his three eighth-grade boys who wouldn't likely be returning to school the following September. Most Amish families took their children out at that age. The girls would work in the houses and gardens with their mothers and boys on their farms with their fathers. The boys sometimes even got jobs in construction. Ethan had been fortunate enough that his father had encouraged him to complete high school, which enabled him to be a schoolteacher.

"Hannah says that's New Mexico," Liz said in *Deitsch*, pointing at the outline of New Mexico.

"English, please," Ethan told her. His policy was to always speak English, unless a child didn't understand something and then he would switch to Pennsylvania *Deitsch*. It was his belief, and the school board's, that one of his duties as the schoolmaster was to be sure all of the students spoke English well enough to function in the Englishers' world.

Liz switched to English. "I told her and told her it was Arizona, but she won't let me write it in." She pointed at the paper on Hannah Gruber's desk. While Liz was currently leader of the four of them, Hannah had been making a move for the position for weeks.

"What do you think, Mary?" Ethan asked, turning his attention to the younger student. Mary Kutz, a nine-year-old, was Hannah's cousin.

Mary nibbled on her lower lip and whispered something. The child was painfully shy.

"What was that?" Ethan asked. His inclination was to lean closer to her, but he was working hard to encourage Mary Kutz to speak up. She was an excellent student; he'd seriously considered moving her up at Christmas to the fifth-and sixth-year group, but he was worried she would wilt amid that set of bossy girls. What Mary needed more was not to be promoted to a higher grade, but to find a healthy dose of confidence.

Ethan waited for Mary to repeat what she'd said.

"New Mexico," she murmured with a slight lisp. She pointed to the correct state. "Arizona." She indicated that state, then rattled off three more, touching with her finger each state that was yet to be identified. "Utah, Colorado, Kansas," she said.

He smiled at her. "Excellent!" He stood to his full height. "So Hannah is correct, Liz." He slid the piece of paper and a pencil to Mary. "Why don't you label them?"

The timid girl took the pencil and immediately began to neatly print the names of the states in the proper places.

Ethan looked to Hannah's little sister Lettice who sat quietly in her seat, hands folded, watching Mary. Lettice was one of his two students who had Down's Syndrome. While families often chose not to send children with disabilities to school, Ethan thought the Grubers had made a wise choice in allowing Lettice and her twin brother, Esau, to begin the previous September. He often put Lettice with the younger girls. She'd already learned to write her name and could count to fifty. But she was more comfortable being with her big sister, so Ethan allowed her to divide her day between the two groups. He didn't know how much geography and science she was learning, but she seemed content. And she never misbehaved, which was more than he could say for some of his students.

"Ethan?"

He felt a tug on his sleeve and looked over his shoulder to see his stepbrother Jesse standing beside him.

Jesse was an average student, but a good kid. "Jamie," Jesse said under his breath.

Ethan exhaled, trying to keep his patience intact, said something encouraging to the girls and then turned to his brother. "What is it?"

"I know we're not supposed to tattle, but…" He nervously tugged at a forelock of his hair.

"Yes?"

"He won't leave us alone. We're trying to take that division quiz you gave us, but he keeps hitting us with… stuff."

Ethan arched his eyebrow. "Stuff?"

"Spitballs," Jesse whispered, looking down. "He got me right here." He pointed to his cheek. There was a distinct red mark.

Ethan glanced at Jamie who appeared to be concentrating on his reader. He looked back at his brother. "Go back to your seat. Finish your quiz." He gave Jesse's shoulder a squeeze and then crossed the room to where Jamie sat alone at a desk. Earlier in the day he'd been with the first and second graders, but he'd scribbled all over his neighbor's book and then tried to lie his way out of it.

Jamie spotted Ethan coming toward him and immediately tucked something into the back of his pants. The boy picked up his pencil and stared at the worksheet in front of him intently.

"Spitballs again?" Ethan asked him quietly.

Jamie didn't respond, which Ethan supposed was a step in the right direction. At least he hadn't flat-out lied to him this time.

Ethan stood over the boy's desk, looking down at the worksheet. Jamie was supposed to have read the next chapter in his reading book and then answered the questions. Had he been able to behave himself, he could have done the assignment with a partner. Instead, he was doing it alone.

Jamie hadn't filled in a single answer. And the answers weren't that difficult. Their reader was a simple one from the 1940s that he'd found six copies of at Spence's Bazaar. The story Jamie was supposed to have read was one about a boy and a dog going fishing. All Jamie had to do was answer questions like what color the dog was and what he had done earlier in the day.

"You haven't answered a single question," Ethan said, pointing at the blank page. The corner of the paper was conspicuously missing.

Jamie said nothing.

"Did you read the story?" Ethan asked. Technically, Jamie was a third grader. The story was written on a first-grade level. By Ethan's calculation, the boy should have been done with the assignment half an hour ago.

Jamie stared at the paper on his desk. He hadn't even written his name on it.

Ethan took a deep breath. "Okay." He placed his finger beside the first question. "What was the dog's name in the story?"

Jamie was quiet.

"What was its name?" Ethan repeated. "Easy question."

"I don't remember," the boy answered softly.

"Okay…" Ethan opened the book to the first page of the story. "Right here, second line." He pointed at the word. Waited.

Jamie lowered his head. "I don't know," he said under his breath.

"So read it out loud." Ethan tapped on the word.

"*F…*" The boy made the sound of the first letter. "*F…*" he repeated. He squirmed in his seat. "Fred!" he declared.

Ethan frowned. "Look again. Sound it out. *F… I…*"

"Fireman?" Jamie asked.

"Now you're just guessing." Ethan looked down at the boy. "Can you see that word?" he asked, wondering if the boy needed glasses. "What are the letters?"

Jamie groaned and ran his finger under the word. "*F… I… Um… D.*" He exhaled loudly. *"O?"*

"*O*, that's right. Which spells what?" Ethan asked when the boy was quiet again.

Jamie pressed his lips together staring at the page.

"Fido," Ethan said. Then he squatted down, looked into Jamie's eyes and knew at once what was happening. "You can't read, can you?" he asked softly.

Still Jamie didn't speak.

How had Ethan missed this? He thought back to the times he'd believed Jamie was misbehaving for not being attentive to reading assignments. He'd attributed his lack of progress to mischievousness, his blank assignment papers as just more willful disobedience.

Feeling guilty that he hadn't been more attentive to the child, hadn't recognized it sooner, Ethan stood and squeezed Jamie's shoulder. "We'll get back to this tomorrow. Why don't you gather the erasers and pick a buddy to go outside with you and clean them?"

Jamie popped out of his chair, needing no further encouragement.

Ethan watched him go. They had only another twenty minutes until school was over. The erasers would keep

Jamie busy until it was time to gather his things. And then Abigail would be there to pick up her son.

And Ethan and Abigail were going to have to have a talk.

Chapter Four

Abigail stood off to the side of the driveway as children left on push scooters in groups of three or four. They had all hooked their lunch bags, baskets or pails on the handlebars and wore fluorescent orange vests so that motorists could spot them on the country road more easily. She could see that most of the students *did* have scooters, but not all of them. Some of the children left on foot by the road while others took a path through the woods behind the schoolhouse.

As she waited for Jamie to come out, she thought about whether or not she should buy him a scooter, rather than holding it over his head as a reward for better behavior. It wasn't as if she didn't have money to buy one. Unlike many widows, her husband had left her with a tidy bank account, and after the sale of their house and one-hundred-acre farm, she had more money than she had the need for. But her father had cautioned her about spending too much on Jamie. He thought it would spoil him, making him feel as if he was in some way better than other children, isolating him from his community. Her father had even criticized her for making her son new clothing and buying him new boots. She'd reminded him that he was an only child and that she had no hand-me-downs to give Jamie, but he'd stubbornly maintained that a boy shouldn't look so fancy.

One by one, the students left the schoolyard and soon it was empty. But Jamie didn't appear. Abigail had wanted to wait for him outside so she wouldn't have to encounter Ethan again. She'd made her apology to him. She saw no need to speak with him again. But she supposed she was going to have to go into the school to retrieve her son. She hoped he wasn't in trouble again. With a sigh, she walked along the oyster shell driveway, up the steps and pushed open the door to the cloakroom—almost running right into Ethan.

"Oh!" she exclaimed, backing down the steps. "I didn't— I was waiting for Jamie. He hadn't—"

"Here I am," Jamie piped up from behind the schoolmaster.

She stood in the grass looking up, feeling flustered and she didn't know why.

Ethan held her basket in his hand. He didn't look happy, but he didn't seem angry either, so maybe her son wasn't in trouble. "Jamie was helping me put some books away," he said.

"Was he?" Abigail asked, relieved his behavior wasn't the issue.

"Ya." Ethan stood on the top step and let Jamie go by him, then locked the door with a key. "We thought we'd walk home together." He shrugged, coming down the steps. "Since we're going the same way. Right, Jamie?"

Abigail looked at Jamie, finding it hard to believe her son had agreed to walk home with his schoolteacher, considering how he felt about him. Jamie hadn't come right out and said he disliked Ethan, probably because he knew better than to say such a thing. But it was clear the schoolmaster was not her boy's favorite person in Hickory Grove.

"That okay with you?" Ethan asked Abigail, slipping the key ring into his pocket. "Your place is on the way to mine if I go by way of the road."

"You…you didn't bring your buggy?" she asked, feeling silly the moment the words came out of her mouth. Of course he hadn't driven his buggy this morning. If he had, he'd be taking it home. And she'd certainly have seen his horse tied up at the hitching post. A horse that color couldn't be missed. She groaned inwardly, wondering what on earth had gotten into her. She was usually so levelheaded. Never flighty.

"I walked. Thought I'd enjoy the nice weather," Ethan said, not seeming to think her question had been silly. "I like walking when the weather is decent. On the walk here in the morning, I get my lesson plans straight in my head. On the walk home, I… I think Englishers use the word *decompress*." He met her gaze, still solemn but not annoyed.

She wondered what made him such a sober man. Was it his job as a schoolmaster? She thought not. But there was definitely a sadness in his eyes. She wondered if his marriage was an unhappy one and that thought saddened her. She and her husband, Egan, had married for love. Her parents, as well. But not all Amish couples had that luxury. Sometimes marriages were arranged by parents, sometimes they were made for financial reasons and sometimes women like her, *often* women like her, single with children, married a man suitable to be a husband and father. Their faith believed in the responsibility of all men and women to be married; romance was only a secondary consideration.

"I think about whatever has gone on that day and then I try to let it go," Ethan continued. "Helps me look at things fresh the next day."

She nodded, imagining taking that time to *decompress*, as he called it, helped him to be a better husband, a better father. If he had children. She didn't know if he did. She'd not been in the community long enough to have knowledge of such details of her neighbors yet. It was on the tip of her tongue to ask, but for some reason, she didn't feel like she should. It somehow seemed too...*personal* to be asking such a question of her son's teacher.

Instead, she turned her attention to Jamie as the three of them set out for home. "What did you do in school today?"

"Um." Jamie held up his lunch pail for her to take. "We played softball during recess. I got out two times. But I made a good catch at third base," he added, seeming pleased with himself.

"Sounds like you had fun." Abigail reached out to take his lunch pail, then pulled her hand back. "Carry it yourself." She looked back at Ethan. "I can take my basket."

"I'll carry it as far as your place. It was good, the lunch. And the whoopie pie?" Ethan made a sound that was very near to delight, which took her by surprise. "Delicious. *Danke.*"

She couldn't help but smile. So maybe he wasn't always such a sour man. "I'm glad you liked it." She almost blurted that her husband, Egan, had loved her whoopie pies, too, but she caught herself before she said it. She didn't speak often about Egan, and never to strangers. At first, she was afraid it was because she hadn't cared enough for him. It had been her mother who had pointed out that sometimes the deepest feelings are the ones that are the hardest to share.

"Your timing was perfect," Ethan continued. "The John Yoder twins both forgot their lunches. So they shared my bologna sandwich and potato chips and I had your chicken salad. I think I got the better deal for once. I like the little peppers in it. What were they?"

"Pimento," she said. "And I always add a pinch of cayenne pepper."

"Take it, *Mam*." Jamie stubbornly bumped her hand with his pail. "Please?" He drew out the word.

"Carry it yourself," she said a little sternly. "You're old enough to carry your own lunch, to and from school."

"But you used to always carry it for me when we lived in Wisconsin."

Jamie's whining tone embarrassed her and she took a breath before she responded. "But now you're older and you can do it yourself." She glanced over her shoulder at Ethan again. The grassy patch that ran along the side of the road was wide enough for two to walk side by side, but not three so he had taken up the rear. She looked forward again. "What else did you do in school, *sohn*?"

"Um… At lunch we watched a bunch of ants eat part of the crust of Jesse's bologna sandwich. They took away little tiny pieces. To their house, Jesse told us. They leave something behind so they know their way back. Fair… Fair somethings."

"Pheromones," Ethan put in. Then to Abigail he explained, "We've been talking about insects in our sixth-grade class. My brother Jesse is in that group."

She nodded. She didn't know that ants left a trail for themselves, but she had always wondered how they could wander so far from their anthills and still find their way home. She was impressed that Ethan knew such a fact and that he had shared it with his students. "That must have been interesting about the ants," she said to her son. "But I meant in school. What did you do *in class* today?"

"I don't know." He kicked at a tuft of dandelions and the fuzzy seeds blew away in the breeze. "Nothing."

"*Nothing?* I think if I asked your teacher, he might say you'd done *something* in school all day."

Neither her son nor Ethan responded, and Abigail let the subject drop. Instead, she walked in silence, enjoying the warm sunshine and the scent of freshly turned soil in the field they walked beside. Jamie slowly made his way forward until he was in front of her and the three of them walked single file.

A buggy approached them from behind and Ethan waved. They slowed down. Abigail didn't know the couple, but she smiled. The passenger door slid open and a woman who looked to be in her fifties smiled and nodded her head in greeting.

"New neighbor, Abigail Stolz, daughter of June and Daniel King. Just moved here from Wisconsin. And my student Jamie—Abigail's son," Ethan introduced. He pointed to the buggy. "Hannah and Albert Hartman."

"Good to have you here, Abigail," the woman called. "We need young families. Too many folks moving away. Will we see you at the Brubachers' Saturday?"

Abigail looked over her shoulder at Ethan questioningly.

"I'm sure you will," Ethan called to the older woman who Abigail took an immediate liking to. Hannah had a sparkle in her eyes that seemed mischievous and kind at the same time.

"I'll let her know all about it," Ethan promised.

"See you there!" Hannah waved enthusiastically and the buggy picked up its pace and pulled away.

"They live over in Seven Poplars," Ethan said when they had gone by. "North of here." He pointed in the general direction. "Interesting man, Albert. He's a veterinarian. Takes care of most Amish families' livestock in the whole county."

"An Amish veterinarian?" Abigail asked in surprise, looking back at him.

"They're pretty amazing, the both of them." Ethan caught up to her and walked beside her. "Second marriage for Hannah," he explained. "Hannah's husband died, leaving her with six girls to raise. She stayed single for years while she raised her girls. Taught school over at Seven Poplars. Albert was a bachelor. He was Mennonite but became Amish so he could marry Hannah. Funny thing is, Hannah was Mennonite, too, before she married her first husband."

"And their bishop allows him to continue to be a veterinarian?" she asked in wonder.

"Sure does. With restrictions, of course." Ethan slid his hand into his pocket as he walked beside her. "No work on Sundays. Not even for his Amish clients. He has someone on call for him on Sundays. But he's allowed to drive his work truck because he just does large animals—cows, sheep, horses and such." He pointed at her. "Oh, and alpacas."

Abigail laughed, "What's an alpaca?"

"Like a llama. Albert has a bunch of them."

She shook her head with a chuckle. It certainly didn't sound very Amish. "Why does he have alpacas?"

"Apparently their wool is worth something. I don't know that he makes much profit off it, but he likes them. Likes the oddity of them, I think."

She nodded, thinking she might like to see these alpacas. And she imagined Jamie would, too.

"Anyway, what Hannah was talking about," Ethan went on, "is a barn raising going on Saturday. Everyone in the area is invited. It's for the Brubachers. They live over toward Marydel, which is west of here. The family lost their main barn in the fall to a lightning strike. The whole thing went up so fast, Abner barely had time to get his horses and cows out. You and your parents and Jamie should come. Good way to meet more folks."

"I haven't been to a barn raising in years," Abigail mused aloud as they made a right-hand turn onto her road. "I bet my *dat* and *mam* would enjoy it." She was learning that it was good for her mother to get out with people. Her mother's head seemed clearer when she didn't spend so much time alone with just their small family.

He shrugged. "Like I said, everyone is welcome. The more folks there, the faster the barn will go up. There will be a big dinner of course, and it looks like we're going to have a good day for it. Sunny and seventy degrees."

Jamie turned around to face his mother. "Can I run ahead?"

Abigail hesitated.

"Please?" Her son bounced on the balls of his feet, his lunch pail banging against his leg. He was obviously a bundle of energy after sitting at his desk all day.

"Fine," she agreed.

The boy took off.

"But you better stay away from Karl's cows!" she hollered after him. Then she sighed. "Boys." She glanced at Ethan. "I suppose you think I should have made him walk beside me all the way home." Her tone suddenly grew prickly. She was enjoying the walk home with Ethan, but that didn't mean she hadn't forgotten the animosity between them. "To *discipline* him."

"I see no trouble letting him run ahead. You'll be able to see him if he climbs Karl's fence." Ethan glanced at her and then ahead again. "I wanted to talk to you alone anyway."

She looked at him and back at the grassy path trampled by others who took the same route to and from school. "What's he done now?" She said it almost as an exhalation. Her day had been a long one already.

She and her father had had words when she had come home from dropping Jamie off at school. She'd arrived to find her mother trying to make bread using a cup of warm vinegar instead of water to dissolve the yeast. Her father had made light of the incident, saying her mother had just "forgotten." Abigail had argued that a woman seventy years old, who had been making bread since she was ten, did not *forget* how to make it. She felt there was more going on with her mother than forgetfulness but no matter what happened, her father insisted there was nothing wrong. He usually countered any argument with Abigail on the subject by recalling an incident where he'd forgotten to pick up an item on the grocery list or left a feed bin open for the chickens to get into. And she always responded with the fact that it wasn't the same, but her father was an obstinate man, especially when it came to the subject of his wife.

Abigail didn't look at Ethan. She just put one foot in front of another. This was probably something trivial again. Obviously the schoolmaster didn't like her son and he was going to take every opportunity he could to pick on the boy.

"I wanted to talk to you about—" Ethan went quiet for a moment and then blurted, "Abigail, I don't think Jamie can read."

She halted and turned to him. *"What?"* she demanded with a mixture of indignation and disbelief.

Ethan met her gaze. He didn't seem angry, only concerned. "I don't think he can read. No," he corrected himself. "I'm sure of it."

"That's ridiculous. I've heard him read," she argued, settling her hands on her hips.

"You've heard him read what?"

"Um…" She thought for a moment. It wasn't as if students brought their reading books home and read aloud to their parents at night. Reading was for school. And understanding that children, no matter their age, had chores to do when they got home, Ethan didn't often give homework. "I don't know. A sign in the grocery store? On…on a feed bag."

Ethan shook his head no. "That doesn't mean he's reading. He's a smart boy. I think he's guessing."

She dropped one hand from her hip, her annoyance with him rising by the second. "What do you mean?"

"He knows the sounds of most of his letters, but

he's using context clues to guess the word. The pictures. Or the item. Sure, he can read a sign that says apples because he can see the apples in the bin. A bag of chicken feed?" He lifted his hand and let it fall. "A chicken on the bag."

Abigail walked. They had almost reached her father's driveway. She could see that Jamie was nearly to the house. "That's ridiculous," she repeated again. "Jamie is… He's bright. Mischievous, but…bright. And he's good with math. He adds and subtracts well. Multiplies."

Ethan caught up to her and walked beside her again. "You're right. Jamie is bright. And he's also good with math in his head. But I've been a teacher here for years now and I know a student who can't read when I see one."

She reached the driveway and turned to face the schoolteacher, feeling defensive. "Jamie started school when he was six, right on time," she sputtered. "His teacher back home never told me he couldn't read."

"Was he getting into trouble at his old school?"

She didn't answer.

"That's often an indication of a problem with learning. Students who aren't learning at the same pace as other students their age, slower *or* faster, act out from boredom. Or sometimes frustration."

"I have to get home." Abigail took her basket out of his hand, being none too gentle.

"Me, too." He walked past the driveway, then turned back to her. "It would be easy enough for you to see for yourself. Test him."

She didn't know what to say, maybe because the thought crossed her mind that possibly Jamie couldn't read as well as he should have been able to. She immediately thought of a couple of instances over the last year when he'd misread something. But she'd just chalked it up to all the changes in his life. The idea that a nine-year-old boy couldn't read, *her* nine-year-old, was absurd.

"Test him," Ethan repeated, heading down the road. "Then we'll talk."

That evening, after the supper dishes had been cleared away, the family had settled in the living room for an hour before bed. Abigail was still fuming about what Ethan had told her. Of course Jamie could read. Maybe he just didn't want to read for Ethan. Maybe the subject in his reading book was boring. There had to be a dozen explanations.

But what if Ethan was right? That thought had been creeping into her head since she'd discussed it with him earlier in the day.

Abigail glanced up from the list she was making for their trip to Byler's store the next day. They needed groceries, including several items to make the macaroni salad her mother wanted to take to the barn raising on Saturday. It turned out that her father had already heard about the community event when he was at the harness shop that morning—the harness shop owned by Ethan's father. At supper, her father had announced that he told Benjamin Miller he would help and that they would all be going to the barn raising in Marydel. He'd been assigned to a work crew right on the spot.

Abigail tapped her pencil on the pad of paper on her lap. Her mother was sound asleep in an old recliner that had been left in the house by the previous owner. Her father and Jamie were playing a game of checkers.

"And that's your last one," her father announced, skipping over Jamie's black checker with his red one. "I won."

Jamie frowned, crossing his arms over his chest. "You never let me win."

"No, I do not. But if you listen to what I tell you, you'll be beating me on your own in no time," his grandfather said, beginning to reset the board for the next time they would play.

Abigail watched her son for a moment and then called his name.

Jamie looked over as he got out of his chair. *"Ya?"*

She waved him over with the pencil in her hand. "Come here for a second." As he crossed the cozy living room, she turned the pad of paper around so that she could point out one of the words she'd printed neatly on the page. "What does that say?" she asked, tapping beside the word *pears*.

Jamie looked down and then up at his mother, suddenly seeming uncomfortable.

"That's…that's your shopping list," he said.

"Ya," she agreed. "And I want you to tell me what that word is on my list."

"I'm tired," he whined. "I want to go to bed."

"You can go in just a second." A feeling of dread was growing stronger inside her with every second. What if Ethan had been right? What if her son couldn't read? "Read the word to me, Jamie," she said, the tone of her voice telling him she wouldn't tolerate disobedience.

He groaned loudly. *"P…p…"* he repeated the sound. "Potatoes!" he exclaimed.

She didn't know what to say. She tapped the next word on the list: *crackers*.

Jamie stared at it. "*K… k…*" He looked up at her. "I don't know. Your writing is messy." He wiped at his eyes that had suddenly turned teary. "May I go to bed? I'm tired."

She hesitated, then rose from her chair and kissed the top of his head. "You may."

"What was that all about?" Abigail's father asked as Jamie hurried out of the room.

"I'll tell you later," she whispered. Then she carried the pad of paper into the dark kitchen, not sure what she was more upset about at that moment. Was it that Jamie couldn't read, or that she was going to have to apologize to Ethan Miller again?

Chapter Five

By eight on Saturday morning, the sound of hammers and saws echoed across the Brubacher farm. The day was bright, the grass still damp with dew and the air filled with the scent of spring blossoming around them. It was a good day, and Abigail was grateful to God for the gentle weather.

Next to the family's farmhouse, women and girls set up tables in the yard, while boys took charge of arriving horses and buggies. At the construction site in the barnyard, eight men were already raising the frame of the first wall on the new barn. According to Abigail's father, because the block foundation was in place and the poured cement floor laid, they would have four walls and a roof by sunset.

Friends and neighbors were coming from every direction, on foot, in wagons piled high with lumber, in buggies, and on push scooters. Abigail and a young woman she'd met that morning, Phoebe, walked among the men offering mugs of steaming coffee and breakfast sandwiches wrapped in aluminum foil to keep them hot.

"Sausage, egg and cheese on an English muffin or

bacon, egg and cheese?" Phoebe asked a handsome young man who looked to be in his early to midtwenties.

Phoebe had introduced herself the moment Abigail and her family had arrived and had quickly steered each of them in a different direction. She'd sent Abigail's father to speak with Abner Brubacher who was overseeing the barn raising. She'd taken Abigail's mother to join a group of older women at a picnic table where they were wrapping silverware in paper napkins for the noonday meal. And to Jamie's delight, Phoebe had waved Ethan's brother Jesse over. The two boys had run off with talk of fetching nails for the men, and Abigail hadn't seen her son since.

"Which ones did you make?" the man asked Phoebe, pointing at the basket of hot sandwiches her new friend was carrying. The way he was grinning, Abigail suspected that he was smitten with Phoebe.

"None of them," Phoebe answered, smiling back at him. "Bacon or sausage, choose quick, or I'll be choosing for you."

Phoebe's brash statement, combined with obvious flirting, confused Abigail. She knew that for an Old Order community Hickory Grove was relatively relaxed, but the way these two were looking at each other was certainly not something she witnessed often. It embarrassed her and tickled her at the same time. And made her miss her husband.

"Abigail." Phoebe turned to her. "This is Joshua Miller. My husband," she added, looking back at him.

Abigail smiled. He was her husband. That made sense, though they were still rather flirty with each other.

"And my husband is getting bacon, egg and cheese

because we have more of those left," Phoebe went on as she took a foil-wrapped sandwich from her basket and offered it to him. "This is my new friend, Abigail. She just moved here from northern Wisconsin. Her parents are June and Daniel King. I know you've met Daniel at the harness shop. They live right down the road from us."

Joshua propped his hammer against the foundation and accepted the sandwich.

"Coffee?" Phoebe asked.

"Sure. Thanks."

"There certainly are a lot of Millers here." Abigail only said it to make conversation. There had been a lot of Amish Millers in Wisconsin, too. "My son's teacher is a Miller, too."

Joshua took a sip of the coffee he'd taken off the tray, his gaze moving from his wife to Abigail. "That would be my big brother, Ethan."

"Oh... I... I didn't know." Abigail looked down at the tray in her hands not understanding why this information surprised her or why she cared. Ethan had already told her he would be there. In fact, she'd spotted him when her family arrived. He was one of the men now securing the first wall of the barn.

"My other brothers are here, too. Well, Jacob, Will and Jesse. Our brother Levi is living in Lancaster, apprenticing as a buggy maker." He cut his eyes at his wife. "At least that's the story he's giving us. We all have a notion he's there because the courting pond is larger. Levi has a bit of a reputation for being a ladies' man."

Phoebe frowned, but only half-heartedly. "You shouldn't say such things, Joshua." She looked to Abi-

gail. "He means a ladies' man in an Amish kind of way."
She shook her head. "Not in the way Englishers mean
it. Levi's a good man, faithful and good-hearted." She
shrugged. "He just likes to flirt."

"He'd be flirting with you, Abigail, if he was here.
I guarantee you that. You being single and all." Joshua
set down his coffee and began to unwrap his breakfast
sandwich. "He keeps trying to give Ethan tips on how
to get a girl's attention. He's been pushing hard lately.
Every time we see Levi, he's trying to introduce Ethan
to a girl he thinks might be suitable."

Abigail knit her brows. "Wait, Ethan is— I thought
he was married."

Phoebe shook her head no, ever so slightly.

Abigail wouldn't have been any more surprised than
if Joshua had just said that the next load of wood coming in from the sawmill would be on the back of an el-
ephant. "But he has a beard," she argued. "Married men
have beards. Single men don't."

Phoebe's face softened. "Widowed." She looked to
her husband. "What? Going on six years now?" Her
tone was soft and kind.

Joshua held his sandwich but didn't take a bite.
"About that." He glanced at Abigail. "His wife, Mary,
had epilepsy. She had a seizure and passed away."

"She's with the Lord now," Phoebe said gently.

Abigail bowed her head. "I… I assumed that because he had the beard," she stammered, "that he…"
She stopped and started again. "Where I come from,
a clean-shaven man is unmarried, a married man has
a beard."

"It's that way here, too." Joshua took a bite of his
sandwich. "But when you get to widowers, the rules

aren't so black-and-white. Our friend Eli is widowed. He had a beard for some time after his wife passed, but now he's shaved it. He said that, for him, it was part of the mourning process. I can't imagine what it must be like to lose your wife or your husband." He looked at Phoebe. "If I lost my Phoebe—" His voice caught in his throat and Phoebe reached out with one hand and rubbed his shoulder.

"I'm not going anywhere, silly," Phoebe murmured to him. Then she looked at Abigail and said, "And I'm sorry about your husband."

"It's been three years," Abigail answered.

"Doesn't matter." Phoebe smiled. "I'm still sorry for you and for your son."

Nodding, Abigail pressed her lips together looking away from them. Joshua reminded her a little of her father. Amish men didn't always talk so freely about such things. She had liked Joshua the moment she met him, but she liked him even more now.

Her thoughts darted from one place to the next. Joshua's brother was Ethan. Ethan who was *not* married. She didn't know why but the idea made her feel completely off balance. Because of the way he had handled Jamie, obviously she didn't care for him. But a part of her suddenly felt almost attracted to him. Which fascinated her and dismayed her at the same time.

"Mam!" Jamie's voice drew her attention.

She turned to see him and Jesse and a boy she didn't know running toward them. "Jesse's *mam* said you had sandwiches," Jamie huffed, out of breath from running. "We're hungry."

Abigail had fed Jamie a nice breakfast of buckwheat hotcakes with honey from Fifer's orchard, scrapple and stewed apples with cinnamon before they came that morning, but his appetite seemed endless these days. Her mother said it was because he was growing. "Do we have enough or are these just for the men working?" she asked Phoebe.

Phoebe gave a wave of dismissal. She was such an attractive woman with light brown hair and blue eyes. She had a son, too: John, who was younger than Jamie. "We have plenty of sandwiches. And Claudia—you met her earlier. This is her new barn. She's got more eggs and meat frying on her cookstove."

"Are you boys helping with the building?" Abigail asked as she nodded, indicating Jamie could take a sandwich from the basket Phoebe offered.

"Ne." Joshua finished off the last bites of his sandwich and handed his wife the crumpled foil. "These rascals would be more in the way than they're worth. Back to the house with the three of you," he ordered, retrieving his coffee mug from the tailgate of the wagon where he'd set it down. "Tend to the horses and do whatever the women ask."

"Good behavior," Abigail warned her son as the three boys took off.

"Joshua!" a man called from the far end of the first wall frame. "We need you on this beam."

"Guess I better get back to work." Joshua nodded to the women and, taking his coffee with him, strode toward the place where the men had begun construction of another wall on the ground.

"You're going to have to put the coffee down," the man who called to Joshua hollered.

Abigail looked up to see a man who looked identical to Joshua speaking to him and she glanced at Phoebe.

"Your husband is a twin." It wasn't a question. Most large Amish families had at least one set of twins. Abigail had known a family in her old church district that had *three* sets of twins.

"That would be Jacob. He's unmarried, too." Phoebe started walking and Abigail went with her. "Very sweet. Good-natured. Loves animals. He'd make a good husband, too."

The look on Phoebe's face made Abigail chuckle. "Who said I was looking for a husband?"

"Actually your mother. She told all of us." She wrinkled her nose. "But I think she has her heart set on Ethan. Who would also make a good husband. I'm not saying he wouldn't. He's just a little more...*reserved* is maybe the right word...than Benjamin's other sons."

Abigail barely heard what Phoebe had said about Ethan. She knew she was blushing. She could feel the heat rising from her neck upward. She imagined her face had to be bright red. "I can't believe my mother would—" She was so embarrassed that she didn't know what to say.

"Oh, Abigail, don't be upset." Phoebe stopped and touched Abigail's arm. "You know women. We talk. It's only natural. Mothers want husbands for their girls. Girls want husbands, families. It's one of our favorite things to natter about when the men aren't around. She meant no harm."

Abigail stared at the ground. "I know I'll marry again. That I should. I only wish my mother wouldn't—" She exhaled. "It's awkward that she would bring up Ethan. He and I, we haven't—" She searched for the right thing to say without being critical of Phoebe's brother-in-law. "There's been a bit of trouble at school with my Jamie. Ethan and I had words. I suspect I'm not exactly his favorite person right now."

"*Ne?* Then why's he waving to you?" She pointed.

Abigail looked up to see Ethan, not twenty yards away. He had just lowered an armful of timber to the ground. He was wearing a straw hat like the other men, but he'd rolled up his sleeves to bare his arms. The thought went through her head that he was awfully muscular for a schoolteacher. Then she was embarrassed all over again.

"Good morning, Abigail," Ethan called to her. "You have a minute?"

Before Abigail could respond, Phoebe took the tray that had only two coffee mugs on it from her. "Go on." Then she whispered, "He doesn't seem upset with you to me."

Abigail offered a quick smile at Ethan and walked toward him. The dew was beginning to dry from the grass and the sweet smell of fresh-cut lumber filled the air. The sound of hammers hitting nails rang out and somehow the familiarity of it all, even though she was now so far from home, comforted her. It reminded her of the goodness in God's world. "I'm helping with the breakfast," she said as she approached him.

"I've got another load to haul." He pointed to the lumber in the grass. "Just take a second." When she was close enough that no one else could hear them, he said, "Listen, Abigail… I feel like I owe you an apology."

She looked up at him. Into his brown eyes. For the first time, she noticed his blond hair was a little long. Which made sense because he was obviously in his thirties; a man in his thirties usually had a wife to cut his hair. But he was widowed. And his mother was dead, too. She wondered who did it for him. His father's new wife?

"An apology? What for?" she asked. "I was the one who was rude to you."

He shook his head. "I shouldn't have blurted it out that way. About Jamie. His inability to read."

"But you were right," she told him, holding his gaze. "And I was wrong. I was wrong to snap at you the way I did, and I was wrong not to trust you as his teacher."

He shook his head. "Doesn't matter that I'm his teacher. It was unkind of me to tell you that way. It was just that I was…frustrated."

"I know how trying Jamie can be." She gave a chuckle, feeling herself relax. "Believe me. I of all people know."

He smiled at her. "So you tested him?"

She nodded, looking down at her sneakers damp from the earlier morning dew. She'd worn her favorite everyday dress today, blue, bright like a midsummer sky in Wisconsin. For some reason she was glad she had. She looked up at him again. "I was making a grocery list and I asked him to read it to me. No…" She searched for the phrase he'd use. "No *context clues*," she said. "He thought the word *pears* was the word *potatoes*." To her chagrin, emotion had suddenly clogged her voice. What if Jamie couldn't learn to read? Even in their slower-paced world, Amish men and women needed to know how to read. They needed to be able to read because they still lived in the Englisher's world. They had to use Englisher grocery stores, banks, doctors' offices.

"Hey, hey," Ethan said gently, taking a step toward her. He didn't touch her of course. That wouldn't have been appropriate. But the tone of his voice was comforting. Almost like a hug. "It's going to be okay. I promise you."

"Ethan!" someone called. "We need a hand here! Something's not quite square. Jacob says it Joshua's fault. Joshua says it's Jacob's," he finished good-naturedly.

Ethan glanced in the direction of a group of men. "Coming!" He looked back at her. "I have to go but—"

"*Ne*, it's fine." She took a step back, suddenly feeling self-conscious. The thought went through her mind: *He's not married. He's widowed like me. He understands what it's like to be alone.* "I have to get back to help with the…the coffee and breakfast sandwiches."

He walked away, calling over his shoulder, "Let's talk when we break for dinner." He pointed. "I'll come find you. And don't worry. Jamie is going to be fine. I promise."

Oddly enough, there was something in his voice that made Abigail think he was right. Her boy really was going to be fine.

Carrying his plate heaped with sandwiches, salads and assorted casseroles, Ethan walked around the side of the house in search of Abigail. The grass here was nearly knee-high in places, and the previous year's dried up Queen Anne's lace and black-eyed Susans lingered, adding their brown and gold stalks to the green carpet sprouting up all around. He'd spotted Jamie's mother walking this way a moment ago. He couldn't miss her in that blue dress that made her eyes seem even bluer.

"There you are," he called, spotting her as she walked away from a group of his students sitting under a blossoming peach tree. He was pleased to see that Jamie was among the boys. He'd specifically asked Jesse to be sure to include Jamie in the day's activities, reminding his little brother what it had been like when they'd moved here to Delaware and he hadn't known anyone.

"Ethan." She smiled at him and he was relieved to see that even though they had gotten off to a bad start, maybe she wasn't the sort to hold a grudge.

He walked up to her. The voices of men and women talking and laughing drifted from the backyard where tables were set up to eat. They'd had such a great turnout, though, that there weren't nearly enough seats for the men who would eat at the first sitting.

Ordinarily, at this type of event, the men ate first, then once they had returned to work, the women and children ate. Due to the limited seating, one of the women had made the decision that the elders and those with physical issues would take seats at the tables. The younger men and teenaged boys, and those children who couldn't wait another moment to eat had found steps or a shady place under a tree to enjoy their meals.

"I thought maybe we could talk while we eat," Ethan told Abigail.

"Oh, I don't know. I should…" She glanced over her shoulder. "I should probably go back to help serve. I was just checking on Jamie. I was going to eat later. With the other women. Once the men go back to work," she explained, working her hands together.

She had pretty hands, shapely. The skin looked smooth and he imagined they would feel soft. He had no doubt she worked as hard as any woman in the community, but it appeared she took care of her hands. Her nails were neatly cut and he guessed she used a lotion just like his stepmother and sisters did. And suddenly he had the strangest impulse to touch her hands, to see if they were as soft as they appeared.

"Come on," he cajoled, not quite sure what had gotten into him. He did want to talk about Jamie, but for some reason he just wanted to…to talk to her. To Abigail. This wasn't like him at all, to seek someone out. Certainly not a woman. An unmarried woman.

The evening before, Rosemary had filled him in on Abigail's husband's passing. How she had nursed him through his cancer until his death. That she had tried for years to run their farm on her own. According to his stepmother, it was only after her parents moved to Hickory Grove that she'd decided to sell her place and leave Wisconsin. And that had apparently been more about her parents than herself. Ethan had gotten the impression that June had some health issues. What they were, his stepmother hadn't said but from his couple of encounters with June, he could make a good guess. Rosemary *had*, however, expressed her opinion that Abigail had done the right thing, that her parents needed her.

"Come on, sit with me for a few minutes." Balancing his plate in one hand, Ethan waved in the direction of the yard beside the house that was planted with flowering bushes and clusters of herbs. "They've plenty of help and I've kept my eye on you. You haven't sat down since you got here at seven this morning. And we really should talk about Jamie," he added, hoping that would win her over.

She looked up at him, obviously torn.

"Ten minutes," he said. And then he walked away.

"Fine, but just five minutes," she told him. And followed.

He found a little wrought iron bench along the side of the house, nestled between clumps of pink and white flowering azaleas. "Sit." He dropped onto the bench. "I bet you're as tired as I am."

"I'm not tired," she said.

He pushed back the brim of his straw hat and looked up at her. "You know what I mean. It will feel good to sit a minute and talk. I already have a plan worked out. Jamie's going to be reading at grade level by Christmas if he'll cooperate."

The idea of that seemed to be enough to convince her to join him because she sat down on the far end of the bench.

"What a spread," he said, looking down at the china dinner plate in his lap.

Someone had brought a church wagon from one of the larger districts. The wagons were moved from house to house where services were held. They contained tables, chairs, dishes and even silverware, enough to feed the sixty-odd people who were there, and probably then some.

He pointed at his plate. "Ham sandwich, potato salad, rice salad, macaroni and cheese, chicken salad sandwich. Which I suspect you made because it has pimentos in it." He slid a rolled napkin of silverware from his pocket. "I took too much. We can share."

She shook her head. "Thank you, but…" She smiled at him. "I can eat later with the other women."

"Forget that," he told her, surprising himself with his joviality. "If you don't help me eat this, I'll have to eat it all myself." He nodded in the direction of a silver maple whose branches were filled with leaves about to burst. "And then I'll be asleep under that tree the rest of the day."

She laughed. "Guess you shouldn't have put so much on your plate."

"Eyes bigger than my stomach, that's what my wife used to—" He halted midsentence, surprised he would mention his Mary. And to someone who was a complete stranger. Nearly.

Abigail was quiet for a moment and then said, "Phoebe told me your wife had passed. I didn't know. I'm so sorry. And I'm sorry for that comment I made to you earlier this week. I saw your beard and assumed you were married, and I was upset and—" She exhaled, looking down.

"You don't have to apologize. You already did. It's fine. Forgotten. I've seen a mother hen protect her chick in the barnyard."

"It's still not okay. For me to have said something like that when your wife was dead. I know…at least, I have some idea how that feels. What it's like. And I know it must have been hurtful. Because I know how much you must miss her," she added softly.

He stared at his plate for a moment. She did know what that was like, didn't she? Her being widowed, as well. Maybe that was why he had brought it up? Because somehow, he felt some sort of kinship to her. Sure, he had known others who had lost spouses. His own mother had died. His father had been widowed. As was Rosemary. But they were older, had thirteen children between them and somehow that seemed different. To lose a spouse when you were older. Having a wife die so young. It made you feel like you should have died with them. Sometimes wish you had.

"Look, someone put two forks in this napkin," he said trying to lighten the conversation. "I guess it was meant to be, you and I sharing this plate." He offered the fork.

She took it, which surprised him and...pleased him.

For a moment they were both quiet. Ethan cut the ham sandwich on a roll in half and then the chicken salad sandwich. He picked up half the sandwich and offered it to her. "My hands are clean. I promise. I washed up at the hand pump, soap and all."

She laughed but hesitated.

"You better take it," he warned. "Best chicken salad I've ever had. It was already almost gone when I went through the line. No way there's any left by the time the women sit down to eat." He held it out.

She accepted the sandwich and took a bite. "Do you really think you can teach Jamie to read?" she asked, and he felt himself exhaling, not realizing he'd been holding his breath, hoping she'd let him help her and her son.

Chapter Six

"I can absolutely help him. I only have a high school education, but I've done a lot of reading. A lot of studying on teaching methods and such. I think Jamie knows the sounds of most letters," Ethan explained. "And some of the digraphs."

"Digraphs?" She took a bite of the sandwich. Ethan was right. She had made the chicken salad. And brought slices of bread and soft rolls so folks could make small sandwiches and have a taste of more things. She chewed thoughtfully. She'd never heard the word *digraph*. She'd been a good student but had only completed the eighth grade. One of the things her father had taught her was to never be ashamed of admitting she didn't know something. The shame was in *not* learning, he always said. "I don't know that word. *Digraph*."

"Nobody does. It's just a fancy way of meaning the sounds certain consonants make when you put them together." He set the plate down between them on the bench. "Like *TH* in *thank*."

"*Ya*, I see. Like *ST* in *stop*." She nodded surprised to find how hungry she was. She took another bite of the sandwich and then, without being invited, dipped into the potato salad on Ethan's plate with her fork.

"Right." He took a bite of macaroni and cheese. "But Jamie doesn't understand the sounds *diphthongs* make. Those are combinations of vowels, like *EA* or *OU*. Like in *mean* or *shout*."

Abigail turned this idea over in her mind, fighting a feeling of failure. How had she not known her son was struggling? She hesitated, then glanced at him. "I feel bad. What kind of mother am I that I didn't know Jamie couldn't read?"

Ethan reached for his half of the chicken salad sandwich and took a bite. "This really is good. Want a pickle? There are pickles in there somewhere." He poked at the plate with his fork, then looked up. "You can't feel guilty about this, Abigail. Jamie's a smart boy. He had me fooled for weeks and I'm his teacher. And it's not as if you haven't had anything else to do. Your husband was sick. You were taking care of your farm." He took a napkin from the two the cutlery had been wrapped in.

She watched him, wondering how he knew so much about her. Had her mother told everyone in Hickory Grove her whole life's story? She probably should have been embarrassed about that, too. But she had to keep in mind what mattered here. And that was Jamie.

"And now you have your parents to look after," Ethan continued.

"Well, my *dat* doesn't need looking after, but my *mam*, that's another story. It's really why we came when we did. You've probably heard, she—" Abigail was quiet for a moment. "She's beginning to forget things. Sometimes words. Other times how to do things she should know how to do." She accepted the napkin he offered. "I suspect she's the one who wrapped this silverware—two napkins, two forks, one knife, one spoon. It's the sort of thing she does. My grandmother, *Mam*'s mother, got the same way. Eventually, she didn't know our names."

Abigail had no idea why she was telling Ethan all of this. She hadn't talked about her mother's memory problems with anyone but her *dat* and her next-door neighbor, Sarah, back in Wisconsin. She and Sarah had been best friends since first grade. Sarah had a husband and four children now, but no matter how busy she was, she'd always been there for Abigail: in the end with Egan when she'd been running the farm on her own, when she'd made the tough choice to move to Delaware.

"I'm sorry to hear that." Ethan wiped his mouth with his napkin. "My *grossdadi* on my mother's side got like that, too. It was hard. He used to get so upset that the sheep weren't laying eggs."

Abigail giggled, then covered her mouth with her hand. "I'm sorry. That's not funny."

"Sure it is." He grinned. "And the same grandfather used to tell me that sometimes you'd better laugh, otherwise, you'd cry."

"My mother keeps putting salt in my *dat*'s coffee every morning. And he drinks it that way because he doesn't want to upset her."

Ethan laughed as he met her gaze. "That must taste terrible."

She suppressed a giggle, having no idea what had gotten into her. She couldn't believe she was sitting here laughing with Ethan when she had been so angry with him only days before. And talking about her mother.

It was so unlike her to share with someone this way. And a man, no less. She hadn't talked to a man this way since Egan died. That thought sobered her and she took a bite of broccoli casserole from the plate. "So Jamie. You think you can help him with his…digraphs and diphthongs?" she asked.

"Positive. He just needs some one-on-one. What I was thinking, if you would be okay with it, is that Jamie could stay for a little while after school a couple of days a week. Maybe just Monday through Tuesday or Wednesday." He started on half the ham sandwich. "And only half an hour each day. I don't want to over-whelm him or make him feel like he's being punished."

"That would be fine, it would be wonderful, but—"

"But what?" He pointed at the plate between them. "Try the ham. It's good. And there are two brownies." He grimaced. "You can only have one, though. I've a bit of a sweet tooth."

"I can't eat another thing," she told him, holding her hand to her stomach. "Ethan, I appreciate your offer-ing to help Jamie, but you have a whole schoolhouse of students five days a week. I hate to ask you to work longer days."

"You'll be doing me a favor. I feel bad that I didn't catch it the minute Jamie came to my school. And his behavior, I think a lot of it has to do with his frustra-tion in school."

"I don't know about that. He was always a bit naughty, even as—"

"There you are!"

Phoebe approached them on the bench. "I was look-ing for you. Your mother, she, um…" She smiled. "She's looking for you. I think she's a little overwhelmed. So many people she doesn't know."

Abigail jumped up. "I would be so thankful if you'd help Jamie," she said to Ethan. "When do you want to start?"

"How about Monday?"

She gave a nod. "Monday." She stood there smiling at him a moment longer than seemed proper and then she hurried off after Phoebe.

Abigail walked up the schoolhouse lane to find Ethan and Jamie sitting on the steps of the cloakroom. Jamie was supposed to walk home alone after his reading lesson, but she'd decided at the last minute to meet and walk back with him. She'd been working in the garden and her father had been gone all day so she and her mother needed a break from each other. It had taken Abigail longer to hoe two rows and plant radish seeds and broccoli plants with her mother's help than without it.

Abigail had talked to her father about growing some vegetables in hills instead of rows, just to see if there was a difference in the size of the plants or the ease of keeping them watered midsummer. They had agreed. Her father had even sketched a layout of the garden with rows and hills, but June would have none of it. And no matter how many times Abigail had reminded her mother how to dig a small hole and gently place the broccoli seedlings in it, June had either buried them completely or laid them on the ground allowing the roots to dry out. By the time her father returned from his errands in Dover, Abigail had needed a few minutes to herself and walking to school seemed like the perfect opportunity to grab them.

That was what she told herself.

She'd baked cookies and wanted to give Ethan some, just as a thank-you, and if she picked up Jamie, she could give them to him. She knew she could have sent them the next day, but cookies were always so good when they were fresh. And Ethan was being so kind to be working with Jamie this way. They were on week two of his lessons and she was already seeing improvements. Ethan had sent a reader home with him and each night after supper either she or her father read with Jamie for ten minutes. At first, her son had fought her on it, but she was beginning to realize that she could be as stubborn as he could be, and she wasn't giving in on this one. If Ethan said Jamie needed ten minutes of practice five nights a week, he was going to do it.

"Excellent," Ethan said to Jamie as Abigail walked up the oyster shell driveway. He took a book from her son's lap and closed it. "You're just in time," he said, looking up at her. "All done."

"Working outside, are you?" she asked.

Ethan shrugged. "A change of scenery is good sometimes. My older girls did their social studies work sitting in the grass this afternoon." He nodded in the general direction of the back of the white clapboard schoolhouse.

Jamie popped up from the step. "Why are you here? You said I could walk home myself today." He pursed his lips. "I haven't ridden anyone's cows again."

She and Ethan both chuckled.

"Who says I came to walk you home?" Abigail approached them, carrying a little cloth shopping bag she'd made from a scrap of fabric from her mother's sewing room. It was handy for groceries or a task like this one. "I brought Ethan some cookies I made this morning." She held up the gingham bag.

"Cookies?" Jamie ran toward her. "What kind?"

"Oatmeal with chocolate chips."

"My favorite! You bring some for me?"

"*Ne.* I told you, these are for your teacher. Yours are home on the kitchen table."

"Can I run ahead?" Jamie asked excitedly.

"Please." She motioned down the driveway. "Run home. Get rid of some of that energy."

He grabbed his lunch pail from the grass and raced past her.

"I'll be right behind you," she called after him. "I have yeast rolls rising on the counter. Don't fuss with them or they'll fall. Have your cookies and milk, but then I expect you to get on your chores."

The oyster shells crunched under Jamie's feet as he ran.

"Mind the road," she hollered after him.

And then she and Ethan were alone.

She held up the bag of cookies again. "I hope you like oatmeal with chocolate chips."

"You keep bringing me cookies, and brownies and pie and I'm going to have to ask Rosemary to let out my pants." Reading primer in hand, he went up the steps. "Let me just grab my lunch pail and the keys. We'll walk home together."

Which was just what she had hoped he might say.

When Abigail took the notion to bring the cookies to Ethan herself, she realized he might have come to school that morning in his buggy, but secretly, she'd hoped he'd walked. She'd hoped they might walk together as far as her place. They'd done so twice the previous week and then again two days ago. And thinking back, she realized those had been her best days since she'd moved to Delaware.

Of course Ethan had *also* contributed to some of her worst days, but she was over that. She realized now that their bad first encounters were due to her own quick temper. Now, it seemed like she almost craved his company. Phoebe had said he was grumpier than his brothers and Abigail could see how she might get that impression. She'd seen a bit of it early on, but since Ethan had started tutoring Jamie, he'd been nothing but kind and patient. And she found that she liked talking to him. And not just about Jamie. It didn't matter the subject, whether it was his family's buggy business or farming or the school itself.

Monday on the walk home, he'd asked her opinion on the end-of-the-year school program and then he'd actually listened to her thoughts. He'd explained to her that he wanted to have a spelling bee with students being able to compete in different age groups. Of course anyone in the community would be welcome and he expected a good turnout: parents, grandparents, neighbors and family. He was also thinking about combining it with a fund-raiser, but he didn't know what kind. He said he'd thought about getting people to donate items and then auction them off on a piece of paper rather than by an auctioneer. The Englishers called it a silent auction, but he wasn't sure how the bishop would feel about that. It wasn't gambling, which was strictly forbidden, but the idea might be too newfangled. Ethan told her that Bishop Simon was pretty open to new ideas, but he also liked to caution his parishioners to take care they didn't step too far outside the boundaries their ancestors had set. He said it made it harder to find your way back if you got lost.

Abigail looked up to see Ethan coming out of the schoolhouse. He locked the door and walked down the steps toward her, putting his straw hat on his head. His face was suntanned. He must have worked outside the day before. And she noticed he'd gotten his hair cut. It looked nice, and she considered telling him so, but the idea made her feel awkward for some reason, so she didn't.

"How was your day?" she asked. The minute the words came out of her mouth, she felt her cheeks flush. She used to say the same to Egan, days when they didn't see much of each other.

Ethan didn't seem to notice her discomfort. He thought for a moment. That was something she liked about him. He was thoughtful. He chose his words carefully. She tended to respond quickly, too quickly at times, something her father, and even occasionally her husband, had criticized her for Well, maybe not *criticized*, but gently warned of the consequences of not thinking before speaking. It was how she had gotten herself into trouble with Ethan in the first place. She looked up at him as they walked down the driveway toward the road that would lead them home. She was wearing a pale green dress and she'd put on a clean white apron before she left. The string of her white prayer *kapp*, a loop that fell to the nape of her neck, fluttered in the slight breeze.

"Mine was…good," Ethan said. "Let's see. Peter Fisher, who was never a great student, won the eighth and ninth grade spelling bee today by spelling *unforeseeable*. And… Hannah Gruber sat in her chair and did her *entire* math lesson without raising her hand a single time." He chuckled. "I love her dearly, but she constantly needs reassurance and with twenty-seven students in the class, I don't have the time. Oh—" He held up one finger. "*And* I got to eat my own lunch, for once."

"Twenty-seven students. I don't know how you do it." They started down the path, Ethan walking beside the road and she next to the drainage ditch. "And how about Jamie? How was he?"

"He was pretty good. We had an incident at lunch when the boys were supposed to be washing up and somehow they got into a water fight." He glanced at her. "One Jamie started."

She sighed. "I was hoping his behavior would be better when his reading started to improve."

"You said those cookies were for me?" Ethan pointed at the bag she was still carrying.

"*Ya.*"

"Then how about we have one." He took the bag from her, reached in and pulled out two cookies. He offered her one.

She shook her head. "*Ne.* Thank you."

"Oh, come now. Have one. Otherwise I can't. It would be rude for me to eat what looks like a delicious cookie and leave you to watch me. And they're huge." He held one up. "A meal, practically."

She laughed and accepted the cookie. She'd made them big the way her father liked them. They were the size of the palm of her hand and took more work to make than a simple drop cookie. To make one this size, she had to measure out a quarter of a cup of dough, make it into a ball, and then press it onto the cookie sheet with the bottom of a glass that had been dipped in sugar. And the cookie had to be a uniform thickness, or some would turn out overcooked, while others were undercooked.

He took a bite of his cookie. "Mmm. Excellent. I knew it would be."

She nibbled on hers, trying to suppress the pride that swelled in her chest. It was fine to do a good job at something and recognize one's accomplishments, but *hochmut* was a boastful kind of pride and one to be avoided.

"You're quite a baker, Abby." He hesitated. "Is it okay if I call you Abby? For some reason you seem more like an Abby to me than an Abigail."

She thought for a moment. The way he would. Growing up, she had always been Abigail, named after her maternal great-grandmother. And even as a child, when someone called her Abby, she politely corrected them. She had always been Abigail. But she liked the idea of him calling her Abby. There was no denying she had started to feel an attraction to Ethan, and she sensed it was mutual. She didn't want to get ahead of herself, but what if...what if they were to court? To marry even? It wouldn't happen, of course. But she liked the idea that if she remarried, and she thought she would someday, whoever she married would call her something different than Egan had. And Egan had always called her Abigail.

"No one else does," she said hesitantly. She gave a little nod. "But *ya,* you can call me Abby." She looked straight ahead, taking another bite of the cookie that truly was excellent. "I think I'd like that."

"Well, *Abby,* on the subject of your son, I do think his behavior has improved a bit." An old pickup truck approached and passed them and Ethan waited until the sound died away to continue what he was saying. "I hope you weren't expecting an overnight change. For Jamie to wake up a different boy once he could read the word *pears*."

She smiled, knowing he was teasing her a bit. But also being truthful. "*Ne*, it's only that—" She smiled and took a bite of cookie, lowering her head. "I think maybe I *was* hoping it would be an overnight cure," she said. "Because he certainly can be trouble. Saturday he decided to make mud pies and then use my clean sheets as a target. I don't know what gets into him sometimes."

"Well, I can tell you, as a teacher, there is no overnight cure for naughty boys."

She chewed her cookie, enjoying the crunchy texture of the oatmeal and the smoothness of the chocolate chunks. She never used chocolate chips for her baking. She always bought big bars of chocolate and then chopped them up. "My father says I spoil him. That that's why he misbehaves."

Ethan had finished his cookie and reached into the bag for another. "I'd have to agree with your father. That might be part of it. But I think we also have to keep in mind, as you pointed out to me that day you shouted at me—"

"I did not shout," she corrected.

"That day you *didn't* shout at me," he conceded, a teasing tone in his voice, "that Jamie's had a lot of changes in his life." He looked down at her. "He must miss his father," he said quietly.

The tenderness in Ethan's voice brought a lump up in her throat and it took a moment before she could speak again. "Did you and your wife have children?"

"We did not." Now she heard sadness in his voice. "We'd hoped God would bless us with a flock, but…" He didn't finish his sentence. He didn't need to.

She and Egan had hoped for more children, too. But it hadn't been in God's plan. That's what she always told herself when she was sad that she had only Jamie. But hearing Ethan say that he and his wife had not had children, she realized she should always be thankful for what she had and not what she didn't have. She had Jamie to remind her every day, in a good way, of the husband she had loved. Ethan had no one.

She was quiet for a moment and then said, "I don't want to pry, but… May I ask you what her name was? Your wife's?"

"Mary." He smiled as if just speaking her name brought back a good memory of her. "Mary Elizabeth. She was twenty-five. She had a seizure and died. I had just walked out of the room. One minute she was with me and the next…" He took a breath. "She was with God."

"A pretty name," Abigail mused. "I can't imagine what that was like for you, not being able to say goodbye. With Egan, once he was diagnosed with cancer of his pancreas, we knew pretty quickly that he wasn't going to survive it." She took a breath. She had no idea why she was saying these things to Ethan. She was almost in tears. But it also felt good to talk about her husband. To talk to someone who she knew understood what it was like to lose a spouse so young. "We had time to say all the things we wanted to say to each other. To say goodbye. He…he died in my arms. At home," she finished.

Both were quiet for several minutes. Just walking

side by side, lost in their own thoughts. Ethan was quiet so long that she wondered if she had overstepped some invisible boundary. Maybe he thought her sharing something so personal wasn't proper, but when he spoke, his voice was filled with a tenderness that made the backs of her eyelids sting with tears.

"Thank you for telling me about Egan." He tucked the gingham bag with three more cookies still in it into his tin lunch pail. "And thank you for listening to me tell you about Mary. I don't talk about her much."

"I don't talk about Egan. I feel like no one—" She couldn't go on.

"Understands," he finished for her. Then he looked at her. "I don't know how we got on that gloomy topic. Let's not talk about it anymore. It's too pretty a day. Did you come up with any ideas for the end-of-the-school-year program?"

"I did." A sudden excitement came over her. "I don't know how the bishop would feel about this, but back home, we used to have a pie auction. Women would bake pies and they would be auctioned off. But whoever's pie you won, you got to have dinner with the baker because she would pack a meal. You could have the children do their presentation, have the spelling bee, and then maybe there could be a time for games and visiting before the auction."

"I like that idea," Ethan said, nodding. He narrowed his gaze. "But how about a cake auction. I'm not saying I don't like pies, but I love cake."

"A cake auction would be perfect. We could put up a volleyball net. Throw horseshoes or maybe even that Englisher game with the beanbags. And then we could auction off the cakes and with them the picnic baskets.

Husbands always buy their wives' baskets of course, but it gives the singles a chance to spend some time together. A young man is sweet on a young woman—" She shrugged. "They get to spend time together."

"And—" he pointed at her "—find out what kind of cook she is."

She laughed. They were almost to her driveway already. The walk had gone by so quickly. Too quickly. "I suppose that's true." She stopped at her parents' mailbox.

He continued to walk but turned so he was walking backward. "I like the idea for the picnic supper. Let me check with the school board. I know Bishop Simon will be fine with it because we went to one over in Seven Poplars last year together. Will I see you tomorrow?"

She slid the mail out of the mailbox, looking at him questioningly. Was he asking to see her?

"If you pick up Jamie," he told her, "we can walk back together and make plans."

"Oh, I don't know if I can get away. My *dat* might need me to… I don't know," she repeated.

"Let's just plan on it and if you can't come, I'll understand."

"All right." She found herself smiling at him.

"All right. I'll see you tomorrow, Abby." Ethan turned around and walked away, whistling as he went.

Chapter Seven

Ethan was still whistling when he met up with his father in their driveway.

Benjamin waited for him, watching a stray Rhode Island Red chicken cross their path. "You certainly sound chirpy." He'd just left the harness shop where there were two buggies, a horse and wagon, and two pickup trucks parked in the gravel parking lot. He was walking up the lane toward the house, limping slightly.

Ethan shrugged, switching his lunch pail from one hand to the other, seriously considering having another cookie. It would be hours before suppertime, and they had been so delicious. "I had a good day. One of my students' mothers brought me cookies." He slowed his pace so he could walk beside his father. "To thank me for spending some extra time after school with her son. He's struggling with reading."

Ethan felt no need to go into any more detail. It wasn't necessary that others know Jamie couldn't read. It would be righted soon enough. He didn't want to cause embarrassment to his student or Abby.

"She brought you cookies?" His father stopped and

looked up at Ethan, who was several inches taller than he was. "Who?"

"Abigail Stolz. Daniel King's daughter."

"The one you had trouble with?"

Ethan nodded.

A smile tugged at the corners of his father's mouth. "Nice girl. Pretty. Good cook, Rosemary says. Abigail gave her a recipe for brown sugar tarts. Of course I know you've had trouble with her boy." He narrowed his gaze and he waggled his finger. "Karl Lapp had a tale to tell about that one. You marry a woman with a child, you become that child's father. His behavior problems become yours."

"Who said anything about marrying anyone?" Ethan opened his arms wide, his lunch pail swinging in his hand. "She brought me cookies."

"A way to a man's heart…" Benjamin patted his round belly. "I took one bite of your mother's *rosina boi* at a harvest dinner and decided there and then she was the woman for me. Walked right up to her and asked her to walk out with me. We married six months later."

"You did *not* marry my mother merely on the basis of how good a raisin pie she could bake," Ethan argued. "And Jamie is just a little boy." He shrugged. "Little boys are mischief-makers. I know I was when I was his age. Remember that time I took those watercolor paints *Grossmami* gave me and painted *Mam*'s white goat. Gave her spots?"

His father chuckled at the memory, then cocked his head as he resumed walking. His tone became serious. "Abigail you say… Lost her husband a couple of years ago, didn't she?"

Ethan nodded. "She did. It was cancer. They lived

in Wisconsin. After he passed, she ran the farm for a while before it got to be too much. It wasn't until June and Daniel moved here to be closer to his brother that she decided it was time to sell her farm."

His father started toward the house again, his forehead crinkling. "Who's Daniel's brother again?"

Ethan had to think for a minute. "A King over in Seven Poplars. His boy married Hannah Hartman's daughter Susanna. She and her husband live with Hannah and Albert and both have Down's."

His father snapped his fingers. "Right, right. Ebben King. His son David King rides along with Albert sometimes when he makes veterinary calls." He touched the brim of his straw hat. "Wears a paper crown from that burger place all the time. They were out here last fall to have a look at Toby when he got wrapped up in that bit of wire and cut his hock."

"*Ya*, that's him," Ethan agreed, ambling so his father could keep up with him. In the distance, he could hear the sounds of lambs bleating and a guinea hen that must have had her feathers in a ruffle. "I think Ebben is a younger brother to Daniel. I heard that Ebben convinced his brother to move to Delaware for the better climate. Not as much snow to shovel here in the winter as Wisconsin."

"Or upstate New York." His father shook his head. "We sure did shovel our share of snow when we lived there. And then some."

"We sure did," Ethan agreed.

They walked a piece, just enjoying the peacefulness of the afternoon, and then his father spoke again. "You want to ask her to join us Sunday?"

"Ask who?" Ethan drew his head back, wondering what he'd missed.

"The King girl. Stolz. Abigail." His father stroked his graying beard. "It's a visiting day. No church. Weather is supposed to be good. Rosemary thought she'd make a barrel of iced tea, maybe some lemonade, and we'd sit outside. This morning she had Jacob bring the outdoor chairs from the barn and hose them down."

It was on the tip of Ethan's tongue to say of course he wasn't going to invite Abby to visit on Sunday. He didn't invite women anywhere for visiting Sundays or for anything else. But then he realized that he might actually like that. To see Abby this Sunday. It would give them more time to talk about the end-of-the-school-year program. The walk home from the school to her place was too short. An hour together and they could work out all of the details.

But if he was truthful with himself, the fact was that even if they didn't have the school event to plan, he'd enjoy having a glass of tea with her on Sunday afternoon. He might even take her to see the new buggy he and his father were working on. If she'd be interested.

"You should invite the whole family," Ethan's father continued. "I like Daniel from what I can tell. Them still being new to Hickory Grove, it would be the neighborly thing to do." He halted for a moment, breathing heavily.

"You okay, *Dat*?"

Ethan's father rubbed his right hip. "My arthritis is giving me a fit this week. Rosemary wanted me to stay around the house today. Or at least take a cane."

"But you were stubborn," Ethan said.

Benjamin gave a huff and limped forward. "Too much work to be done to be sitting around the house. I should have been at the plow in the garden hours ago. Headed that way now. To hitch up Blue and Carter."

"You already plowed the garden weeks ago."

"Rosemary wants a couple more rows. Wants to plant some fancy kind of sweet corn Edna Fisher was telling her about." He muttered something under his breath that Ethan didn't catch. "I don't know why I bought a place this big. Rosemary told me we didn't need all this land, but I said I wanted it for our sons. Our daughters, too, if any of our girls wanted to raise their families here." He chuckled. "She teased me about being an old woman, wanting all my chicks under one roof."

"I don't know that that will happen. Rosemary's Lovey and her family are settled at his place down the road. And Mary's in New York. I don't see her and Amos and their brood moving south anytime soon."

His father shrugged. "Never know. Your sister and her husband might get to an age when they are tired of shoveling snow, too. Mary said in a letter last week that she was never so glad to see the first spring thaw. Said they had a hundred and seventy inches of snowfall this year. Glad we left that all behind, but Rosemary was right. I tried to tackle too much here. All this land, the upkeep of a big house, the outbuildings." He threw up his hand. "Then I got it in my head to open a harness shop again. Rosemary asked me why. I told her for the same reason we needed all this acreage. For our children. To give them opportunities for an honest day's work." He looked up at Ethan. "It's a good thing I have you here, son. I don't know what I'd do without you."

"What are you talking about? Doing without me," Ethan grumbled. "I'm right here, *Dat.*"

"Right here with no wife. No grandchildren to see me through my old age."

Ethan started to say he wasn't going around that hoop again, but he held his tongue. Instead, he glanced up at the sun, still bright in the sky. "Why don't I get those rows plowed for you and keep you out of hot water with Rosemary. Maybe you could have a look at that seat upholstery I was working on." He pulled the brim of his straw hat down a bit to block the glare of the sun, now lower on the horizon.

His father stopped again, seeming thankful for the break. "What's wrong with it?"

"I don't know. Folds aren't right. Might be the leather, but I'm afraid it's the padding beneath." Ethan gestured impatiently. "Which means I have to pull out all the tacks, lift the leather without tearing it and fix the padding."

His father rubbed his hip, glancing in the direction of the garden beside the house. Part of it was fenced in, but now they were planting outside that area. He and Rosemary were trying to decide whether or not to extend the perimeter of the fence or just plant some crops beyond it this year and take their chances with the critters. "You wouldn't mind plowing? Four rows are all she needs."

"Don't mind at all," Ethan said. "If you don't mind having a look at that buggy seat."

"All right, then." As his father turned to go, he patted him on the shoulder. "Like I said. Don't know what I'd do without you."

Abigail walked beside Ethan up the lane of his family's farm. It was late afternoon and sun had begun to shift in the sky, but it was still warm on her face and she could smell the freshness in the air that spring brought with it. Ethan was walking beside her, explaining the difference between metal-rimmed and rubber-rimmed buggy wheels. She was only half listening, though she'd asked him the question. Instead, her mind kept wandering as she enjoyed the pleasant cadence of his voice.

Ethan had invited her family over for the afternoon. It was a visiting Sunday for their church district. That meant that instead of spending a full day in one of their homes listening to a preacher's sermon, praying and singing hymns, they used the hours for outings to see friends, neighbors or family members. Or hosted. Because Abigail and her family were new to the community and because of her mother's situation, they hadn't even had anyone over. They'd either stayed home or gone visiting since her and Jamie's arrival. Though on the wagon ride over to the Millers, her father had said he would like to have his brother's family over, and maybe a few of their neighbors. He'd asked Abigail if she'd be up to it and she'd agreed. It was only a matter of deciding when.

As Ethan went on explaining the advantages of rubber-rimmed wheels, a smoother, quieter ride being one of them, she dared a glance up at him. He was wearing his Sunday clothes: dark pants and vest with a white shirt with the long sleeves rolled casually to his elbows. Instead of the usual wide-brimmed black felt hat worn to church, he sported his everyday straw hat. His hair was neat, his beard cut shorter than it had been earlier in the week and his hands were clean, his nails neatly trimmed.

Sometimes on visiting Sunday, folks just wore everyday clothes. Abigail was glad that she'd chosen her more formal black dress with a white apron and white cape that went over her shoulders and pinned into her apron. Because of the warmth of the day and casualness of the gathering, she'd just worn a white prayer *kapp* and forgone the black bonnet. But she'd chosen her church *kapp* with the strings hanging in the front, rather than the more modern single loop in the back.

Ethan had sought her out the moment her family arrived. The two of them had been talking all afternoon. She was the one who, a few minutes ago, had suggested they should join the others in the backyard. They had been gone at least an hour. First, he'd taken her to see the harness shop, which she'd never visited, then to the back of the building to where he and his father were building buggies. It wasn't that she wanted to return to the group of women under the trees talking recipes and babies. She was enjoying her time with Ethan.

They'd talked about the end-of-the-school-year fundraiser and agreed to have the cake and picnic basket auction. He'd already gotten the okay from the bishop. They'd talked about Jamie's progress as well and discussed the possibility of continuing tutoring over the summer in the hopes he would be caught up with the other students his age by the time school began in the fall.

But Abigail was beginning to feel guilty about abandoning her responsibilities and felt the need to return to her family. Ethan had assured her that Jamie couldn't get into too much trouble with Jesse by his side. But she was also concerned about her mother. Her mother wasn't as comfortable being with strangers anymore. She'd refused invitations to go visiting and to join a quilting circle. Her mother's excuse had been that there was too much work to be done in the house and garden, but Abigail had a suspicion her mother was turning into a homebody because that was where she was the most comfortable. When she got outside her own surroundings, she began to forget people's names, words for common objects, simple tasks. She stressed over her forgetfulness and that seemed to make her more forgetful.

Then, there was the issue of decorum. Single men and single women weren't supposed to spend hours alone talking. Even at their age, and even though they were both widowed, the tradition was to have a chaperone. It could be anyone, an elderly aunt, another couple, even a child. It was Abby's opinion that such rules were a bit silly. After all, she and Ethan weren't teenagers. And they both had been baptized long ago. Neither would ever say or do something inappropriate. Still, she was new to the community and she didn't want her behavior to reflect poorly on her parents.

She stole another glance at Ethan. He was a handsome man: larger than his brothers and father, taller. Not stout like Benjamin, but muscular. More muscular than Egan had been. Her thoughts drifted back to her husband, but the stab of pain she had felt for so long wasn't there today. She'd been feeling it ease for the last six months or so. It wasn't that she didn't still love Egan, but she'd noticed a subtle difference. Life without him was getting, if not easier, more comfortable.

"Do you still miss her?" Abigail asked suddenly.

Ethan halted and looked down at her. For a long moment he didn't reply. Maybe he didn't know who she was referring to, but then he answered.

"My wife? *Ya.* Every day."

She nodded thoughtfully. "Me, too. I knew Egan from my school days. His family was in our church district. We saw each other growing up, through our teens. He was always there." She lifted her gaze. "Where did you meet Mary?"

He stroked his beard, seeming to consider whether or not to tell her. "She was visiting a neighbor of ours. We met at singing the first week she arrived. I was there chaperoning more than attending the singing. I was getting a little old for that sort of thing."

A pure white cat with red eyes walked lazily down the lane toward them and they both watched it for a moment.

"Mary was only supposed to stay with her cousins for two weeks, but she stayed four. Which turned to six." Ethan was still watching the cat. "We'd known each other two months and three days when I asked her to marry me."

The cat walked up to Ethan and rubbed against his pant leg. Abigail could hear it purring loudly. "So you didn't court for long?"

He shook his head. "That was spring. We married in November. Most weddings in our community up in New York were in November." He surprised her by squatting down to pet the cat. "Snowball," he said.

"What's that?"

"The cat. Her name is Snowball." He stroked the cat's fluffy white coat. "One of my students brought her to me this winter. She's an albino. His parents were going to drown her, so he smuggled her out of his barn and brought her to school. He couldn't bear the thought. He begged me to take her, so I did."

Abigail smiled faintly, touched by his tenderness.

"Egan and I courted for some time. He wasn't ready to marry. Still sowing his oats. We saw each other all the time, but we'd agreed that if we ever met someone else we were interested in, we were free to get to know him or her."

"That ever happen?" He scratched the cat behind her ears.

"*Ne.* One day Egan just came to me and said it was time. He said he loved me. That he'd always loved me, and that God was leading him to become a husband, a father and he wanted to marry me." The cat moved on to her, purring and rubbing against her ankle. She crouched down to pet it. "We took our time marrying because we thought we'd have a lifetime together," she said softly. When she looked up, he was studying her intently.

"I know what you mean about thinking we had a whole life ahead of us," he said. "We thought the same thing. We had so many plans."

Abigail felt a scratchiness behind her eyelids. She stroked the cat. She had no idea why she had brought up the subject of their spouses. Had God led her here? She'd been praying so hard these last few months for Him to show her the way out of this loneliness. Was He leading now? Was that how she had ended spending the afternoon with her son's schoolmaster? The idea seemed outlandish, yet maybe not. "I was so lost after Egan died."

"Me, too. After I lost Mary."

"And I felt so alone, even though I had my *mam* and *dat* and Jamie."

He gestured in the direction of the house. "We've

got two kitchen tables to seat us all at suppertime. And I still feel lonely."

"For Mary?" she asked.

He nodded. "For Mary but also for—" He sighed. "For a life of my own. Children," he finished, emotion in his voice.

She met his solemn gaze and smiled. "I understand."

"Most don't. But I think you do," he said. Slowly he came to his feet and she did the same. And for what seemed like a long time, he just stood, looking into her eyes.

Abigail felt like she should say something, but she didn't know what.

"Ethan!" a voice rang out.

Abigail and Ethan both looked up the driveway in the direction of the voice. It was Jesse and he was coming at them at a dead run. "Ethan! Abigail! Come quick!"

Abigail's first thought was that Jamie had been hurt. Or done something bad again. She hurried toward Jesse.

The boy cupped his hands around his mouth. "Benjamin sent me to fetch you both!"

"What is it?" Ethan called, taking long strides, passing her. "What's wrong?"

"Is it Jamie?" Abigail walked fast, nearly breaking into a run. Last she'd seen her son, he was headed toward the pond with Jesse and some other boys from down the road. Her son knew how to swim, and he'd begged to be allowed to go with the older boys. Her father had said he would be fine. Ethan, too, but what if—

"Jesse!" Ethan said sharply. "Did something happen to Jamie?"

"Ne." Jesse panted, almost to them now. "It's June."

Abigail clutched her chest with one hand. "My

mother?" She couldn't imagine what could be wrong with her mother. She was healthy as a horse. It was her father who'd had to see a cardiologist once. "Is she sick?"

"*Ne.* Not sick." Jesse came to a halt and leaned over to rest his hands on his knees, panting hard. "She's missing," he finally managed as he gulped for air. "We can't find her anywhere on the farm."

Chapter Eight

Abigail found her father in front of the Millers' barn, buckling their horse's harness. "You lost *Mam*?" she questioned sharply.

Her father glanced at her, then at Jamie who was standing on the other side of their bay. Thankfully, at least she didn't have to worry about her son at the moment.

"Check that side," her father told Jamie. He looked back at her. "I didn't *lose* your mother." He threw up one hand, clearly upset. "She was sitting under the trees with the women. She was fine. Having a good time, I think. I just walked down to the horse pasture with Benjamin to check on his mare that's about to foal. She was right there." He pointed in the direction of the picnic tables and chairs under the shade of a big silver poplar tree.

When Abigail had walked down to the harness shop with Ethan, there had been half a dozen women sitting there, surrounded by small children, talking about the best stitches to use on particular quilt patterns. Her mother *had* seemed fine. She had actually been excited to go to the Millers' and had seemed relatively at ease when Abigail had left her seated beside Edna Fisher.

Now the women who had been sitting in the chairs drinking lemonade and iced tea were bustling around the yard, children trailing behind them, calling, "June? June!"

"Check the garden again," one of Ethan's stepsisters, Abigail didn't know which, called to another. "And around the pond."

Abigail returned her attention to her father. She felt terrible. She shouldn't have been gone so long with Ethan. She should have stayed at her mother's side. It was her duty. "Are you sure she's not in the house?" she asked, pressing her hand to her forehead.

"She's not in the house," her father replied, running his hand over the bay's bridle.

"In the bathroom?" Abigail asked, feeling more anxious by the second.

"Not in the bathroom." Her father was growing terser with her by the moment. "And nowhere that we can find her on the property. We've already looked. Everyone has looked. And called her and looked again."

"How long has she been missing?" Abigail exclaimed.

"I don't know. Half an hour, maybe." Her father looked to Jamie. "Good on that side?"

"Ya, Grossdadi."

"Goot. Hop up." He gestured to the wagon.

"Dat!" Abigail exclaimed. "Where are you going?"

"Abigail," Ethan said, startling her.

She hadn't even heard him approach.

"No need to panic," Ethan said calmly.

"No need to *panic*?" She swung around to face him,

her tone growing shrill. "You don't understand. My *mam*, she doesn't—" She lowered her voice. "She gets confused. I told you that."

"I understand, but it's going to be all right." He brushed his hand across her shoulder blade. "She couldn't have gotten far."

It was only the briefest touch, but Abigail felt the flutter of anxiety in her chest ease. There was something about the gentle tone of his voice that calmed her. She took a deep breath. "You're right. She can't be far. She hasn't been gone long and she's not much of a walker anymore," she said, trying to gain her composure.

Ethan turned to her father. "Jesse just told me that one of the Fisher boys saw June walking across the field, headed for the road. They didn't think anything of it."

Abigail looked at her father. "She must have just gone home."

"That's what I'm thinking," Ethan agreed.

Abigail spotted Jesse leading Ethan's horse and wagon into the barnyard as chickens scattered to get out of their way.

"Here you go, all hitched and ready to go," Jesse called to his big brother.

Ethan grabbed the reins. "You should stay here, in case she comes back here," he told Abigail.

"I'm not staying here! She could be walking along the road. You know how fast those cars go!" She hurried toward her father's wagon.

"Jamie, you stay here. Keep a look out for your *grossmami*," Ethan ordered. "Your *grossdadi* and *mam* will head for home."

"Where are you going?" Abigail asked as Jamie jumped down and she clambered up into her father's wagon. The moment her black Sunday shoes touched the floorboards, her father tightened the reins and eased their bay backward.

"I'm going to follow you." Ethan leaped up into his wagon and remained standing as he took a rein in each hand.

"Why are you following us?" Abigail called over her shoulder as her father pulled around.

"In case she's not there," Ethan called back.

Abigail sat down hard on the seat as the wagon lurched forward, understanding Ethan's meaning. He was taking his wagon in case her mother hadn't gone home. In case she really was lost.

When Ethan saw Abby come running from her house, he knew June wasn't there. And she hadn't been on the road between his place and the Kings', else they would have seen her. If she'd cut across the field as the Fisher boy said, if she was headed home, they should have seen her on the road.

"She isn't here!" Abby called as she ran toward his wagon.

Despite the seriousness of the situation, he smiled inwardly. There weren't many Amish women her age who would run, no matter what the situation. Certainly not on a Sabbath day. He knew his Mary wouldn't have. But there was something about the strength of Abby's love for her mother, for her family that touched him. She would run to look for her mother. She'd go head-to-head with a schoolmaster over her son. The fact that she had been wrong about the situation with Jamie didn't matter. What impressed him was the fierceness of her love for her child, for her whole family.

"*Dat*'s going to look around, but she's not here. If she were, Boots wouldn't have been on her chair on the porch." Reaching his wagon, she hitched up her skirt.

Ethan threw out his hand and she accepted it, leaping up into his wagon. "Who's Boots?" he asked.

"*Dat*'s dog." She pointed at their border collie. "She's not allowed on the chairs. *Mam* won't have it. Boots only does it when *Mam* isn't home."

The black-and-white dog was now on the porch steps barking at him, but with no great menace.

"Drive," she ordered, releasing Ethan's hand.

It was odd, but he almost felt a sense of loss when she let go. All these years since Mary's death, Ethan hadn't been able to bring himself to even think about another woman and suddenly, there was Abby. Abby whom he wanted to talk to. Wanted to be with.

"Drive," she repeated, dropping onto the wooden bench seat as she gestured forward.

"Where we going?" he asked, loosening the reins, but still on his feet. Butterscotch was a mare who had always taken a light hand. At the slightest urging, she broke into a trot, seeming to sense the importance of the situation.

"I don't know." Abby shook her head, her *kapp* strings swinging. "Back to the road. Maybe she was trying to go home and missed our driveway."

He'd noticed Abby had worn her church prayer *kapp* today, not an everyday *kapp* like some of the women, like his stepsisters. The movement of the starched linen strings seemed almost like tendrils of Abby's blond hair and he felt a heaviness in his chest, an urge to protect her, to protect her family. To make everything all right, just as he had promised it would be.

He eased onto the bench seat beside her.

"Let's keep going up Cherry Road, in the direction of the main road." She pressed her hands to the seat to steady herself. "Maybe she—I don't know—I don't know—"

She sounded as if she was close to tears and without thinking, Ethan reached down and covered her hand with his. "I'll find her," he promised.

Abby looked up at him. She wasn't crying, but her eyes were moist. Blue eyes, big blue eyes. He swallowed hard. Then took the reins firmly in both hands and urged Butterscotch to go faster.

And find her he did. They were riding down the road at a trot, him scanning one side of the road and the fields, Abby the other. They'd passed neighbors from another church district, the Yoders from over near Rose Valley, and called to them as they passed, asking if they might have seen June. George and Eda Yoder and their passel of little ones had promised to keep their eyes out for her.

Ethan spotted June as they were passing the school. He almost missed her, but out of the corner of his eye, he saw movement behind the schoolhouse. He made a U-turn right in the middle of the two-lane road.

"What is it?" Abby grabbed the side of the wagon as Ethan whipped it around and it rocked precariously. "Is it *Mam*? Did you see her?"

He came to his feet, slowing Butterscotch down so as not to startle June. If it *was* June, which he was pretty certain it was. What other seventy-year-old woman dressed in Sunday church black, a white apron and white cape would be swinging on a child's swing?

"I think so. Maybe," Ethan said under his breath as he turned into the school's driveway.

Butterscotch stepped high, the oyster shells familiar under her feet. As they came around the corner of the schoolhouse, Abby saw her mother at the same moment that Ethan did.

"Mam!" Abby cried out. She barely waited until the wagon had rolled to a stop to leap down and rush across the grass.

Sighing with relief, Ethan took his time tying down the reins and climbing down from the wagon. He didn't bother to tie Butterscotch up. He knew she wouldn't go anywhere.

"Mam, we've been looking for you." Abby wasn't running now, but she was walking fast, her *kapp* strings fluttering behind her again. "What are you doing here?"

June King was a sight to behold: a tiny, frail bird of a woman dressed all in black and white. Except for her shoes. She'd shed those, and petite bare feet poked out from beneath her dress as she swung forward on the swing. It was a child's swing, chains and a canvas seat, set at a height for Ethan's younger students, but the right height for June who couldn't have been five feet tall.

June gazed at the both of them, a slight smile of something that couldn't be described any other way but satisfaction on her face. And swung higher.

"Mam," Abby said, the relief in her voice turning to frustration. "What are you doing here?" she repeated.

June pumped her legs and flew backward. "Swinging."

Ethan couldn't resist a smile, but he dropped it as Abby looked back at him.

Abby walked closer. "We looked everywhere for you, *Mam*. I thought you were lost or hurt or—"

"Not lost or hurt, as you can see," June responded.

"What are you doing here? Why are you swinging?"

"Haven't been on a swing in years. Not since my school days. The ladies and I were talking about our school days. About the desks all lined up. Learning our numbers. Swinging on a swing at recess. At my school, we didn't have a fancy swing like this." She pointed at the rusty metal swing set a member of the school board had procured from one of the public schools in Dover when they remodeled their playgrounds some years ago. "Ours hung from a tree. Pin oak, I think it was," June mused. "I wanted to swing again."

"*Mam*, you have to get off the swing," Abby said, pointing at the grass.

"Why?" June asked. "I like it. It's fun. You should try it."

Ethan had to look away not to smile this time. He knew it wasn't funny. He understood why Abby and Daniel and everyone else had been so concerned when June had gone missing. He had already gathered from things Abby had said, and from June's behavior the couple times he'd seen her, that she was suffering from some form of dementia. It was evident not so much in her forgetfulness but in her lack of the normal inhibitions most adults had. But…the joy in June's voice just made him want to smile. The fact that she could find such pure pleasure in something so simple as a child's swing lightened his heart.

"*Mam*, get down now." Abby pointed at the ground. "We have to go. *Dat*'s waiting for you." She stepped even closer, close enough for June to almost touch her with her little bare feet when she swung forward. "He was worried. We didn't know where you were."

When June continued to swing, Abigail said tersely, "*Mam*, it's *Sunday*."

With a huff, June leaned backward, allowing the swing to slow.

Abby picked up her mother's black leather shoes and black stockings that were lying in the grass. As she gathered them, Ethan watched her with admiration. She was a good daughter. Certainly, a good mother. He'd enjoyed the afternoon with her. Enjoyed it far more than he had anticipated.

"Let's go home," Abby told her mother and the two women walked toward the wagon.

Ethan helped June onto the back bench seat and waited, his eyes averted as Abby put her mother's stockings on for her and then her shoes and tied them.

"Straighten your *kapp*, *Mam*," Abby said when she was done with the business of the shoes. Then she turned to Ethan and looked up at him. "I don't know how to thank you."

"No need to thank me. I'm just glad she's okay," he said softly.

"Cookies or brownies?" There was a playfulness in her voice. "Or maybe a batch of my blondies. You'd like them. I make them with macadamia nuts and white chocolate chunks."

"She makes a decent blondie," June piped up from the back of the wagon. "But I like her *mandelplaettchen* better. No one makes better almond wafers in all of Wisconsin. That's what all the ladies say."

Neither Ethan nor Abby looked back at June.

"I'll take the blondies," he said.

* * *

Abigail gave a nod, smiling back at him. "Blond-ies it is."

The sound of a buggy approaching caught her attention and she glanced up. It was the Fishers: Edna, John and more children in their wagon than seemed possible to fit in the rear. They slowed, then seeing June, waved as they passed.

"Good to see all's well, ends well," Edna called.

Abby waved back, thankful the Fishers didn't stop to ask where they had found her mother. She didn't know if her mother would be embarrassed by the truth, but even if her mother wouldn't be, Abigail wasn't ready for questions. She wasn't ready to discuss her mother's situation with people she barely knew.

They drove the last half mile in comfortable silence. Then, just as Ethan went to make the turn into their driveway, her mother said from the back seat, "Supper."

"We already planned our supper, *Mam*. We're having the rest of that roaster we made yesterday," Abby said over her shoulder. "And creamed cabbage and greens with mustard sauce. We picked those nice greens yesterday, you and I."

"I'm not asking what we're having for supper tonight," her mother declared indignantly. She leaned forward, thrusting herself between Ethan and her daughter. She looked at Ethan. "Come to supper. Not tomorrow night. Not the next night. The next one." She touched her hand to her forehead. "I don't know what day that is, offhand, but that day. You know which one I mean."

"Wednesday," Abby supplied, not sure if she liked the idea or not of having Ethan to supper. It certainly seemed like the right thing to do. Without Ethan's help, she didn't know how long it would have taken to find her mother.

Nonetheless, once she issued the invitation to supper, she fretted. There was no telling what her mother might say or do. Her mother might be perfectly fine. But she might also come to the supper table wearing her winter wool cloak, or worse, an undergarment over the top of her clothes. Or she might tell a tale of when she grew up living in a cookie house. It had happened before. It was a realistic concern.

"Wednesday," her mother repeated, still addressing Ethan. "Come Wednesday. Have supper, then you and my daughter can take a walk down to the pond." She poked him with one of her tiny, bony fingers. "It's a nice place for walking, our pond."

Abby was sure her face turned bright red. She couldn't look at Ethan. *"Mam,"* she chastised. "Ethan doesn't want to walk to the pond. You invited him for supper."

They turned into the driveway and suddenly Abigail remembered her son. "Jamie," she said. She'd been so caught up in the drama of her missing mother, and then the whole thing with Ethan that she had forgotten about her son. She brought her hands to her cheeks. "He's still at your place," she told Ethan.

"I'll go back, fetch him and bring him home." He glanced at her as they rode up the driveway. "Unless you want to ride back to my place with me. I can bring you both back."

Abigail was tempted. She'd had such a nice day with him that she hated to see it end. But then she thought better of it. She needed to get her mother safely home and rested. At her age, her mother had to be exhausted to have walked so far. And then all that swinging. And Abigail needed to get supper on the table. The whole family had to be famished. "I'd best stay here and get her settled." She tilted her head in her mother's direction. "Would you mind fetching Jamie? I know he could probably walk but I don't think my heart could take it tonight. I've already had enough excitement for one Sabbath."

His mouth turned up in a half smile. "*Ne*, I don't mind a bit."

As they came up the drive, Abigail's father hurried down the porch steps, relief on his face. Boots barked and raced for the wagon wheels.

"Found her. She's fine," Ethan called as he pulled up at the porch.

"June," Abigail's father said, his eyes red. "Where have you been?" He reached up and lifted her down from the wagon.

"The schoolmaster is coming for supper," Abigail's mother announced as her husband ushered her toward the house.

Abigail remained in the wagon, watching her parents go into the house and then she turned to Ethan. "I can't thank you enough for helping us." She shook her head. "She's never wandered off before but something terrible could have—" She exhaled, considering how much more to say, but then blurted, "*Dat*... I think he has his head buried in the sand. He says she's fine but makes excuses for her all the time. Blames himself or us for her mistakes. I keep telling him there's something wrong, but he gets upset when I even try to talk about it. He says I don't know what I'm talking about. That she's just forgetful."

Ethan rubbed his thumbs along the smooth leather of the reins. "Has she been to a doctor about this?"

She exhaled. "*Ne*. Like I said, *Dat* doesn't think there's anything wrong with her."

"Can I make a suggestion?"

She looked up at him. She found it so interesting that he didn't seem much like the man she had argued with at the end of her driveway a month ago. This side of him she had seen today had been so kind, so patient.

"What should I do?" she asked.

"Make an appointment for your *mam* with a neurologist. That's a doctor that knows about the brain. She can be tested."

She considered the idea. While her parents weren't beyond seeing a doctor, they had no health insurance. The Amish didn't believe in health insurance. A person paid their own doctor's bills, or if there was an accident or a severe illness like her Egan's cancer, the entire community pitched in. "That could be expensive. This friend of *Mam*'s back in Wisconsin, she had, you, know—" she waved her hand "—some kind of scans. It was costly."

"I can get the name of a good neurologist Rosemary knows about. A friend of hers over in Rose Valley used her."

"A woman neurologist?" Abigail asked in surprise.

He shrugged. "I guess so. Rosemary's friend talked to the doctor about the costs and the doctor did some tests, but not others. I think a neurologist can talk to someone, ask questions and make a good guess if the problem is just forgetfulness or something else. Like Alzheimer's, that's what my *grossdadi* had. You've heard of that, right?"

She nodded.

"Then there might be some kind of medicine your *mam* could take. I don't think there's a cure, but it might help her."

Abigail exhaled. The idea of convincing her father her mother needed to see a doctor, then tracking down the name and phone number of a neurologist, making an appointment, and getting there seemed overwhelming. But she didn't want to tell Ethan that. She didn't want him to think she was helpless.

Seeming to sense her hesitation, he said, "I could find out the doctor's name. And we've got a phone at the harness shop. You could walk over and make the call."

"I could do that," she agreed slowly.

"And I can give you the names of some drivers we use. Or even…" He hesitated. "I'd go with you if you wanted. If…your *dat* didn't want to. School will be out soon and then I'll just be working on the farm." He opened his arms. "It wouldn't be a problem."

"Thank you." She offered a quick smile. "I'll talk to *Dat*. And to *Mam*," she added. "She knows something's wrong. She gets frustrated sometimes when she can't remember things. She might want to go see a doctor." She clasped her hands looking down at them. "Thank you," she said again softly. "For everything." She stood to get out of the wagon. "So I guess we'll see you for supper." She stepped to the ground and looked up at him. "Wednesday."

"Wednesday supper it is," he agreed. "But I hope I'll see you before that," he called as he pulled away.

Abigail's father was waiting for her on the porch steps, his hands in his pockets, watching Ethan pull away. "You walking out with him?" he asked.

Abigail looked up, her skirt bunched in her hands. "What? *Ne.*" She shook her head. "What would give you that idea?"

Her father continued to watch Ethan go down the driveway. "You've been seeing a lot of him. Walking home together from school most days. And you were gone more than an hour today with him over at his place."

Abigail stopped in front of her father. "He was showing me the harness shop. And…and where he and his *dat* are making buggies," she said suddenly flustered. "We talked about Jamie's progress."

"Showing you the buggy he's making," her father repeated, seeming amused.

"*Ya, Dat.* I wanted to see it." She brushed past him, annoyed he would even think such a thing. What had given him the idea Ethan would be interested in courting her?

He turned to watch her go. "Well, if he didn't ask you to court him, only be a matter of time."

Abigail looked up to see her *mam* in the doorway clap her hands together and squeal with delight. "Abigail's courting the schoolmaster!" she exclaimed, bouncing on the balls of her feet the way Jamie did sometimes. "We're going to have a wedding!"

"*Mam!*" Abigail opened the screen door. "No one's courting anyone. No one said anything about a wedding. *Dat?*" She turned to him, her expression pleading.

But he just laughed and shrugged as he followed them into the kitchen. "You know your *mam.* I can't do a thing with her."

Chapter Nine

"I don't understand," Jamie whined to his mother from down the hall. "Why is *Tietscher* coming for supper?"

Abigail had sent him to wash his face and hands before supper. Ethan would be there any moment and for some reason she was all a jitter. She had nothing to be nervous about. Her mother had invited a neighbor to supper, that was all this was. And she knew how to make supper for a neighbor; she'd done it a hundred times. The table was set, she'd just pulled the *schnitz un kneff* out of the oven and the whole kitchen smelled like the smoked pork and dried apple dish. She had hot potato salad resting on the back of the stove, along with a saucepan of lima beans with bacon to be reheated. The freshly baked buttermilk biscuits were already on the table. She just had to grab the apple butter and the blackberry jam she'd brought from Wisconsin out of the icebox. It was a good weeknight supper. Actually, more suitable for a dinner. But on weekdays, during the school year, her family tended to eat like Englishers and have their heavier meal at the end of the day rather than midday, so Jamie could be included.

Abigail fussed with her apron, worried now that it was too much, such a big meal. That it would seem as if she was trying to show off her cooking skills. Would he think her too prideful? She'd even made two desserts not knowing which he would prefer: a fruit pudding and a German nut cake. She knew he had a sweet tooth, but one dessert probably would have been enough.

"*Mam*, why is *Tietscher* coming to supper?" Jamie repeated, walking into the kitchen. His hands were still wet, and he had missed a smudge of dirt on his face, but he smelled as if he had at least used soap.

Abigail handed her son a dish towel. "Dry your hands." She went to the stove to turn the lima beans back on. Like many Amish homes, they had both a woodstove and a gas stove for cooking, but she preferred the gas stove. The temperatures on the stove top and the oven were more predictable. Her mother, however, preferred the woodstove and had used it to bake corn bread muffins which Abigail was afraid weren't going to be edible. Her mother had added too much salt to the batter and then burned the bottoms. Abigail had considered throwing the muffins to the chickens and just serving the biscuits, but her mother was so pleased with having made them that she couldn't bring herself to do it.

Maybe, Abigail thought to herself, she could move the basket to the far end of the table and hope, with all of the other food on the table, Ethan wouldn't take one.

"*Mam*." Jamie drew out the word.

Abigail looked down at her son in exasperation. "Your grandmother invited him. As a…thank-you." Originally, Ethan had been invited for supper Wednesday, but he'd ended up postponing until Friday because he'd gone with his father to a doctor's appointment Wednesday and had had another commitment Thursday night.

"What's she thanking him for?" Jamie asked, sounding sulky as he dried his hands with the rooster towel. "For finding her when she got lost?"

"Your grandmother wasn't lost." Abigail gave the lima beans a stir, the pools of delicious bacon fat curling around her wooden spoon. "She...went for a walk and...didn't tell us where she was going."

"Liz Fisher, she's in my class, she told me she saw you and Teacher coming from school Sunday with *Grossmami* in the back of the wagon. Her *mam* told her that—"

"Liz Fisher needs to mind her own knitting," Abigail interrupted. She tapped her left cheekbone. "You missed a spot. Right here."

He took the towel and swiped at his face.

"Don't—" But it was too late. Before she could get the words out, he'd already wiped the kitchen towel on his dirty face. "That was clean," she told him. "Put it in the laundry now."

He groaned, dragging his feet as he walked out of the kitchen.

Abigail grabbed a clean towel from the basket on top of the pie safe. It was probably just as well she didn't have her mother's red rooster towel out. What would Ethan think of an Amish kitchen with a red towel?

Boots began to bark from the porch and Abigail whipped around. She hadn't heard buggy wheels. Ethan must have walked. She turned down the burner under the lima beans and ducked into the bathroom down the hall to catch a quick look at herself in the mirror. Tucking a stray tendril of blond hair into her prayer *kapp*, she walked calmly back through the kitchen and out onto the back porch to greet her guest.

Her *parents'* guest, she reminded herself. He wasn't there to see her.

Or was he?

Supper went even better than Abigail had hoped. Ethan ate heartily, complimenting her on the meal, which made her pleasantly uncomfortable. He and her father seemed to get along well. They talked about crops, about the buggy Ethan and his father were making, and the weather. With spring coming late and too much rain, then not enough, the farmers were all worried about planting. It was the same conversation men had every year, had been having since she was a girl.

Ethan had taken one of her mother's corn muffins, despite Abigail's attempt to keep the basket away from him, but if he noticed how heavily they had been salted or how burnt they were, he didn't show it. He ate the whole thing slathered with fresh-churned butter and blackberry jam and told her mother how good they were. June had giggled with glee, promising to pack a sack of them for him to take home. After supper, it was Abigail's mother who reminded her daughter and Ethan that they should go for a walk.

Abigail was pleasantly surprised that her mother had remembered saying that almost a week ago but embarrassed at the same time that she would bring it up. "*Mam*, I'm sure Ethan needs to get home. I imagine he has chores to do," she said, getting up from her chair. She'd relaxed during the meal and enjoyed herself thoroughly. It was so nice to have someone else at their supper table, to have a younger man again. But suddenly she was anxious. It was kind of Ethan to accept her mother's invitation to supper, but she certainly didn't want him to feel obligated to anything else. Certainly not to *go for a walk* with her.

"Ya," Ethan agreed, still sitting at the foot of the table across from Abigail's father. "I should get home. My *dat*'s hip's acting up. He might need a hand with evening chores." He glanced at Abigail. "Want to walk me to the end of the driveway, Abby?"

Abigail froze, the serving dish of the leftover lima beans in her hands. "I… I best help *Mam* clean up."

"Oh, fiddle!" her mother declared sounding more like her old self than Abigail had heard in months. "Leave the dishes and walk to the end of the lane with *Tietscher*. Your father can help me, and Jamie can, too."

"I have chores," Jamie said sullenly. He'd been quiet throughout the meal, picking at his food, which was unusual. He normally had a big appetite for a boy his size.

"You do have chores," Abigail's father agreed, getting up as he reached for the basket of salty corn muffins. "But they'll wait. You can help your *grossmami* clear off the table, first."

"Women's work," Jamie muttered, staring at his plate.

"Jamie," Abigail scolded. "Don't speak to your grandfather that way."

"Women's work you say?" Ethan asked, his tone easygoing. He picked up his plate and utensils and carried them to the sink. "In my father's house, and it's a big household, we all pitch in together. It's the way my *mam* brought us up. My brothers and I aren't above mopping a kitchen floor or weeding in the garden and my sisters work at the harness shop. They even repair harnesses sometimes."

"They do?" Jamie asked, begrudgingly interested. "How do they know how to do that stuff?"

"My *dat* taught them. My brothers and I taught them." Ethan walked back to the table and grabbed two empty buttermilk glasses. "If you like, you can come home with me one day after school and I'll show you around the shop. Show you what we do."

Jamie looked to his mother as he slid out of his chair. She nodded, silently agreeing she'd let him go. He picked up his plate and silverware and took it to his grandmother.

Abigail's mother took the glasses from Ethan's hands and looked up at him. He towered over her, but she didn't seem to be intimidated. "It was good to have you for supper, Ethan. You come again. Now shoo." She made a sweeping motion with her tiny hands, sudsy from dishwater.

Ethan glanced at Abigail, a look of amusement on his face. "I think we've been dismissed," he told her.

"I think *you* have." She smiled to herself. She liked his sense of humor. It was hard to believe this was the same man she had argued with on more than one occasion. Like on Sunday, tonight he had seemed so relaxed. So easygoing. Not so sad.

Ethan said his goodbyes and left the kitchen. Abigail followed. In the laundry room, he grabbed his straw hat and put it on his head. Abigail donned a sweater that fell open across the front and had no buttons. She'd stitched it herself from navy blue sweatshirt material. It got chilly this time of day, once the sun began to set, and there had been the smell of rain when she'd tossed the potato peels to the chickens earlier.

They were just about to go out the door when Abigail's mother came hurrying after them, a small cloth sack in her hand. "You forgot your corn muffins." Grinning, she held them up to Ethan.

"I sure did. And wouldn't I have been sorry when I'd gotten home and realized I didn't have them," he said, taking the bag from her. "Good night."

Abigail's mother trotted back into the kitchen and Abigail and Ethan took their leave. They walked through the barnyard and headed down the lane, side by side. Boots trailed behind them.

"The meal was great, Abby. Thank you," Ethan said when they were away from the house.

She clasped her hands together looking down as she walked. "You're welcome. It was nice to have someone else at the table. Even though our family is small, back home in Wisconsin we always had friends and neighbors joining us. It was nothing to cook supper for a dozen."

"Well, I enjoyed *not* eating with a dozen people." He glanced at her. "And Rosemary and the girls are good cooks but, phew—" he made a sound of approval "—that *schnitz un kneff*, I'd have to say it's the best I've ever had."

She pressed her lips together to keep from smiling. "You even enjoyed the corn muffins?"

"Probably the best part of the meal," he teased, holding up the cotton sack.

She tried to suppress a chuckle. "You like them that salty?"

He nodded, chuckling with her. "I like them with lots of jam. Lots. And two glasses of water."

She laughed. "That's good because it looks like *Mam* gave you enough to take in your lunch for days." Then looking up at him, she said, "I'm sorry. I didn't mean to trick you. *Mam* made them and she was so proud of them. I tried to warn you at the table not to take one, but I couldn't catch your eye."

"It's fine." He gave a wave of dismissal and met her gaze. "I'd have eaten two more if it would have made your mother happy."

His words touched her and she looked away, surprised by the tightness in her chest. The tenderness she felt for him. He had been so kind to her mother, so friendly with her father and he'd even drawn Jamie into a conversation. Ethan had seemed so comfortable at their table, so comfortable that it was as if he belonged there.

Ethan and Abigail walked in silence for a few steps and then, to change the subject, she said, "It sounds like everything is set for the end-of-the-school-year program next week."

"Thanks to your idea. I think we're going to have a good turnout. I hear a few folks from Seven Poplars might be joining us. They've got a matchmaker over there, Sara Yoder, who's got the idea in her head that it might be a nice event for some of her singles she's trying to make matches with."

Abigail was so surprised she stopped short and the border collie nearly ran into her, he was following her so close. "A matchmaker? I didn't know there was such a thing anymore."

He shrugged. "*Ne?* I'm surprised. She's a cousin to Hannah Hartman from Wisconsin. You didn't know her?"

Abigail chuckled and started to walk again. "Wisconsin is a big state. A lot of Amish communities. I don't know her. But now I'm curious to meet her."

"You're in luck because she'll be there." He stopped where the lane met the blacktop and slid his hands into his pockets. "Did you talk to your *dat* about your *mam* seeing a doctor?"

"I did." She exhaled. "He's not happy, but he's agreed to let her go." She looked down. Her father's dog had plopped himself down in the driveway between the two of them and was looking from one to the other as if following the conversation. She smiled and scratched Boots's head. "But he says he'll be no part of it." She hesitated. "If I take her to the neurologist, you'd be willing to…go along?"

"I sure will. Just say the word."

She met his gaze. "I'd like that."

"Done," he agreed. "Come by the harness shop Monday and use the phone. I'll leave the name and number for you and let my sisters know you'll be by."

She clasped her hands. "Thank you."

He backed onto the road. "You're welcome. See you in church on Sunday?"

"See you in church," she echoed, then watched as he turned and headed down the road.

As she watched him go, once again she found herself disappointed that her time with him had come to an end. She was beginning to think he felt the same way. Why else would he have asked her to walk to the end of the lane with him? She wasn't quite sure what was going on between them, but they had fallen into a friendship she certainly hadn't expected when they met. One she cherished. The thought had crossed her mind more than once in the last two weeks or so that maybe she had feelings for Ethan.

And suddenly, all at once, she realized she did. The question was, what was she going to do with them?

On Fridays, Abigail's mother sometimes liked to take butter, eggs, baked goods and seasonal produce to Spence's Bazaar in Dover where they rented a table and sold the items to the English. It surprised Abigail that her mother would want to go to such a public place when she shied from quilting circles and visits with other women in Hickory Grove. It was Abigail's *dat*'s theory that his wife's excuse in going was to make a little money, but the *real* reason she liked going was to buy things. They would go early so that they could set up their stand before the first shoppers of the day arrived, then Abigail's mother would leave her husband to watch the stand while she prowled through the aisles of antiques and yard sale junk Englishers were selling.

June King loved Spence's. She liked to watch the English tourists in their strange clothing, and she loved to poke through the dusty tables of ceramic knick-knacks, kitchen utensils and plastic toys in the flea market. This day, June had, in her eyes, made a real find—an old Amish-style rag doll without a face.

"This is it," June declared, holding up the ragged doll to show her daughter.

Abigail had, at her father's request, trailed her mother at a safe distance, giving her a chance to feel independent without risking her wandering off again. Jamie, who was now on summer vacation from school, had come with them and had agreed to stay with his grandfather and help with the sales.

"She's perfect," Abigail's mother declared, peering into the face of the doll that had no features. "I'm going to buy her and take her home."

"Mam," Abigail said softly. "Jamie doesn't really care for dolls."

Her mother looked at her indignantly. "It's not for *Jamie*." She hugged the doll to her chest. "She's for me. Her name is Annie."

Abigail glanced around. No one seemed to be paying them any mind, not even the two young Mennonite women selling the hand stitched items, both old and new. They also sold embroidery thread and fabric. *"Mam*, are you sure—"

"I'm buying it with my own money," her mother interrupted as she pulled a big white hanky from inside her sleeve where she always kept it. She wrapped it around the doll as if it were a blanket. "She'll have to have some proper clothes. And a prayer *kapp*," she said, walking up to one of the young women. Both Mennonite ladies wore dresses very similar in style to Amish ones, only they were made of calico with a tiny flowered print on the fabric. And instead of a full prayer *kapp*, a piece of round lace rested on top of their hair that they wore in a neat bun at the nape of their necks, similar to Abigail's.

"How much?" Abigail's mother asked.

The young lady responded. Abigail's mother countered the offer and walked away with two dollars saved and two free pieces of fabric big enough to stitch an Amish dress and apron for the doll.

As they walked away from the Mennonites' booth, back toward their own, Abigail shook her head in awe of her mother. Abby had used Millers' harness shop telephone and made an appointment for her mother with the neurologist Rosemary had recommended, but she was wondering if that had been a mistake. Her mother had just been as sharp as a tack, negotiating down the price of the doll. Maybe her father was right. Maybe her mother wasn't slipping into dementia. Maybe she was just stepping further from the confines of Amish rules and customs. She wasn't necessarily breaking them, but like a teenager or young adult preparing to be baptized, she was definitely bending the rules. This had become her father's new theory since the incident where June had wandered off the Miller farm to go swing in the schoolyard.

"Daniel, look what I bought," Abigail's mother called to her husband as they approached him. He was busy taking money from an Englisher woman with hair dyed purple who was buying butter and a bag of chocolate-chip-and-almond cookies Abigail had made. The woman was carrying a cloth bag on her elbow that looked like a handbag. A tiny white dog poked its head out of a hole in the top of the bag.

"Daniel," her mother repeated when he didn't immediately respond.

"Just a minute, June." He gave the purple-haired woman her change and she walked away. "Now let me see."

While her mother showed off her purchase, Abigail glanced around. Spence's seemed busier than any grocery store in town, except maybe the Walmart. Both Amish and Englishers frequented the market on Tuesdays, Fridays and Saturdays, the only days they were open. There were so many things to see and buy and the smells coming from the food area inside the building were enticing. There were homemade baked goods and steak sandwiches, fresh doughnuts and soft pretzels and she could smell the sweet, distinct scent of funnel cakes. The aroma of the funnel cakes made her think of Ethan and his love of sweets. She imagined he liked funnel cake.

It was past lunchtime and her stomach had begun to gurgle. She wondered if it might be a good time to grab something to eat and then pack up what hadn't been sold, though it didn't appear that there would be much to take home. The woman with the purple hair had just bought the last pound of homemade butter they'd wrapped in cheesecloth. There was only a dozen or so cookies left and a couple of bundles of new radishes her father had grown in their hothouse.

Abigail gazed up at the sky. It was clouding up in the west, and it looked as if they might get an afternoon thunderstorm. Better today than tomorrow, she thought to herself. The following day, the end-of-the-year school program and fund-raiser was being held and it would be a shame to get rained out. In the event of bad weather, Ethan had told all of the families they would still hold the spelling bee and the cake auction, but if it rained, it wouldn't be the same because they wouldn't be able to play games and sit outside on blankets and share their picnic suppers.

Abigail turned to her parents. "Anyone hungry? I was thinking about getting a sandwich at the deli." The deli was run by an Amish family that came all the way down from Lancaster and had a reputation for making excellent sandwiches. Her favorite was something they called a Rachel that had pastrami and Swiss cheese and coleslaw on it, of all things on rye bread. And they grilled it on a little griddle that squished the sandwich as it toasted the bread and melted the cheese. "By the time we get home, it will be too late to make dinner. If we're having peas and dumplings for supper," she said, "by the time we get the buggy unpacked and things *ret* up, it will be time to start supper."

"Good idea," her father said. "You know what I like. Italian submarine with pickles and hot peppers."

She nodded. He always got the same thing. *"Mam?"* she asked.

Her mother was sitting on an upturned wooden crate fussing with the doll she had just bought. "If you had a baby, a little girl, I could give her Annie," she said.

Abigail glanced at her father, then back at her mother. She knew her mother meant no offense but the mention of her having another child brought up emotions she tried to keep at bay. Because she did want more babies. She just didn't know if that was in God's plan. *"Mam,* I'm widowed. I… I can't have a baby."

"Grilled cheese," her mother responded. "Pickles on the side. Sweet not sour."

"Hot dog!" Jamie sang. He'd been in a good mood all day, mostly because school was over. Although Abigail had reminded him at the breakfast table that morning that his teacher would still be tutoring him twice a week. The tutoring was coming along well and while Jamie certainly wasn't angelic, she felt as if his behavior was improving. "And potato chips."

Abigail eyed her son. "I don't know that you need chips," she said, though she actually liked them, too. They were homemade and had a better crunch than the kind you bought in a bag at the store. "Want to come with me?"

"*Ne. Grossdadi* and I are playing checkers when we don't have customers." He pointed to the old board her father had had for as long as she could remember.

"Guess I can get them to go instead of on plates." Abigail turned to head in the direction of the deli when her mother popped up off the crate.

"I'll go." She set the doll on the crate and trotted after her daughter.

The line to place orders was long at the deli, but Abigail didn't mind. She actually ended up standing behind Eunice Gruber and her daughter May who looked to be about fourteen or fifteen. They were in the same church district. Despite the warnings she'd gotten from several people that Eunice could be a bit of a gossip, Abigail had liked the woman at once. She was friendly and she was always nothing but kind and patient with Abigail's mother.

"Nice to see you," Eunice greeted as Abigail and her mother got into line.

"Nice to see you. It's busy here today," Abigail commented, nodding in the direction of the deli counter. They must have had half a dozen Amish women working. One took orders, one ran the cash register at the other end of the counter, and four ladies were busy cutting meat and cheese for those who were ordering by the pound or making sandwiches.

"Always like this on Fridays," Eunice said. "But the line moves pretty fast." She nodded to Abigail's mother. "Good to see you out, June. We missed you at the quilting circle this week."

"Not much for quilting," June answered. "Busy. Very busy."

"You just never know who you'll run into at Spence's, do you?" a man said from behind Abigail.

She knew the deep voice and she immediately felt her cheeks grow warm. She spun around to see Ethan with his brother Jacob getting into line behind them. Though Joshua and Jacob were identical twins, Phoebe had pointed out a spattering of freckles across Jacob's nose that Joshua didn't have, so now Abigail could tell the difference between them.

She couldn't resist a big smile. "Never know, do you?"

Ethan met her gaze and she felt a little tingle of… something, something warm and pleasant and…his smile just made her feel good. And the way he looked at her, she realized that he felt it, too.

"Getting sandwiches for the crew." He hooked his thumb in the direction of where dozens of buggies were hitched in a parking lot. "Our little brother James decided to throw a fit when Rosemary told him no ice cream. Then Josiah joined in, so she took them both to the buggy. Almost nap time, I think."

"They're not even two yet." Abigail gave a wave of dismissal. "They've probably had a busy morning."

"Busy morning," Abigail mother repeated loudly to Eunice.

"Good afternoon, June." Ethan pressed his hand to his flat stomach. "I think I'm still full of that supper you cooked up last week."

"Busy, busy, busy," Abigail's mother went on to Eunice, paying no mind to Ethan. "We're planning a wedding, you know."

Abigail froze. Her eyes widened.

Eunice drew back in obvious delight. "I didn't. You hadn't mentioned you had another daughter or is it a son?"

"My little Babby. Abigail," her mother said proudly, standing a little straighter. "Getting married. To the schoolmaster." She grinned and pointed right at Ethan.

Abigail's face flamed so hot, she was sure she was the color of her mother's rooster dish towel. She was so mortified that she didn't know what to say. Even with all the people in line and milling around in the deli with all the noise, there was no way Ethan hadn't heard her.

"Mam," Abigail said quietly, tugging on her mother's sleeve. "No one's getting married," she whispered into her ear. *"I'm* not getting married."

"He's a very nice young man," Abigail's mother went on, paying no mind to her daughter. "He'll make a good husband, a good father to my grandson and the little ones to follow."

Eunice's face had lit up. She looked Ethan's way, then back at Abigail's mother. "He certainly will, and to think everyone in Hickory Grove thought he'd stay a bachelor. Most eligible bachelor in the county some would say."

"Such a busy time," Abigail's mother went on. "We have so much to do, guests to invite…"

Her mother's voice faded in her head as Abigail turned to Ethan. "I'm so sorry," she whispered, so humiliated that she couldn't meet his gaze.

"Abby," he said gently.

"I have no idea where she got such a—"

"Abby," Ethan interrupted, keeping his voice down.

Jacob was looking up, pretending to be entranced by the menu posted on a big white board hanging by chains over the deli counter.

"It's fine," Ethan went on.

She covered her face with her hands. "I don't know what to—" She exhaled. "I'm just glad we have that appointment with the doctor coming up." She dropped her hands, looking up at Ethan, knowing her cheeks had to be bright red. "Thank you for being so nice about this. It's embarrassing for me and for you."

"Embarrassing?" Ethan knit his brows. "Are you kidding? These ladies just made my day. Apparently, I'm the most eligible Amish bachelor in Kent County." He leaned forward. "And speaking of such things, I heard some guys talking about you at the mill the other day."

"Me?" She drew back.

He shrugged. "You're single, too. A pretty, smart woman like yourself, it will only be a matter of time before someone asks to court you." He held her gaze. "Almost makes me think I ought to—" He cut himself off from what he was saying and pointed ahead. "I think you're next in line."

She hesitated. He'd been about to say something, but what? She thought to press him, but then her mother took off for the deli counter and she had to hurry after her. "See you tomorrow," she called to Ethan.

"See you tomorrow," he answered. "Hey, Abby, what kind of cake are you making?"

"Lemon icebox," she responded. She didn't look back, but she could feel him watching her. Had he been about to ask if he could court her? Her heart gave a little pitter pat and she suddenly felt ten years younger.

Chapter Ten

At noon on the day of the school program, Ethan loaded his wagon in the barnyard with a couple of tables he was borrowing from his district's church wagon. His prayers had been answered and it was a bright and sunny cloudless day with the temperature reaching seventy-eight degrees. Most folks attending the program would bring blankets to sit on in the grass to eat, but in anticipation that a few of the elderly might prefer to sit in a chair at a table, he'd decided to haul some over to the school. He also needed a table to display the cakes that would be auctioned off. With the money he was hoping they would raise, he intended to buy some new books for the classroom and maybe even one of those fancy whiteboards to replace the chalkboard that had to be fifty years old if it was a day. The thing was so old and had been cleaned so many times that fresh chalk barely showed on it.

As Ethan started adding chairs to the wagon, his father came walking up from the milk house.

Benjamin's hip had improved with the warmer weather and today he was barely limping. "Good day

for a picnic," he greeted. "Rosemary's girls are all aflut-
ter. Looks like a bakery in our kitchen right now. I hear
Ginger is sweet on someone and hoping he'll bid on
her cake."

Ethan chuckled. "Ginger is always sweet on someone
and there's an endless line of boys wanting to take her
home from a singing. Be interesting to see who she ends
up with when she's ready to get serious about courting."
He walked back to the church wagon. "You're right.
Couldn't have asked for a better day. Warm enough so
folks won't get chilled, but cool enough that the cakes
the women are baking won't melt."

His father had a piece of straw in his mouth and he
was chewing on it thoughtfully. He halted between the
church wagon and Ethan's. "You plan to bid on a cake?"
It was a tradition at this type of affair that husbands always bid on wives' cakes, but single men tended to bid
on cakes baked by women they were sweet on.

Ethan grabbed another wooden folding chair and
added it to the ones he was taking to the school. Once
they were all loaded, he'd secure them with straps so
they wouldn't bang around or tumble out on the ride.
"I imagine I ought to. Me being the schoolmaster and
the one running this shindig today."

His father eyed him. "Anyone's cake in particular
you fancy?"

Ethan took another chair from the church wagon
but lowered it to the gravel driveway, contemplating
what to say. He'd been thinking about that very question since the day before when he'd bumped into Abby
at Spence's. He wanted to bid on her cake. He wanted to
sit on a blanket and share a picnic supper with her and
talk with her and laugh with her, but he didn't know if

that was the right thing to do. The idea of it all was so overwhelming that it had kept him up half the night.

It seemed as if in the last few weeks, his minutes, hours, days were strung together by the time he spent with her. The time he waited to see her again. The last weeks of school, they had ended up walking to her place every afternoon and those times with her had been the best of his day. She was so easy to talk to, whether it was about something as simple as a science lesson he'd taught on the life cycle of a frog, or the more serious topic of being widowed. It seemed like his Mary and her Egan came up in conversation all the time and he was astonished by how easy it was to talk to her about his wife. How easy it was to hear about her husband. Abby understood him, understood his pain in a way no one else he knew understood, not even his *dat* and Rosemary who had lost their spouses, too.

Ethan had been denying it for weeks, but the truth was, somehow on those afternoon walks, at her father's supper table, at the noonday meal at church, standing in line at Spence's, he'd fallen in love with Abby. But how could that be possible? He still loved Mary.

Ethan looked up to see his father watching him intently.

"You going to bid on Abigail's cake?" Benjamin asked. Not much got by his father.

Ethan picked up the chair and carried it to the wagon. "Thinking about it."

"What's to think about?" His father chewed on the bit of straw, fiddling with the end of it with his fingers. "Nice girl. Strong in her faith. Can cook. From what I hear, she can run a farm on her own." He narrowed his gaze. "Why *wouldn't* you bid on her cake?"

When Ethan didn't answer, his father went on. "Why wouldn't you want to snatch her up before someone else does? You know, Eli was asking me about her yesterday. I think he has half a mind to call on her. Next thing you know, we'll be attending their wedding."

Eli Kutz lived down the road a piece and was a widower with four children. He wanted badly to remarry, not just to provide a mother for his children, but because he had told Ethan that he felt like only half a man without a woman at his side. He'd been interested in Phoebe back when she was single, but in the end, it had been Joshua she had married. Ethan had felt bad for Eli, but at the same time, he'd known Phoebe wasn't the woman for him.

"Don't you like her?" Ethan's father pressed. "You seem like you like her. Seems like she likes you. The two of you have your heads together every time I see you."

"I do like her." Ethan took his time arranging the chair just so, stalling as he searched for the right words. He wasn't like his *dat* or his brother Joshua. Talking about how he felt came hard. At least with most people. It was Abby who could get him to talk. To say things he'd never said to anyone else. "It's just that I…" He exhaled and didn't go on.

"You just what, *sohn*?"

Ethan turned to his father, taking off his hat and wiping his forehead. "I… I feel like I'm betraying Mary somehow." His voice caught in his throat and it was a moment before he could go on. He took his time pulling his hat back on his head just so. "I have feelings for Abby, but how can that be possible?" He lifted his gaze to his father and was surprised to see tears in the older man's eyes. "I loved her so much, *Dat*."

His father plucked the straw from his mouth and tossed it on the driveway. He rubbed his eldest son's back as if Ethan was one of his toddlers. "Of course you loved her. She was your wife. But she's gone, Ethan." He looked up, seeming unashamed of his tears. "You don't think I loved your mother? Still love her? But I love Rosemary, too. It's different. She's a different woman than your mother was. I'm a different man than I was when your mother and I married." He shrugged. "I don't think we can only love one person, *sohn*."

Ethan looked away, afraid he was going to tear up.

"I don't think God means for His people to be that way." His father was quiet for a moment and then went on. "You know, after you were born and we were expecting your sister Mary, I worried that I loved you so much, how would I love the next babe? And the next who came along and the next? But I did. And then to have Josiah and James come along at a point in mine and Rosemary's life when we thought there would be no more children?" He gestured in the direction of the farmhouse with a meaty hand. "I love them every bit as much as I love you, as I love your brothers, and your sister. See… God's love isn't limited, and we're made in his image, Ethan. You understand what I'm saying?"

Ethan was quiet for a long moment and then said as much to himself as to his father, "I think I do love Abby. Like you said," he went on, thinking out loud. "It's different, but—I'm falling in love with her. I've fallen in love with her."

His father grinned as he took his hanky from his

pocket and wiped his eyes. "Then I think you best bid on her cake and marry her before Eli beats you to her."

"Marry her?" Ethan drew back. "We haven't even courted."

"What do you think you been doing all these weeks? It's not as if you're kids. You couldn't take her to a taffy pull or drive her home from a singing the way we did in our youth. Those walks you two been taking? That's been your courting time, you've just been too stubborn to see it. Don't you remember how I courted Rosemary? At her supper table. With her at ours. Under the trees after Sunday service when we talked."

Everything his father was saying made so much sense that Ethan almost felt like a dunce. He prided himself, maybe sometimes too much, in being a smart man. He certainly hadn't been smart with Abby. It had been there right in front of his eyes all this time. *She* had been right there.

His father walked over to the church wagon, picked up a chair and carried it to his son. He pushed it into Ethan's hands. "You know nothing would make me happier than to see you bring Abigail and her boy here to be a part of our family. Nothing would give me greater pleasure than to see you raise your own little ones right here on this farm." He adjusted the brim on his straw hat. "So what do you have to say, *sohn*?"

His father's smile was infectious. "I think I'll be bidding on an icebox lemon cake."

Abigail was delighted that Saturday was a perfect day for Ethan's school event; the sun was shining, and there was a slight breeze to keep everyone from getting overly warm. All of the parents, relatives and friends who lived in the community turned out, as well as Sara Yoder, the matchmaker from Seven Poplars. With her, she brought two wagons and a buggy of single young men and women.

The spelling bee had been a great hit with the parents and students alike, and the Fishers' oldest daughter still in school, Miriam, had won the grand prize. The school board had awarded her a gift certificate to Walmart by spelling the word *koinonia*, which meant Christian fellowship, taken from the Book of Acts in the Bible.

After the spelling bee, several students gave presentations and then there was a volleyball game between the girls and boys. The bonnets won, hands down because Bishop Simon decreed that all the straw hats would have a handicap. The boys had their ankles tied together with lengths of corn string so that they were hobbled. It made for many tumbles and even more laughter. After that came an egg and spoon race, adult men against their wives, and the men had been forced to use raw eggs. The losing team, consisting of fathers and grandfathers, would have to clean up afterward.

Eli Kutz brought his red cart and driving goats so that all the small children got rides. There was hymn singing by grades one through three, and a greased pig competition for boys between the ages of four and ten. After a hilarious contest and many near misses, one of the Gruber children caught the pig and got to keep it, much to the delight of his mother.

"Roast suckling pig for Christmas dinner," Eunice cried, clapping her hands. But everyone knew that they wouldn't really eat his pig. Ethan's brother-in-law, Marshall, who had donated the piglet, had promised to trade the greased pig, a male, for a young sow. The boy would use that pig to start his own breeding project. If he was diligent, he'd have the start of his own herd and be earning money from the animals by the time he was a teenager.

Throughout the afternoon, Abigail kept her *mam* at her side as she helped organize the games and prepare for the cake auction. Abigail hadn't taken part in the volleyball because she didn't want to be anywhere near Ethan. She'd taken enough teasing from Phoebe who had heard from Eunice that June had announced that Abigail and the teacher were getting married. It wasn't that Abigail didn't want to talk to Ethan or that she was upset with him; she was just biding her time until she could talk to him alone. She was hoping he would bid on her cake. She thought he would. Otherwise, why else would he have asked her what she was making for the auction?

Once the games had concluded and the women began unloading their picnic baskets, the auction began. It was Benjamin who had volunteered to serve as the auctioneer. He held a three-layer cake high in the air. "So first we have a chocolate-on-chocolate cake with more chocolate, baked by—" He halted and leaned over to whisper to the matchmaker from Seven Poplars who was standing beside him. Abigail had been introduced to her but had barely had time to say more than hello when she was called to settle a spat between Jamie and one of his classmates. Sara, a plump, dark-skinned woman with a bright smile, whispered back to Ethan's father. "Baked by Amanda Beiler, visiting us from Arkansas. What are we bid?" Benjamin called in his deep auctioneer's voice. Though the names of the bakers were announced, bid-ders had to be ready to act fast because no one knew in which order they'd be auctioned off.

"One dollar!" a young man in a blue shirt who Abigail didn't recognize called out.

"None of that," Benjamin flung back. "This is for the school. These boys and girls need one of those fancy chalkboards that you don't even need chalk for. I hear you use some kind of markers. Come on, son, we know you can dig deeper into your pockets. We're starting this bidding at five dollars!"

Six came and then seven. There was laughter and teasing and the boy in the blue shirt bid nine dollars for the chocolate cake. Samuel brought a rubber mallet down on the table and handed Amanda Beiler's supper basket to the blushing boy. Amanda took the cake and the two went off amid whistles and hoots to find a place to spread their tablecloth in the shade.

One after another, the cakes were sold. They fairly flew off the table as money jingled and rustled into a big pottery cookie jar on the auction table. One of the Fisher girls' pineapple upside down cakes sold for twelve dollars, and then Joshua bought Phoebe's pudding dish cake for fourteen dollars. After that, Bishop Simon offered to stand in as auctioneer and got a roar of approval when Benjamin successfully bid on both Rosemary's cream sponge cake and his youngest stepdaughter Tara's jelly roll, paying thirty dollars for the two of them.

Abigail's father bid on his wife's Bundt cake that hadn't risen, paying twenty-one dollars for it, then another four cakes went to single boys the matchmaker had brought along. After that, Abigail lost count of the cakes and the money being raised for the school until the bishop raised her lemon icebox cake high.

"Ten dollars!" Eli Kutz shouted before the bishop had opened his mouth.

Abigail and several others turned to look at the widower who was stepping to the front of the crowd.

"Looks delicious," the bishop said. "So delicious I might bid on it myself if I wouldn't think I'd be in hot water with my wife, Annie."

Everyone laughed.

"So ten dollars," Bishop Simon said. "Who will give me fifteen? Come on, boys. I don't think I've ever seen a lemon icebox cake that looked this good."

Abigail could feel herself blushing. She didn't want to eat her picnic supper with Eli, though he was a nice enough man. She wanted Ethan to bid on it, but what if, being the schoolmaster, he wasn't supposed to bid? What if he didn't want to? She suddenly wished she hadn't made the cake. If Eli won, she'd have to have supper with him and his children. Not that it would be so terrible, but—

"Fifty dollars," came a deep voice from beside the auction table.

Everyone gasped. Abigail knew that voice. It was Ethan's, and she couldn't help but break into an embarrassed grin.

"Fifty dollars?" the bishop gasped. "I'd say that young man likes icebox cakes, wouldn't you?"

Everyone clapped and the bishop brought the rubber mallet down hard on the table. "Sorry, Eli. Sold for fifty dollars to the schoolmaster who's given us all a fine afternoon. Seems like we ought to be paying him, though, eh?"

There was more clapping as Ethan walked up to the table and pushed a handful of bills into the cookie jar. The next thing Abigail knew, she was walking beside him.

"How about over there under that oak tree?" Ethan asked her quietly. No one was paying much attention to them as the last couple of cakes were auctioned off and everyone was finding a place to set out their picnic suppers.

Abigail nodded, not being able to find her voice quite yet. Ethan had bid on her cake! He had paid fifty dollars for it, an astronomical price for a cake, even at a fund-raiser. To pay that much was almost a declaration that they were a couple. The idea made her nervous and excited at the same time as she wondered if he would bring up the subject or if she would be forced to.

"This basket feels heavy enough to be packed with rocks." Ethan looked down at her. "You brought lots of food. Good. I could eat a horse I'm so hungry."

"Not Butterscotch, I hope," she answered as she followed him, keeping her eyes on his back, trying not to make eye contact with their neighbors. Eunice Gruber, in particular, seemed to be interested and watched them go by without even pretending not to be staring.

"Not Butterscotch the horse, but maybe some butterscotch pudding," Ethan told her. "You bring some of that?"

"What? Cake isn't enough dessert?" she teased. "Sorry, no butterscotch pudding, but I did bring fried chicken, coleslaw, and macaroni salad, sweet pickles, corn bread and honey butter."

"All my favorite foods. How's this?" Ethan asked when they reached the oak tree.

"Good." She set the cake down on level ground and glanced up to see Jamie settling down with her folks on an old blue quilt her *mam* had made many years ago. From there she could keep an eye on him. She was annoyed that he'd caused trouble earlier and didn't want him getting into any more altercations.

Ethan waited for her to take out the checked yellow tablecloth she'd brought and spread it on the ground. Most people were already eating.

Abigail knelt and began removing the fried chicken and macaroni salad from the picnic basket.

"You know I'd have bid a hundred dollars to beat Eli out of that cake," Ethan said to her.

Abigail met his gaze and knew that she'd not imagined her feelings for him. Or his for her. Suddenly she felt shy and she busied herself preparing the feast. He sat, stretching long legs out while she still knelt. "You didn't have to buy my cake for that much money," she said. She unfolded foil-wrapped chicken and passed Ethan a plate and several paper napkins.

"Sure I did. Otherwise, Eli would be having supper with you and I wouldn't." He sprinkled salt and pepper on a chicken leg and looked up at her. "Can I drive you home after supper?"

Abigail served him a large portion of macaroni salad and gave herself a smaller one, then handed him a fork. "We'll have to clean up after supper. Load the tables and such."

"After we clean up? Just the two of us?"

She lifted her gaze to find Ethan studying her intently and she realized something had changed in him. Something had changed between them. "I suppose Jamie could just go home with *Mam* and *Dat*."

"He could."

Ethan was still smiling two hours later as he eased Butterscotch down the schoolyard lane. Everything had been cleaned up and they were the last folks to leave. "Nice night tonight," he said, the sounds of insects and peepers clicking and croaking all around them. When he reached the blacktop of the road, he reined his horse in. "Feel like taking the long way home?"

"I don't know. I should get home to be sure Jamie's in bed."

"Come on," he cajoled. "Jamie will be fine." He shrugged. "He's already been in trouble today. Bet he's in bed, as well behaved as any nine-year-old boy can be."

She hesitated.

"And I want to talk to you."

She gave a little laugh but inside she was pleased. "Talk to me?" she teased. "We talked for more than an hour over supper. Most everyone else had eaten, packed up and headed home and there the two of us were still talking."

He glanced at her. "Nice wasn't it?"

She nodded.

He must have taken that to mean they could take the long way home because instead of turning right to head for her parents' place, he turned left. For several minutes they rode side by side on the wagon bench in comfortable silence. Of course, the evening wasn't really silent because of the clip-clop of Butterscotch's hooves, the creaking of the wooden wagon wheels as they rolled, and the sounds of the insects, critters and creatures that came out after the sunset.

"So what I wanted to talk to you about." Ethan

cleared his throat. "I've been trying to think all afternoon how to say this, Abby, and I can't think of any way to do it but to just come out and say it."

She looked at him and was about to speak when he blurted, "I think I'm falling in love with you."

Her breath caught in her throat.

"Ne," he said, gripping the reins tightly in his hands and pulling the wagon to stop right there in the middle of the road. "I *have* fallen in love with you. I… I'm in love with you, Abby, and I think—" For a moment he just held her gaze and then smiled. "I guess I've known it for weeks, I just… I didn't understand."

She nodded, knowing exactly what he was talking about. "You didn't understand how you could care for another woman when you loved Mary. When you still do." She nibbled on her lower lip, amazed she could speak so freely with him.

The sound of a car and a flash of headlights came from behind them and Ethan made a clicking sound between his teeth to urge Butterscotch forward again. Even with the electric lights on the back of the wagon, run by a battery under the seat, it wasn't safe to sit on the road. He waited until a blue sedan passed them and glanced at Abigail again. "It was my *dat* who set me straight. You know Rosemary isn't my *mam.* My *mam* died. And Rosemary's husband died. The way *Dat* explained it to me was that a man can love more than one woman, a woman can love more than one man in a lifetime. He said God made us in his image and He can love many."

She wiped at her eyes that had gone misty. When he explained it like that, it made so much more sense to her. Made her feel so much better because somewhere in the back of her head she had been thinking she was somehow betraying Egan by caring for Ethan, but suddenly she knew it wasn't true.

They rode in silence for a few minutes before Ethan spoke up again. "I'm sorry if this is too much. Too soon, Abby. I know we haven't known each other but what, two or three months?"

"Well, three months ago we'd just arrived in Hickory Grove and you were telling me what a naughty boy my son was," she said with amusement.

"And you weren't having any of it, were you?"

"The first couple of times, I had patience with you, but that last time. The outhouse incident…"

"Phew," he said. "I don't think I've ever had a parent quite so angry with me."

"I wasn't angry."

He cut his eyes at her.

"Okay," she confessed, "I *was* angry, but I'm not anymore. You were right but none of that matters because—" She took a deep breath, feeling the way she had the first time she'd ever run off the dock at home back in Wisconsin, held her breath and jumped into their pond. It was a light-headedness that was scary and exhilarating at the same time. "It doesn't matter, Ethan, because…because I love you, too."

"You do?"

"Ya," she said bashfully.

He slid his hand across the wooden bench and covered her hand with his. "Tell me something about Egan."

"What?"

"I want to hear more about Egan."

"Like what?" she asked.

"Anything you want to tell. The way I see it, the

more I know about him, the more I'll know about you. I guess I want to know everything."

His words touched a place in her heart that she didn't know could ever be touched again and she began to talk. By the time they were back on her parents' road, the subject had changed to talk of his Mary. He told her about the log cabin quilts she used to make, that she added honey to her applesauce instead of sugar and how she'd always been one for losing things. And with each thing he told, Abigail felt strangely closer to him.

By the time they drove up her father's lane, Ethan was holding her hand. There were rules about unmarried men and women touching, but Abigail didn't care. It just felt right.

In the barnyard, Ethan climbed down from the wagon and walked around to help Abigail down. The only light on in the house was the glow of a lamp from her parents' upstairs bedroom. As he walked her toward the house, he kept hold of her hand.

Abigail felt as if she was floating. It had been a long time since she had remembered being this happy. "So," she said stopping just beside the porch. All the openness between them had suddenly made her bold. "What are we going to do about this?"

"This?" he asked.

"Us," she said.

He took her other hand and stood facing her. They were both smiling, and she knew, just *knew*, he was going to ask her to walk out with him.

"What are we going to do?" he repeated. Then he shrugged. "I guess the only thing to do is for me to ask you to marry me."

Abigail was so shocked that, for a moment, she

couldn't respond. "M-marry you? Ethan, we haven't even courted yet."

"According to my *dat*, we have been. For weeks, months, by his tally and… Abby, I know you're the right woman for me and I think I'm the right man for you. I haven't been able to talk to someone else like this since Mary—" He stopped midsentence and looked away.

The moment the words came out of his mouth he drew his lip tight as if he wished he hadn't said that. "I'm sorry," he told her. "I shouldn't have said that. Here I am trying to woo you and I'm talking about my dead wife." He closed his eyes for a moment shaking his head. "I'm sorry," he repeated.

"Ne," she whispered, taking her hand from his to brush it against his cheek. Her eyes were welling with tears again. As ridiculous as it seemed, hearing him speak of his wife made her love him more. "Don't ever apologize for speaking her name. Promise me." She gazed into his eyes. "And I'll never hold back from talking about Egan. They're a part of us, Ethan. Don't you see that? Mary is who made you who you are in some ways. She made you the person I love."

"Is that a yes?" Ethan asked. "You'll marry me?"

He was so close at that moment that Abigail thought he might kiss her. It was prohibited of course. They weren't unbaptized teenagers. Kissing was for husbands and wives, but she found herself leaning toward him anyway.

"Ya," I'll marry you," she whispered.

Their lips had almost touched when suddenly Ethan cried out and they were splashed with what seemed like a bucket of cold water.

"Oh!" Abigail cried, stepping away from Ethan to look up in the direction the water had come.

And there, leaning out the window, was Jamie, ready to toss another water balloon.

"Jamie Stolz!" she called up at him.

He disappeared from sight and slammed the window shut.

"I'm so sorry," she said as Ethan removed his hat, dripping with water. Her face was covered in water and so was her dress. And so was Ethan's shirt.

He started to laugh as he wiped his face with a dry spot on his sleeve.

"It's not funny!" she told him, marching toward the back porch.

"It's not, but don't be too hard on him," he called after her as she went up the steps.

He was still laughing when she walked into the house and closed the door.

Chapter Eleven

The garden soil was warm between Abigail's bare toes and she took a moment to appreciate the blessing of the warm day, the final crop of fragrant strawberries she was dropping into her bucket and her betrothal to Ethan.

In some ways, it seemed as if everything had moved so quickly between the two of them. It was mid-June and she and Ethan had already been to see the bishop and set their wedding day for the last Thursday in August so that they could be married before the school year began. At the same time, it seemed as if she had known Ethan a lifetime and their impending marriage was simply the next stepping-stone in their lives. She couldn't wait to be his wife and walk through the life they had been given by God, hand in hand.

Both of their families were thrilled with the match, which made the engagement all the more exciting. Abigail's mother couldn't wait for the wedding and had her husband busy sprucing up the interior of the house with new coats of paint in anticipation of the upcoming ceremony, which would be held in their home.

Abigail glanced across the strawberry patch at Jamie.

He was kneeling, bucket beside him for strawberries, but he wasn't picking. Something had caught his interest in the soil. "Move along," she told her son gently. "The sun's climbing higher in the sky. You'll soon be complaining it's too hot out here and we have the rest of the patch to finish."

"Ants," Jamie said pointing.

"Ah, you found an anthill." She'd seen several that morning; everyone on the farm was busy. She plucked a fat red berry and eased it into her tin bucket so as not to bruise it.

"Did you know that ants are some of the strongest creatures in the world for their size?" Jamie asked still watching the ants. "They can carry up to like three *thousand* times their weight before their heads fall off. And they can even get other ants to help them and carry heavier things."

She nodded, moving up a little and parting the leaves in search of more ripe berries. There were no green ones left. She doubted there would be another picking. The only reason they still had *any* strawberries the third week of June was that spring had come late that year. "You learn that in science class at school?" she asked.

She knew for a fact that ants had been a topic of discussion the final week of school because Ethan had told her how well Jamie had done on his test. Not only had his reading improved, but his writing, as well. He'd gotten an A on the test and Ethan had tacked it to a bulletin board with the other A's in the classes from that week.

Jamie shrugged, losing interest in the ants, and turned back to the strawberry patch. "I guess."

"Ethan said you liked the unit on insects." She placed another strawberry in the pail. "Is that true?"

He lowered his head so that she couldn't see his face beneath his straw hat. "All you do is talk about him," he grumbled.

"Talk about who?"

"*Ethan*. It's all Ethan this and Ethan that." He took an irritable tone to his voice. "*Ethan's* coming for my reading lesson. We're going to *Ethan's* house for supper. We have to walk with *Ethan* to church on Sunday."

She sat back on her heels. "I thought you liked Ethan. Jamie, he's helped you so much with reading. He says at the rate you're going, you'll be reading at the same level as the other boys in your class by Christmas. He says you're very smart."

Jamie threw a strawberry into the weeds beyond the garden.

"I hope that was a rotten one." Abigail pointed in the direction of the strawberry he'd just tossed. "We don't waste food."

"It was. A bug got it." He batted at the strawberry plants as he searched for another ripe berry, his picking only half-hearted now. "And see what I mean. *Ethan* says I'm smart. Ethan. Ethan. Ethan."

Abigail took a moment to gather her thoughts before she spoke. She had sensed her son wasn't keen on her betrothal, but she had been telling herself he just needed time to adjust to the idea. They hadn't really talked about it. "You know Ethan and I are going to marry in August, and then we'll live around the corner at his place. So you may as well get used to him."

"He's not my *dat*." There was anger in her son's voice now.

"No, he's not," she said gently. "And we'll never ask

you to call him that. No one can ever replace your father, but I hope that you'll come to care for him as my husband. And as your stepfather." She hesitated and then went on, though what she was about to say wasn't something an Amish woman usually discussed with her son. "You know, God may bless me with more children. You would be a big brother to them. And Ethan would be their *vadder*, so…he could be as much your *dat* as you want him to be."

Jamie chewed on that for a moment. "I don't want brothers and sisters. And I don't want to move." He met her gaze stubbornly. "I want to stay here."

"But we're going to have a new house." She kept her tone upbeat, trying not to get frustrated with him. She knew this had to be overwhelming for him. "Ethan's already broken ground. It's going to have a big wraparound porch and—and we'll be close enough for you to walk over to see your grandparents. You can stop every day after school if you like."

It had been decided that Ethan would build them a *grossdadi* house of sorts, one smaller than the big farmhouse where he currently lived with his father and Rosemary and their children. It would be set on a little knoll, through the orchard behind the big house. Eventually, Ethan and Abigail and their children would take the larger farmhouse and Rosemary and Benjamin and whoever was left at home of their children would move into the little house. With their twins being ten years younger than Rosemary's youngest by her previous marriage, it made sense that eventually there would just be the four of them and they would take the smaller house. It was what Benjamin and Rosemary wanted, according to Ethan, and because it was what *he* wanted, it was what Abigail wanted. Besides, it really did make sense.

"I want to stay here with *Grossmami* and *Grossdadi*," Jamie whined. "Can't I stay here with them? You can go live with Ethan at his place."

"You can't stay here," she said gently. "Because I'd miss you too much. And because you're my son and I'm your *mam*. Children live with their parents."

"Then you should stay here, too." He threw another rotten strawberry, harder this time. "I don't see why you even have to get married at all."

She dropped her hands to her lap. Her fingertips were stained red with berry juice as was her apron. "It's what men and women do, *boppli*," she said using a childish endearment. "It's God's wish that when we grow up, we marry. Someday you'll marry and then you'll live with your wife."

"I like it here," he argued. "I don't want to get married. I don't want you to get married. I just want things to stay the same."

She glanced away in frustration. As if she didn't have enough to worry about with her *mam* this week, now Jamie was going to act out? It wasn't that her *mam* had been overly difficult the last few days. Actually, she'd been pretty good. The wedding had given her something to focus on and she'd even been doing a little cooking successfully. But Monday she and Ethan had taken June for her follow-up appointment with the neurologist and the doctor had confirmed that it was likely her *mam* was showing early signs of Alzheimer's. Abigail had tried to listen to the doctor as she gently explained that there was no way to predict how quickly or slowly the disease would progress. It was Ethan who had comforted Abigail on the way home by saying that no matter what happened with her mother later down the road, he would be there to help the family.

Abigail shifted her gaze to her son who was just sitting there now, not even attempting to pick strawberries. She felt bad that Jamie was upset about her impending marriage, but the fact of the matter was that a nine-year-old boy didn't get to play a part in that decision for his mother. And as for not wanting siblings, had Egan lived, she and Egan certainly wouldn't have consulted Jamie before having any more children. It wasn't a child's place.

"Jamie," she said, surprised how strong her voice was. She wasn't being unkind, but she was definitely being firm. "I'm sorry you're not happy about the changes in our lives, but you'll adjust with time. In the meantime, I expect you to be respectful of Ethan and of my decision."

Jamie just sat there.

"Do you understand me, *sohn*?" she said.

When he didn't respond, she repeated herself a little more sharply.

"Ya," Jaimie conceded.

She looked down and parted the strawberry leaves in front of her, in search of another berry. "*Goot.* Now get to work. Finish that section of picking and then you can go play for an hour before you finish the rest of your chores."

And with that, she returned to the task at hand and tried to decide what she would take for dessert to Ethan's house for Friday night supper.

* * *

Ethan walked beside Abigail, her hand in his. It felt good. Not all couples held hands before marrying but he had gotten so used to seeing the physical affection between his father and Rosemary, and Phoebe and his brother, that he wanted that kind of warmth in his and Abby's courting and later in their marriage. If that was acceptable to Abigail, of course. It seemed to be.

Ethan and Mary had never been physically affectionate in front of people because that wasn't how she had been raised, but he liked the fact that Abigail was more open to the idea. Maybe because her parents weren't shy about showing their feelings for each other. While Ethan had not tried to kiss Abigail again since the night they'd become engaged and Jamie had dropped the water balloon on them, he had made it a point to hold her hand when they were alone together. They were still talking a lot, getting to know each other, which was bringing them closer together, but for some reason her touch also made him feel closer to her. It seemed to form a connection that lasted long after they had said goodbye.

"I can't believe you got me out of washing dishes again," she chastised gently as they walked through the orchard that he and his father and brothers had expanded that spring.

The summer solstice was almost upon them so the sun was just setting, though it was eight thirty at night. It was a nice evening, warm and humid but not hot. Fireflies flickered between the branches of the trees. There was an orchard on the rear of the large property but this one was only about five years old. He liked the idea that they would have to walk through the field of Liberty and Golden Delicious apple, Clingstone and

Lorin peach, and sour cherry trees to go from the big house to their smaller one. It would give them a little privacy, the kind a newly married couple needed. An orchard also made a nice front yard, he had decided.

"Rosemary and your sisters will think I don't know how to *ret* up a kitchen after supper," Abigail went on. She was complaining about not staying back to clean up, but it was only half-hearted. He had a feeling she enjoyed these stolen moments of time alone together as much as he did.

He squeezed her hand. "It was Rosemary who told me to take you out to see the foundation we laid this week. So you've officially been excused from cleanup. And she was going to get June to dry dishes, so you needn't worry about your mother."

"That's so kind of Rosemary," Abigail said, glancing at him. "She's so patient with *Mam*." She smiled up at him. "With me."

Abigail was as pretty as a picture this evening in a rose-colored dress and white apron, her prayer *kapp* string looped and dangling beguilingly at the nape of her neck. Blond tendrils of hair peeked from beneath her *kapp* and made him smile. He was so happy. After being so sad for so long, he just couldn't believe this was all real. That Abigail was real. He wished now that his faith had been stronger, that he had believed God would bring him happiness again. It was a mistake he would learn from. One he believed had made his faith stronger.

"Rosemary likes you," he went on. "And so do the girls," he added, referring to his stepsisters and Joshua's wife, Phoebe, who lived with them, too. Eventually Joshua and Phoebe intended to build on a plot of land at the back of the property near the old orchard, but for now, they were using their money to expand his greenhouse business. "Why wouldn't they?" he asked. "You're smart and kind and you're going to take me off their hands." He chuckled and she chuckled with him.

"I guess they're tired of seeing you mope around."

He drew back. "Mope? I don't mope."

She arched an eyebrow. "And I suppose you've never been grumpy either?"

"I—" He stopped and grinned. "So maybe I can be grumpy once in a while. But you changed all that, Abby." They ducked under a low-lying walnut tree and the foundation for the house he and his brothers had been laying came into view.

"Wow," she breathed. "You've really made progress this week." She let go of his hand to walk closer to the cinder blocks set on the footers.

"No rain and things weren't too busy at the harness shop. Charley Byler came over from Seven Poplars to give us some pointers, him being a master mason." Ethan pointed to her. "I think you met his wife the other day. Miriam?"

"That's right. Miriam Byler." She turned to him, her smile warming his heart. "So show me what's what. Where's the kitchen? You showed me the sketches, but it isn't the same as standing here," she said excitedly. "Show me again. Take me through our rooms."

Ethan clasped her hand again and led her forward. "So here we are on the front porch that will wrap around the house this way and that." He pointed in each direction with his free hand. "And this is the front door and the hallway." He took a big step forward. "Parlor on this side." He indicated the right. "Living room behind it with doors that will open up both rooms when

we host church services. And the kitchen is this way."
They turned left and walked across grass that had been
trampled by many boots that week. "The pantry and
mudroom are behind the kitchen. The back door will
be in the mudroom, which will also have room for a
washing machine and dryer that will run on propane.
In the middle of the house, beyond the front hall, will
be the staircase and beyond that is a first-floor bath and
bedroom. *Dat* and Rosemary's request. At some point,
they figure they'll be too old to want to climb steps."

Abigail nodded and kept smiling.

He was so pleased. Because making her happy made
him happy. "Upstairs will be another big bathroom and
three bedrooms." He took her hand again. "I figured
we'd sleep upstairs with Jamie." He moved very close to
her and without thinking, kissed her temple. "And with
the little ones I hope God will bless us with someday."

She looked at him for a moment, but he couldn't read
her face. He was afraid maybe he had crossed the line,
kissing her like that, but it had been an act of tenderness more than anything else. As for speaking of children, they'd talked about wanting a family, even about
how many children they would like to have.

She took his other hand in hers and faced him. "It's
going to be beautiful."

"How can you tell?" he teased, wanting to lighten
the mood. "I've not even yet finished the—" Something
struck him, stinging his back, and he whipped around
trying to figure out where it had come from. It was
nearly dark but as the sun had set in the sky, the moon
had risen. He could make out the shapes of the trees in
the orchard, the pallets of cinder blocks that had yet to

be laid and a wheel barrel used for mixing mortar, but he couldn't see—

He was struck again, this time in the chest. "Ouch!" he said, instinctively rubbing where he'd been hit.

"What is it?" Abigail asked. "Did a bee sting you?"

He leaned down and in the semidarkness found a pebble. "Not a bee. Someone just hit me. Look!" He held up the rock.

"Who would hit you?" she asked incredulously. "Maybe we just kicked it up or something?"

Ethan studied the shadows. He was willing to take a guess as to who was pelting him with pebbles, but he didn't have to risk making any false accusations because at that moment he spotted a little boy's face peeking over the wheelbarrow.

"Jamie!" Ethan said.

Abby grabbed his arm. "Jamie wouldn't—"

"Jamie!" he repeated more sharply, calling into the darkness.

Before Abigail could finish her thought, Jamie stood up from behind the wheelbarrow, revealing himself.

Abigail gasped as she saw her son appear. Why would he do such a thing? It had to be a mistake. Maybe he'd been aiming at a predatory animal.

"Come here, please," Ethan said to her son, pointing at the place in front of them.

Jamie slowly came forward, hanging his head. He wasn't wearing his hat.

"Do you understand how dangerous what you did could have been?" Ethan asked, keeping his tone low. "You could have hit your mother. You could have hit me in the eye."

Abigail looked at Ethan and then at her son. "Apologize," she ordered, feeling embarrassed. Ethan sounded awfully harsh, and she still wanted to believe it was all a mistake.

"Sorry. I was just goofing around," the boy said, and she relaxed. He hadn't meant harm.

"It's not playing when it's dangerous, Jamie," Ethan said, looking down at him. "I don't want to see you throwing rocks again unless it's skimming them in a pond. Do you understand me?"

Abigail crossed her arms over her chest. There was no need for Ethan to rub Jamie's nose in his mistake. He'd apologized.

"Do you understand me?" Ethan repeated.

"Ya," Jamie mumbled.

"Goot. Now go back to the house. I would guess your grandparents will be ready to go home soon. We'll be there shortly."

Ethan stood there watching the boy go before turning back to Abby. She could tell from the confused look in his eyes that he was questioning himself, perhaps wondering if he had overstepped his bounds. Yes, he had. They weren't married yet.

When he looked at Abby, she looked away.

He exhaled, and she could hear the frustration in his trembling breath. "Out with it," he said.

She hesitated, gathering her thoughts. Eventually, he'd be a father to Jamie. But he wasn't one yet, and she'd disagreed with his leap to judgment.

"Abby," he said quietly. "Just because we love each other, it doesn't mean we're always going to agree. But when you're upset with me, you have to tell me so and you have to tell me why. You can't think I can read your mind or guess right. And I'll vow to do the same." He opened his arms, looking as disappointed as she felt. Their romantic walk to see the home he was building for her had turned into what appeared to be a disagreement. "It's the way a marriage should be. Don't you think so?"

"All right." She lowered her arms. "You were quick to snap at Jamie."

"I didn't snap. Actually, I think I was pretty calm considering the fact that he hit me with rocks. Twice."

"More like pebbles," she argued. "And he said he was just playing."

He looked down at her but didn't say anything. Instead, he waited for her to speak again.

She sighed, thinking how foolish it was to defend anyone for throwing something at someone. It didn't matter that it was Jamie. He could have hurt them. "I'm sorry. I'm just not used to hearing someone else correct my son. I know that at school it's your job but..." She let her sentence trail off.

"You think because I'm not his father, I shouldn't speak up when he's done something wrong?"

"*Ne*, you shouldn't," she said quickly. "I'm his mother. I should be the one—" She went quiet for a moment, realizing a time would come when she wouldn't be the only one responsible for Jamie, that people in the community would expect that Ethan, as Jamie's stepfather, would be accountable for his stepson's behavior.

Ethan waited. When she didn't speak, he asked her quietly, "Once we're married, will we share the discipline with Jamie?"

"Of course," she said.

"Okay, so..." He drew out his last word. "Do you want me to keep quiet until after we're married, or do you think it would be better if Jamie begins getting used to it now? You start getting used to it."

She crossed her arms again, ready to argue, then released them as she realized how patient he was being with her, not forcing her to accept this new reality, but leading her gently to it. "You're right," she said in a rush. "I'm sorry, Ethan. You're absolutely right." How blessed she was to have found such an understanding man.

"It's not about being right, Abby. We're talking here about how we want our marriage to be. What you expect of me." He hesitated and then went on. He wasn't acting upset with her. He obviously did believe, as he'd pointed out, that these kinds of conversations were important, even if they weren't easy.

It wouldn't be long before they were married. They needed to settle things like this before the wedding day. Not every issue that could possibly come up could be dealt with now, but when faced with a question, they should at least talk about it. Even if they came to no conclusion yet. Ethan was being wise and prudent, forcing her to confront this important question now: how to handle parenting Jamie.

She took a deep breath and looked up at him. When she spoke, the annoyance was gone from her voice. "I want us to share the parenting. I do want you to give Jamie guidance when he needs it. It's only that... Like you said, I have to get used to it. You know?" She looked up at him. "It's just been me for a long time." And since it had been her alone, she'd often felt the need to be Jamie's defender, to take his side against the world.

"I understand." He took a step closer, smiling down

on her. "Think we better get back?" He put his hand out to her.

She took it. *"Ya,"* she agreed. "We best get back before Jamie does something else bad." She shook her head. "I don't know what gets into him. Throwing things at someone? He knows better."

"Sometimes little boys know better and they do things anyway. They can't help themselves," Ethan said as he led her back through the orchard that was now quite dark. "I once threw eggs at my grandmother's friend's buggy. Sadie Basler was her name. Big woman with a *big* voice."

"You didn't!" she exclaimed looking at him, seeing his eyes gleaming in the moonlight. "What would ever possess you to do such thing? Now I'm learning the truth about you, Ethan Miller," she teased, poking him in the chest.

He shrugged. "She tattled on me for snitching snickerdoodle cookies from the pantry before supper. Told my grandmother and got me in trouble. I was about Jamie's age, maybe a little younger. I guess I thought I'd teach Sadie a lesson."

Abby laughed. "By throwing *eggs* at her buggy? And you didn't think you'd get caught?"

"That's where I hadn't quite thought things through. The moment she came out of the house and saw the raw egg running down the sides of her buggy, she knew it was me. I was the only child there visiting my grandparents that day." He was laughing with her now. "Who else could it have been?"

"What happened?" Abby asked. "Did you get a spanking?"

"Worse," he told her, leading her between two blossoming apple trees that smelled fragrant, even in the dark. "I had to clean her buggy head to toe with a scrub brush and buckets of water and then I had to go to her house with her and muck out her goat stalls."

"Oh, no," she laughed.

He shrugged. "I never did it again, so I guess it worked."

"So maybe that's a mistake I've been making." Abby grew more serious. "I talk and talk to Jamie, but maybe there need to be consequences to his actions."

"Maybe," Ethan agreed. Ahead, they could see the lights of his father's farmhouse. It looked like Daniel and June were on the porch saying their goodbyes. "But whatever you want to try, I'll be with you on it."

She stopped and looked up at him. She was still letting him hold her hand. *"Danke,"* she said softly.

"For what?" he asked.

"For being you." Wise, patient, gentle. He would be a good father to Jamie.

And then he smiled at her and her heart swelled with love, as she realized that their wedding day couldn't come soon enough.

Abigail and Phoebe walked side by side down the Millers' driveway. Phoebe was walking her to the road after Abigail had paid her a visit to ask her to stand up with her as her witness at the wedding. Ethan was going to ask Joshua. It had been a tough decision but he had chosen his married brother, thinking it would be wise to have a young couple with some experience, not just beside them the day they were wed, but there to support them in their first weeks and months and years of marriage.

Phoebe had been so thrilled when Abigail had asked her that she had cried. And then she had laughed and hugged Abigail. She had said she would be honored to serve as a witness to the marriage and knew that her husband would feel the same way.

"I wish you could stay awhile longer," Phoebe said as they neared the blacktop road. Halfway down the lane, it had begun to rain, but she had grabbed an umbrella on her way out the door. "It seems like we never have time to visit."

"I know, but I have bread to get into the oven and Jamie isn't feeling well today. When I left, he was playing with his toys on his bed upstairs. But come fall," Abigail said cheerfully, "we'll be living just across the orchard from each other, won't we?" They walked side by side with Phoebe holding the umbrella between them. It was black and plenty big enough to protect them both.

"*Ya*, I suppose that's right," Phoebe agreed. "We'll practically be sisters then."

At the mailbox, the two young women halted. Abigail could hear the sound of hoofbeats, and she spotted a buggy pulled by a bay coming down the road toward them. Because the buggies were all black in Kent County and several families had bay driving horses, she couldn't tell at that distance who it was.

Phoebe backed out from under the umbrella, looking upward. "It's still coming down. Here, take the umbrella." She thrust it toward Abigail.

"I couldn't." Abigail felt silly that she'd left the house without one. The sky had been dark all day. It had only been a matter of time before the rain began. "You'll get wet going back to the house."

"I'm only going as far as the harness shop. Take it." She passed the umbrella to Abigail. "I was going to stop by to find Joshua. He's either there or in the greenhouse."

"You sure?" Abigail asked, holding the umbrella over both of them.

"Positive. I only—"

"Abigail!"

Abagail turned in the direction of the road. Some-one was calling her name. A man. Someone in the approaching buggy.

"Abigail!" The driver hung out of the buggy's open door. "Come quick!"

Abigail saw it was Eli as he reined in his horse. "What's the matter?" she called, passing the umbrella back to Phoebe as she hurried toward the buggy.

"You have to get home. Get in. I'll take you."

"But why?" Abigail demanded as she ran for the buggy.

"Your *Dat*'s house," Eli told her, panting. "It's on fire!"

Chapter Twelve

As Eli turned his buggy around in front of the Millers' harness shop, Abigail heard the sounds of the fire engines. By the time Eli turned onto her father's lane, there were already two neon-yellow fire trucks in front of the house and several firemen on the lawn spraying water on the roof of the back porch. Wanting to keep out of the way of the fire trucks, Eli drove his buggy right up over the grass, headed straight for the house. Abigail spotted her mother first, wrapped in a blanket, standing behind a paramedic truck. A young woman in a blue jumpsuit was taking her blood pressure.

Abigail jumped out of the buggy while the wheels were still rolling and raced across the wet lawn. Her mother was there. But where was Jamie? Had he been upstairs on his bed when the fire started? What if… She couldn't bear to think what might have happened. And where was her father?

"I'm sorry, miss!" a fireman called after her. "You can't—"

Abigail paid him no mind. *"Mam!"* she cried, rushing toward her mother. "Are you all right? Where's Jamie? Where's *Dat*?"

June turned to her daughter. Her face was covered in soot as was her dress. She also looked to be soaked, maybe from the rain that was falling lightly, but it seemed like a lot of water.

When Abigail reached her mother, she grasped her thin shoulders. Abigail was shaking from head to foot. "Where's Jamie?" she repeated.

"Bread didn't rise right," her mother answered. "Thought I'd make it into fry bread. Just a little oil is all you need." She smiled at Abigail, obviously having no sense of what was going on around her.

Abigail turned to the paramedic. "I have a son. Nine years old." She could barely catch her breath, she was so frightened. "Do you know where—"

"Found him!" Eli shouted as he led his horse past the fire trucks toward the barn. He pointed in Abigail's direction. "I'll find your *dat*," he hollered. "I'll find Daniel."

"Mam!" Jamie called from behind her.

Abigail swung around to see her son running toward her. Unharmed. Instead of his straw hat, he was wearing a plastic fireman's hat. She opened her arms and hugged him tightly against her. "Where's your *gross-dadi*?" she whispered against him, squeezing him so tightly that the hat fell off.

Jamie squirmed out of her arms and bent down to pick up the hat. "I don't know. Around here somewhere. I just saw him. The firemen had to spray this foam in the kitchen and they were worried the laundry room roof was getting hot so they were shooting water, but

Grossdadi doesn't want them wetting down anything that didn't have to be wet."

Abigail squeezed her son's cheeks between her hands. "I'm so glad you're all right. How did the fire start?"

She was afraid to ask if he'd done something bad. The other day he'd tried starting a fire in the wood-stove for his grandmother. His heart had been in the right place, but Abigail thought she'd made it plain to him that he wasn't to try to start a fire on his own, not without proper instruction and even then, only when his mother or grandfather was around. "Jamie, what happened?" she repeated.

The barnyard was chaos. Eli's horse had gotten spooked and was dancing sideways as he tried to calm her. There were the two fire engines, the paramedic truck, an ambulance, and now a state police car was coming up the lane. There were chickens running all over the lawn and one of her mother's goats had escaped and was standing on top of the old well house bleating. But none of that mattered. All that mattered was that her family was safe. Abigail took a deep breath and then another.

"It wasn't me this time. I promise," Jamie exclaimed. "It was *Grossmami*," he whispered behind his hand.

Abigail glanced over her shoulder. Her mother was too busy chatting with the paramedic to be paying anyone else any mind. She was explaining how to make blackberry syrup without too many seeds.

Abigail looked down at Jamie. "Tell me what happened, *sohn*."

"I don't know exactly. I was playing upstairs and I fell asleep on my bed and the next thing I knew," he said, placing the plastic fireman hat on his head,

"*Grossdadi* was picking me up and running down the steps with me."

"Your grandfather *carried* you?"

"He was so upset, *Mam*. I've never seen him like that. The smoke alarms downstairs were going off and they were so loud."

Hearing that, Abigail said a silent prayer of thanks. When she'd arrived in Delaware, there had been no operational smoke detectors in the house. She'd gone to Walmart and bought several and the batteries to go in them and helped her father mount them on the ceilings and walls, upstairs and down.

"Where was your grandmother when he came upstairs for you?" Abigail asked.

"*Grossdadl* took her outside and then went upstairs for me. We couldn't find her at first. He got so scared that she had gone back in the house. But she hadn't. She was in the henhouse getting eggs. She wanted to make cupcakes, she said," he explained.

"You said she started the fire. Do you know how? Where?"

"In the kitchen. She put too much oil in the frying pan and I guess it dripped? That's what *Grossdadi* said. Then when she lit the gas burner… Whoosh!" He threw his hands up in the air. "I guess when the fire started, she tried to carry the pan out of the house. That's how the laundry room caught on fire."

"Wait." Abigail glanced in the direction of the house. "So the fire was in the laundry room, not the kitchen?" That made more sense now. That's why the firemen were keeping the roof of the porch wet. The porch came off the laundry room.

"I guess," Jamie said. "*Grossdadi* wouldn't let me

go inside. I think he put the fire out in the kitchen with the extinguisher we brought from home, but the fire in the laundry room was too big."

"Who called the fire department?"

"Some Englisher who was driving by. She used her cell phone."

Abigail glanced over her shoulder at the house again. She was finally breathing easier. She didn't know how much damage the fire had done, but the house obviously wasn't engulfed. In fact, the firemen had stopped spraying water and were now milling around, talking. She spotted a wagon coming up the driveway at a fast clip and saw that it was Ethan, along with his brother Jacob, as well as Benjamin and Phoebe.

"Can I go see how much of the house *Grossmami* burned down?" Jamie asked his mother.

"You may not." She put her arm around his shoulder and gave him a quick hug. "I'm going to check on *Grossmami* and then *Grossdadi*. You go tell the Millers what happened." She met her son's gaze. "I'm so glad you're all right," she said, emotion choking her.

He made a face and pulled away. "I'm fine."

She watched him run toward the wagon coming up the lane and then she took a breath and walked to where the paramedic was caring for her mother. She saw now that one of her mother's hands was wrapped in white gauze. She couldn't believe her mother had nearly burned down the house. With Jamie in it. Tears filled her eyes.

This changed everything.

That Sunday, Hickory Grove had a visiting preacher because both of theirs were out of town. While Barnabas Gruber led the morning services, Preacher Reuben Coblenz came from Seven Poplars to preach in the afternoon, following the dinner break. He spoke on the Good Samaritan, a story from the New Testament that apparently, according to Phoebe, he often chose for his message and one that he could speak on at great length. It was one of Abigail's favorite passages, but she had found it hard to concentrate on his message that day. In fact, she'd had a hard time concentrating on much of anything. She'd been avoiding Ethan since the fire earlier in the week and he knew it.

She had chosen a seat near an open window in Eli Kutz's parlor, beside her *mam*. Phoebe was sitting on her other side. Outside the window, a monarch butterfly fluttered. She saw one, then a second and then a third and she realized they were settling in the purple flowering butterfly bush beside the house. She wondered what it was like to be a butterfly. They seemed so free and unencumbered. Like humans, they were one of God's creatures but without the same responsibilities. It was the matter of responsibility that was heavy on her heart today. Had been for days.

Abigail felt someone tug at the sleeve of her black church dress and she glanced at Phoebe.

"You all right?" Phoebe murmured.

Abigail stared straight ahead and nodded.

"Ethan said he tried to talk to you," Phoebe whispered, "during the dinner break, but you told him you were busy."

"I was serving," she whispered back, her gaze shifting to the butterflies again.

She'd not spoken with Ethan since he had come to her at the fire, and even then, she'd been so overcome with worry and fear that she barely remembered what she'd said. He'd offered consolation and help, and she'd thanked him but told him she needed to tend to her parents. He'd understood and told her he'd wait to hear what repairs he could assist with.

Preacher Reuben's voice thundered out, echoing off the rafters as he warmed to his subject and began to repeat himself for the third time. Abigail tore her attention from the window and tried to focus on his words. But as her gaze swept the room, she spotted Ethan sitting across the aisle from her with the other men. As had been the tradition in her church district in Wisconsin, the men sat on one side of the room and the women on the other for services. Ethan wasn't watching Preacher Reuben either. He was staring directly at her. And when their gazes met, Ethan frowned questioningly.

Startled, Abigail averted her eyes, but when she glanced back from under her lashes, Ethan was still watching her. She knew she couldn't keep evading him. That they were going to have to talk, but it was going to be such a hard discussion to have. And she still didn't know what she was going to say. How she was going to say it. When the preacher finally wound up his sermon and the congregation rose to offer the final hymn, she looked at Ethan and found him looking at her again instead of his hymn book.

The hymn ended; everyone sat down, and Bishop Simon offered a traditional prayer in High German before dismissing the congregation to head home to do chores. Because it was Sunday, the only chores that would be done would be those absolutely necessary, mostly involving caring for the children and farm animals.

When everyone scattered, Abigail made a beeline for

the kitchen. She'd already told Jamie and her parents she would meet them outside. She just had to pick up the baking dishes she'd brought her rhubarb cobbler in.

There was a crowd of elders at the back of the spacious room, so she turned left to leave by another door, thinking she would go the long way around. When she reached the hallway, however, she found Ethan alone, arms folded, blocking her way.

"What's going on, Abby?" he asked. He met and held her gaze, his face solemn. He was dressed in his Sunday best with black pants, a white shirt and black coat. He wore his wide-brimmed black hat on his head. He was handsome in his church clothes, so handsome that a lump rose in her throat. She had thought she would marry this handsome man. Handsome, good man, but it wasn't to be. Because she didn't have the freedom those butterflies outside the window possessed.

"Why are you avoiding me?" he asked.

"I haven't been avoiding you."

He stared at her, making it clear he didn't believe her. She lowered her gaze. "All right. I have been."

Before she could protest, he grabbed her hand and led her to the rear of the hall where there was an alcove. It appeared to have once been a small room before an addition had been added. Where they stood, no one could see them.

"I thought we were going to be honest with each other, Abby. I thought we agreed that was the kind of marriage we wanted to have."

She clasped her hands in front of her, staring at the floor. She'd chosen her black Sunday dress instead of the dark blue she could have worn because the black was more somber. Because it was a reflection of how she was feeling inside.

"Abby?" he begged. "Please talk to me."

"There you are, *Mam*!"

Abigail turned around to see Jamie coming toward them. He'd grown so much since winter that his black church pants were well above his ankles. The only reason he wasn't flashing bare skin was that he was wearing a pair of his grandfather's black socks that went up higher. "*Grossdadi* says to tell you we're hitched up and ready to go. *Grossmami*'s tired." He made a face. "She says she's tired from wiping down walls at home, but she hasn't cleaned up any of the soot. You and I have been doing it."

"And I'm thankful for your help," she told her son. "You've been so responsible this week. I'm proud of you."

"They can go. I can take you home," Ethan said quietly. "We can take one of the buggies or I can walk you."

Abigail turned back to her son. "I'll be right there."

Jamie hesitated, seeming to sense something was wrong.

"Go on," she told him.

It wasn't until she heard his footsteps in retreat that she turned back to Ethan.

"Abby, what is going on?" he repeated, opening his arms wide. "I know you're upset about the fire, but the house is fine. There are only a few days of work there and the laundry room will be as good as new. Better. And your mother is fine. A few blisters on her hand, that's it." He shook his head. "I don't know how, but it wasn't worse. The Lord keeps an eye on little ones and the elderly, that's what my grandmother used to say. Now I know…"

Abigail barely heard what he was saying. She had to force herself to look up at him. To meet his gaze. Her chest ached. Her heart was breaking. She could almost feel it shattering. She loved him. She loved him more than she ever thought she could love a man again. She loved him and she wanted to marry him and live out the rest of their days together. But life wasn't that simple.

"I can't marry you," Abigail said, interrupting him midsentence.

He stared at her. "What?"

"I changed my mind," she heard herself say. "I can't… I *won't* marry you, Ethan."

He just stood there staring at her for a moment. As if he couldn't comprehend what she was saying. "Abby, we've talked about this. I know Jamie is struggling right now, but he's going to be fine. You heard what Bishop Simon said last time we went to talk with him. That this is typical for a boy his age and to be expected. I think Jamie's already coming around. He came to me during the dinner break and asked me if he could come over this week and help with the framing of the new house."

"It's not Jamie," she whispered.

"Then *what*?" he asked, raising his voice.

His tone made it easier for her to find the words. "I can't leave my mother. She almost burned the house down, Ethan. I have to take care of her."

"You can't live down the road and take care of her?" he asked incredulously.

"Jamie could have *died*," she told him. She shook her head. "I need to stay home and help *Dat* take care of her. You heard the doctor. She said she's only going to get worse. They're my parents. I'm their only child. I have a responsibility to them. Just like as your father's eldest son you have a responsibility to him."

"So that's it?" he demanded. "We're not going to talk about it?"

"There's nothing to talk about," she said, staring at the polished wood floor.

He stood there a moment and then, without another word, brushed past her and walked down the long hall, his footsteps echoing all around her.

Chapter Thirteen

❧

"I figured you'd know what to do," Rosemary said quietly. "I don't know where your *dat* is, but I know your family had beehives back in New York. I know you helped him out."

Ethan's stomach did a flip-flop as he stood at the edge of the orchard and looked up at his little step-brother Jesse. Rosemary had come to the house site and fetched him just a moment ago.

Jesse, who was almost twelve, had climbed into the branches of a Golden Delicious apple tree and sat with his back against the trunk and his legs swinging down on either side of a branch. He was at least eight feet off the ground, but the distance ordinarily wouldn't have worried Ethan too much. Jesse was strong and agile, and climbed like a squirrel. Like Ethan and his brothers, the boy had been scrambling up ladders and into trees since he'd learned to walk. What scared Ethan at that moment was that Jesse was surrounded by thousands of honeybees.

"Please, Ethan, get them off him and get him down," Rosemary murmured under her breath.

"You stay back," Ethan instructed his stepmother. It was his belief that bees could sense it when people were afraid of them and it made the bees nervous. Nervous bees could be dangerous.

He took a step closer to the apple tree. "Jesse, I need you to sit still and not move," he called to his little brother. "Don't do anything to startle them."

Jesse shrugged. "I don't think they'll hurt me. They like me." Bees surrounded him, walking on his bare feet, his arms and fingers. They buzzed around his head and face and crawled in his hair. And only inches from Jesse's head of brown hair, a wriggling cluster of the winged insects, thicker than the boy's body, swayed on a branch.

"Don't make any noise," Ethan warned, trying to think back to his days of beekeeping with his *dat*. His heart thudded against his ribs.

"They tickle," Jesse said, seeming more fascinated than afraid. He lifted one finger covered in bees and studied them.

"I told you not to move." Mentally, Ethan went through his options. Did he try to brush them off the boy with a broom? Run the hose from the house and spray them with water? But Ethan knew that was foolishness. The bees were already crawling all over Jesse.

Besides, if they startled the swarm, they might all attack both of them. He didn't care about himself, but his brother was still so young. And he was small for his age. The child could be stung hundreds of times in just a minute.

"Please help him," Rosemary said quietly from behind Ethan. "You know how I feel about bees. A snake doesn't bother me. Nor a rat, but bees... When I was a girl, a friend tried to rob honey from a hive. He died. I still remember his swollen body in his coffin."

"No one's going to get hurt here, Rosemary." Ethan took another step closer to the tree, still racking his brain. It was true, they had kept bees back in New York, but that was years ago. He'd never dealt with a swarm himself.

"Could you use smoke?" Rosemary murmured. "I've heard that calms them."

"It probably wouldn't hurt. But I don't think we brought any of our equipment when we moved here. I think *Dat* sold it."

"Where did the bees come from?" she asked.

Ethan glanced up at the swarm. "They've left someone's bee box somewhere, or a hollow tree or maybe an abandoned building."

"Why did they do that?" Jesse asked.

"Probably because their queen was old or the hive got too crowded. They're being so friendly because they don't have honey to protect." He stroked his chin. He'd not grown his beard back. "They're just looking for a new home."

"I see," Rosemary said, staying at a safe distance back, but never taking her eye off her son.

"Were they in the tree when you climbed up there?" Ethan asked Jesse.

Jesse made a face, obviously afraid now that he was in trouble. "I was coming to see you to see how the house was going and I spotted them. I just wanted to see what they were doing."

"Jesse, you're not supposed to mess with bees," his mother called from behind Ethan. "You know better."

"But the bees didn't sting me," Jesse argued as little boys will with their mother. "They like me."

Ethan thought for a moment, then said, "Rosemary, could you do something for me? Could you go to the new house site and get my stepladder? I think it's near the wheelbarrow. Can't miss it." He pointed in the direction of the house he was still working on even though more than a week ago Abigail had told him she wouldn't marry him. Why he was still building it, he didn't know. Maybe because it gave him something to do while he went over and over in his mind how he could change Abby's mind. Which was already proving to be difficult because she wouldn't even speak to him. He'd gone to the house several times to try and even attempted to corner her at Spence's Bazaar, but had been unsuccessful.

"Be right back," Rosemary said, backing away slowly before she cut around a peach tree, moving quickly for a woman in her late forties.

"Honeybees are wonderful creatures," Ethan said, turning back to the apple tree. He kept his tone low and even. "But you have to respect them, Jesse. You have to give them their space."

"So I shouldn't have gotten so close?" His little brother blew a bee off his nose.

"You should not have," Ethan agreed. "Did you know that a community of bees thinks all together, like they have one brain?" he asked him, in an attempt to keep his composure, as well as Jesse's as they waited for Rosemary to return with the ladder. "This swarm has drones and workers, and in the middle, a queen. The others all protect her, because without the queen, there can be no colony."

"Why did they land in this tree in a big ball?"

"They're looking for a new home. For some reason, and we don't know why, they couldn't live in their old house anymore. They won't stay here in the tree. They need to find a safe place where they can store their honey, protect the queen and safely raise baby bees."

"Who taught you about bees?" Jesse asked.

"My *dat*. And his *dat* before him." Ethan heard Rosemary come up behind him and without turning his back on Jesse or the bees, he reached back for the ladder. "I'll take that."

He lifted the ladder onto his shoulder and carried it slowly over to the apple tree. "Hey, Jesse, did you know bees like singing?"

"They do?" he asked.

"Sure do," Ethan said softly. "Why don't you sing to them? Maybe something we sing at church."

In a high, sweet voice, the boy began an old German hymn.

Ethan settled the legs of the ladder into the soft grass and put his foot on the bottom rung and joined his brother in the song. He continued to sing as he slowly, one step at a time, climbed the ladder. When he was almost at the top, he put out his arms. "Swing your leg over the branch," he murmured. "Slowly. Keep singing." His little brother did just as he instructed, and Ethan nodded encouragement. "Easy. That's right. Come to me," Ethan murmured. "Slowly. And keep singing." A bee took flight, leaving the child's arm to join the main swarm. Then several more. Ethan caught Jesse by the waist, and the two of them waited, unmoving, as bees crawled out of his hair and flew into the branches above them. He brushed two more bees off his right arm. "Good. Now we'll start down. Slow and steady."

Sweat beaded beneath Ethan's shirt and trickled down his back. Step by step, the two of them inched down the ladder, and as they withdrew, it seemed that the tone and volume of the colony's buzzing grew softer.

When Jesse's bare feet touched the grass, the last few bees abandoned the child's mop of brown hair and buzzed away. "Go on," Ethan told his brother. "It's safe now. Go to your *mam*."

Jesse ran the fifteen feet or so to his mother and Rosemary gave a little cry of relief as she hugged her son.

Ethan left the ladder where it was and backed up. "We should fetch Eli. He's got bees. He can probably move the whole colony back to his place. They might even be his. Unless you want to keep them," he told his stepmother.

"Eli is welcome to those heathen beasts," she replied.

"Can I go get a snack?" Jesse asked, pulling himself away from his mother, looking embarrassed by her attention.

"*Ya.* But don't eat too much," she called after him as he took off across the grass toward the farmhouse. When he was gone, Rosemary walked toward where Ethan stood, keeping him between her and the bees in the apple tree. "Thank you, Ethan. I'm sorry I pulled you away from your work, but I didn't know what to do."

"It's fine." He took off his hat and fanned himself with it. "I don't know why I'm even bothering with the house at this point. I'll be having no wife to take to a new home."

Rosemary exhaled. "Benjamin told me to hold my tongue and let you and Abigail work this out. But I have to say, Ethan, I think you're being foolish to mope around here when you could be at her house trying to change her mind. That boy will adjust to his mother's marriage. And to you. And you'll adjust to him. He's really not that naughty."

Ethan looked down at his father's wife, contemplating what to say. She was barefoot and wore a midcalf-length dress, an oversize apron with large pockets and a wide-brimmed straw bonnet over her prayer *kapp*. Despite being middle-aged, she was still a pretty woman with brown hair and green eyes. He could see what had attracted his father to her physically, but the person she was inside was even more attractive. Rosemary was smart and fun and she was easy to talk to. She had a way of getting him to tell her what he was thinking when no one else could. Like Abby.

He put his hat back on his head and gazed out through the orchard in the direction of the foundation of a house he feared he would never live in. A house he didn't want to live in without Abby. He hadn't told his father and Rosemary exactly what had happened between him and Abigail. He hadn't told anyone, not even Joshua. He'd just said the wedding was off and refused to say more, even when Joshua had cornered him in the buggy workshop, demanding to know why his brother would let a girl like Abigail get away.

Ethan surprised himself when he looked at Rosemary and said, "We didn't break up over Jamie."

Rosemary appeared startled by the news. "You didn't? I just assumed—we assumed—" She glanced at her fish pond in the backyard that was surrounded by rocks that were covered in moss.

It was twenty by ten feet maybe, oblong, with a bubbling cascade, miniature lily pads, cattails and decorative rock border. The pond, the Irish moss and the wrought iron bench were already there when his father had bought the farm. One of the reasons he said he bought it was because Rosemary had loved that pond with its running water. It reminded her of the streams in upstate New York, he had said.

Rosemary took her time in speaking. "Your father and I just assumed… The way Abigail is with the boy, spoiling him so, him throwing rocks at you here and then after the fire at their house, we thought—" She sighed. "Ethan, we just assumed he had set the fire."

He considered remaining silent, but after spending months talking with Abby, he was finding it harder to hold back his thoughts and feelings. With anyone. It was as if a dam had broken and he was tired of feeling so isolated and alone. "Jamie didn't start the fire."

Rosemary dropped her hands to her hips. "He didn't? Then who—" She halted midsentence, raising one hand to her forehead. "*Ach.* Of course. It was June, wasn't it?"

"You know she saw the doctor. The diagnosis isn't good, Rosemary." Ethan shifted his gaze to the swarm of bees in the tree that was still undulating. He'd quit work for the day and go see Eli. If Eli couldn't come himself, Ethan would borrow the equipment he would need to capture the bees. All he really needed was a nuc box and maybe a little lemongrass oil to lure them in. The bees would find their way into the temporary home within a few days and he'd either give them to Eli…or maybe start his own hive. He had enjoyed working with bees when they'd lived in New York.

"So…this is all because of the fire?" Rosemary

asked. "Because Abigail doesn't want to leave her mother?"

"Exactly," Ethan agreed still staring at the swinging, wriggling mass of bees hanging off the apple tree. "She needs to stay home with her *dat* and help take care of her *mam*."

"Okay…" Rosemary spoke the word as if there was something she didn't understand.

"Okay what?" He opened his arms wide, frustrated more with the situation than Rosemary, but unable to keep it from his tone. "It's over. The betrothal is broken and we won't be marrying."

Rosemary frowned, her hands on her hips again. "Have I missed something here?"

"What do you mean?" he asked impatiently.

"You love her, and she loves you, *ya*?"

He looked away, surprised by the emotion that had suddenly welled in his throat. *"Ya,"* he managed.

"Then why don't you just marry and live there instead of here?"

"Live there?" Ethan wiped his eyes with his hand, embarrassed by the wave of emotion he felt just talking about Abigail. He gave a little laugh that was without humor. "You know I can't do that. I'm the oldest son. *Dat* is depending on me. *Dat* needs me to take care of the farm, to care for the two of you when you get older. He's even got me building the house you'll live in someday so I can take over the big house. I can't live at the Kings' farm. My responsibility is here."

"You have all of these brothers and sisters. I don't think all these chickens are going to fly the coop, Ethan."

"But I'm the oldest son," he repeated. "You and *Dat* are my responsibility."

She narrowed her gaze. "You haven't talked to your father about this, have you?"

"Nothing to talk about," he answered doggedly. "I know my duty."

"Ach." She shook her head, walking away almost as if she were fed up with him. "You Miller men, you're a stubborn bunch. Your mother always used to tell me that. She loved you all dearly, but you sorely tested her patience sometimes."

She turned back and was quiet for a moment, as if trying to decide what to say next. That was fine with Ethan because it gave him a moment to regain his composure.

Rosemary made a clicking sound between her teeth. "I need to get back to the house to check on the little ones. I'll thank you again for getting Jesse out of that nest of bees." She waggled her finger at him. "But I have one thing to tell you, Ethan Miller. You best think on this matter of you and Abigail and talk to your *dat*. Because most people don't get the chance to love again. And you'd be a fool to let her go."

Abigail glanced at her *mam* and then turned her attention back to Rudy, one of their driving horses. She eased him onto the shoulder of the busy road to allow a line of cars to pass. The gelding was a young horse, and Abigail didn't completely trust him yet, so she liked to keep a sharp eye out for traffic.

"We going for groceries?" Her mother's soft voice carried easily over the regular clip-clop of Rudy's hooves on the pavement and the rumble of the buggy wheels. The rain, which had held off all morning, was coming down in a spattering of large drops.

"*Ne*, to Edna Fisher's for a quilting frolic." She almost added "remember" but caught herself. There was no need to say it. Her mother obviously hadn't remembered where they were going even though they'd left their house only half an hour ago. An ominous roll of thunder sounded off to the west and Abigail flicked the reins to urge Rudy into a trot as she pulled back onto the road.

"I don't quilt much," her mother announced, folding her hands neatly in her lap. "At least I don't think I do. My sister May, now *she* was a quilter. Log cabin, bear claw, diamond, she could sew all the patterns. Gave your father and me a quilt as a wedding gift, she did. Still have it."

Her mother smiled at her, and Abigail was struck by how pretty she still was even at seventy. This afternoon she was wearing a lavender dress with her black apron, and her black bonnet tied over her starched white *kapp*. "You must have been a beautiful bride, *Mam*."

Her mother giggled. "What a thing to say. I hope I was properly Plain."

Her mother had had a good life, but certainly not an easy one. She had lost more babies than she cared to count, and Abigail had come at a time when her parents had thought there would be no children. But her mother had always been a positive person, kind, faithful and she never resented or bemoaned what she didn't have. She'd always told Abigail and anyone who would listen how God had blessed her and her husband with a child at the age when parents could truly appreciate such a gift.

Unexpected tears suddenly welled in Abigail's eyes

and she fixed her gaze on the black pavement spattered with rain ahead of them. What if she was like her mother? What if Jamie was the only child she would ever have? She and Egan had dreamed of a houseful. And then, after she met Ethan, after they had fallen in love, they had talked of filling their home with children, of welcoming, with open arms, as many as God saw fit to give them.

Abigail swallowed hard as she guided the buggy onto Edna and John Fisher's long dirt lane. She hadn't spoken to Ethan in nearly two weeks, not since she had ended their betrothal at Eli's house. He'd come by her father's place three times and then tried to corner her at Spence's Bazaar on Friday, but she'd refused to speak with him. What was the point? She'd made up her mind.

Abigail's father had questioned her about the breakup, but she'd given him no explanation beyond that it had been a mutual decision. As for her mother, no matter how many times Abigail reminded her that there was to be no August wedding, June went right on making plans and talking about the event to anyone who would listen. For that reason, Abigail had been hesitant to bring her mother to the quilting frolic. What would she do if her mother started a conversation about the marriage in the quilting circle? But the creases around her father's mouth and his clipped tone that morning had suggested he needed a break from his wife, so she'd yielded to his suggestion. He had said it would be good for Abigail and her mother to get out of the house, but what he really meant, she suspected, was that it would be good for him to have a few hours' break from June.

When Abigail had agreed to go to the quilting frolic, her father and Jamie had made plans to go fishing on their pond where bass had been stocked by the previous owners of the property. Originally, her father had planned to put another coat of paint on the remodeled laundry and mudroom, but Jamie had cajoled his grandfather into playing hooky for an hour. When Abigail and her mother had gone down the lane in the buggy, she'd spotted her father and son cutting across the meadow toward the pond, fishing rods on their shoulders.

When the buggy neared the two-story farmhouse, Abigail saw several of the Fisher children in the yard taking charge of the guests' horses. As she reined in Rudy, she spotted Phoebe standing near the back door. Waiting for her.

Suddenly, Abigail wished she hadn't come. Not only had she been avoiding Ethan, but she'd been avoiding Phoebe, who was her best friend there in Delaware. The look on Phoebe's face as Abigail took her time getting out of the buggy and then helping her *mam* down was easy to read. Abigail wasn't going to be able to dodge Phoebe this time.

"Sarah!" Phoebe called to one of the teenaged Fisher girls who was hustling across the driveway, carrying a pie brought by the Gruber girls. "Take June inside before she's soaked." Phoebe marched across the driveway, ignoring the rain, and put her arm around Abigail's mother. "Go with Sarah, June. We'll see you inside."

June bobbed her head and went along quite readily. "My daughter's marrying the schoolmaster, you know," she started off, telling the teen.

Abigail groaned and reached into the back of the buggy and pulled out the dish of blackberry buckle she and her *mam* had brought.

"Give me that." Phoebe grabbed the dish out of her

hand and passed it to another one of the Fisher girls. Abigail didn't even know which one she was, though she seemed to be close in age to Jamie.

"Now you come with me." Phoebe grabbed Abigail's hand and tugged, making it clear she wasn't going to take no for an answer.

"Where are we going?" Abigail protested.

"Somewhere where we can talk alone." Phoebe impatiently pulled her along beneath the overhang of the barn roof. "Because Joshua and I, all of us, have had about enough of Ethan's moping. And if he won't do anything about it, you're going to have to."

"Ethan's moping?" Abigail asked as Phoebe led her around the corner of the barn, away from the prying eyes of the women arriving for the frolic. She knew he had been upset, but somehow she'd convinced herself that she was suffering more than he was. She could stand her own sorrow, but to think of her beloved in pain...

"Honestly," Phoebe said when they were out of earshot of anyone else. "I don't know what I'm going to do with you. Why did you two break up? What's going on?"

"What does Ethan say?" Abigail murmured, pulling her hand from her friend's.

"No more than you." They stood near a Dutch door. The top was open and the comforting sounds of cows chewing their cud and chickens clucking came from inside. Rain pattered on the tin roof over their heads.

Abigail wrapped her arms around her waist and gazed out into the yard, watching the raindrops fall into a puddle and disperse in circles. "This is between

Ethan and me. There's no need for anyone to be involved. We're not teenagers."

"Well, you're acting like teenagers!" Phoebe stared at her for a moment, then exhaled. "Maybe if you could tell me what happened?" She hesitated and then went on. "Eunice is telling everyone that Ethan decided Jamie was too much for him to handle. That that was why he broke up with you. I bet she's told the story about him riding Karl Lapp's cow a dozen times in the last week. I asked Ethan straight out what happened, but he basically told me to mind my own knitting."

Abigail peevishly wiped at a tear that slipped down her cheek. She wasn't ordinarily a crier, but she'd certainly become one since the breakup. "Ethan didn't end our engagement. I did."

The words came hard for Abigail. She didn't understand how once a heart broke, it could keep breaking. But that was how she felt. Every time someone mentioned Ethan's name, every time she saw him, even from her bedroom window when she pretended not to be home, another tiny piece of her heart broke off. She knew she had done the right thing, but that didn't make it any easier.

"Are you mad? Why would you end the betrothal?" Phoebe asked incredulously. "The two of you are perfect together. Even his brothers say so."

Abigail met her friend's gaze. "We should go inside. You don't want to catch a chill." She lowered her gaze to Phoebe's belly that had the slightest roundness to it. She and Joshua were expecting their first child together. It wasn't something talked about openly among the Amish, but Phoebe had shared her secret a few weeks ago and Abigail had been thrilled for her. At the time, she had prayed she would be expecting the following year, but now that hope had gone out the window with so many others.

"We're not talking about me right now. We're talking about you." Sadness crossed Phoebe's face. "Oh, Abigail. I hate to see you like this. So sad. But this is just further proof that you and Ethan belong together. I can't tell which of you is more miserable without the other."

Abigail reached out and grasped her friend's hand. "Can we please not talk about this anymore?" She met her gaze, her eyes filling with tears. "Because I just don't think I can bear it."

Phoebe threw her arms around Abigail and hugged her tightly. "It's going to be all right. I'm praying for you and Ethan. We all are. God will make it right," she whispered in her ear. "He has a solution to our troubles. He always does. Even when we can't see it."

Abigail nodded, taking a shuddering breath. Praying Phoebe was right.

Chapter Fourteen

Ethan heard his father call his name, but he was sorely tempted to pretend he didn't.

He raised his ax and swung downward, relishing the feel of the resistance of the log. He lifted the ax and swung again. His hands were blistered from the rub of the wooden ax handle, his shoulders were aching from the exertion and his eyes stung from the sweat on his face. But none of it compared to the agony in his heart.

He missed Abigail so much… He missed the life they could have had. The life they had dreamed of together. And to think it was all because they both felt so strongly about their responsibility to their families. Once his initial anger had passed, he realized that even if he didn't agree with Abby, he understood her decision. And respected it.

"*Ya*, here," Ethan called. This time, when he struck the log squarely, it split with a satisfyingly loud crack and the smell of fresh-cut applewood filled the air. He had halted work on the *grossdadi* house days ago and started a project he and his brothers had been talking about since they moved to Delaware: cleaning up the old orchard.

"Could you hide a little closer to the house?" his father asked as he came around the wagon, limping slightly. Just after sunrise Ethan had driven the horse and wagon across the pasture and down the old logging road to the orchard on the rear of the property. The trees were all dead, disease ridden or too old to bear fruit and needed to be cut down. It was barely noon and he already had the wagon half-filled with split wood. Ordinarily, he would have loaded larger logs into the wagon and taken them to the woodshed to cut there, but he wasn't in the mood to be near his family. Truthfully, he figured he was doing everyone a favor by staying away and sparing them his "storm cloud," as his stepsister Ginger was calling it.

"I'm not hiding," Ethan grumbled. Setting the ax into another log, he picked up the splits of wood, carried them to the wagon and stacked them neatly.

"Ne?" His father glanced in the direction of their plow horse, Carter, grazing contentedly in the shade of a walnut tree. "Looks like you're hiding."

Ethan wrenched the ax from the applewood stump. "You shouldn't be walking so far. Your hip is just starting to get better." He swung the ax into the wood so hard that the force of the impact reverberated up his arms to his shoulders.

"Enough." His father leaned on the wagon with one arm and raised his other hand. "Put the ax down, *sohn*. We have to talk."

Ethan sank the ax into a stump and rubbed his hands together, easing the soreness of his palms.

"I spoke with Rosemary."

Ethan met his father's gaze. *"About?"*

Benjamin frowned. "You know well what about."

Ethan pulled his hat off, tossed it on the tailgate of the wagon and reached for the jug of water he'd brought with him. He took a couple of swallows and wiped his mouth with the back of his hand. "Rosemary has no right to interfere."

"She has *every* right," Benjamin answered firmly. "As my wife and your stepmother." He waggled his finger at his eldest. "You'll understand one day when you have children. It doesn't matter how old they get, it doesn't even matter once they have children of their own. You're always still a parent and you always want what's best for your child. Even if he's too foolish to realize himself what's best for him," he added.

Ethan eyed his father and then took his time pulling his handkerchief from his pocket and pouring water on it. He wiped his face with the cool, wet cloth. The July heat was oppressive. It had to be well into the nineties.

"Rosemary could tell me that Abigail's mother has been diagnosed with a serious illness. That Abigail made the decision she needed to stay home and take care of her."

Ethan said nothing. He was angry that Rosemary had told his father about their conversation from the other day. But he should have expected that. His father and Rosemary were like that. They never kept anything from each other. And he didn't blame them. It was the way a marriage ought to be.

"We're not like Englishers," his father said. "We don't accept social security or Medicare or any of those trappings. We take care of our own. That said, as an only child, Abigail is right to choose to stay with her parents."

Ethan looked up. For some reason he had expected his father to say he disagreed. To tell Ethan he should go back to Abigail and persuade her to marry and come with him because that was what God intended. For a woman to marry and go with her husband, wherever that might be. Men liked to quote from the Book of Ruth, "Wherever you go, I will go. Wherever you live, I will live." Of course it wasn't referring to a wife, but that was a detail not often picked up on.

"I agree that she needs to be with her parents," Ethan responded quietly. "So that's that. The end of the matter. There will be no wedding." He tossed the wet handkerchief over the side of the rough-hewn wagon's side and walked back toward his dwindling pile of logs.

"What are you talking about? That's not the end of the matter," his father barked, crossing his arms over his chest. "The solution is simple. If Abigail can't come to you, then you go to her." He motioned impatiently in the general direction of Daniel King's farm. "You marry her, and you take on her family as your own. You take her burden on your shoulders, lightening her load."

Ethan stared at his father in disbelief. It seemed as if his whole life his *dat* had been telling him he had a responsibility, as the oldest son, to remain at his side. "But I have to be here for you and Rosemary and Josiah and James."

"Says who?" Benjamin asked.

"You." He pointed at his father. "You made all of these plans for me to stay here and raise a family. Won't you be disappointed in me if I don't remain here to care for you?"

"I don't say this unkindly, but you're not my only child. And Abigail *is* June and Daniel's only one." Benjamin threw his arms around Ethan who was a full head taller than his father. His voice choked with emotion, he said, "I'll only be disappointed in you if you *don't* marry Abigail. If you don't go and care for her family." He drew back, gazing into Ethan's eyes, obviously unashamed of his tears. "I'll be disappointed if you don't take the gift God has given you. The gift we've all been praying for since you lost Mary. And that's a new life. With Abigail."

There was no doubting his father's sincerity. Ethan knew his *dat* wasn't just saying these things to make him feel better. He truly would be disappointed if Ethan didn't act. He believed God had sent him Abigail, and to ignore this gift would be like turning his back on a true Godsend.

With crystal clarity, he realized how right this was, and how it was his responsibility to convince Abigail of its rightness, too. To continue to mope and brood would be selfish.

Ethan took a shuddering breath and hugged his father back. He was nervous, but prepared to act.

An hour later, he was showered, dressed in his Sunday clothes and walking up the Kings' driveway. The old border collie, Boots, greeted him and served as escort, taking him right to the backyard where the family was having dinner at a picnic table beside the house, shaded by a giant silver maple tree.

"Ethan?" Daniel half rose from the bench when he spotted him. "Good to see you. Would you like to join us for dinner? There's still a little something left." He pointed to the remnants of the meal on the center of the table. "We've got cold fried chicken and salads here, and blueberry pie for dessert in the kitchen."

Abby sat quietly beside her son, keeping her eye averted.

"I didn't come for dinner." Ethan removed the black hat he reserved for his Sunday best. And for marriage proposals. His gaze shifted to Abigail. "I came to…" He took a breath. "Abby, I came here to ask for your forgiveness for being so thickheaded. And to ask you to marry me. Again."

Abigail just sat there for a moment stunned. She was so happy to see him, but nothing had changed. Why would he come here and—

"Now, before you say anything, Abby, I want to tell—I want to tell all of you," Ethan said, opening his arms wide, his hat still in his hand. "That I want to come here to live. To help you, Daniel," he said to her father. "To be the best son-in-law and stepfather I can be," he said, addressing first her mother and then Jamie.

Abigail rose from the bench, her heart thudding in her chest. She was afraid she was dreaming but Ethan offered his hand to her and she took it and felt the heat of his touch. This was real. He was there in flesh and blood.

"Would that be agreeable?" Ethan asked her father. "For me to join your family after we're married? To live here and help you take care of the farm?"

"It would be more than agreeable," her father answered. "I'd be proud to have you here. Now come on you two," he said waving at Jamie and his wife. "Let's leave Abigail and Ethan to themselves for a few minutes and we'll see to that blueberry pie."

"Pie!" Abigail's mother declared. "I love a good pie. With a big scoop of ice cream on top."

Jamie giggled. "Me, too, *Grossmami*. Lots of ice cream."

He glanced over his shoulder and it was on the tip of Abigail's tongue to ask him how he felt about the idea of Ethan living there with them. She decided against it, though, and turned back to the man she wanted to spend the rest of her days with. Who she married wasn't up to Jamie.

"Are you certain this is what you want?" Abigail heard herself say. She looked into Ethan's dark eyes, losing sight of her family. The only person that mattered right now was Ethan. "It's a big sacrifice."

"I'm certain I want you," he said, taking her hand. "So not a sacrifice at all. I just—" He exhaled. "I'm sorry I made a mess of things. I'm sorry I wasn't thinking clearly. I wasn't communicating clearly. It didn't occur to me that I could join you here because I thought my *dat* expected me to remain on the farm with him. And care for him and Rosemary in their old age."

"But he's okay with it?" she whispered, looking up at the face she hoped she would be looking into for a very long time. "He's not disappointed?"

"When I finally confessed what had happened, he thought I was a fool." He chuckled. "He said he'd be disappointed in me if I *didn't* marry you and join your family here."

"But you're the oldest son."

Ethan shrugged. "Apparently Rosemary and my father are even less conventional than I thought. Their answer was that they had plenty of other children, so apparently as the firstborn, I'm not all that important to them."

For some reason that struck Abigail as funny and she tipped her head back and laughed. And when she opened her eyes, Ethan was very close to her.

"So, will you?" he asked, taking both of her hands as he faced her.

"Will I what?" Of course she knew what he was asking, but she wanted to hear it again.

He smiled, seeming to understand. "Will you be my wife, Abigail? To have and to hold until death parts us?"

Abigail met his dark-eyed gaze as she leaned closer, looking up at him. "I will marry you, Ethan. Because I love you."

"And because I love you," he whispered.

And then, even though they both knew better, when he lowered his head and brushed his lips to hers, she accepted his kiss. He released her hands and wrapped his arms around her and just as they were about to kiss again, something struck them on the tops of their heads and they were both suddenly soaked with water.

With a squeal of surprise, Abigail stepped back. "Jamie!" she cried. "I thought I told you—" She looked up to see that the culprit was not her son, but her mother!

"Ethan and Babby, sitting in a tree," her mother sang, hanging out the upstairs' window. *"K-I-S-S-I-N-G!"*

"Mam!" Abigail shouted up, wide-eyed.

"I'll get her!" came Jamie's voice. Then he pulled his grandmother out of the open window and slammed it shut.

Abigail lowered her gaze until she was looking at Ethan again. He was soaking wet with water running off the brim of his Sunday hat. She covered her mouth to keep from laughing aloud and Ethan began to laugh with her. Her *kapp* was wet, her hair was wet and so was her blue dress.

"Well," Ethan said, pulling a handkerchief out of his pocket and handing it to her. "If nothing else, being married to you is going to be full of surprises."

"Ya," she agreed, wiping her face.

"And also love," he said.

And then he kissed her cheek gently and Abigail realized that God had given her all she had prayed for, and much, much more.

Epilogue

Two years later

Abigail dipped her brush into the bucket of whitewash and drew it across the clapboard siding. The new school year would begin in less than a week and Ethan was determined to get the entire exterior of the schoolhouse painted before his students arrived.

"Have enough paint?" Ethan asked, coming up behind her. He pressed his hand to her shoulder.

"Plenty," she told him, smiling as she dipped her brush again. "Where's Jamie gotten to?"

"He went back to the wagon to get a roller for me. Joshua is using one on the back wall and he says it's going faster." He gazed down at her. "You really don't need to do this, you know. We have plenty of help. You could go sit under the tree with your mother. She's keeping an eye on Joshua and Phoebe's new baby."

She cut her eyes at him and brushed the paint on the wooden siding. "You want to park me under a tree with elderly ladies and newborns?" she asked.

He gazed down at her swollen abdomen and made

a face, indicating it was not him who was being ridiculous.

Abigail was two weeks short of her due date and was enormous. Twins, according to the midwife. But she felt good. And she wanted to be there with Ethan to help him prepare the schoolhouse for the new year. "Stop fussing over me. I'm fine," she told him shaking the paintbrush at him.

He plucked the paintbrush from her hand, wrapping his other arm around her. "Stop fussing, you say? Isn't that a husband's job to fuss over his wife when she's about to give him not one but two more sons?"

His words made her tear up. She'd been so sensitive these last few weeks that she knew her time was growing near. The fact that Ethan referred to Jamie not as his stepson, but his son, filled her with emotion every time he said it. Because he meant it.

When Abigail married Ethan, she loved him, and he loved her. And he had been serious in his promise to join her family. He was up at dawn with her father, milking cows. He plowed, he mowed, he did whatever work was needed on the farm. He and her father had become good friends and Ethan couldn't have been kinder to her mother, even as time passed and she was less aware of the world around her. But Abigail had expected all of that. What she had *not* expected was the love that she had seen grow between Ethan and Jamie. In the first days of the marriage, things had sometimes been tough between the two of them. But Ethan had continued to tutor Jamie and to act as a substitute for his father, not as his father, and against his will, Jamie had begun to soften toward Ethan.

And now, they were the best of friends. That didn't

mean that issues didn't arise when Ethan had to discuss Jamie's words or actions with him, but there was no resentment like the early days. Jamie now accepted Ethan's guidance the same way he did his mother's or grandfather's. And Jamie was so excited now about the prospect of having little brothers to take care of and to act as a role model for.

"I'm serious," Ethan said, kissing her temple. "You've been on your feet for hours. Why don't you take a break? Go check on your *mam*. On the baby. I'm sure Phoebe would appreciate it. She's on the back wall with a paint roller. I think she paints faster than Joshua."

Abigail laughed. The truth was that she was getting a little tired and her back was beginning to ache. She rubbed it absently. "Think we'll finish today?"

"At this rate, we'll be opening those picnic baskets early," he said leaning down to pour paint into a tray. The painting of the schoolhouse had become a family event with the Millers and Kings joining forces.

"Found it, Ethan!" Jamie called, running across the driveway with the roller in his hand.

"Oh, goodness," Abigail said, watching her son come toward them. "He's sore in need of new pants. Everyone in school will be saying he wears high-waters."

"Told you I thought he'd grown a foot this summer," Ethan said, watching him, too.

At eleven years old, Jamie was already beginning to look more like a man than a boy and Abigail was so thankful for the new babies. Because before she knew it, her eldest son would be a man. A fine man, who read well, thanks to her husband. And was kind and well behaved…at least most of the time.

Jamie halted in front of them, out of breath. "I

thought you were going to use the roller," he said to Ethan. "What are you doing with a paintbrush?"

"Your mother was using it, but now she's not." Ethan took the roller from Jamie and handed him Abigail's brush. "I thought you could help for a while. Your mother needs to rest."

"You trust me to paint the school? Sure," Jamie said excitedly.

"I'm not tired," Abigail said with exasperation. "I don't need to—" She halted midsentence as her husband and son turned their backs to her to begin tackling the task side by side. Maybe she wasn't too tired to paint, but it made her so happy to see them working together that she gave Jamie a kiss on the cheek.

"Ew, *Mam*!" her son groaned, pulling away from her.

But she just laughed and turned to plant a kiss on Ethan's cheek. "Thank you," she whispered, looking up at her handsome husband.

He turned to her, paint roller in his hand. "For what?"

"For loving us," she said and then she turned and walk away, stroking her belly, knowing that as good as life was with Ethan, it was only going to get better.

* * * * *

AMISH RECKONING

Jocelyn McClay

Always, thanks to God for this opportunity. Thanks to Audra and Moriah for your candid and heartfelt input on sisterhood. Oldest grandchild Judah, you are a precocious inspiration. Lorelle and Debi, your valued feedback improved the story. Kevin, you showed me that romance can be as simple as reading my first novel when I was traveling because you missed me. And Genna, here's to treasured Wednesday chats.

Casting all your care upon him;
for he careth for you.
—*1 Peter* 5:7

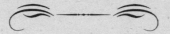

Chapter One

Today was going to change his life. The certainty thrummed through Samuel Schrock as he looked over the farmyard in the predawn darkness of the July morning.

A pinpoint of light pricked the horizon. The muted rumble of a large engine climbing a hill was an odd accompaniment to the growing whistles and calls of waking birds. Samuel stepped off the porch and rubbed his hands together. It was finally happening. He'd longed for this opportunity his whole life.

Smiling wryly, he acknowledged that twenty-two years might not be much of a lifetime according to some of the long-bearded elders in his Amish community. But for Samuel, it seemed like forever since his earliest memory—playing around the legs of his *daed*'s tall Standardbred, an adventure that almost got him kicked for his enthusiasm—instilled in him a love of horses.

Earning a living working with them had been his dream ever since.

When he and younger *bruder*, Gideon, had moved to Wisconsin to join their eldest *bruder* at the furniture business Malachi had purchased last fall, Samuel figured the dream would be put on hold while they established themselves in a new community. But thanks to the savvy of the operation's previous owner, Schrock Brothers' Furniture was already humming along successfully.

It just had one less Schrock brother working in it.

Watching the headlights' steady approach, Samuel strode to the top of the lane. To the east, a seam of gold heralded the sun's arrival, promising a beautiful day. Of course, today could be pouring down rain, and it would still be beautiful to him.

The engine picked up speed. Its rumble would probably wake up Gideon when it pulled into the yard. *Ach*, well. His *bruder* would survive. Those in the barn were already up. If the livestock had minded being fed a little early this morning, as Samuel had been awake for hours, they'd kept it to themselves.

Malachi agreed to let Samuel leave Schrock Brothers' earlier than anticipated when old Elam Chupp retired from procuring horses for Miller's Creek and other small Amish communities in the region. Kicked one too many times, Elam had explained, but it'd been said with a smile. Samuel had swiftly arranged to take over the business.

He loved his big brother dearly, but he'd lived his whole life in Malachi's shadow. Now was his chance to break free. Earn his way, both economically and psychologically. Prove that he was more than just the charming Schrock brother.

The glow of light split into two separate beams. Samuel retraced his steps to the porch. He didn't want to look too eager, too excited, too inexperienced. The outline of a pickup and a gooseneck trailer approached on the country road.

He'd hired the freight hauler Elam had used and recommended. Gale someone. According to Elam, the hauler was reliable and fair priced, the latter particularly important as margins on sales were slim. Samuel had inquired about other freight outfits and found them to be too expensive for his fledgling business to handle. Elam also said this carrier was decent company, a factor as the Milwaukee racetrack and other locations they'd travel to might be some distance away. Hence the early start.

The truck slowed, presumably looking for addresses as many of the Amish farms in the area looked similar with their big white barns and houses with no electric line connections. Remaining on the porch, Samuel waved an arm, unsure if the driver could see him. The pickup's blinker came on. It turned into the lane.

Watching the truck's approach, Samuel recalled Elam's surprising principle advice. The older man had cautioned that trust—not a good eye for horseflesh or the ability to drive a hard bargain—was the biggest part of the job. Samuel sucked in a deep breath of the early-morning air. Folks had always liked him. He was aware, though, that there was a disparity between liking someone versus trusting and respecting them. Thoughtfully exhaling, Samuel pondered the difference. He didn't anticipate any issue bridging that gap. There wasn't any reason folks shouldn't trust him. He was a man of his word.

Samuel raised an eyebrow as the rig made a circle in the farmyard. Not what he was expecting, although he didn't know why he'd assumed the outfit would be brand-new. It wasn't. The black quad-cab Dodge Ram, although certainly robust enough to handle the goose-neck trailer behind it, had been on the road a number of years. As had the trailer. But both looked in good working condition and were free of rust. Trailer rust and the potential resulting holes were deadly in hauling four-legged animals.

His other brow rose when the driver opened the door and descended from the cab. Well, that would teach him to make assumptions. Apparently, Gale was Gail. There was no mistaking the tall, trim figure encased in jeans and a long-sleeve shirt, or the curly brunette ponytail swinging at the back of her head as anything but female.

Or the pitch of her voice when she asked warily, "Samuel Schrock?"

"Ja." Samuel stepped off the porch, anticipating the smile that always greeted him when he met a woman. This one frowned. She looked disappointed.

The reaction was a new one for him. Bemused, he offered his hand, something Amish didn't normally do, but was a common custom among the *Englisch.* After a moment's hesitation, she reached out her slender one and clasped his for a single brief shake before snatching her hand back and sliding it down the front of her jeans like she was trying to wipe off something distasteful. Samuel blinked. He'd expected numerous new experiences today. But a woman finding him repulsive hadn't been one of them.

He wasn't upset that Gail was female. Women drivers passed him all the time on the road. Though they whipped by his buggy as fast as men—turning to gawk just as frequently, except for the ones who were on their phones in some manner as they drove—he had no issue with them. He was just surprised to see this one climb out of the robust pickup. She looked younger than he was.

But she had a problem with him for some reason. Women, particularly young ones, never had problems with him. Usually it was the other way around.

They stared at each other across a few feet of gravel in the farmyard. Him, with a friendly smile on his face. Her, with anything but. From the chicken coop, a rooster crowed, apparently deciding it was light enough to get about the day's business. At the sound, Gail started, apparently deciding the same thing.

"Get whatever stuff you need and put it in the back of the cab." She pivoted and reached for the door handle.

Samuel found himself facing her swinging ponytail. When she climbed into the cab without looking back, he shrugged. As his notebook, pen and bishop-approved cell phone were in his pocket, he headed for the passenger seat. Rounding the front end of the Dodge, he glanced through the windshield to where Gail already sat on the driver's side. Her expression looked like she'd taken a bite of a fruit, expecting an apple and finding a lemon instead. Samuel sighed softly at the reality that a pretty girl didn't always mean a pretty disposition. It could be a long ride to Milwaukee.

But not if he could help it. She was still female. He was good with women. Whatever issue she might think she had with him, he'd charm her out of it. Opening the door, he entered the truck and buckled himself in.

Shifting in the seat, he faced her now-solemn profile with its delicate brow and dainty nose. Particularly intriguing was the graceful shell of her ear outlined by hair pulled back into a high ponytail, a sight he didn't often see. Frequently, Amish women's ears were at least partially covered by their *kapps*.

"Elam told me about you, but there were some obvious things he left out," Samuel cajoled.

Instead of the flirtatious response he expected, he got a muttered, "He didn't tell me enough about you."

It was a start. "I can tell you more, if you like."

"That's okay." Gail quickly dismissed his offer as she reached for the key in the dash. The engine roared to life. She shifted into gear and the truck started down the lane. As they rolled past the white painted posts of the farm's fence, a grin creased Samuel's cheeks, his companion's perplexing attitude temporarily set aside.

It had begun. His new adventure. His new job. This was his chance to make his life's dream work. To prove himself as more than just a younger brother. And he would do everything in his control to make it successful.

They weren't even out of the lane and Gail was already missing Elam. When he'd announced someone else was taking over his horse-trading business, she'd been expecting an Amish man like him. One wearing a gray beard of some length, indicating he'd been married for years. Slightly homely. Shorter than she was. Sweet. Not charming. Not attractive.

This one made the Ram's cab feel like it had shrunk to the size of a fifty-five-gallon drum, and all the air had been sucked out of it. He made her feel small. And female.

A betraying warmth started in her cheeks and journeyed from there down to her toes in her worn work boots. The long-sleeve shirt she'd donned due to the cool morning now stuck to her flushed skin. Slanting a look at her passenger, she resented that he was so attractive he made her sweat. She cracked the driver's window, causing her ponytail to flutter in the breeze. Bonnie's air-conditioning system had been finicky lately. Gail didn't want to push her luck with it now when she'd need it later in the heat of the afternoon. She prayed that the old pickup wouldn't leave them sweltering.

"Gonna be a warm one today." Her passenger's rich baritone rolled through the cab.

His alluring voice was as disconcerting as his appearance. Gail clicked on the radio. Pop music blasted over the rumble of the engine and the wind's rush through the window, making it difficult to hear. Therefore, difficult to talk. All the better.

They were both slung forward against their seat belts when she braked hard at the stop sign to the highway. It was a good thing there were no horses in the trailer yet. They'd have been knocked off their feet and possibly injured. The thought churned her stomach.

She smoothly pulled onto the pavement. *Get a grip, Gail. Or you won't have to worry about how much you don't want to be around him. He'll take his business elsewhere, and then where will you be?*

Not in a good place. More broke than she was now. She needed this job. She'd been sick with worry when Elam announced he was retiring. The Amish hauls were critical in helping extremely frayed ends meet, especially with fall and the closing of the track for the winter approaching. Gail had already missed one payment on the truck and trailer when the Amish hauls stopped during the business transition. If she missed another payment, she'd lose her rig. The only jobs available to her with an eighth-grade education—waitressing, clerking and other part-time jobs—would barely support her.

On her own, she might be able to survive, but not with Lily. Gail had worked too hard to make it this far. No charming young Amish man, too attractive for his broad-fall britches, was going to upend her life.

Again.

Since he was her customer, a desperately needed one, Gail tipped her head toward the dash and raised her voice to be heard over the chirpy female one coming through the speakers. "Do you mind the music?"

He grinned at her across what had once seemed like a wide seat and shouted back, "No, not at all."

Gail faced forward again, eyes on the road in front of her, resenting his charming smile.

He looked like a younger version of an actor. The big, brawny blond one who carried a hammer in the superhero movies she'd watched on her streaming service, the one perk her meager budget allowed. He should look ridiculous—Samuel, not the actor—but he didn't.

He wore a flat-brimmed straw hat, suspenders, dark blue pants and work boots. His hair was a little shorter and cut differently than the long bowl style normally worn by Amish men. That indicated he was in his *rumspringa*, when a few more liberties were allowed. The sun-lined creases bracketing his crinkling blue eyes indicated the charming smile was frequently in place. Eyes that were about the same blue as the awakening sky beyond the windshield.

She despised blue eyes. She despised charming

young Amish men. Blond ones were the worst. Shifting on the cloth seat, Gail scowled. He was attractive. She was attracted. Therefore, he was off-limits, as she'd proved herself a lousy judge of character with attractive men. Besides, it didn't matter to her. It couldn't. Because he was Amish. And she wasn't.

Not anymore.

And although she longed to, she couldn't go back. Not if she was going to keep her daughter.

A muffled boom merged with the reverberating percussion of the music and rush of the wind through the lowered window. The steering wheel jerked and began vibrating, pulling hard toward the side of the road. Gail tightened her grip like she was trying to hold on to a wild animal instead of a circle of plastic. Instantly nauseated at what it meant, Gail flicked on her blinker and let up on the gas. When she noted the intersection for a country road, she puffed out a breath in relief. Turning cautiously onto it, she pulled the truck off to the side and shut it down. In the ensuing silence, broken only by the cooling tick of the engine, she slumped back against the seat and closed her eyes.

"Oh, Bonnie. How could you do this to me? I was going to take care of you," she muttered. "You were supposed to last just a little longer."

"Is everything all right?"

No. Far from it. Opening her eyes, she glanced at Samuel and forced a smile, hoping it didn't look as sour as her stomach felt. "It'll be fine."

Although his brow furrowed, he seemed satisfied with her assurance. "You named the truck? We name our animals, but—" his eyes bounced around the cab's interior "—this is a piece of metal."

Not to Gail it wasn't. All her hopes, dreams and sacrifices were tied up in the truck and the trailer behind it. Her and her daughter's future were literally riding on the Dodge's wheels. One of which was now most assuredly flat. As was her bank account, which couldn't afford to replace it or the other three of matching condition.

At the moment, her too-attractive passenger was the least of her worries.

Chapter Two

With a heavy sigh, Gail set the parking brake, unbuckled and climbed from the truck. Pushing the door shut, she found the bottom third of the truck's front wheel level with the road surface. Her shoulders sagged in relief when it looked like the rim had escaped damage. Gail strode to the back of the truck to get the spare tire.

She'd feared this was coming. She'd been pressing a penny into the truck tires for the last month, wishing that somehow Lincoln's hairstyle would morph into something tall enough to reach the shrinking treads. Gail knew the tires wouldn't make it through winter, but she'd hoped they'd at least make it into the fall before she needed to spend money she didn't have.

Gail blinked back a threat of tears. *Gott* would provide. He always had. She just wished she didn't have to be such a nuisance to Him.

Dropping the tailgate, Gail reached for the spare, only to see work-calloused hands grab hold of it first.

"I got it."

Samuel's arm brushed her shoulder. Gail's startled inhalation caught a whiff of soap and the pleasant musk of horses. Hastily stepping back, she bumped her head on the gooseneck of the trailer. It made less of an impact to her equilibrium than finding herself the focus of Samuel's blue eyes and dazzling smile.

"I knew this day would be full of new adventures. Just didn't expect them to start before we got to the track." Lifting the tire from the truck bed, he added, "We can't leave Bonnie here lingering with a broken leg." He nodded toward the flat tire. "What do you use to lift the truck?"

"I'll get the jack." Gail ducked under the gooseneck, dashed to the front passenger door and uncovered the jack assembly. When she turned in the V of the open truck door, he was there. She held the jack in front of her like a shield. It wasn't much protection against her escalating heartbeat that hammered away at his nearness. "Got it," she said unnecessarily. To her relief, he stepped back and she skirted around him to the tire, pulled off the hubcap and began setting up the jack. Seconds later Samuel crouched at her shoulder.

He was too much like the Amish charmer she'd fallen for years ago, too close for her ricocheting senses and too tempting for her obvious poor judgment in men.

"Do you…ah…know what it is to block a wheel?"

Samuel smiled at her as if she'd asked if he knew what shoofly pie was. "*Ja*, I think I can handle that."

"Can you block the far rear one?" The errand would give her a moment of space. Working quickly, she had the jack in place and the nuts loosened by the lug wrench. Gail was starting to loosen the nuts the rest of the way manually when Samuel's fingers reached for the next lug nut and their hands brushed. Gail jerked hers back. As he quickly loosened that one and moved on to the next, she dropped the nut she held into the upturned hubcap with a clang and stood.

The remaining bolts were quickly stripped of lug nuts under his capable fingers. Samuel pulled the flat tire off and set it aside. "It's pretty much like changing a buggy wheel—" he grunted as he lifted the spare onto the bolts "—except with rubber, heavier, wider and the buggy has a name." He shot her a grin over his shoulder. "Where'd you come up with *Bonnie*?"

"Ah." Gail wasn't going to mention that Bonnie, a big Percheron mare, had been her favorite among her *daed*'s draft horses. "Um, black truck. *Bonnie* starts with *B*. Just popped into my head when I was driving." *One time when I was traveling long miles by myself, trying to support a child, so homesick I cried for about sixty miles. I just needed something from home.*

Gail slid the hubcap with the lug nuts within his reach. Grabbing the deflated tire, she maneuvered it to the truck's tailgate, wrestled it into the bed and slammed the tailgate shut. Samuel had stepped back from the wheel by the time she returned. Kneeling, Gail released the jack and used the wrench to finish tightening the nuts.

"I can do that." Samuel's voice came from just off her shoulder.

Gail switched the wrench to the next nut, her brow lowering as she stared at the tread of the spare. It wasn't in much better condition than the flat they'd removed. Reality settled in like the weight of the truck on the unjacked tire. "I got it. My truck, my responsibility. But thanks for your help." He must have heard the dismissal in her tone, as he stepped aside. Gail could feel his gaze on the back of her head.

Concern for her and Lily's future chased away the long-dormant feelings of awareness and attraction that'd fluttered like a newly caged bird through her. She had no time for such frivolous things when their livelihood was at risk. Without another word, she stored the jack assembly, leaving the front passenger door open in unspoken invitation for him to get into the truck. As she rounded the hood, Gail glanced dejectedly at the other front tire, apprehensive now that it'd blow out as well before they reached the city. She'd let it go too far. They all needed replacing. There was no more postponing the inevitable.

With slumped shoulders, she climbed into the truck. Returning to the highway intersection after finding a lane in which to turn around, Gail looked to the right and found Samuel watching her. Giving him a weak, warped smile, she turned on the radio again. Upbeat music, contradictory to her mood, reverberated through the cab as she pulled onto the road.

As they headed toward Milwaukee, Gail didn't know which was more detrimental to her peace of mind—the attractive Amish man beside her or her nonexistent finances that were about to get worse.

Finances won. With risky tires, she couldn't make any income. Without the income, she'd lose the rig. Without the rig—Gail inhaled sharply through her nose—she could lose her daughter.

When Samuel asked a few questions, Gail cranked the music to avoid conversation and the distraction it brought. Hands firm on the steering wheel in case another of Bonnie's tires decided to go, she sent up a simple prayer. *Gott* said not to worry about tomorrow, but that was hard to remember when your future was riding on four bald tires and an empty bank account.

Unfortunately for her bank account, but fortunately for the sorry turn of events, Gail had no extra hauls scheduled that day. At the track, she took a moment to introduce Samuel to a few key people, primarily trainer George Hayes, before leaving the trailer in the track's back parking lot and heading for the tire dealer George had recommended.

Safety first. The thought drummed through her head in concert with her fingers that rested on the open window. Her daughter was an occasional passenger. Her reputation transporting horses depended on it. Gail's heart pounded at the possibility of a blowout and loss of control when Lily was in the truck, or an equine passenger was in the trailer.

She could live without air-conditioning. She had for years growing up. She couldn't live without safe tires. Getting a complete set was the right thing to do. Even knowing that truth, her stomach twisted as later she handed over the credit card that already had a balance higher than her bank account.

She'd have to get an extra job. Gail's stomach wrenched further. That would mean more missed time with her three-year-old daughter. It felt like she was rarely home as it was.

Home. Gail flattened her lips at the thought of it. Not the tiny basement apartment she shared with Lily, but the well-kept farm Gail had grown up on. If only she could go home…

Picking up the newspaper in the waiting area, she flipped to the want ads. There were jobs, but nothing she was qualified for. Gail dropped the paper and crossed her arms. Hopefully, Samuel knew what he was doing and was more than just a pretty face. Although Gail made some money with him as a passenger, the real money was when she was hauling horses. If he bought even one or, better yet, two today, it would help her desperate finances. She'd be thrilled enough to ignore her hard-earned wariness and hug Samuel Schrock's handsome neck.

If he'd only buy a horse.

Samuel waited outside George Hayes's stable block where Gail had left him that morning.

It'd been a *wunderbar* day. Knowing that he looked strange even for a stranger, Samuel had been uncharacteristically nervous when he'd first arrived at the track, but the few brief introductions from Gail had set him on an effective course for the day. He'd even bought a horse, an older gelding that no longer made the time trials, from George. It was a risk on his first day, but Gail obviously respected the older man, so Samuel figured it was safe to do so, as well.

He smiled at the thought of his freight hauler. Old Elam must've had something he didn't, because if Gail was what Elam called decent company, the man hadn't gotten out much. Or had spent too much time with only horses.

Of course, maybe she didn't get out much, either, if she was naming her truck. He snorted at the memory. Samuel almost wished there'd been four tires needing changing instead of just the one. She'd seemed almost friendly there by the side of the road.

But as soon as they'd climbed back into the truck, it was back to business and ear-ringing music. Samuel liked *Englisch* music, but he liked a good conversation, as well. Particularly one with a pretty woman. With her dark hair and expressive blue eyes, Gail-the-freight-hauler was definitely a pretty woman.

One who was as skittish around him as an unbroken filly. Old Elam had indicated that trust was paramount in his new position, but Samuel had never figured that would be an issue with women. He'd never had a problem with them before, Amish or *Englisch*. He didn't expect one now, but it was hard to flirt with a woman while shouting. And every effort of his had been deflected. The woman certainly had a way with words. A way of speaking as few of them as possible.

The July afternoon sun beat down on him. Using a knuckle to tip his flat-brimmed hat farther back off his sweating forehead, Samuel watched the horse and the human traffic that flowed around him. It was quieter in the stable block now than it'd been earlier. A number of equine athletes were already returned to their stalls for the day. Latecomers from the track passed, some with jog carts, most with racing bikes; their nickers of greeting to their stablemates along with the stomps of shod hooves, rattle of stall doors and murmur of distant conversations were muffled in the sultry air.

Glancing down the shed row, Samuel caught sight of Gail, immediately recognizable from her long but feminine stride and graceful lean figure. She walked like she had someplace to go and was intent on getting there. His lips curved into an admiring smile. Although he enjoyed the efforts of the young Amish women who'd vied for his favor, none had caught his attention. But this one might. Samuel's smile widened. Then she'd throw it right back at him.

She'd been in the back of his mind all afternoon, which was disconcerting as so many *wunderbar* new things had been peppering the front. His driver was very attractive indeed, but Samuel wasn't about to do anything to risk their professional relationship. He needed Gail for his business. And based on the age of the truck, the trailer and her worn blue jeans, she needed him as a customer.

While it'd been a *gut* day for him, as Gail got closer he could tell from her drooping shoulders that it hadn't been such a *gut* one for her.

She stopped several feet away from him. "Ready?" Distressed or not, she wasn't one to dawdle.

Samuel nodded and tipped his head back toward George's stable block. "Need to pick up a horse first."

"Really?"

For a moment Samuel thought he was seeing a second sunrise in the day, the way Gail's face lit up. She lunged forward, her arms lifted like she was going to throw them around his neck.

Chapter Three

They were inches apart for a breathless moment before Gail took a step back, her face as red as some racing silks that he'd seen on the track that day. Releasing a quiet sigh, Samuel regretted that she hadn't come to her senses a few seconds later.

Samuel knew he'd love this job. And if this was the way his pretty driver reacted when he made a purchase, he envisioned himself quickly gaining a small herd of horses, the big white barn at the farm bursting at the seams.

Gail awkwardly rubbed her hands together. "Let's, ah, let's go get him, then."

Nodding, Samuel turned and headed for the stall that held his new purchase, with Gail falling in step beside him.

"He's a sweetie." Gail ran a hand down the sleek neck of the gelding while Samuel obtained a lead rope from the attending groom. "I can tell by his eyes. They're patient. Approachable. Calm." She smoothed the horse's forelock over the bay's broad forehead.

Samuel suppressed his responding snort. That was

at least three qualities the gelding didn't share with the woman petting him. Snapping the lead rope to the horse's halter, he unhooked the half door and led the horse out. "Those characteristics might be the very reasons he's coming with me instead of staying at the track." The steady clip-clop of the bay's steps accompanied them as they headed for the parking lot.

"Different realities in life require different strengths. I'm sure he'll do fine in his new role. You have a prospective buyer for him?"

"I've got a neighbor who mentioned he was looking for a new horse for his wife. I'm thinking this one might be a good fit."

On the other side of the horse, it was quiet a moment before he heard her murmur, "Good. Sometimes it's hard to find the right fit for your life."

When they reached the truck and trailer, the gelding loaded like the pro he was. After watching Gail secure the trailer latch, Samuel walked the length of the trailer, pausing when he reached the rear of the truck and noticed the tires, all dark and shiny.

He raised his voice to be heard across the truck where she was approaching the driver's side. "You didn't just replace the one?"

From the far side of the truck he heard the slam of the cab door. Gail didn't respond until Samuel climbed in beside her. "They all needed to be replaced. It's safer." She gave him a lopsided smile. "Don't want to give our new passenger a ride like this morning." She started the engine and rolled down the windows. "Or worse."

They pulled out of the parking lot, the open windows letting in a hot breeze. As they took the ramp to the interstate, the truck's speed picked up, as did the rush of air into the cab. Although loud, it didn't prohibit conversation like the music had on the way in.

Gail glanced over, frowning apologetically. "Sorry about the windows. The air-conditioning is misbehaving."

Samuel grinned. "S'all right. It's about the only thing I've faced today that I'm used to. At home, instead of the breeze blowing in the side windows, it's coming through the front. And it doesn't come as fast."

He thought her lips tipped up toward a smile, but he wasn't sure. "Bonnie seems a bit cantankerous."

Gail patted the weathered dash. "She's all right. Just needs a little support and TLC now and then, like all of us."

"Speaking of support, thank you for the introductions this morning."

"No problem." For a few miles, except for the streaming wind noise, it was silent. Samuel saw Gail glance at the radio, like she was thinking of turning it on, but didn't. Instead, she pitched her voice above the cab noise and asked, "Elam didn't mention much about you. Are you originally from the Miller's Creek area?"

"*Nee.* Moved up to Wisconsin from Ohio last year. Followed my older *bruder*." He shrugged. "Seems I'm always following him in some manner. This is my first solo adventure. Malachi's very successful. He's…" Samuel struggled with words that would accurately describe his *bruder*. "I admire him greatly, but it's time for me to strike my own path. That's why this job opportunity is *wunderbar*. It's a chance to make my own way doing something I love." He rested an elbow on the edge of the open window. "You ever feel like a sapling under the shade of a huge oak tree?"

Samuel glanced over at Gail. Her mouth was slightly open, as if she was about to say something, but all the conversation was in her eyes. It must have been a difficult one. Samuel didn't speak, waiting to hear what she wanted to share. When she remained silent, he took pity on her.

"What? No music this time?" To him, it was a victory. The comment earned him another small smile.

Gail clicked on the radio and adjusted it so it was just a quiet thrum under the sound of the breeze. Her shoulders rose and fell under a slow, deep sigh. "So what does your oak of a brother do?"

Samuel grinned at the reference. It was an apt description of Malachi. "He owns a furniture business. A shop and the attached store in Miller's Creek. Used to be Fisher Furniture."

Gail remembered Fisher Furniture. It'd been a fixture on Miller's Creek's main street. She used to love going into town on shopping day. "What happened to the Fishers?"

"Amos Fisher died sometime back. Don't know the cause, but he'd apparently been sick awhile. Bishop Weaver wouldn't allow his daughter to continue to own the shop that employed several men, so she had to sell. Malachi bought the business and a farm—the one you picked me up at this morning—and we moved in."

Gail's fingers tightened on the wheel as she recalled her own encounters with the Weaver family. She wasn't surprised to hear Bishop Weaver had forced another Amish community member into something against their wishes.

From her peripheral vision, Gail could see that

Samuel was smiling. He always seemed to be smiling. Didn't the man take anything seriously? "What?" she pressed when he didn't say any more.

"In the move, Malachi ended up with the business and a wife. He married the previous owner's daughter. I'm not sure how that happened. Most of their interactions that I witnessed had her fluffed up like an outraged cat. But one day she was making arrangements to leave the community and seems like the next, their upcoming wedding was announced in church."

Gail remembered Ruth Fisher, as well. She was glad for her. She'd always liked the energetic Ruth. Glancing over at her passenger, she found Samuel watching her pensively, like he was going to ask her something. Possibly something about her own history.

That wasn't going to happen.

"So, what? You flunked at making tables, chairs and dressers?"

"If *flunk* is the same as *fail*, I didn't flunk at anything. Not to be *hochmut*, but I was a pretty good furniture maker."

Gail's own lips twitched at the wry grin on his handsome face.

"Most of the time," he conceded. He shifted in his seat, turning more to face her. "Ruth caught occasional, very minor—" he held his fingers a hairbreadth apart "—errors and made me correct them. When they were married, they moved to Ruth's farm. With settling into the farm, the furniture business and now a new wife, my *bruder* has his hands full. One of the reasons that Malachi released me from the business was that I'm taking on more of the farmwork for both places. I'm *gut* with that. My *bruder* is a fair boss, but I'd rather be working outside and with livestock instead of being under a roof all day."

That was something Gail easily understood. She missed being part of a working farm. The baby animals in the spring. The warm earth beneath her bare feet in the garden. Lily would've loved those and other aspects of a close-knit family farm life. If only they could go home…

"So who's your oak?"

Although Gail's eyes were on the road and the sweeping Wisconsin countryside, her older sister immediately came to mind. She hadn't talked about her family to anyone in years. The vehicle slowed as a tsunami of homesickness swept over her. Glancing over, Gail found Samuel watching her again. There was no judgment in his gaze. Only a speck of…commiseration? She returned her attention to the highway in front of her.

"My sister. She's perfect. Never puts a foot wrong no matter the situation." The words escaped before she realized it. Puffing out a breath, Gail continued, "Which was the opposite of me growing up. I was more impulsive, which sometimes got me in trouble." She frowned. "I'd like to despise her perfection, but in addition to being perfect, she's…sweet. Really nice. Sincerely nice."

Recollections of her older sister made Gail swallow hard. She shot a look at Samuel again. He was nodding his head solemnly, as if he understood.

"*Ach*, I see what you mean. She isn't like you at all."

Gail blinked and dropped her jaw as she processed what he'd said. Without thinking, she reached out and bumped his shoulder with her fist. He didn't try to dodge, just grinned his magical grin.

"So how did you become such a fine, sturdy tree, then?" There was humor in his voice, but all thoughts of responding to its playful timbre evaporated from Gail at the memory of how she'd had to change so much, so fast.

"I moved away." Leaning forward, she flicked up the volume on the radio. "And never went back."

To her dismay, he reached out and turned it back down. "Why not?"

Gail strove to ignore the warmth that ran up her spine at the rich tone of his voice. She attributed it to the thought of revealing her history. Wasn't going to happen. An expert in redirection, she responded, "I'd always heard that men liked to talk about themselves."

Although her eyes were fixed on the windshield in front of her, she could hear the smile in his voice. "You must be thinking of *Englisch* men. It would be too *hochmut* for an Amish man to do so."

Gail snorted. "And you aren't proud?" There was an unexpected silence where she'd expected a quick retort.

His voice was thoughtful when he finally responded. "Not *hochmut*. Just…confident. Sometimes it takes confidence to get things done. To face new situations. If I didn't have some level of confidence, how could I have the courage to leave my old job and start a new, uncertain one?"

Gail pulled off the highway onto the country road that led to his farm. She was surprised at his insight. If she hadn't had some level of confidence in herself, she'd never have made it as a pregnant teenager leaving the Amish community. It had tested every minute amount she'd had. Still did.

She'd already succumbed once to a charming Amish man. Look where that'd gotten her. While she couldn't afford to lose this man as a customer, she couldn't afford any attraction to him. Gail tightened her grip on the steering wheel. As long as Samuel limited his obvious passion to his job and not his driver, they wouldn't have a problem.

Slowing for the turn into his lane, she glanced toward the big white house. What she saw in the farmyard drove the breath from her body.

Climbing into a buggy were two women, one petite with auburn hair, the other tall and blonde.

Hissing in a breath, Gail made the careful turn off the road and pulled to the edge of the two-track gravel lane. Not wanting to stop—that might prompt the approaching buggy to do so, as well—she kept the truck inching along as far to the side of the driveway as she could. Blindly, she flipped up the armrest beside her and dug in between the seats until she closed her fingers on the brim of her ball cap. Snatching it, with one hand still clenched on the steering wheel, she awkwardly tugged it on, pulling the brim as low on her forehead as possible. Whipping her head toward the pasture that bordered the lane, she tried focusing her gaze on the two placid Belgians grazing there, only to see Samuel watching her, a puzzled frown on his face.

"It's my sister-in-law, Ruth, and her friend Hannah Lapp. Every once in a while they take pity on my younger *bruder*, Gideon, and me and bring over some food. Unfortunately, they draw the line at housecleaning and doing laundry. They've seen female *Englisch* drivers before. Don't worry."

He lifted a hand to wave. Gail captured his hand, surprising them both. Jerking hers back, Gail grabbed the wheel with both hands. Unrestrained, Samuel gave a friendly wave to the pair, his eyes remaining on Gail. His look said he probably thought she was jealous. *Let him.* It was the least of her concerns.

Gail glanced up the lane. From the corner of her eye, she saw the two women wave back. Beneath the *kapps* whose ribbons floated in the breeze of the moving buggy, Gail could easily make out their smiling faces. Hunching her shoulders, she sank lower in the seat. When the two vehicles were side by side, she put her hand by her face, ducked her head and stared at the footwell under Samuel's seat. Breathing shallowly, she could hear the clip-clop of hooves and the buggy wheels crunching on gravel as they passed a few feet away. *Please don't stop, please don't stop...* The mantra echoed in her head as she counted the eyelets on his brown work boots.

The truck inched forward. When the sounds of the rig faded, Gail dragged in a deep breath.

"They're gone."

Lifting her head, Gail checked the rearview mirror to ensure the buggy wasn't turning around. Only when their Standardbred sprang into a ground-covering trot did her anxiety ebb. Silently, she drove up the rest of the lane and circled the farmyard to back the trailer toward the barn. Shifting into Park, she reluctantly faced Samuel.

His eyes were hooded. "Do you have a problem with Amish women? The choices they've made? Maybe they

don't have the liberties you do in the *Englisch* world.
But it's a noble life."

Now dizzy with relief, Gail shook her head. No, she
had no problem with Amish women. She'd intended to
be one. She'd planned to take her place in the Amish
community. But sometimes life changed course on you.

The Belgians in the pasture welcomed the newcomer
with a chorus of neighs, which he energetically returned
from the trailer, jolting her back from the past. "No
problem. I just need to get your horse unloaded so I
can get back on the road."

Never before had she unloaded a horse so quickly.
Usually, she loved an opportunity to explore big Amish
barns, but not today. As she drove down the lane ten
minutes later, Gail tugged off the cap, tossing it on the
passenger seat. Her head flopped back against the head-
rest. Yes, she had a problem with those women. One in
particular. The blonde one. She was the most beautiful
Amish woman Gail had ever seen.

Her older sister hadn't changed at all.

Chapter Four

The empty trailer rattled down the lane. Hands on his hips, Samuel watched the truck turn and accelerate down the country road. She was going faster than normal. What'd upset her?

Returning to the shadowed interior of the barn, he unhooked the halter and tugged the lead free from where he'd hastily tied the gelding in a stall when he realized the clanking that'd followed him into the barn was Gail securing the door of the trailer at lightning speed. By the time he'd reached the double doors of the barn, she was pulling out.

He'd wanted to say farewell. *Ach*, more so, he'd wanted to probe a little about her strange reaction when Ruth and Hannah passed them in the lane. The usual *Englisch* response when they saw Amish was either to stare outright or pretend they weren't when they really were. Perhaps Gail had worked with Elam so long and delivered enough horses to his farm that she had a more nonchalant response? But her actions had been anything but disinterested. She'd almost slunk all the way to the floorboards. He doubted she could see over the dash as the truck crept up the lane.

Gail didn't seem to have a problem with him. Well, she had a problem with him but not in that way. Maybe she had an issue with strangers? If she had, she was capable of getting over it, as the folks at the track appeared to like her well enough.

His new purchase wandered around the unfamiliar stall, nosing the fresh straw cushioning the floor. Samuel hooked the stall door closed. Ascending the ladder to the hayloft, he dropped down a fresh bale. When he climbed back down, his mare, Belle, and the new gelding were eyeing him with interest.

He snorted at their avid attention, the dust motes kicked up by the dropped bale swirling about him. "Too bad women aren't as easy to understand as you two. I can tell by your ears what you want." Unbidden, the vision of Gail's ears under her high ponytail sprang into his mind. Samuel tripped over the bale as he went to get the knife that hung on the barn wall to cut the twine. Quickly recovering, he glanced sheepishly back to the watching bays.

"You don't mind a quiet conversation instead of a loud radio." He snorted again. "You answer about the same amount of questions. In fact, I probably know as much or more of your history, even upon our short acquaintance, than I do hers." Samuel rubbed the gelding's forehead when the horse reached over the stall wall to lip some loose hay from his shirt.

Bending, Samuel cut the twine from the bale. It relaxed into an accordion of separate flakes, releasing a strong scent of fresh-cut hay.

"I'd like to say I like you better for your straightforwardness. But I don't want to lie. There's just something…" Samuel breathed in the sweet hay aroma, one of his favorite smells. He realized, though, as he tossed a few flakes of it into each horse's manger, that a more intriguing one now was the clean soap fragrance that'd greeted him this morning when he climbed into the truck's cab with Gail. Samuel frowned as he straightened up the open bale.

"A mysterious woman just makes a man wonder." Ambling over to Belle, he stretched out a hand to scratch her between the ears. She jerked her head up and swung it out of reach, avoiding his touch. Shaking his head, Samuel retreated, giving her space to return to the hay in the manger. "Or maybe I'm just a fool for skittish females."

Turning his back on the mare, he crossed to a large pen in the back of the cavernous barn, vaulted the low gate there and strode through the pen to open the door that exited to an attached pasture. Jeb and Huck, the two Belgians, were waiting just outside. Gabby, the Guernsey cow, wasn't far behind. "It'd be nice if she'd trust me like you all do." Stepping aside as the trio entered the barn, he looked down the road in the direction the truck and trailer had taken. "Something for me to work on, I figure."

Gail hadn't seen Hannah in years. Four, to be exact, when Gail's pregnancy was getting too difficult to hide. The day her folks were gone to an auction, when she'd walked down the lane with her eyes full of tears and her hands full of the few possessions she could carry to the bus stop.

Hannah had followed her to the road, her normally

pristine apron wadded in clenched fists, trying to convince Gail to stay. But after a lingering final embrace, Gail had started walking. She hadn't looked back.

With only an eighth-grade education, as per Amish practice, even part-time jobs for her were scarce. Somehow she'd ended up at the racetrack and *Gott* had answered her fervent prayers. Standardbred trainer George Hayes had needed a stable hand. Or maybe George hadn't. Maybe he'd just known that Gail desperately needed a job. He gave her one.

She'd learned to drive, as a license didn't require a high school diploma and it was something she could do while roundly pregnant. She'd scrimped together enough to put a small down payment on Bonnie and the trailer. Although the years since had been tough, she thought they'd finally be able to make it.

Until she hit a rough patch and missed some payments.

Scouring the rural area she traveled in for cheaper rent and childcare, *Gott* had again answered Gail's prayers when she found a widow with a small basement apartment who was thrilled to watch Lily during the day. The downside was its proximity to Miller's Creek. If the wrong person found out about Lily, she risked losing her daughter. But if Gail couldn't keep a roof over their heads, she could lose her anyway. And that would happen if the truck and trailer were repossessed.

She'd worried Elam would recognize her. When he didn't say anything, Gail allowed herself a sliver of hope. Later in conversation he admitted that he didn't pay a lot of attention to the *youngies* and she breathed easier, casually probing him for news of home. That was how she learned about the death of Atlee Weaver, Lily's father.

No. No one from Miller's Creek could know she was nearby.

The buggy had fortunately turned down another road. Gail stopped at the intersection, shifting into Park. Crossing her wrists over the top of the steering wheel, she dropped her forehead against them.

She missed her family.

Seeing Hannah was like having a swollen river top a levee and weaken it, threatening to wash away the whole protective barrier.

She wanted to go home.

Gail raised her head at the sound of a passing car. Her eyes blinking back tears, she considered the roads before her. If she turned one way, it led to the small town where she lived. If she turned another…it would take her down the country road that led to her family's farm.

Shifting the truck into gear, Gail turned on the country road and drove by well-remembered territory.

Her pulse started throbbing when her family's white-painted buildings topped the landscape. *I'm not going to turn my head to look as I pass. Too much like* Englisch *gawkers.* Even so, the truck slowed to a crawl when she reached the beginning of her *daed*'s property, as Gail scanned the neat farmyard.

The wash was on the line. Oh my, the pants were getting long. Her younger brothers must be growing so big. Aprons and solid-colored dresses fluttered in the breeze. Dropping a quick glance to her jeans, Gail tried to remember the last time she'd worn a Plain dress.

She dashed a hand across her tear-blurred eyes when

she saw the apron-wearing figure in the garden. *Mamm*.
Against her resolve, Gail twisted her head, continuing to look as she drove past. A loud blare of a horn
had her swerving the pickup back to her side of the
road. A driver glared at her through the window of
a passing SUV. A tug on the steering wheel warned
the wheels of the trailer had dropped into the shallow
ditch. She'd lose her livelihood if she tore up her rig.
Berating herself, Gail eased the trailer back onto the
blacktop surface.

Maybe some church Sunday when she knew they'd
be gone, she'd drive by with Lily. Nothing would be said
about unknown grandparents, but Gail could point out
what a beautiful and carefully maintained farm looked
like. Yes, they could do that. Lily would enjoy it and
she…she needed to show her.

Did *Mamm* have any grandchildren beside Lily?
Surely Hannah was married by now. Or was the reason Hannah was coming over with Ruth to the Schrock
farm because she was interested in Samuel?

The truck shot forward with the sudden pressure on
the gas pedal. It slowed again when Gail forced her foot
to relax. What girl wouldn't be? Gail's stomach twisted
as she vividly recalled being second choice for an attractive Amish man before. And the bleak outcome.

Get over him, Gail. She shouldn't be dreaming about
an Amish man. If Samuel happened to marry her sister, well…it wasn't like she'd be around to see them
together.

She longed to head straight home to where Lily
waited for her. But the black-and-white Holsteins in
her *daed*'s pasture had reminded her of their milk-
less refrigerator. She'd intended to grab some groceries

while in town, but the flat tire and her new customer had driven everyday things from her mind.

Even with the warm breeze that blew through the open window, a cold sweat broke out over Gail. She couldn't afford to drive the many miles out of the way to another grocery store when there was one almost in her path. If she went into Miller's Creek.

Surely *Gott* had tested her enough today? Surely she could run into a store without seeing someone she knew? The meager amount in her checkbook persuaded her that the odds should be in her favor.

Gail pulled into the small grocery store's parking lot. Her left foot bounced in the footwell when she saw the horse and buggy hitched to the rail made available for Amish customers. She stilled the action with a hand on her leg. *It's not* Mamm *or* Daed. *Hannah wouldn't have had time to get into town. I look different. No one else knows me as well. As long as it isn't... But what are the chances that out of all in the community, it's Ruby Weaver's buggy? The woman probably doesn't do anything as mundane as grocery shopping. She's too busy manipulating lives.*

Retrieving the baseball cap from the passenger seat, she tugged it low on her forehead. With a deep breath, Gail exited the truck and hurried across the parking lot. Slipping through the sliding doors, she ignored the carts and scanned the produce section for anyone wearing a dress and *kapp*. The coast was clear. Exhaling slowly, Gail peeked into the first aisle. Finding it empty, she headed for the back of the store.

Gail flicked her gaze down the aisles as she passed. Clear. Clear. Noting the sign indicating box goods, her breath hitched at the sight of a woman in an aisle until she quickly identified the shopper by attire as *Englisch*. She trotted down it to grab a box of mac and cheese. Returning to the refrigerated coolers at the back of the store, she snagged a package of hot dogs and a gallon of milk. Gail's shoulders relaxed as she rounded the end-cap of the last aisle. Just a loaf of bread and she was done. *No one is going to recognize me. It's been four years. I'm an unreasonable coward, except the stakes are so high. But that's only if I see...*

Gail stood motionless, almost as if she'd become one of the items in the hip-high freezer at her side. Atlee's mother, Ruby Weaver, was halfway down the aisle, wearing a frown like a required piece of clothing as she stared at the shelf in front of her. While the years had changed Gail, time hadn't made a difference to Ruby. The belt of her apron sagged at the waist of her gaunt figure. Her *kapp*, pressed in iron folds, was anchored scrupulously to her steel-gray hair. Ruby's eyes were narrowed on the container in her hand, as if she planned to recommend shunning it for offending her in some manner.

It was a look Gail remembered well. An amplified version of it had pinned a sixteen-year-old Gail to a barn wall where Ruby had cornered her alone after the church service announcing Atlee's engagement—to another girl. Calling Gail a jezebel, the bishop's wife warned her to leave her son alone, or Gail would regret it, as would her family.

Later, Gail wished she'd retorted that Ruby's cherished son had been the seducer, probably of many young Amish women, but at the time, she'd been shocked and scared. She still was, because Ruby was the neck that turned the head of the bishop. A bishop who interpreted the community's *Ordnung* in a manner that best suited his own family.

Ruby pivoted and stared unblinkingly at where Gail stood rooted. Ducking her head, Gail stared at the bags of frozen chicken breasts in the freezer, her fingers white-knuckled on the groceries in her hands. *She won't recognize me. The hat. The ponytail, the jeans. It's my imagination that she's watching me. I'm just an* Englisch *girl.* Gail forced herself to move along the far side of the freezer, working her way to the front of the store.

From under the bill of her cap, she sneaked a glance at the older woman. Ruby's eyes, under the center part of her hair, were hooded as she watched Gail. The older woman's pursed lips gathered up the loose wrinkles from her face. Gail ignored the bread section and hastened to check out. Thrusting her items onto the conveyor belt, she looked back to find the bishop's wife had followed her to the end of the aisle and stood, hands on narrow hips, staring at her.

Foot tapping a rapid tattoo on the tile, Gail waited for her change. When she had it, she grabbed her items and fled the store, feeling a burning stare between her shoulders with every step. Shoving her purchases to the passenger seat, she jumped into the cab. Moments later the truck and trailer rattled out of the parking lot.

Gail was half a mile out of town before her heart rate slowed down. Ruby Weaver was the reason she couldn't return to the Amish community. The threat the bishop's wife posed to her daughter forced Gail and Lily to stay in the *Englisch* world. If Ruby ever found out her precious dead son, Atlee, actually had a daughter, she'd use the bishop to gain custody of the child.

Elam lived on the fringe of the Amish community.

Samuel's farm was closer to the center. Somehow, Gail needed to avoid Miller's Creek while supporting her new—and very distracting—customer.

Pulling into the main street of a town so small it couldn't boast a gas station, Gail circled a block and parked the pickup and trailer along a side street lined with small, neat houses.

Grabbing her groceries, Gail shut the door with her hip and headed for the sidewalk. She had greater things to worry about than a man. Yes, Samuel Schrock was tempting, but he didn't fit into her life. And he didn't hold a candle to what did. Gail smiled as she crossed bright-colored chalk marks on the cement pavement, the tension of the day easing from her shoulders at the unidentifiable drawings. Before she reached the screen door, it flew open and a small blond-haired girl bounded down the steps and launched into her arms.

"Mommy! You're here! I love you so much!"

Dropping the grocery bags, Gail closed her eyes and embraced the girl's precious, warm weight. Inhaling the soft, sweet scent of her daughter's hair, she murmured, "Me, too, Lily. Me, too."

The double barn doors were open, ostensibly to let in light from the glow of the early-morning sun, but primarily so Samuel could hear the sound of a truck and trailer pulling up the lane. He pitchforked a flake of hay in front of their cow, Gabby. He'd been think-ing about his driver since she'd dropped him off three days ago with barely a wave in his direction. His trip today might have more to do with the ride to and from the track than the Standardbreds there. But he wasn't going to tell his *bruder* that.

"I ran into Elam at the hardware store yesterday." Gideon's muffled voice came from the far side of Gabby, where he leaned his head against her flank as he milked the fawn-and-white cow.

Samuel stabbed the pitchfork into a nearby bale of alfalfa. He'd made time to see Elam the day before to ask his opinion on the trainers at the track. "He told me he's not regretting his decision to quit the business. Hope it wasn't just to make me feel good in taking it over. Seems hard to believe, but I look forward to today with even more excitement than I felt on my first one."

"*Ja*. Really hard to believe." The hiss of milk pinging against the metal sides of the pail punctuated his *bruder*'s words. "When were you going to tell me that the driver, Gail, was a woman? And a *yung* one at that?" Although his hands never stopped their steady rhythm, Gideon leaned back and shot his brother a glance. "Is that why you've been working like a madman the past few days? So you could fit in another trip to the track this week? I half expected the barn to be repainted when I arrived home yesterday, the way you've rushed to get work done."

Samuel couldn't deny the accusation, as it was the truth. "The past few days were clear and the low humidity was good for cutting and drying the hay at our farm while it was down. I've got to get to Malachi's fields after that. And with the long evenings, there was plenty of light left after you got home yesterday to help me put up the bales. Just because I'm doing the majority of work on the farm doesn't mean that you can't occasionally get your hands dirty with it anymore."

"*Ach*. That's not what I mean, and my hands feel pretty full of farmwork right now." After a few final squirts, Gideon grabbed the handle of the bucket and stood from the three-legged milking stool where he'd been perched. "And after talking with Elam, I just wanted to know what I'm working for."

Samuel took the pail from him and poured its contents through a strainer into a metal milk can. "You're working for the farm." He set the pail down and shot his brother a grin. "And maybe a bit for your *bruder* to see a pretty girl again this week."

Gideon didn't share his smile. "As long as my *bruder* remembers that the pretty girl is *Englisch*."

Samuel's smile slipped. "Your *bruder* is very aware of that fact and doesn't need to be reminded." He stepped away to disinfect Gabby's udder and release her head from the wooden stanchion. The Guernsey stayed put, munching on the hay. "We met *Englisch* girls at *rumspringa* parties in Ohio before we moved. She's not the first girl who wasn't Amish who I've flirted with. Though I may stretch them at times, I know where the boundaries are." He placed a hand on Gabby's bony hip and met his brother's eyes. "When the time comes, I'll be baptized. I'm not leaving the Amish faith."

His younger brother's shoulders visibly relaxed and his mouth tipped up at the corners. "That's a relief. I thought so, but after watching the spring in your step even after the past few long days and finding out that the driver was a *yung* woman…and pretty—" his smile expanded "—your word, not Elam's, I was a little concerned over the glint in your eye when you spoke of your new business."

"*Mamm* will be glad you're here to take her place as mother hen. Malachi hasn't even been married a year yet and you're trying to get me married off, too? I said, when the time comes I'll be baptized into the church. Then I'll be married. But the time hasn't come, *bruder*. I'm not ready to settle down yet with *Gott*'s chosen one for me. This girl—" Samuel didn't know how to describe Gail, or his unaccustomed feeling for her "—is a challenge, that's all. Can you believe that she might not like your charming *bruder*?"

"It makes me think she has good sense."

Patting his brother on the shoulder, Samuel stepped back to pick up the milking stool and hang it on pegs on the barn's wall. His ears had picked up the sound of a vehicle approaching in the quiet morning. "No worries, then. Who wants to marry a sensible woman? Isn't Ruth enough to scare us off from that?" He winked at his brother, knowing that Gideon cared for his sister-in-law as much as he did.

His attention already on the approaching truck, he absently instructed, "Take some milk in for Ruth and Malachi and drop the rest off at the cheese factory."

"Like I do every day?"

He waved away Gideon's response, which followed him out the barn's double doors, and watched Gail's truck and trailer pull into the lane. Maybe he was more than a little eager to see how long it would take him to get past this woman's defenses.

He'd sold the gelding. Made a slim profit, but a profit nonetheless. Although the Amish seemed a patriarchal society, the adage "happy wife, happy life" still applied. The wife had been happy with her new transportation, happy enough the husband had talked about it with some friends, drumming up a few more potential customers for Samuel.

The truck pulled into the lane and swung around in

the farmyard. A moment later Samuel was sitting next to Gail in the worn cloth seat. He was immediately wary when she shot him a hooded look. He was used to women watching him closely, but not like they were just waiting for him to put a foot wrong. He hadn't been the recipient of a look like that since his *mamm* had to run an errand, leaving him alone in the kitchen with the cookies she'd just finished baking for a Christmas exchange.

"What?"

Gail didn't reply, just shifted the vehicle into Drive and the rig rattled down the lane.

That was when he realized they weren't alone.

Chapter Five

Samuel didn't know what prompted him to twist around to look in the backseat of the truck's cab. If it'd been a noise, it'd been a quiet one. But having turned, he stared for a moment. When he faced the front again, even though her eyes were on the road, he knew Gail was conscious of every breath he was taking. She was like a baseball batter in the box, braced for whatever he might pitch at her.

He casually leaned back into his seat. "Your sister?"

"My daughter." Eyes trained on the windshield, Gail's delicate jaw was shot forward, daring him to make a retort. And when he made one, it would be like shaking a wasp nest out of a tree. Although sometimes Samuel liked to poke at wasp nests, he knew this wasn't the day or the time.

Keeping his face neutral, he twisted around to take another look at the sleeping child.

"She's a beauty." And she was. Blonde where her mother was brunette, the little girl made a dainty portrait in her pink shirt, blue shorts and white tennis shoes. Her little rosebud mouth was relaxed in sleep.

The dark fan of her long eyelashes rested on porce-
lain cheeks.

Samuel faced the windshield again. "How old?"

"Three and a half." Gail's response was succinct but
her graceful fingers relaxed their strangle of the steering wheel. From his angle, he had a clear view of them.
No rings. Something he'd checked on day one. Amish
women never wore jewelry, but *Englisch* women did.
It still didn't mean anything, as some folks who did
physical work didn't wear rings, either to protect the
jewelry or to retain their fingers.

Samuel was surprised at the sudden sick feeling in
his stomach at the thought that Gail's ring, one that
proclaimed she belonged to another, might currently be
in some esteemed place, waiting for her to come home
and put it on. Surely it wasn't disappointment that was
hollowing out his middle? There were always available
girls out there; why would he feel so disappointed that
Gail wasn't one of them?

Besides, she was *Englisch*. Samuel didn't know what
his short-term future held in regard to women, but he
knew his long-term one included baptism and raising
a family in the Amish community.

His fingers drummed on the leg of his blue pants.
After a few moments of silence, he could contain the
question no longer. "Does your husband work in the
horse business, too?"

"There is no husband, and her father's not in the picture." This time Gail did look at him. The intensity in
her eyes reminded him of a doe with a fawn he'd accidentally cornered once in a field—defensive, wary,
protective. He'd backed away then, giving them space
to work their way out, escape to where the doe felt safe

and secure. He did the same now. But for some reason, her statement made the day a little brighter, like the sun peeping back out after a threatening thundercloud.

Although he didn't see single, unmarried parenthood much in the Amish community, he knew it was there, although generally frowned upon. He also knew there were sometimes wedding dates moved up from the traditional late-fall wedding season because a *boppeli* was on the way. He didn't know how the Amish community in Miller's Creek handled those situations.

Amish or *Englisch*, it wasn't for him to judge. That was made clear in the *Biewel*.

"She like horses like her *mamm*?"

Gail's eyes flicked to the rearview mirror as she glanced at the sleeping girl. The hint of a smile touched her lips, and her shoulders eased back into the seat. "Loves them. Hard to keep her from walking right up to an unknown horse." She sighed. "I don't usually bring her to the track on workdays, but her babysitter was sick this morning and I had some jobs today that I couldn't afford to lose…"

While he was sympathetic to her situation, Samuel couldn't help but think that would never happen in the Amish community. Family was everything. There were always grandparents, older siblings, aunts or cousins on either side to help care for the *kinder*. The Plain life was wonderfully supportive. Being a young mother alone with a *kind* would be incredibly difficult. The prickly nature of his companion was becoming understandable, much like the doe at the fence.

Gail glanced in the rearview again. "Usually she drifts off after riding in the truck for a while. Hopefully, today will be one of those days. Otherwise—" she shook her head "—she can be a handful."

It was his turn to look in the rearview. The tiny girl didn't look like a handful. She looked sweet. Innocent. Samuel generally got along with women of all ages. He wanted the one sharing the front seat of the truck to like him. Maybe assisting with the one in the back would help.

"If she decides that today is not one for resting, she can stay with me."

Gail looked at him as if one of her equine passengers had spoken to her. "You're kidding."

Samuel was mildly insulted. "Why would I be kidding? I have several younger siblings, I've been around *kinder* before. My *bruder* Malachi is going to be a father. Maybe I want to practice at being an *onkel*?"

She snorted. "They don't start out this size. Let me tell you, there's a big difference between a *boppeli* and a three-year-old."

"But they do get there. And to me, they're less scary at this size." He cradled an arm like he was holding an infant. "That initial small bundle is more frightening than anything. I'd rather handle a fractious thousand pound Standardbred. Your daughter, I won't be afraid to drop."

Gail shot him a skeptical glance.

"Not that I would, but at least she isn't as helpless."

"No, she isn't that." Her lips curved into a rueful smile. "It's when she's insistent on being helpful that problems usually arise."

They rode in silence until they reached the outer edge of Milwaukee. If Gail's bouncing left leg and gnawed bottom lip were any indications, she was deep in thought about his offer. "If you're sure?"

"I'm always sure."

She snorted in response. "If you have any trouble, most of the folks in George's stable block know her. They're too busy to keep her for long, but someone there might be able to give you a break."

"I'm sure we'll be fine."

They pulled into the track's back parking lot. "I have a couple of local hauls." Gail checked the rearview mirror. Samuel didn't turn, but the little girl must still be sleeping, as she continued, "Hopefully, she'll be good through those. I'll look for you when I get back."

Samuel nodded. "I'm serious about my offer."

He pulled the door handle and started to slip out of the cab when a sleepy little voice murmured from the back. "Who are you?"

Standing at the open door of the still-running truck, he looked across the front seat at Gail. Hand poised over the gearshift, her blue eyes were round with apprehension.

Samuel heard the childish voice again, a little less sleepy, a little more indignant. "Mommy. I want out."

"Hey, sweetie. Mommy needs to drive for a bit. I've got an appointment. We'll get out later." Gail left the truck in Park and turned toward the backseat.

"I want out *now*."

Through the back window of the truck, Samuel could see miniature legs kicking against the seat, the action coordinating with the thumping he could hear from inside the cab. He had to smile. The daughter was as direct as her mother.

"We'll just ride for a bit longer, then we'll get out."

"Been riding. I want *out*." The little girl bent her head, and her hands went to the buckle at the center of a number of straps on her car seat. Samuel raised his eyebrows when, after fiddling a moment with the buckle, the straps came loose. A second later she was wiggling out of the seat.

"Lily! We talked about not getting out until Mommy said it was okay. You need to get back into your seat, young lady." Looking at Samuel, Gail shook her head in bewilderment. "I don't know how she does that."

"Please say it's okay to get out, Mommy, please?"

Samuel didn't know about Gail, or being a *mamm*, but he melted at the pleading in the child's voice.

Apparently, her *mamm* wasn't unaffected, either. Gail looked to where Samuel silently stood at the door. "I got her up so early after the sitter let me know she was sick and couldn't watch her today. As we're in the same building, usually Lily stays in bed until she wakes up. I guess I can't blame her for wanting out now." Gail's features went from a guilty uncertainty to piercing him with an accusatory gaze like he'd disagreed with her. "She's not spoiled. I try not to spoil her. She's usually a pretty happy girl."

At the swirling emotions, Samuel felt a moment of gratitude that in an Amish community the women raised the *kinder* and the men raised the barns. You might bang your head barn building, but it probably wouldn't impact your mental state as much as child-raising seemed to. He hadn't spent that much time with his younger siblings during the day when they were little; he'd already had responsibilities working outside. If this was the way it felt to care for a child, he was rethinking his suggestion. But it was too late; he'd made it.

"My offer still stands."

Gail looked torn. "She won't stay in her car seat and I'll be at places where I don't know the horses or the people. If she gets out when I'm not looking…" She inhaled raggedly.

A pint-sized hand reached through the space between the seats and rested on Gail's arm. "Please let me out, Mommy. I'm hungry."

Gail closed her eyes and seemed to come to a decision. When she opened them and pinned him with a look, Samuel knew the decision included him. "Lily, I'd like you to meet Samuel."

Leaning back into the cab, Samuel came face-to-face with the wide-awake Lily, who'd poked her head over the folded armrest into the front seat. Her bright blue eyes solemnly took him in. "Why does he wear a hat? Can I wear a hat?"

"You have a hat in your backpack." Gail reached between the seats to pull out a dainty purple pack from the floor and set it on the passenger seat. It was a small version of what Samuel had seen *Englisch* schoolchildren wear. "There's a banana and some peanut butter crackers in there, as well as a juice carton. That should hold her until I get back for lunch." Gone was the indecisive mother. Now that a decision had been made, she was all business. "You do have a cell phone, don't you? Your bishop lets you carry a phone for your job? Elam did. Of course you do. You've contacted me on it. Give it here." She reached out her hand.

"Uh, yes." Actually, like many men in their *rumspringa*, he'd carried a phone before he'd undertaken the job. He just wasn't used to a woman demanding it. Samuel fished it out and handed it to her. Without a word, her fingers worked rapidly over the screen before she handed it back.

"Okay. I just sent a text to myself so I'm the first message up. Call me if you need anything. I also put in George's phone number. He's well acquainted with Lily. Depending on what he's doing, he might be able to get to you faster." She frowned. "Maybe I should just call him and see what he's got going on today."

Samuel was a bit stung that she didn't think he was capable. "I can do it." He turned his attention to Lily. "We'll get along just fine."

Two matching sets of big blue eyes regarded him skeptically.

"I want out."

"There's also an extra set of clothes in there, in case of an accident, or she gets into something. And a little coloring book and crayons. She'll tell you if she has to go potty. Most of the female grooms know her and can help."

Samuel's eyes widened. Maybe he should have kept his mouth shut. He was trying to build a business here, and Elam had said that required building trust. How much trust could he build while stopping a potential transaction to arrange a bathroom trip for a little one? But he'd offered, and in his business and life, a man was only as good as his word. He cleared his throat. "Okay. Anything else?"

Gail's forehead wrinkled for a moment. "No, she's pretty good about communicating what she needs." For the first time that morning, a real smile crossed her face. "Be prepared for questions." She reached out her hands to her daughter, who scrambled through the opening over the armrest into the front seat. "Lily, you're going to spend the morning with Samuel. He likes horses, too. In fact, last week I took a nice gelding to his place. Maybe he'll tell you about him."

She reached out her hand and Samuel found himself holding the purple backpack. "I'll call or text you later to check on her." Gail glanced at her watch. Her eyes, looking from her daughter to Samuel, held uncertainty and guilt. "I have to go."

Samuel opened his arms and, at her mother's encouragement, the girl went warily into them. He ducked back out of the cab, shut the door and stepped away from the truck. Gail pierced him with a stare through the open truck window. Samuel almost took a step back. If he'd have been a lesser man, he would've wilted under the intensity of her blue gaze.

"I'm trusting you because I don't have a lot of choice and Elam trusted you. And for all I've seen, you're a good guy. But if anything happens to my daughter..." Her tone and narrowed eyes left no guesstimate necessary on his condition should Lily not be hale and hearty at the end of the day. Samuel grinned. He'd experienced half-ton cows charging him when he was trying to take care of their calves that were less intimidating.

Bouncing the little girl in his arms, who was regarding him as suspiciously as her *mamm*, he assured them both, "We'll be fine. It'll be an adventure for both of us."

Gail turned her attention to her daughter. "Bye, sweetie. I'll see you later. Love you. Be good for Samuel." She put the truck in gear, and it and the trailer

rolled away, leaving Samuel and his small charge looking after it.

If he was such a good guy, why had there been tears
sparkling in the backs of her eyes? Samuel turned
to look at the pint-sized passenger in his arms. She
reached out and poked the brim of his straw hat with a
tiny finger, pushing it back on his head.

"Can I wear a hat, too?"

Samuel took a deep breath as he met Lily's blue eyes.
His whole day would be based on how he handled the
next few moments. *Ach*, the first thing he'd learned
about women was to start with a smile. The second,
somehow you needed to give them what they wanted or
at least make them think you would. Shifting the little
blonde in his arms, he pulled up the backpack so he
could unzip it. "Let's check in here. Your *mamm* said
you had a hat. She's been right about many things so
she's probably right about this, as well."

He rummaged past a banana, some other snacks
and a few bright-colored clothes to find a petite purple baseball cap. "Is this it?" Triumphantly, he pulled
it from the pack.

"I want a hat like yours."

"Well, one would be difficult to find here today.
But if we get along well, later I'll let you wear mine
for a while."

She considered the bargain for a moment. "Okay."

He slipped the purple hat on her head and, one-
handed, worked the little ponytail through the back.
Now what? Fishing out the banana, he offered it to her.
"Are you hungry? Your *mamm* said you were up early."

"She's not my *mamm*, she's my mommy."

"*Ach*, you're right. *Mamm* is the word I grew up using for *mother*."

"Why didn't you use *mommy*?"

Samuel sighed as he looked into her curious eyes and thought wistfully about barn-raising. "Would you like to see some horses?"

Lily smiled. "I like horses."

Slinging the pack over his shoulder, he shifted her onto his hip and started for the entrance to the stable block. "Let's go see them, then. Let's see lots and lots of horses."

By the time they reached the main avenue, Samuel understood Gail's warning regarding questions. After a short hike, when he was carrying her again—too much human and equine traffic for her to be down on the ground—Lily tugged on the black suspenders that ran across the tops of his shoulders.

"What are these?"

"They're suspenders."

"Why do you wear them?"

Samuel blinked. He'd never imagined talking with a girl about clothing articles. Lily stared at him from her perch in his arms, waiting for an answer. "They keep my pants from falling down."

Her rosebud lips frowned. "My mommy doesn't wear them and her pants don't fall down."

Ach. "They're for men." It seemed like a pretty good response, until Lily began twisting her head this way and that. He smiled as her soft ponytail repeatedly brushed his cheek.

"He doesn't have them. And he doesn't have them. And they're boys." Lily pointed to men working nearby as they walked from the stables to the track. She looked up at Samuel, as if daring him to refute her observation.

"You're right, Lily. I wear them because I'm Amish."

Her brow furrowed. "What's an A… Amiss?"

Ach. "Well, Amish people are people who choose to live a certain way." Samuel suppressed a smile. The next question would be how and why people choose to live differently than others. Samuel didn't think he had the capability of explaining that to a three-year-old.

He slipped the purple cap off her head and replaced it with his own straw one. Lily's head disappeared underneath it. "How about you wear my hat for a while?" His distraction proved a success when she tipped it back and gave him a toothy grin. It expanded when he set the purple cap on his head. "We'll switch." At Lily's giggle, Samuel thought he might have the knack for *kinder* care as well as barn building.

A while later they'd worked their way to the rail along the track, where he wanted to watch the horses run time trials. Gail had already texted to check on them. Twice. Samuel assured her they were fine. Lily was fed, content wearing her own hat and seemed intrigued enough with the current surroundings that a few moments were free of question asking.

Samuel watched the trio of horses coming around the curve of the track, their gleaming brown coats in contrast to the white rail behind them. One was falling behind as they came down the stretch. Cocking his head, Samuel focused on the mutterings of the trainer leaning on the fence a few yards away. A pearl of wisdom from Elam, the previous Amish trader, was the more the trainer complained about a horse, the cheaper the price. Based on the man's conversation to his companion, this one might go pretty cheap indeed.

A few minutes earlier Lily had insisted on being set down. She'd been busy in the powdery dirt by the fence, making little piles and then tramping on them with her miniature sneakers. Puffs of dust had drifted up with each stomp to coat her bare legs. Samuel hoped the rules of the day hadn't included keeping the little girl clean. If so, he was a failure at *kinder* minding.

"Well, Lily. Think we ought to inquire about that gelding?" He glanced down to where she'd been playing at his feet.

There was no purple ball cap over a blond ponytail between him and the fence. Samuel peered up and down the fence row before spinning to look behind him. "Lily?"

Chapter Six

Samuel frantically scanned the corridor between the rail and the stands. People passed by alone and in groups but everyone was hip high or taller. Spying a flash of purple, Samuel dodged around a pair of trainers only to discover the bright color had been the silks of a passing driver. Swiveling his head, Samuel searched the surrounding area. "Lily!"

Where could she have gone? She was there a moment ago. Samuel's heart pounded so hard he felt the accelerated beat in his ears. "Lily!" Grabbing the rail, he vaulted into the stands and ran up several rows of empty bleacher seats to get a better view. A group of eight trotters took the track and were warming up before their time trials. Samuel caught his breath at their churning legs. What if Lily wandered onto the track in front of the racing horses? He scoured the track, the infield and the surrounding perimeter. Nothing.

Cupping his hands around his mouth like he would when calling cows at the farm, Samuel hollered as loud as he could, "Lily!" People stopped and looked at him askance, but he didn't care. What should he do? He didn't even know her last name. Not seeing Lily's diminutive form from his current position, Samuel raced up to the top row of the stadium, chastising himself with every lunging stride for being more interested in flirting with her mother than learning about his small charge. *Please,* Gott, *help me find her. Help her to be all right.*

When he reached the top railing, he gripped it with white knuckles and looked out toward the stable block and parking lot. The panorama before him laid out the racetrack in miniature.

How could he find her? How could he not?

A cold sweat trickled down the indentation of his spine as he scrutinized the area below for a little girl in a pink shirt and purple hat. Nothing. Nothing. But... wait! A small figure was threading its way through the horse and human traffic between the track and the stables. A few folks turned to watch as it flitted by. Could it be? *Please,* Gott*!* Samuel cupped his hands around his mouth again.

"Lily!"

The figure paused and spun around.

"Lily! Stay right there!"

Faces were upturned in his direction. Samuel pointed to Lily and called again, "Lily, stay right there!" He held his breath until a passing groom, leading a Standardbred from the horse walker, directed the bay over to the girl and said something to her. They both looked up toward Samuel. He waved frantically and they both waved back.

Whirling, Samuel sprinted down the steps of the bleachers three at a time, his work boots clanking on the aluminum planks. He wove his way through the human and equine crowd at a jog and finally reached the waiting groom and little girl. Swinging Lily into his arms, Samuel was so thrilled to find her the words that spilled out were the first language he'd learned and not English. The groom regarded him curiously.

"*Denki, denki.* I can't thank you enough."

The groom nodded and moved on with his charge.

"*Ach*, Lily, I couldn't find you. I was afraid I lost you."

"I was right here." Lily frowned at him.

"*Ja*, that might be so, but I didn't know that. Why did you leave? Where were you going?"

"You said we could get a hot dog when we got hungry." She pointed toward the snack shack they'd passed earlier that morning. "I was hungry so I was getting a hot dog."

"Ah…" She had him there. "When I said that, I meant we'd go together."

"You were busy."

With his heart still pounding at his scare and relief in having found her, Samuel didn't feel capable of reasoning with a three-year-old. He inhaled his first full breath since he'd looked down to find her missing. It shuddered out of him, taking the tension with it. "Let's go get one now." So what if it was before ten o'clock in the morning.

Moments later, hot dogs in hand, they wandered to George Hayes's section of the stables. They found the trainer by one of his stall doors, frowning at the occupant inside. At Lily's enthusiastic greeting, he turned as they approached.

"Well, hello there, Lily. How are you?"

"We're eating because Samuel lost me."

Samuel winced as the blonde passenger in his arms patted his shoulder.

George eyed him closely. "He did, did he? Looks like he found you again."

"Yup, he didn't lose me for long," Lily acknowledged before finishing her last bite of hot dog.

Flushing, Samuel finished his own before responding, "*Ach*, there's not many secrets, is there? She was hungry. I'm hoping eating at this hour doesn't break any rules."

The trainer smiled. "No, no secrets at that age. You might want to tell Gail your version first, before someone else—" he tipped his head at Lily "—reports it. It'll be all right. She's pretty forgiving."

Samuel blinked at the surprising assessment of the intense woman he was getting to know. "Maybe on food. But probably not if I lost her daughter."

"Well, you're right about that. She'd do about anything for her little girl." The man's eyebrow was raised, probably wondering what Samuel, apparently an incompetent *kinder* minder, was doing with Lily.

Aware of the poor impression he might be giving this friend of Gail's, Samuel hastened to explain, "Her sitter was sick. She was in a bind."

George nodded. "Single parenting is tough. I don't know how she does it."

After spending part of the morning with her daughter, neither did Samuel.

Conversation stopped when a horse stuck its head over the stable's half door. Eyes ringed with white, it snorted at them and disappeared back into the stall.

George leaned on the stall's half door. "Got a bit of a bind myself. An owner wants to reduce his animals by one. I'm trying to determine which one goes. This filly's got promise, but she might need too much work to get it realized."

Securing Lily on his hip, Samuel stepped closer and looked over the door, as well. A bay filly stood at the back of the stall, head high, watching them warily. Her beautiful lines and attitude reminded him of his mare, Belle, who was also nervous, flashy and not for everyone. But for a few adventurous young men in their *rumspringa*, the filly would be a perfect fit.

"I must be quite the problem solver today, because I think I can help you out with your situation, as well."

Having someone fall asleep against his shoulder was a unique sensation. The afternoon sun and busy day had tired Lily out. Her hat was off and stowed in the backpack. Some of her blond bangs were clumped together, slightly sweaty from the warm day. Samuel tried to imagine the level of trust it took to let someone relax like that. He'd had girls lay their heads on his shoulder on rides home after Sunday night singings, but those situations had been edged with conscious ardor instead of sincere trust.

Lily hadn't been out for long. The steady rhythm of her breathing, the miniature hand curled under his chin, shifted something in Samuel. The urge to guard her sleep like a Great Pyrenees dog protected its sheep was overwhelming.

It'd been a great day in spite of, or maybe because of, his pint-sized companion. Gail had called several times to ensure they were doing all right. She called at noon, her distress evident through the phone, explaining another job opportunity had come up for the day, but she wouldn't take it if there was any problem what-soever with Lily. Samuel assured her they were fine. And they were, now that he always kept one eye on the little girl no matter what they were doing. In the early afternoon, Gail texted him to meet her by George's stable block. He and Lily found a bench in the shade and sat down to wait.

He'd managed to buy two horses during the day, the gelding that'd been slow down the final stretch and George's filly. Samuel didn't figure to keep the fret-ful horse long, but expected she'd be a nuisance while he did.

Seeing Gail stride into view with another trainer down the stable row, Samuel carefully shifted his sleeping burden and stood. By the time he quietly ap-proached, Gail was bent at a makeshift table outside the stalls, flipping through some paperwork. Coming up on her right side, he saw her scrawl her signature at the bottom of a page.

Curious as to her full name, since she hadn't yet mentioned it, Samuel tilted his head to read the paper. He froze at the sight of it.

Abigail Lapp.

He darted an assessing glance at the ponytailed, jean-clad woman beside him as a number of curious things now made sense.

As the Amish culture had begun with a limited num-ber of families and for all practical purposes remained a closed society, there were still a limited number of surnames across the communities. Some were more prevalent than others.

Lapp was one of the most common.

Of course, *Lapp* could be a surname in the *Englisch*

world, as well. But Samuel recalled how easily she'd spoken and pronounced Amish words. He'd thought at the time it was because of her hours riding with Elam. Now he wondered.

And there was her abruptly changed behavior when they'd met Ruth and Hannah... Hannah *Lapp*, coming down his lane. And he wondered some more.

The *Englisch* would be surprised how many Amish youth chose to stay in their community at the end of their *rumspringa*. A small percentage, though, for various reasons, did leave. The woman beside him was apparently one of them. And Samuel figured the little girl in his arms was at least part of the reason.

Gail flipped the sheets back down after confirming the delivery. Aware that someone had approached, she looked over as she straightened from the table. Her breath caught at the sight of her sleeping daughter in Samuel's strong arms. A bolt of longing for that kind of security shot through her. She reached for her daughter.

"How was she? I can't thank you enough for watching her today. I feel so terrible leaving her with you but she would've been miserable with me all day."

"I've got her if you don't want to risk waking her in the exchange." Samuel kept his arm under the little girl. "And don't scold yourself. It must be difficult to raise a *kind* alone, unlike in the Amish community, where there's always help around."

Gail's gaze flew to Samuel's blue eyes as she dropped her arms. Surely he didn't know? No secret could be kept with Lily around, but she'd never talked with her daughter about her past. Lily wouldn't have known any secrets to spill. Gail smiled weakly.

"She hasn't been out that long. She must've run out of questions." Samuel's lips curved. "For the moment."

Gail winced. "Was she a handful?"

"*Ach*, we got along. She probably now knows more about the Plain people than most of my *Englisch* neighbors."

Was there an emphasis on some of his words? Tensing again, Gail searched Samuel's eyes. They revealed nothing.

"I bought a couple of horses today. When do you want to load them?"

Grateful for the change of topic, Gail nodded. "I'm ready to go now, if you are."

Casting another glance at her sleeping daughter, she fell in step beside Samuel as they traveled down the shed row to collect his purchases. She took control of the horses while Samuel continued to carry Lily to the truck. When they reached the rig, they switched; Samuel loaded the Standardbreds without incident while Gail fastened her still-sleeping daughter into the car seat.

When Samuel was quiet all the way out of town, Gail covertly glanced at her passenger. He was looking out the window, seemingly deep in thought. Sighing, she left him to them. She'd almost hyperventilated this morning about leaving Lily with him at the track. Sanity had kicked in again but she'd worried all day that she'd done the right thing,

He wasn't a stranger. He had several references. Elam, who was as honest as they came, had spoken highly of Samuel. Ruth Fisher, whom Gail respected, had married his brother, so she must've thought the family was all right. And Hannah, her own sister, who was as sweet and perfect as they came, apparently associated with him. The man couldn't drive and didn't have a vehicle, so it wasn't as if he was going to abscond with her daughter.

Besides, Gail knew about everyone at the track and many knew Lily, so they'd had support on hand.

It would've been a miserable time for Lily, cooped up all day in the truck. And losing this day's business and related prospects would've put Gail much closer to losing the rig and their livelihood.

Gail sneaked another glance at Samuel. Yes, she'd made the right decision. She just needed to stop wishing she could've spent the day with them, as well.

They rode in comfortable silence except for the wind blowing in the open window, until they almost reached his farm. Not knowing when she'd see him again, Gail was surprisingly reluctant to completely let the afternoon go without talking to him.

"I like the gelding. What made you buy the skittish filly?"

She felt his gaze on her as she slowed to turn into his lane. "I've got someone in mind for her. Benjamin Raber admired my mare, Belle, when he and I worked together at my *bruder*'s furniture business. I thought he'd like a similar sort. If not him, there are plenty of young men in their *rumspringa* who wouldn't mind a flashy ride."

Gail remembered Benjamin Raber. Years ago, if she'd walked out with the quiet, dark-haired man, instead of being bedazzled by the blond, charismatic Atlee, she wouldn't have left the Amish community. Her lips twisted for what might have been. But then she wouldn't have had Lily. She couldn't imagine life without her daughter.

As they drove up the lane, a young Amish man, most likely Samuel's brother from the similar build and blond hair, stepped out of the barn. Gail circled the yard and backed the trailer toward the big double doors. Samuel got out. Glancing toward the backseat, he carefully swung the passenger door in, leaving it open a crack.

Upon rolling the windows the rest of the way down and shutting off the truck, Gail twisted in her seat to check on Lily. Head propped against the side of the car seat, mouth slightly open, her daughter was still sleeping hard. It must've been a big day. Surely she'd sleep for the short time it'd take to unload the horses before they were back on the road. Gail smiled before glancing at her watch. Lily would be raring to go when she woke up. And talkative. If her mother asked a few probing questions about her daughter's day with her handsome companion, well, it would be perfectly understandable.

With one last look at Lily, Gail slid from the truck and closed the door with a quiet click.

Samuel was releasing the latch on the back of the trailer when Gail rounded its corner. Seeing her flick a glance toward Gideon, he nodded toward his brother. "Gail, my *bruder* Gideon. He's not always sitting around the barn waiting for company. Sometimes he's actually in town working."

"I'm working whether I'm in town or home. Which I wouldn't have to do if you'd just get things done a little faster around here," retorted Gideon as he pushed the double barn doors behind them farther open.

"I'd have more time outside to get things done if I

didn't have to do most of the cooking. I can't even get the hogs to eat what you make for supper."

Gail's lips twitched at their good-natured bickering. She nodded at Gideon and stepped out of the way as Samuel opened the door at the back of the trailer and swung it with a squeal of stubborn hinges to the right. The thud of hooves against metal rang as the two horses inside shifted at the activity. Not surprisingly, most of the thuds came from the fractious filly fastened nearest the trailer's front.

Samuel stepped inside and untied the gelding, who, although head up and ears twitching, backed smoothly out. Giving the bay a soothing pat as the horse took in his new surroundings, Samuel wheeled him around and led him toward the double doors, where he handed the lead over to his brother.

"Would you take him on in, Gideon? The filly's like a twin sister to Belle and probably won't come out of the trailer so calmly."

Gideon ran a hand down the gelding's neck. "Don't know why you're attracted to that type."

"Probably because they're fast and flashy and I get requests for them. In fact, I may let you have a chance at this one before I tell Benjamin about her." Gideon snorted and headed through the barn doors with the gelding. Samuel turned back toward the trailer. Gail was already inside, untying the filly's lead. "*Ach,* I'll get her out," he called, striding back to help.

"I got her." Gail finished untying the lead and eased the excited filly from the mobile stall. Stepping to the right, out of the way of the pair, Samuel watched warily as the bay kept throwing her head as Gail gently and competently backed her from the trailer.

He knew the Standardbred had been transported many times, but one wouldn't know it to watch her antics. The other horses in the barn and pasture called out greetings to the newcomer, adding to the filly's agitation.

Once they were on the ground, Gail turned the sweating filly toward the large barn doors. With a loud creak, the trailer door started to swing shut, just as Gideon emerged through the double doors from the shadow of the barn's interior.

It was too much for the horse. She reared, almost lifting Gail from the ground.

As Samuel lunged toward them, he saw a flash of pink beyond the swinging trailer door. To his horror, he realized Lily had gotten out of the truck and was approaching them.

Without hesitation, he whipped around the swaying door and swept Lily into his arms. A loud clang of hooves striking metal rang in his ears an instant before the door slammed into his back, a sharp edge plowing into his shoulder.

The blow jolted him forward. He heard Gail's sharp cry behind him as, clutching Lily to his chest, he staggered toward the ground.

Chapter Seven

Samuel went down hard on one knee.

Seconds later Gail was at his side. "Are you okay?"

Eyes closed, teeth gritted, Samuel breathed through the explosion in his shoulder blade a moment before he could speak. "Check Lily. If she's all right, we're all right." Easing down to both knees, he loosened his arms from the rigid grip he had on the little girl.

His anxious gaze matched Gail's as they searched Lily's pale face. The child turned her wide eyes to Samuel before breaking into a toothy grin. "Do it again!"

Samuel winced as he exhaled sharply. "I think not." Carefully releasing her, he ensured she was on her feet before dropping his arms. Gail immediately snatched her daughter into a tight hug. Shifting back onto his heels, Samuel pushed slowly to his feet. Once there, he rested a hand against the trailer as he dropped his head and panted in time with the throb in his back.

Gail looked up from where she held her daughter, gratitude evident in her blue eyes.

"Mommy, you're hugging me too tight." Lily wiggled free of Gail's embrace.

Samuel sent a prayer of thanks to *Gott* for the little girl's safety. Feeling a light touch on his shoulder, he turned to Gideon.

"Your shirt is ripped and bloody." Concern was etched on his *bruder*'s face. They worked enough around livestock and farming to know injuries could be frequent and debilitating. "Better see if you can get Ruth to wash it out for you, as I'm not going to try."

Samuel forced his wince into a smile. "You'd do a poor job of it anyway. Where's the filly?"

"I put her in one of the open stalls." At Samuel's relieved nod, he continued, "I think I'll pass. Give Benjamin a chance on her. You don't seem to be enough judge of horseflesh to bring one home yet that I'd be interested in." Gideon mirrored Samuel's false smile, but his eyes asked how bad it was.

Shifting away from the trailer, Samuel hissed in a breath as he straightened his back. "Sore, yes. Broken, no."

"Gut." Gideon's tense shoulders eased under his suspenders. "Then I won't have to take off work to help you finish the haying at Malachi's."

"I want to take a look at your shoulder." Gail joined them, an interested Lily by her side.

"Ach, it's not the first bruise I've gotten from a horse. It won't be the last."

"That may be, but it's the first one you've gotten while protecting my daughter. Let's go into the house. We're going to take a look at it." Gail tipped her head toward the white farmhouse, indicating that Samuel should lead the way.

Samuel and Gideon exchanged a look. Gideon smiled. "What is it about my *brieder* and bossy women?" He hooked a thumb toward the barn. "I'll get the new arrivals settled in. " Nodding to Gail and Lily, his smile expanded to a face-splitting grin. "Pleasure to meet you. I look forward to seeing you again sometime. Holler if he doesn't behave while you're patching him up. Try not to make him cry."

Samuel rolled his eyes. "Just go take care of my horses," he tossed over his shoulder as he started for the house. "I'll see if I can find a little pony in my travels and buy him for you to drive. Maybe that'd be something you could handle. In case you're worried, I'll have Lily here check it out to make sure the pony is safe enough for you."

"She'd be a better judge of horseflesh than you." Gideon's response followed them across the farmyard.

Samuel smiled, although it probably looked more like a grimace. His shoulder was on fire. While walking beside Gail toward the house, he slowed when he saw Lily dodge around her mother to come along his side. To his surprise, the girl reached for his hand. Her small one only wrapped around two of his fingers, but the feeling that rushed through him at the miniature grip almost made him stumble. She looked up at him, her blue eyes as concerned as his *bruder*'s had been.

"I'm sorry you have an owie."

Samuel touched her hair with his other hand. "It's all right, Lily. I'm just glad that you don't." He'd take his throbbing shoulder and more if it meant Gail and her daughter were safe.

Gail cleared her throat against the sudden lump that'd lodged there at the sight of her daughter walking hand in hand with Samuel. As Gail had no time and even less interest in men, it meant, other than George and some of the grooms at the track, Lily had no male figures in her life. To see her daughter connect so strongly and quickly with this particular one, who made her mother feel the same way... Pressing her lips together, Gail relived seeing the metal door hurling toward the pair. She forced back the tears of relief that they were all right. A glance at Samuel's bloody back amended that. Well, mostly all right.

Recalling the first time she laid eyes on him in this farmyard, Gail acknowledged maybe she'd misjudged the charming Amish man. Certainly, he was pretty on the outside, but there were depths that she hadn't anticipated.

Upon reaching the farmhouse, Gail looked through the screen door into its shadowed interior. Rooted on the porch, she took a few shallow breaths and cleared her throat again before she pulled the door open with a squeak. Heart hammering, Gail crossed the threshold.

It could've been her parents' kitchen. The gas-powered stove and refrigerator, a fireplace situated between the kitchen and living room, kerosene lamps and gaslights positioned at key locations. Pegs on the wall bordered the doors, ready for hats and coats. Even if the ample windows hadn't let in the late-afternoon light, Gail wouldn't have bothered looking for a light switch. She knew there wouldn't be one.

She also knew the plainness of the decor wasn't just because it was a bachelor household. Her family's home had been spartan, as well. The Schrock home had no decorations on the walls, no pictures; only a few wooden shelves held a lamp and a windup clock whose ticktock followed them as Samuel guided them through large, sparsely furnished rooms. Rooms big and open enough to be used for church services when it was the owner's turn to host.

The bare walls weren't lost on Lily. "Why don't you have any pictures? Do you need some pictures? I can make you some. I'm a good drawer. Mommy says so."

Samuel grinned down at her daughter. "Thank you. That would sure make a difference in here, wouldn't it?" He led them across a large living area to push open the door to a small, utilitarian bathroom.

Samuel turned on an overhead gaslight and they stepped in. There wasn't much space in the room for one, much less two. When Lily squeezed in as well, pressing Gail against Samuel's solid frame, she inhaled a startled breath of sun-warmed flesh and a whiff of horse. Unthinking, Gail put a hand on his upper arm to catch herself, before dropping it like she'd touched a burning coal when she felt the lean muscles tense under her fingers.

"Lily! What do you say?" Embarrassed, Gail shuffled back in the limited space and directed Samuel to sit on the edge of a simple white tub.

"Excuse me," Lily offered disinterestedly as she continued to explore.

Shifting out of the way so Samuel could remove his shirt, both he and Gail hissed in a breath when he managed to do so. Him, surely in pain; her, in sympathy of the angry wound.

Samuel regarded the torn and bloody garment remorsefully. "I'm running out of shirts."

Gail reached out a hand. Having been one of two older sisters with several young brothers in the house, cleaning and mending shirts was something she well remembered how to do. "I'll take it home and mend it."

She almost smiled at the hopeful look Samuel gave her as he handed it over. "I have some other shirts and socks that need some help, as well…?"

As a distraction, it helped. Anything to take her mind off the bare torso in front of her. "Can't coax your sister-in-law to take care of them for you?"

"*Ach, nee.* Ruth's too strong-minded to be coaxed into anything she doesn't want to do."

"Don't you have a sweetheart? Why haven't you married?" Gail could've bitten her tongue at the questions that popped out. The prospect gave her a pang. Amish courtships were generally kept secret until the couple's betrothal was announced at church. Her pang became a stab at the memory of how well she knew that fact.

What stung more now was the possibility that Samuel could be walking out with someone and she wouldn't know it. It wasn't as if she was attending Sunday night singings to witness if he was driving someone home afterward, but even that wasn't always a telltale sign.

Gail edged her way past a fascinated Lily to the simple sink. Using the soap there, she washed her hands before she rinsed the basin, set the plug and ran water into it, grateful that it was plumbed for hot water. A quick look around revealed a basket of well-worn washcloths on a shelf under the sink. "Do you have iodine? Or antiseptic ointment? The skin's broken. The handle must've hit you. The door on my trailer probably has enough germs on it that I'd feel better if we treated you with something."

Samuel grunted as she dabbed the gash on his shoulder with the soapy washcloth. "Check the shelf under the sink. There should be a first-aid kit somewhere close. We get poked or stepped on enough that we usually keep something around."

He stiffened as she gently probed the broken skin over his shoulder blade. Although bloody and angry-looking, to her relief, it didn't look like it would need stitches. But it was going to be sore.

"What's that? It looks like cheese." Lily squeezed her way to the sink and poked a square white block sitting on the back of it.

"That's soap, sweetie." Gail remembered making similar bars many times over.

"Why is it so white and square?"

"Because it's homemade."

"Like ice cream?"

"Kind of. Don't eat it, as it probably has lye in it." Gail glanced at Samuel for confirmation.

"*Ja.* My sister-in-law Ruth's efforts. She was making all sorts of things when she first stopped working at the shop after she got married. The woman can't sit still." He touched Lily on the nose. "Like someone else I know."

Lily giggled before looking solemnly into Samuel's face. "Are you going to cry?"

"I'll try not to. But if I do, don't tell my *bruder.*"

Gail appreciated her daughter's presence. If it'd been just the two of them, it would've felt too intimate in the small space, even with his injury. She was trying to be as gentle as she could with the wound, but under her touch, she could feel Samuel's occasional flinch.

He'd never responded to her wife question. Had that

been accidental or intentional? Gail wondered how many old female friends and acquaintances had him in their dreams, if not in their sights. It brought back memories of excitement she'd felt when she'd entered her *rumspringa*. Of her pounding heart when handsome, charming Atlee started paying attention to her. She'd thought at first that his insistence on a secretive relationship was exciting. Now she knew why they'd had to sneak around. He'd convinced Louisa, who he'd been seeing first, of the same necessity. Stomach twisting, she recalled Atlee's betrayal and the fool she'd been. She dabbed at the back before her more fiercely. Samuel recoiled and slanted her a look. Instantly contrite, Gail gentled her touch.

Lily slipped out of the bathroom. Hands on nonexistent hips, she glanced around the living area of the house. "Where's your TV?"

Samuel's lips twitched. "Don't have one. They take electricity, which we also don't have."

"Huh." Lily took a few steps farther into the open area room. "Well, that's weird."

"Remember, we talked today about Amish choosing to live differently? That's one of the ways we live differently."

"How do you watch cartoons?"

"We don't. We do other things." Samuel's attention was focused on Lily, but his voice had gotten huskier as Gail administered to his back.

Gail was glad she didn't have to speak. She didn't know if she could've at the moment. Setting the washcloth on the edge of the sink, she washed and dried her hands again before rummaging on the shelf under it for the first-aid kit. Finding it, she extracted the antiseptic ointment and squeezed some on her fingertip.

Exhaling a stream of air through pursed lips, she stared down at the tanned, muscular back. As she touched the angry wound without the barrier of the washcloth, a flush crept up her cheeks. Gail trained her focus on her daughter's chatter.

Lily's words reminded Gail that her choices for her life would be Lily's life, as well. Much as she longed for home and Plain life, could she take her daughter from the world she'd grown up knowing? Lily didn't know the world Gail had grown up in. One of playing Scrabble or checkers with siblings instead of watching TV. Of hard work, but taking much joy in that work. Of community, of family unity, of visiting friends and frolics.

What was right for them both?

It wasn't the man whose back she ministered to. Gail cleared her throat twice before she could speak. "Um, there're some large bandages in the kit that I'll use to cover it to keep it clean. Then I think I've done all I can. I encourage you to have a doctor look at it."

"We'll see how it is tomorrow. I'll have Gideon take a look at it before he heads out. If he falls over from shock, I might go to the clinic in town. Don't worry. We've got hay to put up at Malachi's place. Gideon won't let it turn gangrenous, as he might have to do more of the farmwork."

"Don't joke about it."

"I'll be fine. Especially since you're fixing my shirt."

Gail secured the oversize bandages over the wound as best she could. "Do you have another one to wear in the meantime?"

"Ah, there should be one in my dresser." Samuel

stood up from where he'd been perched on the edge of the tub. Overwhelmed by his immediate closeness in the small space, Gail shuffled a step back and stumbled over the toilet behind her. Samuel reached out a hand and grasped her upper arm, catching her before she fell.

"I'll get it." Gail slipped out of his grip toward the door and hastened through it into the living area. Lily skipped over to join her as she crossed the room to hesitate in front of two open doors, one opening into a bedroom, the other leading up some stairs. Glancing back toward the bathroom, Gail saw Samuel at the door. Aware of her dilemma, he nodded her toward the open bedroom door. Entering, she found another spartan room, with only a double bed covered in an old quilt, and a dresser.

She took a moment to marvel at the workmanship of the dresser. If this was something Samuel had made, he had indeed not defaulted to horse-trading because he'd flunked out of furniture-making. It was simple, yet beautiful. As Lily investigated the room, Gail made a guess and pulled a middle drawer open.

Samuel was right. He was getting low on shirts. Gail's fingertips itched at the thought of having the right to make shirts for him. Shaking the sensation, she reached in, pulled out the top one and nudged the drawer shut. With a quick self-conscious stride, she crossed the bedroom and living area, stumbling at the sight of Samuel, his blond head bent as he listened to a chattering Lily, who'd preceded her from the room.

Gail handed him the shirt, then said, "Time to go, Lily-bug." Needing something to do with her hands, she lifted her daughter onto her hip. With the familiar feelings the big, open house evoked and the different ones the man who'd saved her daughter prompted, Gail was glad for the weight and barrier of the little girl.

Unfortunately for Gail's peace of mind, Lily wasn't finished with her conversation. "Do you get to have toys, since you don't have a TV?"

Samuel's lips twitched. "Yes, we have toys. But they're Amish toys and might be a little different than you're used to."

Starting to turn away, Gail paused when Lily reached out her hands to bracket Samuel's lean cheeks. "I'm going to call you my Amiss man."

Samuel's white teeth were evident in the smile that stretched between her little hands. "I'm honored, Lily."

With a stiff smile, Gail said goodbye and hustled out of the house and across to the truck. Hurriedly, she buckled Lily into her car seat. As she rounded the front of the truck, she waved an arm to a now-shirted Samuel, who'd stepped out of the house. Gail needed to get going. Before she did something foolish, like echoing her daughter's remarks that she'd like to call him her Amish man, too.

Chapter Eight

Gail shielded her eyes with a hand against Friday's late-afternoon sun. The other hand rested on her stomach, pressed against the butterflies that darted there at the sight of a straw-hat-wearing man riding in a cart behind a fast-moving horse. She didn't question that the driver behind the bay was Samuel, not his brother Gideon. She just...knew.

She shouldn't have come. She didn't have any excuse to be here other than the very lame one of returning his shirt. He wasn't expecting her. Yes, she'd made a delivery close by. Somewhat close by. But surely her concern was understandable? The man had gotten hurt protecting her daughter, after all. She'd just wanted to check on how he was doing from his injury earlier this week. Make sure he was healing and taking care of it, which—as her eyes followed his broad back as man and horse started a wide turn—he obviously wasn't.

She could've called. Samuel carried a phone and Gail had his number, but years of culture that prohibited phone use kept her from using the device for extraneous things. Like calling a man you were interested in, just to hear his voice.

Obviously serious about this horse-breaking business, he'd created a makeshift track around a hayfield. When the pair came out of the back turn, Samuel must've seen her, as he swung the horse toward where she stood at the wooden gate.

"Should you be doing this?" She'd waited until he was near enough to hear without shouting.

"I should if I want to know more about a horse that I plan to sell to my neighbors."

"No, I mean, should you be driving with your injured shoulder?"

"Not to be *hochmut*, I am a *gut* driver, but I haven't yet learned to drive with my feet so I have to use my hands and shoulders."

Gail rolled her eyes at the old joke, her nervousness evaporating with his teasing. "You know what I mean."

He secured the reins. Although it was difficult to leave the sight of Samuel's handsome, broad-shouldered figure, when the bay flicked its tail, she darted a glance at it. With relief, she saw that it was the gelding he'd bought that day, not the filly.

Samuel noticed the object of her attention. "Already worked with the filly. Figured I'd rather try her when I was fresher."

"You going to be able to sell her?"

"Without a doubt. She's what I expected. Not as fast as my Belle, but she's fast enough that some might buy her because they'd think so."

"You're not going to race them, are you?" When did she start acting like a mother to more than a three-year-old? Gail shifted uneasily at the possibility that it began when she'd started to care for a certain someone.

"Not where anyone can see." Samuel grinned at her, his blue eyes twinkling.

Gail inhaled deeply, both to forestall her frustration at his recklessness and to settle the bounding butterflies that'd taken flight again at being the recipient of his dazzling attention.

He glanced at the truck parked in the barnyard. "You done for the day?"

My wits are if I can't do anything but bubble and fizz when you look at me like that. "Um, yeah. On my way home."

"Would you like to take a turn with us around the track? It'd give him a feel of different weight in the cart before I try him with the buggy."

Gail's heart rate immediately accelerated as she glanced at the jog cart Samuel sat on. Used for training, it was bigger and bulkier than a racing bike used at the track. Also unlike the racing bike, it had a seat big enough for two. If the two were sitting very close together. Probably not a good idea as the man already made her nervous and was firmly rooted in the Amish world while she and Lily would have to go wherever they could survive together. She pushed back the surge of longing to ride behind a strong trotter in the open air, the ground skimming by beside her and the breeze teasing her face.

Glancing back to his distracting face, Gail opened her mouth to say no, and blinked when a breathless yes came out instead.

Samuel nodded in apparent satisfaction and scooted

over the few inches the seat allowed. "You have a stop in the area?"

Gail considered the miles she'd driven out of her way as she stepped forward. "Reasonably close. I brought your shirt back. I'm surprised to see you out working today."

"Why? You're working. Sundays are days of rest. The rest of the week, there is always much to be done."

For a moment memories of Sundays growing up washed through Gail. Visiting Sundays, spent seeing friends. Church Sundays, where many voices lifted up the songs of the *Ausbund*, before long sermons followed by community dinners and singings in the evening for the *youngies*.

Don't forget the singings where another charming blond man shanghaied your life.

Leave those memories in the past but don't forget their lessons to protect your future. You have enough challenges managing the present. You don't need to add him to them.

"But your back is injured." Standing beside the cart, she again dubiously eyed the narrow seat. Up close, it seemed even smaller.

"Doesn't stop the need for work." Samuel stretched his torso and shifted his shoulders, grimacing fleetingly as he did so. Gail dropped her eyes to the reins in his work-calloused hands. It was safer than his distractingly broad shoulders.

"But now that you mention it, it feels like I've been kicked by a horse."

"How does it look?"

Samuel grunted. "According to Gideon, it looks

like a spring sky before a tornado touches down. With blacks, purples and some greenish yellow thrown in."

Gail winced in sympathy, biting her tongue against the offer to check it herself, just to make sure he was okay. Obviously he was, as he reached out a hand to help her into the cart.

Hesitantly, she placed hers in its warm grasp.

"Put your foot there, and there." He guided her into the simple cart. Years ago she'd climbed into many buggies in a dress. It was much easier maneuvering into this one in jeans. An instant later Gail was seated beside him, her hip brushing his. Slowly opening her fingers, she reluctantly released his clasp. She felt him take a breath beside her. "Okay, rest your feet on the bar."

The gelding shifted, taking a step forward. Gail swayed on the seat, shooting out a hand for balance. With no back or sides on the cart, there was nothing to hold on to except…him. She brought her hands to her lap and clenched them, trying to contain her irrational excitement at being in any kind of buggy again.

"Ready?" At her nod, Samuel lifted the reins and urged the gelding forward. The horse took a step and stopped, questioning the unaccustomed load. Samuel gently urged him forward again. The bay's ears twitched and he took another step, gaining confidence as they headed toward the first turn at the end of the field.

"Ready for road gear?" Samuel tossed her a wide smile.

"Do I have a choice?" Gail couldn't help grinning herself.

"Nee!" He signaled to the gelding. They lurched on the seat as the horse sprang into a fast trot. Gail's

shoulder bumped Samuel's arm. One hand remaining in her lap, she curled the fingers of the other under the wooden seat to keep steady on her precarious perch.

The gelding might no longer make the time trials, but he was fast. The muffled thud of hooves on the packed dirt of the homemade track was a metronome matching her heart rate. Their speed created a breeze that swept over them, lifting the bay's black tail to stream behind him and causing Gail's ponytail to flutter about the back of her neck. Oh, how she'd missed this! Her smile was probably as wide as the grille on her Dodge.

The ground whizzed by under their feet. Automatically, they both leaned into the curve as the bay swept around it. As they cornered, even bracing her arm, Gail slid toward the outside. Hissing in a breath, she tangled the fingers of her free hand into the rolled-up sleeve of Samuel's shirt to keep herself from slipping off the seat. Once they entered the straight length of the field, she dropped her hand again and edged away a fraction of an inch. She was ready for the second turn.

Samuel eased the gelding into a slower trot as they completed the final turn, approaching the gate where he'd picked her up. "He'll do. He'll do pretty well, in fact. Do you want to drive?" Samuel lifted the reins in her direction.

Gail's fingers itched for the feel of the supple leather. Relinquishing her grip of the seat at the slower pace, she clenched her hands in her lap to keep from reaching for the reins.

"He's got a soft mouth and is well behaved. I'll look for more horses from this trainer." He nodded at the reins in his hand. "Go ahead. See what it feels like to drive a horse instead of your truck. You'll be all right with him, and I'm right here to help you."

Gail glanced over to meet his eyes. Her heart beat heavily. Not because she was afraid. But because she wanted it too much. Uncurling her fists, she reached for the reins.

"Hold them like this."

He cupped her hands in his, guiding the brown leather through her fingers. Gail regretted the loss of the breeze, as she suddenly felt hot all over.

"Okay. Got it?" When he let go, the gelding bobbed its head as if to ask what the holdup was. The reins slid through her hands. Automatically, Gail worked her fingers to gather them up again.

When she glanced at Samuel, he was watching her speculatively. "Ready to go?"

Using her voice and hands, Gail urged the bay ahead, bracing herself for when he surged forward into a fast walk. As they headed into the first turn, Gail clicked the gelding into a faster gait. The gelding drove like a dream, much better than the stubborn Standardbred she'd driven before she left home. She tried to come up with a word to describe her elation as they flew along. The one that came to mind was one she couldn't say. *Wunderbar!*

She asked more speed of him as they raced the quarter-mile length to the back turn of the hayfield. Just as they approached it, a brown figure scurried across the homemade track from the recently cut hay in the center of the field. Gail absently recognized the large marmot as a groundhog. The gelding saw it as a threat. Shying heavily, he jerked Gail halfway off the seat and sent the cart swaying on the uneven ground as he swerved.

Even as Gail instantly and unconsciously regathered control of the horse, she could see Samuel reach a hand toward the reins to assist her. Before he could do so, Gail regained her seat and smoothly returned the gelding to the track while the marmot hurried across to the tall grass of the fencerow.

When she felt through the leathers that the bay had settled down from his surprise, she gave him a little more rein as they came out of the turn. Samuel had pulled back his hand, but she could feel his attention on her. As they approached the gate, she eased the horse into a slow jog before turning him and walking him back to where she'd gotten into the cart.

Swiveling in the seat toward Samuel, Gail returned the reins to him. "Obviously, he doesn't see many groundhogs on the track, but if I was buying a horse, I'd buy him. That was…" She sucked in a deep breath and blew it out in a long stream. "Thank you."

While his mouth smiled, to her surprise, his eyes did not. "You're a natural. Where'd you learn to drive?"

Gail jerked her hands back into her lap, twisting them into a knot. "Uh, um, when I first worked for George, he let me do a little driving to and from the track."

Samuel nodded. "He taught you well."

"Yeah, I guess." With a weak smile, Gail scrambled from the cart. As Samuel drove the gelding through the gate and to the barn, she walked beside them. He drew the gelding to a halt in front of the big double doors, secured the reins and sprang agilely from the cart.

Facing him, Gail started backing toward her truck. "Thanks again for the ride. I'll… I'll remember it for a long time. And I'm so glad you're feeling better." At his ironic expression, she amended, "Well, maybe not feeling better, but functional at least." Bumping into the rear quarter panel of the Dodge, Gail pivoted and headed for the cab door. By the time she was in and buckled, he was at the driver's window. With reluctant eagerness, Gail rolled it down.

Samuel put his hands on the door when the glass disappeared into it. "I won't be able to get to the track for a bit. There's haying to be done at Malachi's farm." He nodded toward the barn. "And as my operation's still pretty slim, although I enjoy looking, before I buy any more, I need to sell these two. Besides, I have a mare that should be foaling any day now. I need to be here when it arrives in case she has any issues."

A pang shot through Gail at the thought of not seeing him for a while. She cleared her throat. "Take care of your shoulder."

"*Ach, ja.* I'll get it healed in time for the next kick." Their eyes held a moment before he glanced toward the barn again. "Would you like to know when the mare has her foal? Maybe bring Lily out to see the little fellow?"

"She'd love that." *I would, too. Stop it! He's a distraction, that's all. A mirage that reminds you of what once was and what you thought would be.* Gail turned the ignition. Samuel stepped back when the truck roared to life.

"I'll let you know, then."

"That'd be great. Thanks. Good luck on selling those two." Gail rolled up the window, sealing him out. She wished she could seal him out of her thoughts as easily. Driving down the lane, she adjusted her rearview mirror in order to keep him in view. He hadn't moved from when he'd stepped away from the window. She couldn't see his eyes under his flat-brimmed straw hat, but he seemed to be watching her, as well. Only when she was on the road did she notice something on the seat beside her and realized she still had his shirt. Reaching out a hand, she curled her fingers into the soft fabric.

The truck and trailer pulled out of the lane and accelerated down the road. Samuel turned toward the bay that waited, slouch-hipped, by the barn. Reaching the cart, he bent to unhitch it and flinched. His back, which the filly had done a good job of irritating when he was driving her today, had been throbbing steadily by the time he worked with the gelding. Up to the time he'd rounded the corner and unexpectedly saw Gail by the gate. At that moment his heart started beating faster than the gelding's quick gait. If he'd been on foot and it'd been a side-by-side competition against the retired track horse, Samuel figured he'd have reached the slender brunette first.

His offer for the drive had generated from his desire to keep her from leaving. And to have her close beside him. He'd been distracted with those sensations. Until she'd handled the Standardbred unerringly and her signature from earlier in the week flashed into his mind.

Abigail Lapp.

With the injury and the inability of getting anything else in his brain other than the feel of her gentle fingers on him since she patched him up in the bathroom, he'd forgotten that feminine scrawl. The offer to drive had accidentally become a test. One she'd overwhelmingly passed.

Abigail Lapp drove better than some Amish men he knew.

It could be, as she'd said, that she'd learned while working for George at the track. But she was Amish, or had been. He'd eat his straw hat and his winter felt one, too, if she wasn't. From the absolute exuberance on her face during the ride, more joy than he'd seen there since he'd met her, for whatever reason she'd left, she wanted to return now.

Upon leading the unhitched horse into the dim light of the barn, Samuel began removing the harness. For reasons that he wasn't going to examine, it was important to him as well that she return. Slipping the collar from the bay, he remembered Gail's odd response when they'd met Ruth and Hannah Lapp coming down the lane. As he had Gail's face memorized, it wasn't difficult to imagine her bouncy ponytail as blond instead of brunette. The resulting image looked a lot like his sister-in-law's best friend. Although he hadn't paid much mind at church, as they were younger than him, Samuel knew Hannah had a number of brothers. It would be interesting to discover if any of them had dark hair.

Grabbing a brush from its shelf on the wall, he ran it over the gelding. Maybe he'd pay the Lapps a visit. Perhaps they were interested in buying a horse.

Chapter Nine

Another song was started. Voices joined in. Mainly female voices, as was the norm. Taking a sip from the glass of water in front of him, Samuel glanced around the room. Other young men in the room were using the same excuse to not be singing. Some were talking quietly with their neighbors, but their attention was on other occupants present. Female occupants. Behind the glass, Samuel's lips curved in a slight smile. The young men didn't come for the singing. They came because the girls were here. The Sunday night singings were a primary form of accepted socializing in their community for those in their *rumspringa*. And the primary purpose of the *rumspringa* was to find a mate.

His gaze settled on a couple at the end of the long table. Even though Amish courtships were usually kept quiet, all the *youngies* knew that Aaron Raber was walking out with Rachel Mast. Were it not for the fact that Rachel's *daed* was ill and she was needed at home to help on the family farm, theirs would be the first engagement announced come fall. Samuel's attention drifted to a couple of young men standing behind those sitting in chairs at the table. Acknowledging Benjamin, his coworker at the furniture shop, he nodded. When his friend didn't acknowledge him, Samuel looked to see what held the young man's intent interest. Benjamin was staring at his older brother and Rachel. *Ach, looking at a particular woman who's not looking back at you, you're heading for nothing but heartache.*

Samuel's smile twisted before dropping completely. Wasn't he doing the same thing? Setting the glass down, he scrutinized the room again. There were plenty of female smiles aimed at him. Usually the sight and knowledge of the attention encouraged him. Flattered him, in fact, even though he knew it was wrong to be *hochmut*. Maybe that was part of the problem. He'd grown too proud and *Gott* was punishing him for it. Because even though most of the female eyes in the room were focused on him and would love to engage in the verbal dance of arranging to have a ride home, for the first time since he could remember, Samuel couldn't generate any interest in asking.

He lowered his lashes, not wanting to make any eye contact and thereby create any expectations. They almost popped open again at the image that immediately entered his head. A ponytailed dark brunette frowning at him. Gail. His lips curved again. She always started out frowning. Samuel took it as a personal challenge to tease a smile out of her. Most of the time, he succeeded. He got more enjoyment out of a few moments of her snipping at him than he did in an hour of other women concertedly flirting.

His smile faded. He wished he was with her now.

"Something wrong with your drink? Can I get you another?"

Samuel looked up to see a red-haired young woman at his elbow. The singing had stopped and the *youngies* were milling around. There were a few other women behind her, anxiously yet covertly watching, but of course Lydia Troyer was in the lead. He had to admire her tenacity. She'd made a play for Malachi first. Since that'd failed, he was apparently next choice on the menu. Well, this was a time when he'd intentionally follow in his brother's wake.

"*Nee*, the drink is fine."

"The singing isn't to your liking?" The girl was persistent, to say the least.

"*Nee*, just thinking of something else." *Someone* else.

"Something that troubles you, then?" Lydia was acting like she was going to sit down beside him.

"*Ach, ja*, it troubles me." Everywhere he went on the farm and in the house, he thought of Gail, saw her there. In the field, in the house, in his bedroom. Except for the barn; she hadn't been in there yet. But he couldn't spend all his time in the barn trying to find peace from unfamiliar longings for one particular woman.

Samuel pushed up from the table, careful not to bump into the group of girls behind him, all adorned in solid-colored dresses under aprons. "*Ja*. In fact, it requires some heavy thinking." He smiled apologetically to the array of upturned faces under matching *kapps*. "I'm afraid I'm not fit company for anyone tonight." Through the chorus of murmured denials, Samuel made his way to the door. He tried to catch Gideon's eye on the way out, but his brother was too absorbed in his conversation with a young woman. Only seeing the back of her *kapp*, Samuel couldn't identify who she was to tease his *bruder* about later. To his surprise, teasing wasn't the thought that chased through his mind.

Was Gideon serious about a girl? Samuel's brow furrowed at the possibility that his younger *bruder* might get married and settled down before he did. Earlier, he would've laughed and needled him about the situation, while content to divide his own attentions among several girls. But now the possibility made him feel… envious?

Stepping out onto the porch, Samuel closed the door behind him, muting the chattering voices. Striding across the wooden boards, he descended the steps to the sidewalk, his chest rising with a deep inhalation of the night air. He should've thanked his hosts for their hospitality. He'd always made sure to do so before, slipping away briefly from the girl he was driving home that evening. But tonight he didn't pause as he headed where he could see Belle, standing with a cocked hip in the diminishing light.

He was going home from a singing while it was still light outside. Probably the only single male in the community to do so. Certainly the only time he'd done it. What was the matter with him that he was more interested in a solitary buggy ride home than in staying to flirt with a bevy of willing young women?

Gail. It was bad enough that she filled his senses when he was with her. Even worse that she filled his mind when he wasn't.

Belle hung her head over the rail from where she was secured to a post. Samuel scratched her behind the ear. When he went to untie her, she reached around to nip at him, something she hadn't done in months. Distracted, Samuel winced at the pinch on his biceps before he could jerk away. Fortunately for him, she hadn't been serious about the bite.

He rubbed at the wet spot on his sleeve. "What is it with the females in my life being so bothersome tonight?" he murmured.

Belle's ears alerted him to the presence behind them. Samuel turned to see that Lydia had followed him out of the house. Of course. He usually didn't bother regretting things in his life, but at the moment, he really regretted that he'd driven Lydia home after a singing one night some weeks back.

"I figured maybe I could distract you from your troubling thoughts if you gave me a ride home." The smile on her face indicated she'd had a little practice in being distracting.

Samuel stepped back, closer to the fence and within reach of Belle's teeth. He figured the mare was a safer alternative. Another past action to regret—that he'd kissed the red-headed girl. Although in fairness to him, it hadn't been his idea. He'd just accepted the very obvious invitation to do so.

"That's kind of you to offer, Lydia, but I couldn't ask you to do that." And wouldn't, either. Short of climbing into his buggy—by the look in her eye, he wouldn't put it past her—there wasn't much the girl could do.

Or so he'd thought. When she moved closer, he wasn't so sure.

"It's all right. Maybe you could distract me, too." Reaching out, her hand curled around his biceps.

Samuel shot a glance at the house behind her, the glow from the gaslights inside visible through the windows. Fortunately, the windows didn't contain a silhouette of anyone looking out on what could appear to be an embracing couple.

"*Ach*, you are a distracting woman, Lydia. But my mind is somewhere else and I can't give you the attention you deserve. I don't want to keep some other fortunate fellow from giving you a ride home tonight." Were these his words coming out of his mouth? Samuel almost turned around to see if someone was speaking behind him. Was he really turning down an obvious opportunity to do some kissing?

Shuffling back a foot, he winced when the top board of the fence pressed into his sore shoulder blade. Still, he preferred that over being pressed against the tenacious young woman before him.

Lydia eased in, trapping him against the fence. Her hand slid to his shoulder.

Samuel inhaled. The woman was taking the running-around definition of the *rumspringa* years literally. Just off his ear, Belle snorted. The mare's head was up, white rings showing around her eyes. Samuel figured his eyes were showing a lot of white, as well. It gave him an idea. *Sorry, girl.* Slipping a hand toward the post, he gripped the coarse weave of the rope tethered there and gave it a subtle tug. Belle jerked her head, laid back her ears and bared her teeth. A short foot away, Lydia paused, glancing apprehensively at the mare.

"Careful. She bites."

The warning could apply to both females. When Lydia jumped back, Samuel took the opportunity to deftly hop over the board fence. Shouldering Belle aside, he began untying the bay. It seemed safer to have some type of barrier between him and the redhead. He looked up from his work to see Lydia, now a yard from the fence, eyeing him and the mare doubtfully. Freeing the rope, Samuel patted Belle's sleek neck as they crossed to the gate of the pasture. For the rescue, she'd get an extra measure of oats when they got home. Once through the gate, he gave an intentionally casual wave in Lydia's direction as he headed for the shadowed row of buggies. After a moment of hesitation, the redhead turned toward the house. Two steps in, her pace accelerated.

Samuel heard the closing of the door in the quiet night as he maneuvered Belle between the shafts. Even now, the girl was probably angling for a different ride home. She made him feel old. Only the knowledge that whomever the girl Gideon had been speaking to was he seemed intent about kept Samuel from using the excuse of thanking the evening's host as an opportunity to warn his younger *bruder* about Lydia. Might say a word to Benjamin, though. He didn't want to see a friend tied to the girl for life. Men could sometimes be fools for flirty eyes and smiling lips.

Securing a trace to the shaft, he paused, visualizing eyes, more wary than flirty, meeting his. *Ach*, men could sometimes be fools for those, as well. At least he was.

Was he a fool? He shouldn't even be thinking of her in that way. Gail was living in the *Englisch* world, while he didn't plan on leaving the Plain community. He had to tread carefully. He needed her freight service for his business. He was barely making a profit as it was. Although Malachi was a decent boss, Samuel didn't want to have to go hat in hand back to work for him.

As for his disturbing *Englisch* driver, he'd taken a

close look at the Lapp family during church and over the noon meal today. He'd made a point to visit with Zebulun—who was brown haired, as were some of his sons. Automatically finishing his task, Samuel absently leaned against Belle. The Lapps all had blue eyes, similar to a pair that continually haunted him.

Although tempted to do so, Samuel hadn't pried or gossiped about their family history. He didn't need to. He was certain they had a daughter named Gail who'd left the Amish community for some reason, probably because she'd been unmarried and with child. She'd managed to live in the *Englisch* world for years. She might never want to return.

And he shouldn't try to convince her. But *ach*, the prospect was appealing. Would it be wrong? She seemed lonely for family and needed help with Lily. Besides *Gott*, there was nothing more important than family for the Amish.

Belle stomped a foot and shifted away from him.

"Easy there," he soothed as he gathered the reins and took them back to the buggy. Climbing in, he acknowledged he needed to take his own advice. He needed to take it easy. Not push her. Let Gail choose what she wanted in life. But his agile mind started thinking about how he could solve her problems and help his, as well.

Adjusting the leathers in his hands, Samuel lifted the brake, slightly disturbed at how much he wanted Gail to decide that what she wanted included him.

Gail pulled into the lane, her attention on Lily's chatter behind her. Her daughter was thrilled at the prospect of seeing a baby horse. Samuel had called to advise that a foal had been born on Monday. It was hard to tell who was more excited: Lily to see the foal, or Gail to see the foal's owner. But whereas Lily could express her enthusiasm, Gail wouldn't have done so even if she could've. She tried to suppress her own eagerness.

Focused on the barn, she didn't notice the Amish buggy and bay tethered by the house until she'd parked the truck and Lily was already fumbling with her seat belt. Upon seeing the rig, Gail's hands automatically went to the ignition to start the truck again and escape. Fingers squeezing the key, she hesitated, sick at heart of the constant fear and her propensity to run. She'd been fearful and running for four years. Running from her family and community because of fear and shame. Barely outrunning destitution. Falling behind in bills. Being swallowed up by loneliness. *I used to be brave. I used to be cheerful. What happened to that Gail?* Still, she began to twist the key head. It could be anyone in the Amish community, but she couldn't take the risk.

Too late. Through the windshield, Gail saw Samuel coming out of the barn, followed by two women wearing *kapps* and dresses covered by aprons. Gail froze at the sight of the smiling blonde walking beside the shorter red-haired woman.

"Come on, Mommy! Let's go see!" Lily had wiggled out of her seat and was tugging at the door handle.

Gail reached a hand between the seats and rested it on her daughter's back. Panting, it took her a moment before she could speak. "Just a minute, sweetie. Um, let Mommy come around and get you, okay?" The numb fingers of her left hand curled around the front door handle. Samuel must've seen her face, because, before she gave the handle a tug that would change her life, she saw his charming smile fade and a look of concern drop over his handsome features. One tinged with anticipation. And guilt.

He hadn't planned this, had he? How could he have known? How could he have done such a thing? Cold sweat beaded down Gail's back as her stomach twisted at the thought of being betrayed again by a handsome Amish man.

"Let's get out, Mommy!" Lily tugged at the door handle again. A muffled click heralded her success in getting it open. Before Gail could stop her, Lily scrambled down from the truck and ran around to the front of it.

It took three tries before Gail could get her door open. She hung on to it for support when she climbed out. Lily, impatient with her mother's delay, ran to her, grabbed Gail's hand and pulled her forward.

Obviously, the blonde woman wasn't party to any preplanned arrangement. Stumbling to a halt, her rounded blue eyes never left Gail's face. Her lips parted as her jaw sagged. For a moment she uttered no sound. Then joy broke over her lovely features like she'd just been given her heart's desire and she surged forward, voicing the name Gail never figured she'd be called again.

"Abigail?"

Chapter Ten

Gail remained planted in front of the truck as surely as if she'd taken root there. When she didn't move or speak, the wonder on Hannah's face faded to be replaced with uncertainty. Her sister slowed before stopping a few yards away.

"We were so worried about you. Why didn't you write? Any kind of message. Just to know that you were alive and well would've meant so much." Hannah's words were barely above a whisper.

Gail's lips trembled. "I couldn't," she finally got out. "It would've been too hard."

"You know I would've helped you any way I could've."

"I know." Gail rolled her lips inward and bit them. The hurt on her sister's face devastated her. "I… I just had to make a clean break. If I'd written to you, I…" She sniffed sharply. "I couldn't have done it. I would've had to come back. But I couldn't, because of…" Her eyes dropped to her daughter, who stood uncharacteristically silent beside her.

Hannah's eyes dropped to Lily, as well. "Is this…?" Her hands came up to steeple against her mouth.

Gail nodded. Gently grasping Lily's shoulders, she shifted the little girl to stand before her. "This is my daughter, Lily. Lily, I'd like you to meet…" Her voice drifted off. How did she explain to Lily that she had an aunt, her mommy's sister who'd never been mentioned? And where could it go from there? Gail still couldn't come back to the community. Not with the risk of losing Lily. Clearing her throat, she continued, "Lily, this is Hannah, a good friend of Mommy's from when she was a little girl." Gail's nose prickled against unshed tears. She was being so unfair. Hannah had certainly been that, but she was also so much more.

Hannah flinched at the deception as her eyes lifted to meet Gail's. Drawing a deep breath, she knelt to Lily's level and did what Hannah always did best. Gracefully composing herself, she made the others around her comfortable. "Hello, Lily. How are you? Your *mamm* is right. I knew her before you were born. I'm so glad to meet you because—" although Hannah smiled brightly, she paused on a little hiccup of air "—I've always wondered about you."

Gail relaxed her fingers from their stiff grip on Lily's shoulders as the girl stepped forward. "How did you know my mommy?"

"We grew up together." Hannah glanced again to Gail and smiled more naturally. "She was my best friend."

"Really?" Lily stepped closer. "My best friend is Miss Patty."

Gail crossed her arms over her chest at the stab that shot through her at her daughter's admission that her best friend was the fiftysomething woman who watched her during the day. Lily didn't have any playmates her own age. No siblings. Didn't attend any community frolics where kids ran and interacted with those their age. What a lonely life for a child. Her daughter should have more friends.

"Miss Patty must be very wonderful to have a good friend like you."

"She is. We bake and color and go to the store and watch TV." Lily now stood a foot away from Hannah, who lifted her arms like she wanted to embrace the child, before carefully returning them to her lap.

"I like to bake, as well."

"What's on your head?"

Hannah reached up to the pleated organdy that covered her hair. "This? It's called a *kapp*. I wear it when I pray, and since I am to pray without ceasing, I always have it on."

"I have a purple hat. Would you like to wear it for a while?"

Hannah smiled, a sweet expression that enhanced her gentle beauty. "That's very generous of you to offer, but I've grown used to this one and while I might struggle to put your purple one on, I'm sure it's a perfect fit for you."

Lily giggled. "Samuel put it on and he looked funny."

"My dignity is under attack here." Samuel stepped forward from where he and the red-haired woman Gail recognized as Ruth Fisher had stopped outside the barn's open double doors. His watchful gaze shifted between Gail and Hannah before he spoke to Lily. "Hey, Lily, would you like to see the foal?"

"Yes!" Lily skipped over to him and, without hesitation, reached for his hand. They disappeared into the shadows of the barn, Ruth Fisher, now Schrock, turning to join them. Gail had felt the woman's eyes on them, as well. No doubt the intention of the two adults entering the barn was to give her and Hannah some time alone.

Glancing at her sister, she found Hannah watching her, a slight, compassionate smile on her lips, but a wary look in her blue eyes.

Gail didn't know what to do with her hands. First tightening them across her chest, she then dropped them to her sides before crossing them over her chest again. She felt like she was flying apart at the bombardment of emotions. She wanted to run to her sister, shouting with joy at seeing her again. Giggle together as they used to do as young girls. Cry with happiness at meeting someone from her family once again. Cry with fear at the repercussions this meeting might bring. Four years of facing life alone left her braced in front of the truck, rubbing her hands along her upper arms.

And Hannah, sweet Hannah, seemed to understand her dilemma. She rose to her feet. "You are looking well."

"Thanks. You, too," Gail replied stiffly.

They stared at each other a moment before Hannah nodded to Gail's jeans. "Are they as comfortable as everyone says?"

For the first time since she'd seen the buggy in the yard, Gail had the urge to smile. "Hotter in the summertime than a dress, but easier to get around in for some things."

"I always envied our *brieder* for their ability to wear pants when we did chores in the wintertime. I wonder if they envied me for being able to wear dresses in the heat of the summer."

Now Gail's numb lips did stretch into a smile. "I doubt it. They were probably thinking instead about escaping to the pond to go swimming." Her smile ebbed and she drew a ragged breath. "How are they? How are *Mamm* and *Daed*?"

"All well. Our *brieder* have grown so much you'd hardly recognize them. Jonah is a few years into his *rumspringa*, with Josiah just about to start. *Mamm* and *Daed*—" Hannah paused and sighed. "They miss you. I missed you. I know why you didn't say goodbye. But it hurt them."

"I couldn't. If I had, I wouldn't have had the strength to go."

"I know." Hannah looked toward the barn before returning her eyes to Gail. "She's *wunderbar*. *Mamm* would be so thrilled to have a *kinskind*."

Gail nodded as her face crumbled. "I'm so sorry," she sobbed.

In two strides, they were in each other's arms, both laughing and crying simultaneously. Gail almost wept anew at the feel of being the center of someone's embrace. Of being supported instead of always being the support. She hadn't allowed herself to cry like this since years before when she was in Hannah's arms, sobbing after she'd heard Atlee and Louisa's betrothal announced at church and knowing that left her with child and alone. When Gail's ragged breathing steadied, she held her sister a moment more before grasping Hannah's forearms and stepping back.

"I've knocked your *kapp* awry. I've never seen you out without it being pinned perfectly."

"It's probably knocked askew because all the prayers I've prayed while wearing it have been answered. Well, most of them anyway."

Releasing Hannah's arms, Gail slid the back of her hand under her nose. Hannah linked her elbow with Gail's and led her into the shade at the side of the barn. "Our faces look about the same as the day you left. I watched you until I couldn't see you anymore. From what I'd heard in the community, no one saw you leave Miller's Creek. What happened?"

"I was so afraid that someone I knew would see me walking down the road. But after about a mile, a passing *Englisch* woman, fortunately not a neighbor, stopped. I told her some tale of going to visit my cousins in Indiana. She took me to the bus stop. From there, I got on a bus to Milwaukee."

"Why not Madison?"

"Too close. I knew Madison would be too tempting to come home and relatively easy to get a ride from there when things got hard." Gail paused a moment, remembering how hard things had gotten. Even being very careful, she'd quickly burned through her meager savings from part-time jobs working at a vegetable stand and waitressing at the Dew Drop restaurant. She blinked away the memory. That was in the past. If they didn't lose the truck and trailer, she and Lily would survive. Somehow.

"Anyway, being farther away was better. You said no one saw me leave?"

Hannah shook her head, but her smile faded.

"But things were said, weren't they?"

Hannah leaned back against the weathered white paint of the barn. "It's amazing how much talking about someone gets done when we all know gossiping is a sin."

Gail folded her arms across her chest and waited. It was what she'd expected, after all. She widened her eyes against tears that threatened over what her parents must have gone through after her abrupt and secretive departure. A bitter taste of remorse filled her mouth.

"*Ja*, there was talk. It hurt *Mamm* and *Daed*, but not as much as it hurt them having you gone. I hope that you'll see them and let them know you're all right?" Apparently interpreting Gail's set face, Hannah sighed softly. "I don't know what was going on with Ruby Weaver, but she wasn't very kind."

Gail snorted, remembering some of the things the bishop's wife had said to her. "That's her nature."

"I think hurt people hurt people."

Gail's lips twisted. The woman must be very pained indeed. A bit of it, she could understand. A large family was considered a great blessing to the Amish. Ruby Weaver only had one living son. Still, Gail recalled past situations in the community where questionable rules had been enforced that punished some while benefiting others. "Are all bishops like this?"

Hannah's brows furrowed before she shook her head. "I don't think so. Our leaders are chosen by lot. Some seem to handle the responsibility better than others. I correspond with someone in another district and she writes very highly of their bishop." Hannah hesitated a moment. "I heard…" Her voice trailed off and she glanced away.

When her *schweschder* didn't continue, Gail dropped her arms and took a step forward. "What? What is it? You're still as readable as a book, Hannah."

Meeting Gail's intent gaze, Hannah began again with obvious reluctance. "Bishop Weaver stopped by the farm shortly after you left. I was in the milk house, but I heard him telling *Daed* that if any gossip was spread about how Atlee might have…*treated* you, he would know where it started and would ensure our family regretted it."

Gail's fingernails cut into her palms as she clenched her fists. It was what she'd feared. "Any threat against her favored son would've come straight from Ruby. *Daed* and *Mamm* would never say anything, but they can't control how the community talks."

Hannah winced. "I keep expecting the Weavers to become more compassionate, but since Atlee died they seem to have only gotten worse."

Gail frowned. "What happened to Atlee and Louisa's *boppeli*? I know there was one, as Louisa was… more evident than I was when I left."

"I think the whole community knew she was with child. Ruby seemed as happy as anytime I've known her. The couple never made their public confessions of sin, but there were subtle signs of an accelerated wedding to accommodate the situation. I would imagine, given a choice, Ruby wouldn't have agreed. But other women of the community would have none of her son being the exception when Ruby had ensured over the years that any other expectant couples' weddings were somewhat slighted.

"As for the *boppeli*…" Hannah shook her head. "I don't know. Shortly after they got married, Louisa was ill and in the hospital. The community held fund-raising frolics to help pay the bills. There was no *boppeli*.

And there's been no *boppeli* in the two years she's been married to Atlee's older *bruder.*"

Gail sucked in a breath. No other *boppeli* meant Lily was the Weavers' only grandchild. It was worse than she thought.

She tried to distract herself with Hannah's last statement. It was news to Gail that Atlee's widow had married his older brother. She didn't know Jethro Weaver well. Several years older, although unmarried, he hadn't interacted with the *youngies* when she'd been in the community. Already baptized, he'd hung out with the married men. As opposed to his charismatic and outgoing younger *bruder,* Jethro had been quiet and withdrawn.

"You know how it goes. After a while something else comes up for people to talk about." Slanting a teasing smile at Gail, Hannah tipped her head toward the double doors of the barn. "He's created quite a stir in the community, at least for the young women. He and his *brieder.*"

Gail's gaze slid to where Samuel and Lily had disappeared a while ago. Her mouth firmed into a thin line. The reasons the women might be interested in the attractive Schrock *brieder* were obvious. But all Gail could think of was that the man had manipulated her via her daughter to come here today. Which made him untrustworthy. Just like the man who'd caused her to leave the community years ago.

"He's little! And fuzzy!" Lily pointed a finger to the spindly-legged foal peeking around her mother's tail at the back of the wooden stall.

"He's a she. A girl, which makes her a filly." Samuel steadied Lily from where she perched on the rail by the manger.

"I'm a girl. Am I a filly?"

"No, that's what a young girl horse is called."

"I'd like to be a horse."

Samuel touched a finger to her nose. "I'm not surprised, but you're *wunderbar* the way you are."

"Does she have a name?"

"Not yet. I've been trying to think of a special one."

"Can I name her? She could be Princess. Or Brownie."

"Those are both good names, but giving a special name takes time." He lifted her from the rail to set her down outside the stall. "You go home and think of some possibilities. We'll discuss them next time I see you."

"Okay," Lily agreed over her shoulder as she scampered over to get acquainted with the orange-and-white barn cat. As the cat was a friendly one, and Lily looked like she'd had some experience as a cat petter, Samuel rested his elbows on the stall's top rail, facing the barn's open double doors. No one was in view outside, but Ruth made her presence known beside him.

His sister-in-law stood with hands on her slender hips, bracketing her apron and the slight bump underneath it. "Now I know why you invited me here at this specific time and urged me to bring Hannah. I thought for a moment that you'd had the good sense to be interested in Hannah. I almost warned her off you, but I knew I didn't have to because Hannah has more sense than to be interested in you." Ruth's green eyes narrowed. "But it's not Hannah you're interested in, is it? It's her sister. Who's now *Englisch*. She didn't know about this little arrangement, did she?"

When Samuel silently shifted his stance in response, Ruth slid her hands off her hips and shook her head. "I don't know what your game plan was, but this might not end up quite the way you expected."

Samuel was thinking the same thing. From the look on Gail's face when she'd spotted Hannah accompanying him from the barn, he'd been surprised a plume of dust hadn't followed the speeding truck down his lane. It was far from the joyous reaction he'd anticipated.

He inhaled sharply as the sunlight through the door silhouetted two figures entering. As they were arm in arm, he took it as a good sign.

Lily noted her mother and, leaving the cat, ran to her. "Mommy! I saw a filly! It's a girl horse. I want to be one, but Samuel says I'm okay as I am."

Gail picked up her daughter and settled her on her hip. "That you are, sweetheart." She shot a look at Samuel. It wasn't nearly as friendly and welcoming. Neither was her tone of voice as she added, "We both are."

Samuel straightened from his slouch against the stall. He flinched when Ruth clapped her hands together a single time before striding over to mother and daughter.

"Lily, I have a girl horse, too. She's older, so she's called a mare. Her name is Bessie. She's a grouchy old girl, but would you like to meet her? And maybe sit in the buggy she pulls for me?"

Lily scrambled down from her mother's arms. "Yes. I like horses."

"*Gut.* And we'll take your new friend, Hannah, with us." With an Amish woman on either side of the little girl, they strolled out of the barn.

Never had Samuel appreciated his sister-in-law

more. He wanted to step closer to Gail, but her posture warned against it.

"You used my daughter to manipulate us into coming today. Did I ever give you any indication that I wanted to have more contact with the Amish community?" Apparently seeing the answer on his face, she continued, "I didn't think so."

Samuel drew in a deep breath. "I thought it would make you happy. I see how much you struggle. I see how hard it is parenting Lily without family and I wanted to help you, because I—because that's what we do in the Amish community."

"How did you know?"

He didn't ask what she meant. "I saw your name the other day and guessed from your reaction the day Ruth and Hannah came down the lane. Also, you're a very *gut* driver for just a few lessons." Samuel tried a teasing smile but scrapped it when he saw how Gail's hands were trembling.

"You should've asked me first."

"I figured Lily needed a family."

Gail went rigid at that. "Lily has me." She shook her head. "You don't understand what you've done."

"I wanted to help."

"You can help by paying attention to what I want for my daughter. When you do the exact opposite, it shows that you feel your opinion is above mine. I have no problem with that when it's in regard to your life, but when it's about mine, it's hurtful and shows a lack of respect for me. And also shows that I can't trust you with things that are important to me."

Gail wrapped her arms around herself, like she was cold in the summer heat of the barn. "It's probably a good thing, as I was beginning to trust you. Maybe you did me a favor. I needed a reminder not to let a man hurt me again. Or, worse, hurt Lily. This isn't some kind of flirtation, this is our lives. My world turned upside down when I learned I couldn't trust a man I was…" She stopped abruptly before going on hoarsely. "I can't trust you. I should have known better once I saw your handsome face."

Samuel was stung. This was far from the dulcet tones and flirtatious smiles he got when he did something to please a woman. "I was only trying to help."

"I don't need this kind of help." Spinning on her heel, Gail strode for the door.

Dropping his head back to stare at the weathered gray boards of the hayloft above, Samuel inhaled deeply. Why couldn't Gail understand that he'd done it for her? Her and Lily. When he looked toward the door again, she was gone. He kicked at a chunk of straw that'd dropped from a bale, creating a shower of golden stalks. The mare and foal watched him warily from the back of the stall.

Ach. Chagrined at himself, Samuel crooned to the pair until they settled down, forcing himself to do so, as well. *Ja*, he'd done it for Gail, but hadn't he done it for himself, as well? Because for reasons he couldn't explain, he wanted her to return to the Amish community. What if she wouldn't haul horses for him anymore? It was entirely possible. He grimaced. Although it would cut into the slim profits of his growing business, he could find someone else to transport his horses. But could Gail find hauls to replace the revenue she'd lose? He knew she needed the money.

Striding to the wall of the barn, Samuel grabbed the

pitchfork that hung there before he marched across the barn to muck out Jeb's and Huck's stalls. If that didn't take the edge off his righteous energy, he'd find another physical task to do. Farming was full of them. Good thing summer evenings were long because it would take a lot of daylight to work off his frustration.

Chapter Eleven

Samuel rubbed at the grime in the leather, his ears tuned in for the sound of a large engine coming down the road. Keeping harnesses in good shape took maintenance. But today the job was more for him to be occupied than for the leather to stay in condition.

He hoped she'd come. He hoped she'd taken the job. If she hadn't...

Thoughts of their conversation in the barn on Thursday afternoon had distracted him for the past few days. Initially hurt and affronted by Gail's reprimand, by Thursday night he'd been honest enough to acknowledge there'd been some truth in what she'd said. It'd been obvious by her reserved behavior that privacy was important to her. If she'd wanted to interact with Hannah, she certainly wouldn't have hidden herself behind sunglasses and a hat and slunk so far down behind the wheel that she was barely visible.

He'd been a fool. An arrogant fool to think he knew better than what Gail obviously wanted. And it cost him what he was realizing that he wanted.

By Friday morning Samuel was thinking of ways to

apologize to Gail, or at least ascertain that they could still do business together if nothing else. Calling her would've been fruitless—it would be too easy for her to ignore. He knew she lived somewhere reasonably close, but he didn't know where. He thought about asking Hannah if she knew, but as he'd already muddied that up, he thought better of it.

Which was why this morning he'd gone to an auction. He'd approached Malachi and Gideon with the need for more draft horses for their two farms. Jeb and Huck were eager and hardworking, but the farms were more than the two Belgians could handle alone. In fact, it was past time to increase their horsepower, as they'd had to borrow horses already for some of the work. And if the two geldings he bought today were on the far reaches of their community, far enough out that the new purchases would need to be hauled home, well, he knew a good buy when he saw it. He was a horse trader, after all.

He'd paid in advance for the transportation, arranging that the auction barn would contact a hauler, specifically Gail, to deliver the animals. Samuel only hoped that she took the job. If she transported the horses, maybe it was a sign she'd forgiven him. Surely Gail still had enough Amish in her to practice the principle of forgiveness? Or maybe she'd take the job because she really needed the money. Hate him she might, but she was a practical woman. Either way, he could see her and apologize.

Samuel jerked his head toward the barn door at the rumble of a motor and the muted rattle of a trailer under a heavy load. Dropping the leather on the counter as he strode out of the tack room toward the barn's double doors, he willed it to be a black pickup coming up the lane, even if its brown-haired driver refused to talk with him.

His shoulders sagged in relief at the sight of the familiar rig pulling into the farmyard. Through the windshield he could see Gail's composed face. It revealed no trace of their emotional conversation. Circling the yard, she backed the rear of the trailer toward the barn doors. Clanks rang through the trailer as his new purchases stomped their bucket-sized feet.

When the trailer stopped, Samuel went to work opening the gate, all senses on alert should Gail come into view. Would she stay in the truck and leave him to unload the Belgians by himself? It was entirely possible.

She didn't.

"I don't suppose Mr. Klopfenstein just happened to have my name and number." When Samuel swung open the gate, Gail stepped inside to untie the first gelding from the trailer's modified setup to handle the oversize passengers.

"It's possible. You worked with Elam and have a growing reputation." Samuel held the gate wide to avoid a repeat of last week. Draft horses were normally gentle, but they were huge. It was difficult for anyone to handle a ton of excited animal and he didn't know the personalities of these geldings.

"Possible, but not probable. Where do you want this big fella?"

"Going to let them settle down outside." When Gail cleared the back of the trailer, Samuel strode over to open a gate along the white fence that lined the pen next to the barn. He'd already moved Jeb and Huck to a lot behind the barn until he had a chance to get everyone acquainted.

While she was leading the first gelding through the gate, he returned to the trailer to get the second. Once they were both inside the pasture, Samuel closed the gate. His charge had his head and tail up, looking around his new home. The gelding was so tall the top of Samuel's hat just barely reached the Belgian's throat-latch, where the horse's head joined its neck. Samuel looked over to see Gail's arm fully extended as she held her horse.

"Go ahead and release him," Samuel directed as he freed his own. The Belgian swung away to trot across the pasture, quickly joined by the other gelding. Drawing in a long breath, Samuel waited while Gail walked toward him. Now that they didn't have four thousand pounds of horseflesh between them, it was time to apologize.

"They're magnificent, aren't they?" Her eyes were on the giant chestnuts trotting along the far fence.

Samuel watched the horses' excited explorations, as well. "I think so."

"You did it again, you know." When he returned his attention to Gail, she was still looking at the Belgians. He couldn't read anything from her expression.

"You manipulated me to do what you wanted."

Samuel closed his eyes and leaned back against the fence as the realization stabbed through him. "*Ach*, you're right. I'm sorry. I wanted to see you and I didn't know if you would want the same. And I thought the money from the haul would help."

"It does. But I'm trying to figure out if the right

action for the wrong reason makes the action right or wrong."

Samuel opened his eyes, awaiting his judgment. "Which way are you leaning?"

With a sigh, Gail turned to meet his gaze. "Although you should've figured out that I'd have contacted my family if I'd have wanted to, I didn't tell you that I specifically was trying to avoid them. So I guess I have to give you another chance." Her lips hooked in a self-mocking smile. "Besides, I need your business and your money."

Relaxing more heavily against the fence, Samuel sighed, as well. "I'm glad." He returned her smile. "And likewise, in reverse." Exceedingly relieved that she had a forgiving nature, he studied her face a moment. She seemed calm. Maybe it was safe to ask. "Why?"

She didn't answer for a while. The way she perused him in return, Samuel knew she was trying to determine if giving him another chance meant trusting him, as well. When she finally did speak, Gail didn't try to prevaricate. "Why didn't I want to see them? Partly because I'm ashamed. I made a mistake. A big one. Partly a bit of fear that they'll resent Lily. What if they won't accept her? She's my daughter. I'll fight like a… Well, Amish might be a nonviolent society, but mamas still will protect their babies." Gail smiled without mirth. "But mostly because I knew it'd be too hard to continue to stay away once I'd contacted them. I feared it'd create the little crack in the dam that eventually brings the whole barrier down."

He furrowed his brow. "If you want to come home, why do you have to stay away in the *Englisch* world?"

"Because if I come back, I might lose Lily."

Samuel abruptly straightened from the fence. "What? Why?"

Gail shook her head as she regarded him. "How many unwed Amish mothers do you see in the community?"

Blinking, Samuel searched his memory for the various community members he'd met or heard about since they'd arrived. The only single mothers he could come up with were widows. He didn't say anything. The Amish were a forgiving society, but there were certain expectations regarding behavior.

"Exactly." Gail read his face. "I think the community would accept them, or some would at least." Gail crossed her arms in front of her. "But probably not in my case." Her eyes were fixed on the geldings. Having explored the perimeters of the pasture, they were settling down to graze. "I don't know why I'm telling you this. Probably because I'm so...tired of not talking with someone. Tired of running away. And you made me face the past."

She glanced at Samuel before returning her attention to the horses. "I was a fool when I began my *rumspringa*. I wanted to find *Gott*'s chosen one for me. But I was too *hochmut* to let Him do the choosing. I never gave Him a chance. I went for the good-looking, sweet-talking fellow who paid attention to me." She slanted Samuel a droll look. He returned it with a wince and a crooked smile as he recognized himself.

"I'd heard things about him that weren't...flattering. But to me, he was. Very much so. He told me everything an awkward girl with a beautiful older sister wanted to hear. I thought that meant he cared for me. He might not have been *Gott*'s, but he was my chosen one. And so I…did things I shouldn't have." Gail looked back at the grazing horses.

"A short while later I discovered I was with child." She shook her head. "I was so excited. I was going to tell Atlee after church that Sunday, figuring it meant we would get married soon. Before I had a chance to, the deacon announced that Atlee was betrothed. To the girl he'd been walking out with before he turned his eye to me." Gail snorted. "I barely made it out of the Zooks' barn before I was ill."

Again, Samuel searched his memory, this time with a twinge of something—surely not jealousy—for an Atlee among the young men he knew in the community. He came up blank. But he'd heard the name. Narrowing his eyes, he tried to recall where and when it'd been mentioned. He inhaled deeply when it came to him. "The bishop's son who fell during a barn-raising?"

Grimacing, Gail nodded. "Yes. I heard about his fall from Elam."

"The bishop's son," Samuel repeated flatly.

"Do you know Bishop Weaver and his wife, Ruby?"

"Haven't met his wife. Met the bishop a time or two. He was the one who wouldn't let Ruth keep her *daed*'s furniture shop, which is what brought us to Miller's Creek. After which, Malachi and Ruth met and ended up getting married. I guess that makes the bishop something of a matchmaker." The last was said tonelessly. Samuel felt like he'd taken a blow to the stomach. It was one thing to know Gail had a daughter. It was another to hear her tell of falling for another man. And how he'd treated her. The bishop's son.

A bishop, by enforcing the *Ordnung*, held considerable influence over a community. Some were fair and rational; some not so much. Bishop Weaver fell more into the latter category. Although Amish chose to live life a certain way to be closer to *Gott*, they were still humans. Humans who sometimes let power and control go to their heads. He was beginning to see Gail's dilemma.

Gail couldn't imagine the stern bishop as a matchmaker. As for the bishop's wife, well, the prospect was impossible. She'd done a lot of thinking in the past few days. Seeing Hannah had made her realize she'd never be whole or happy without some of her family in her life. If she wasn't whole, how could she be the mother that Lily needed? What was she doing to her daughter to narrow her life so? Could she see her family and still avoid the bishop's wife?

"I guess that was the silver lining for me. Not having them as in-laws." A mother-in-law who'd thought of her as the worst sort of jezebel. Gail didn't know what Ruby Weaver had seen or been told of their secret rendezvous, but the thought of how foolish she'd been in her infatuation for the older and charming Atlee made her flush with shame. Her remorse was quickly followed by a flash of anger that Ruby had thought less of Gail's family, even going so far as to threaten them when her son was at least partially at fault.

"So when my…situation was getting too much to hide, I left."

"I understand it would be difficult, but why would you lose Lily if you returned?"

"The Amish society is based on *gelassenheit*. Yielding oneself to a higher authority. The welfare of the community is more important than individual rights

and choices." Gail's mouth twisted as Samuel acknowledged what she said with a nod. "I know the bishop
and his wife would ensure it deemed necessary in the
community for Lily to be raised by a two-parent family instead of a single mother, especially one who's
been *Englisch* for some years. And from what I learned
from Hannah, I even know who the family would be.
Jethro Weaver and his wife are childless. This way,
Ruby could manipulate things so she'd end up with her
own grandchild without everyone knowing of Atlee's
and my shame." Gail rolled in her lips to keep them
from trembling.

"Not your shame." Samuel's words were adamant,
and opposite of the compassionate look he gave her.

Now Gail's chin trembled, as well. "I thought he
loved me. I was such a weak fool."

"You were young. He shouldn't have done what
he did." Reaching out a finger, Samuel tipped up her
chin. "You are an incredibly strong woman." When he
opened his arms, it was the most natural movement in
the world to be gathered into his warmth and strength.

Leaning her head against his chest, Gail relaxed for
what felt like the first time in over four years. She didn't
know if she fully trusted Samuel, but at the moment,
she needed him.

She'd wanted to stay angry with him. But she
couldn't. He was right. It'd been too good to see Hannah again.

When today's haul opportunity arose, she'd known
it wasn't an accident. That Samuel was behind it. Yes,
she'd needed the money, but just as much, she'd wanted
to see him again.

"I can understand why she wants a grandchild." Gail

spoke into the center of his shirt. She didn't know if he could even hear her. "But I'm not giving up my daughter."

Samuel's arms tightened around her. "She won't get Lily."

Tears prickled at the backs of Gail's eyes at his flat statement. She'd spent years without anyone in her corner. She'd been afraid that if she told Samuel of her history, it would drive him away, but the opposite seemed to be true. The notion gave her courage to bring up something else that'd been troubling her for the past few days.

"Speaking of a *grossmammi*, Hannah thinks I should bring Lily to meet my parents. Or at least come and see them myself. So they know I'm all right."

She felt his chest rise under her cheek as he took a deep breath. "What do *you* want to do?"

Gail closed her eyes and just let herself be held against the steady beat of his heart for a moment. She wanted to do what she'd always wanted to do. Be with her family. But should she? What of the repercussions to her and Lily if she opened that door? Once would not be enough. She took strength again in his supportive statement.

"I want to introduce Lily to my family. But I'm scared. It's been so long. I didn't tell them I was leaving. It would've been too hard to go, then." Gail leaned back in his arms. His blue eyes, usually so flirtatious, were solemn when they met hers. "What if they don't want to see me?"

"They will." When she nodded hesitantly, mutely, his customary glint returned. "Abigail, huh?"

Gail's lips twitched. "I want you to go with me."

"What?"

"I want you to go with Lily and me when we see my folks. Another person around to dispel the awkwardness in case it doesn't work out."

"I'm not family."

"But you got me into this. So you're going to be there." When Gail stepped back, Samuel loosened his embrace, but didn't fully release her, sliding his hands down her arms to cup her elbows. Gail relished the continued connection.

Samuel's gaze flicked out into the pasture, where he watched the Belgians for a moment before returning to her. She saw his throat work as he swallowed. "All right."

Later, in the truck driving home, Gail knew Samuel could be trusted to be there. But could she trust the feelings she was beginning to have for him? Could she trust her ability to protect Lily if something went wrong? She was barely keeping a roof over their heads now as it was. But the door to home had been opened and she couldn't resist peeking through it.

Chapter Twelve

Samuel knew he was nervous when Belle stopped fighting him and started flicking her ears back toward him in confusion. Usually the mare was high-strung enough for both of them, but today she was surprisingly calm, or at least confused by the tension that ran down the lines from his hands to her mouth. Samuel didn't know if he wanted Belle to keep up her ground-eating stride and arrive sooner in case Gail needed him the moment she pulled into the Lapp farm, or slow her trot, delaying his arrival until after the emotional gathering. After their conversation the previous day, he was almost as anxious about the reunion as she was.

How would the Lapps take his presence? It wasn't like he and Gail had an understanding that might justify it. Samuel's pulse jumped at the thought. Previously, anytime a girl he was seeing mentioned commitment, or broadcasted that they were together, he went out of his way to ensure they no longer were.

Fingering Belle's reins, he searched for any temptation to flee. And was surprised to find none. More surprised to discover that he was glad to be there for

Gail and Lily. To take his cues from Gail. If she needed him to forestall an ugly situation, he was ready to step in. If she needed him to give her an excuse to leave promptly, he'd provide that, as well.

Gail wanted to arrive during milking time. Before she left yesterday, she'd said she felt more comfortable showing up when her family would be distracted by chores, hoping they'd be less likely to make a fuss. Samuel had questioned her strategy. He figured it would take a lot to distract parents from the return of a prodigal daughter, with her own daughter in tow. *Ach*, well. If needed, the fatted calf could conceivably be nearby.

Surely they would feel like celebrating? He didn't know Willa Lapp, and her husband not much better, but if Willa was anything like Hannah or Gail, she'd at least be reasonable, if not pleasant. As was Zebulun Lapp, Gail's *daed*. Reining Belle into the Lapps' lane, Samuel's stomach lurched at the possibility that Gail's family would give her a poor reception. If they did, it would be his fault for pushing her back into a situation she'd wanted to avoid. He admired her bravery in facing uncertain circumstances. Continuing up the lane, he slowed Belle to a walk. No truck, with or without a trailer, was in the farmyard. He'd arrived first. Or she wasn't coming.

If she didn't, it was no more than he deserved for tangling up her life. After securing the reins and setting the brake, Samuel sat for a moment, his mouth dry at fears for Lily that Gail had revealed yesterday.

As it was Visiting Sunday, he'd been out visiting. While doing so, he'd subtly asked around. Gail's fears had merit. Bishop Weaver's wife was a force to be reckoned with. With the authority of her husband that she used as a tool, few succeeded in disputes with her. As Amish, any disputes should be few and far between, but they were still people with human weaknesses. Samuel had been told of a disturbing number of situations where Bishop Weaver had subverted members' personal needs for the needs of the community. Needs of the community that seemed to benefit some—usually those close to the bishop—more than others.

If Gail lost Lily because of something he'd inadvertently set in motion… Samuel clenched his hands. He didn't know what he'd do. He thought he'd been helping her reunite with a family she obviously missed and needed. Blowing out a tense breath, Samuel stepped from the buggy. He was getting ahead of himself. No use borrowing trouble. But if it came to that, he'd do everything in his power to prevent the situation. In the meantime, he was a horse trader, so he'd go inquire if a farmer was interested in a horse.

After tying Belle to the hitching post, Samuel entered the barn through the milk house. Whereas he only kept one cow for personal use and some surplus to sell, the Lapps milked several, selling the milk to the local cheese factory. Rows of clean milk cans lined the wall in preparation for use. The truck must've picked up today as there were no full cans cooling in the enclosure. Samuel carefully stepped across the pristinely scrubbed floor into the attached barn.

"Hallo?" Samuel lifted his voice to be heard in the cavernous structure. Visiting between farms was a common occurrence in the Amish community.

"Ja?" The response came from farther down a long alleyway. On his way to it, Samuel passed several stalls of Belgians, recently fed. Although tempted to linger

with the gentle giants, he recognized it as a delaying tactic and continued on until he stepped into the milking parlor.

Twelve black-and-white cows were in stanchions contentedly munching hay, six on one side of a center alley, six on the other. They paid him no attention, but the older man, older woman and teenage boy crouched beside the cows as they hand milked looked up as he came in.

"Samuel Schrock. *Wie bischt du?*"

"It's going well. I came to see how your family was doing." Despite his hearty greeting, Samuel's palms were sweaty. He slid them down his pants before he stepped farther into the alley.

"Bin gut." Zebulun Lapp responded without breaking rhythm on the hiss of milk filling the stainless-steel pail.

Samuel hoped it stayed that way when the man experienced the shock of a returning daughter and grandchild. "Saw Hannah the other day. She mentioned one of your horses was getting a bit long in the tooth." It was a bit of a stretch, but it provided him a reason for stopping by. "I was wondering if you might be in the market for another Standardbred and what you'd be looking for, so I could keep an eye out for it."

It was quiet except for the hissing of milk and a few stomps of the cows as Zebulun considered his question. Samuel took the moment to nod at Willa Lapp and one of Gail's younger *brieder*. It was when he'd really looked at Willa last Sunday at church that he'd known Gail was a missing part of the family. She was a brunette replica of her blonde *mamm*.

"*Ja.* I suppose it's time to think about using Daisy more for the shorter trips. What have you been seeing?"

I've been seeing members of your family and soon so will you if the childish voice I hear from the direction of the milk barn is who I think it is.

"This isn't Samuel's house. Why are we here, Mommy?" Lily chirped from the backseat as she looked out the window at the pristine farmyard.

That was a good question. Gail pressed a hand to her stomach as she unbuckled her seat belt. Why were they there? They almost weren't. Even now, parked in the yard, she considered starting up the truck again. But she didn't. She'd run away four years ago. And she was getting tired of running.

"Is this another Amiss place?"

Gail could hear Lily shifting in the backseat. Any minute now she'd work her magic and be free of the car seat. Heart pounding in her throat, Gail opened the door and slid from the truck. At least Samuel was here as she'd requested. If she hadn't seen his mare tied to the hitching post, she might not have pulled in. But she was learning that, unlike a previous charming Amish man she'd known, Samuel was a man of his word.

When she opened the back door of the truck, Lily was slipping her arms from the straps. Gail reached in and lifted her down. "Yes, sweetie. This is another Amish place. This is the first Amish place Mommy ever saw." She inhaled deeply. "And we're going to go see some people Mommy knew a long time ago. Before you were born."

No one came out of the house, which was a relief. Just before they reached the door that Gail knew led to the milk barn, it swung open. Hannah stood at the opening, her smile as broad as the door she was standing in.

"I came out of the house when I saw Samuel go into the barn. I was hoping you'd come." Tears welled in her blue eyes. *"Denki."* She stepped forward to engulf them both in a hug.

The tension around Gail's neck and shoulders loosened. Oh, she'd missed this. She'd missed family. She'd missed home. Maybe finally coming here was the right thing, after all. But what would it lead to?

"It smells funny in here. Why does it smell funny in here?"

The two sisters leaned back with watery chuckles at Lily's insistent questions. Lifting Lily into her arms, Gail stepped over the high threshold and into the dimmer light of the barn.

"There's lots of different smells in a barn, sweetie."

"Samuel's barn doesn't smell like this."

Gail had to admit that a milk house had its own unique aroma. "This room stores fresh milk, which does smell different when there's a lot of it together. Also, they work hard to keep this room very clean, so the milk stays clean. It's a mix of a lot of different smells rolled into one special smell."

Lily took an exaggerated sniff. "I don't like it. I like Samuel's barn better."

Hannah laughed. "It does take some getting used to." She let the door swing shut behind them. Her eyes met Gail's. The look in them told Gail that she could do this. Gail figured the message was sent because stark fear was probably reflected in hers.

They walked down the alleyway of the barn, with

Lily commenting on everything. She wanted to stop and pet every horse they passed. Gail let Hannah respond to her daughter's chatter while keeping them moving.

As for herself, she was sensitive to the rattle of stanchions ahead, knowing that her folks were in the milk parlor a few yards away. Her stomach was sick with tension as she walked down the familiar passage. *Don't expect much. Even if they're glad to see you, Amish aren't physically demonstrative people. So if no one approaches, or gives you more than a nod, it's still good. If they reject you, or Lily, just say you were looking for Samuel about a transportation job. You can offhandedly apologize for the shame you brought upon them as you leave.* Although she knew an offhand apology would nowhere near absolve her of the guilt she felt for what she'd done and how she'd left.

So much for a quiet approach. Thanks to Lily's jabbering, when they stepped into the milk parlor, they had the full attention of everyone there.

Throat tight, Gail's glance swept the familiar scene. She'd come to the milk parlor since she was able to walk, probably earlier, before stopping abruptly four years ago. Ignoring the cows and surroundings, her gaze lingered on the people. She almost didn't recognize her *bruder*. Surely that wasn't Paul? Her heart swelled when she saw her *daed*. But it was the sight of her *mamm* that caused the tears to well in her eyes.

"Mommy, you're holding me too tight!"

Her mouth open and her face as white as the cow beside her, Willa Lapp lunged to her feet. She stood immobile for a moment before stumbling from the Holstein's side toward them, kicking over a full pail in the process. Just for an instant, Gail's gaze followed the milk as it poured down the gutter before she hastened toward her mother and was enfolded in a tight embrace.

Tears rolled down Gail's cheeks as she inhaled the fresh scent of her *mamm*'s dried-on-the-line dress that, up close, overruled the cattle aroma of the milking parlor. All too soon, her nose was stuffed from her crying. But it felt right when she felt her mother's tears against her neck, as well. She tightened her arm about her *mamm*'s lean, work-hardened frame.

"Too tight! Too tight!" Gail could feel Lily wiggling between them. Sniffing, she leaned back and self-consciously swiped at her nose. Her tears continued to roll down her cheeks at the strong grip Willa Lapp had of her shoulders, like she was never going to let her go.

"You came back." It was barely a whisper. "Oh, I missed you so."

Gail nodded. "I am so, so sorry." Through blurred vision, she saw that her *daed* had stepped up beside her *mamm*. Placing a hand on her *mamm*'s back, he scrutinized Gail's face. After a moment a slight smile curved his lips. Knowing her taciturn father, for Gail, it was like the sun breaking through after a heavy thunderstorm.

"*Welkom* home, *dochder*."

Tears sprang anew at the warm weight of her *daed*'s hand on her back.

"I knocked over the bucket." Her *mamm* sniffed self-consciously.

"*Ach*, Willa, no use crying over spilled milk."

After they all chuckled over the joke, her *mamm* reached up to gently touch Gail's face. "*Nee, nee*, there isn't. We're so glad you're back."

Gail swallowed. She couldn't tell them right now it was only temporary. "Me, too."

Willa turned her attention to Lily, who clung, round-eyed, to Gail. "And who is this?"

Gail inhaled a shuddering breath as she tightened her arms protectively around Lily. "This is my *dochder*, Lily." Seeing nothing other than wonder in her parents' eyes, Gail continued hoarsely on the words she'd figured never to be able to say. "Lily, this is your *gross-mammi* and *grossdaadi*."

Willa silently pressed her fingers to her mouth as she blinked back tears. Zebulun's hand moved up to tighten on his wife's shoulder. Gail could see her *bruder* Paul in the background, quietly nodding his head. What was he, fourteen now? Oh, he'd gotten so tall.

"Are these my Amiss, too?"

Gail bit her trembling lip before she could respond. "Yes, sweetie. These are your Amish, too. They're very special. This is Mommy's mommy and daddy."

"You wear a hat like Samuel. He let me wear his hat."

Gail caught her breath when her reserved father lifted his straw hat from his head, leaving an indented ring in his gray-brown bowl-cut hair. "Would you like to wear my hat?" With a smile and an eager nod, Lily slid down from Gail's arms and reached for it. "I like horses. Could you show me your big horses?"

Zebulun's mouth tipped up at the corners. "*Ja, ja*, I can do that." Careful to give the little girl space, he reached for his wife's hand. "Come, *grossmammi*." Keeping one hand on the oversize hat to secure it to her head, Lily reached out with the other to grasp a few fingers of Zebulun's free hand. Gail heard her mother gasp softly at the action. The trio headed back toward the draft horses' stalls, Lily already chattering with excitement about the barn, cows and big, big horses. When they passed Hannah, standing at the end of the alley, she sent a grateful smile to Gail and turned to join them.

Gail watched the group pass the last stanchioned Holstein and leave the milking parlor. She'd never seen her parents stop in the middle of doing chores. Slack-jawed, she turned to find Samuel's eyes on her.

"Better go with them." He winked and nodded to the exit behind her. "They're new at this." He clamped his hand on Paul's shoulder. "I suppose that makes you an *onkel*. Better get in there in case they're setting up the rules of these new relationships."

Paul stepped forward without hesitation. Reaching out, he awkwardly patted Gail's shoulder as he passed. Gail lingered a moment longer, her gaze on Samuel. "Thank you," she mouthed, not even having any air in her tight chest to vocalize the words. "*Denki*. For giving me my family back."

"Go catch up," he encouraged. "Or they'll be so enthralled by Lily they won't even know you're here." With a wobbly smile, Gail hurried to join her family.

When they returned to the parlor later, after having met all the farm's horses, the chickens, the rest of the cows, the fattening hogs and the two Border collies, Samuel was finishing milking the last Holstein.

"Samuel Schrock, you didn't need to do that."

"*Ach*, no problem, Zebulun. I've milked a few cows before. And you were busy."

Nodding, Zebulun glanced at Gail and Lily before

returning a speculative gaze at Samuel. One Samuel apparently read as well as Gail did.

"And speaking of milking, I have chores of my own." With a wave and a single nod himself, Samuel headed down the milking parlor toward the alleyway that led out of the barn, hesitating only briefly when Lily called out to him.

"Bye, my Amiss man!"

He turned to walk a few steps backward. "Bye, Lily." Then he was out of sight.

But not out of mind.

He'd made this possible. He'd done what Gail had thought impossible. She'd been reunited with her family. And it was *gut*. Very *gut*. For a moment longer her thought was on the man and not the family that now surrounded her. *Oh, Samuel. If she wasn't careful, a girl could so easily fall in love with you.*

Chapter Thirteen

The sun was already inching up the sky in front of them. It was a little later than normal when Gail picked Samuel up that Thursday. Extremely aware of his presence on the other side of the truck's worn seat, Gail wondered if the days since she'd last seen him had seemed as long to him as they had to her.

Sunday had been *wunderbar*. She and Lily had stayed long into the evening, past Lily's bedtime, in fact. Her other three brothers had returned from visiting friends and joined them. They laughed at supper, talking of things they'd done as a family when Gail was still there. When her *brieder* had teased Gail that she'd surely forgotten how to drive a horse and buggy, she'd reminded them that she drove more horsepower than they did every day.

Everyone had fawned over Lily. Gail figured her daughter had more piggyback rides with her new *onkels* than the drivers at the track had harness races during the season.

Although Willa Lapp had worn a smile all evening, Gail caught a few gazes where, although joy was at the forefront in her *mamm*'s eyes, apprehension framed the backdrop. Willa didn't look surprised when, at a quiet moment while doing dishes, Gail told her that their return wasn't the beginning of something permanent and added that the visit needed to be kept quiet. Although Gail didn't elaborate, it seemed her *mamm* had an inkling as to the reason why, when her gaze drifted to Lily, who was sitting on Hannah's lap, trying to darn her first sock.

It was a teary farewell when everyone followed them out to the truck to say goodbye. But Gail's heart was full that the whole thing had come about in the first place.

Because of the man beside her.

Thanks to him, her business had picked up, as well. Samuel's request to use her for his purchases at the auction barn had led to other jobs from there. In fact, if business stayed at this level through the fall, she'd be able to catch up on the truck and trailer payments. She'd received a letter from the bank, reminding her of missed payments and laying out consequences if she missed another. The additional revenue would definitely help in catching up. *Gott* was answering prayers she'd been too ashamed to voice.

And using a surprising person to do it.

While she'd enjoyed working with Elam Chupp, Samuel was proving much more dynamic with the Amish horse business. It was obvious he loved what he was doing. Just in the few hauls she'd already made related to the auction barn, she'd heard his name mentioned a few times. Always positively. Behind her sunglasses, Gail slid a glance over to her companion, taking in his broad shoulders under the black suspenders and his perfect profile under the flat-brimmed hat. Unseen was the surprising strength of character the attractive exterior contained. Gail hid a sigh in the wind rushing through the open window. She could understand. He was having a pretty positive impact on her, too.

Her attention focused on the four-lane highway in front of her, Gail debated dropping her right hand to drape it on the armrest between the seats. Just in case Samuel might notice and take it in his work-hardened one that rested close by. Her folks had held hands that night in the barn. The memory of that simple connection with another filled Gail with a contrary mix of joy and longing.

She was relaxing her grip on the steering wheel when she saw a vehicle approaching the upcoming rural intersection from the oncoming lanes. The green SUV didn't even pause as it turned left at the intersection. Pulling right in front of Gail, it straddled her two lanes.

The driver must have realized what they'd done. For a split second, the SUV hesitated. Gail knew in an instant they were going to collide.

Banging the horn, Gail slammed the brakes. Her heart froze at the sight of a child's face in the front passenger seat, directly in her path. She heard Samuel's sharp gasp just before the harsh squeal of the SUV tires accelerating joined the screech of the truck and trailer brakes.

It wasn't going to be enough. Aware the lane beside her was empty, Gail jerked the wheel, steering the truck to the left. Skidding through the lane, they barreled into the intersection.

Gail's knuckles were white on the wheel. The foot

not on the brake was braced against the floorboard, her leg stiff as iron. There was a blur of red out the open window as they shot past the stop sign. With a jolt, the truck hit the curb that marked the edge of the intersection. The cab shuddered and a chilling rasp echoed through it as they bucked over the curb, the racket of the trailer lurching over behind them. Gail's seat belt tightened as she slid toward the door at the slant of the median they now bounced along. Only when the truck—slowed by tall grass and soft soil along with her braking—lumbered to a halt, did she draw a breath.

"Are you all right?" Her shaking voice matched the tremors that raged through her system. Contrarily, her body felt almost too stiff to move.

The airbags hadn't deployed. Steadying herself on the steering wheel, Gail turned to see Samuel and sagged with relief. His right hand on the handgrip by the door, the other braced on the dash, he looked tense but okay. "*Ja.* You?"

"*Ja.*" She echoed his response automatically. Heart pounding, she struggled to release her rigid grip of the steering wheel. "I need to check the SUV. I saw a child in the front window. I was afraid I'd hit them. I was afraid I couldn't avoid hitting them." Gail was babbling, but she couldn't stop.

"But you didn't. Praise *Gott.*" Unlike hers, Samuel's hands were steady when he unbuckled first his seat belt and then hers. Flipping up the armrest between them, he slid down the slight decline caused by the truck's tilted position and pulled her into his arms. Gail didn't resist. She drew from his calm strength. A few moments passed while her tremors dissolved to sporadic shudders before she felt capable of pulling back.

Praise *Gott* indeed. For so many things. Praise Him that there wasn't anyone else at the intersection, that she'd known there was no one in the passing lane when the SUV pulled out. That there'd been no horses in the trailer, as they'd surely have been hurt.

They'd been blessed. Thank You, thank You, thank You, *Gott*. Now if only the other driver and child were safe, as well.

"I have to make sure they're all right."

"You okay getting out on that side?" At his question, they both looked out the windshield beyond the slanted dash. The incline the truck was parked on wasn't that steep. Not like fifty yards farther, where the median dropped into a deep ravine.

"I'll be okay." When she lifted the handle, the door swung hard and bounced on its hinges. Cautiously climbing out, Gail looked behind her to see the trailer jackknifed at an odd angle, tipped in the median so she could see the top of its sun-faded roof. Although her new tires seemed unaffected, at the front one's skewed appearance in the wheel well, Gail knew she wouldn't be as lucky with the axle. Her legs felt heavy as she waded through the knee-high vegetation and rounded the front of the pickup. The truck's grille had grass wedged in crevices and the front bumper tipped up like a curled lip, along with some other new scraps and dents. The aesthetic factors were the least of her worries. The truck wasn't going anywhere. Neither was her future at the moment. But more important now was the condition of the passengers in the green SUV parked on a subsidiary road.

Samuel joined her. Forcing a deep breath into still-tight lungs, Gail checked for traffic before crossing the pavement to the crossroad. The SUV's doors were open. A woman on a phone paced a continuous route between the two open doors on the driver's side.

"I pulled right out in front of the truck. I didn't even see it." The woman was talking in a high, rapid voice with someone. "Yes, yes, we're okay." The woman paused and propped herself against the open front door of the SUV. "We're all okay, but I'm still shaking." She turned toward Gail and Samuel's approach. "I have to go. The other driver is here. Yes…yes. I'm able to drive. I'll see you at home. I know. I love you, too." Beneath the woman's sunglasses, tears were streaming down her cheeks.

As she approached where the woman sagged against the door, Gail glanced into the open car. Her stomach lurched and she stumbled into Samuel, who caught her with a hand at her side. There was not only the child of around ten that she'd seen through the front window, but two smaller children in car seats in the back as well, one facing forward and one, still a baby, facing the back of the seat. The possibility that they might've all been injured had she not cleared the back of the SUV almost made Gail slump against the vehicle, as well.

Lifting her sunglasses to the top of her head, the woman straightened from the door. "Thank you. My husband owns a freight company and I—I know I'm not supposed to say anything that might admit guilt or something but…" She teared up again. "I can't thank you enough for missing my kids. I don't know what I would've done. I thought I'd looked but… Thank you." She sniffed loudly. "Are you okay?"

Gail could only nod. Her lips twisted at the question. Physically, yes, but not financially. "Are you? And the little ones?"

"Yes. Thanks to you." The woman looked over at Gail's rig, parked in the grass on the slanted side of the median. "How's your truck? And trailer? Any damage?"

Gail's gaze followed the woman's to where her now-broken financial future rested. "Yes, but I don't know the extent yet."

"I'll get you my contact number and insurance. Whatever's damaged, we'll get it fixed. Again, I can't thank you enough for missing my kids." Anything else the woman said was lost as she leaned into the SUV for the purse that rested on the console. While she was in there, the two older children chattered in high, excited voices.

Numbly, Gail turned and stared across the road to where Samuel had returned to the truck and trailer. The woman's insurance might cover the repairs, but how long would Gail be without them? She'd needed every job she could get to pay bills. Bile coated the back of her throat when she recalled how she'd been mentally paying bills with money she didn't have just a short time ago. Would she be able to recover from this loss of business while her rig was in the shop? Or get the jobs back that she'd lose in the meantime to someone else? Was the truck repairable?

Shakes now receded, Gail felt mentally and physically exhausted. Her breath left on a shuddering sigh. However she got home tonight, on the way there, she'd need to pick up a paper to check the help-wanted ads. The sooner she started on one, probably two, the better. Even then, her and Lily's financial outlook was dire.

But at the moment at least the children in the SUV were safe. She could live with that. As to the other, time would tell.

After she and the woman exchanged information, Gail crossed back to the median, where Samuel waited by the wheels of the trailer.

"I don't know," he responded to her questioning look. "On a buggy, I could see a problem. On this…" He shook his head. "Got some new dents, which probably isn't an issue for you, but something metallic smells hot, which probably is."

Gail mutely nodded. She'd smelled it, too. With unfeeling fingers, she punched in the phone number of the insurance company on her cell.

Hours later, hands braced on the counter of a repair shop that'd been recommended, Gail glanced at the clock. It seemed like forever but was only early afternoon when the repairman apologetically told her the bad news on the trailer. The truck was even worse and it would be late next week before parts were in and both were repaired. She'd told the shop to go ahead and fix it. She had no choice. Even if they were repossessed, they'd need to be repaired.

Mentally and physically sick, she stumbled from the counter to where Samuel stood at her approach in the small waiting area. "I'm so sorry. You wanted to go to the track. I can call and get someone else to take you. You might be able to salvage a bit of your trip."

"Don't worry about it. I've already had enough adventure today. I imagine that next week there'll still be a horse or two that has more of a future pulling a buggy than a racing bike." While she stuffed the paperwork into her purse, Gail felt his eyes on her. "What are you going to do?"

It was a good question. Gail really didn't know. First step would be to somehow get a ride. She needed to go home to Lily. She needed to hug her daughter. After that… She'd have no means of transportation in a small town. Not planning on using her high deductible insurance, she wasn't familiar with the options, and even less with the woman's insurance company.

Blinking back tears, Gail put a hand on her leg to stop its frenzied shaking.

"I'll call an *Englisch* driver. They can take us both back toward Miller's Creek."

"I couldn't let you do that," Gail automatically protested through numb lips.

"I'm going back anyway. I'm assuming you live somewhere in the same direction."

At the mention of Miller's Creek, the warm, comforting sensation of how she'd felt with her family washed through Gail. In its wake was emptiness at the thought of—with no transportation—being limited with Lily to their stark basement apartment. Yes, Miss Patty would welcome them to join her upstairs, but it would still be cramped for the three of them. In their small village, she'd be lucky to find any work. No buses ran in town. She couldn't reach another town without a vehicle. And they'd still have daily living expenses. With nothing to live on.

Gail closed her eyes, wishing for a place to just… be somewhat whole. When she opened them, Samuel was watching her. Even in the shade of his straw hat's brim, she could see the concern in his blue eyes. And she knew where she wanted to go.

"*Denki.* See if they would mind me picking up Lily before taking us to my folks' farm. I'll call the babysitter to let her know what's going on."

Samuel nodded solemnly, but Gail could tell he approved of her plans.

In a daze, Gail walked out of the repair shop and sat down on the curb to call Miss Patty. A week ago staying with her family would've been the furthest possibility in her mind. Now they were a sanctuary. But it could only be a temporary one. Her financial problems and the threat should a specific someone in the community learn of her daughter raged like dark thunderheads on the horizon.

Gail hoped she could weather the storm.

Chapter Fourteen

"**Y**ou always go for the border pieces."

Hannah pressed a blue puzzle piece into place. One the color of Samuel's eyes, Gail couldn't help thinking. Pushing a flat-edged piece in her sister's direction, she chided herself to get him out of her mind, where he seemed to have become a permanent fixture.

"Maybe it's because I like clearly defined boundaries." Hannah matched the edges on another two puzzle pieces before discarding one. "Maybe it's because they're the easiest to find. Or…" She smiled sweetly at Gail while she leaned down to run a hand over the head of the black-and-white dog lying on the floor beside her. "Maybe it's because it's related to my dogs."

Gail giggled at the absurdity as she nudged pieces around with a finger, trying to sort them by color, her go-to when working on puzzles. She couldn't remember the last time she'd allowed something so foolish to make her laugh.

Despite everything, it had been a *gut* day. Gail blinked in surprise at how quickly she'd reverted to thinking in Amish terms.

Her family had been surprised and delighted yesterday afternoon when the *Englisch* driver had dropped Lily and her off. After ascertaining that Gail was physically all right from her frightening experience, the Lapps assured Gail that she and Lily were welcome to stay. Gail made a point to tell them that it would only be for a few days. She wondered later if that was more to remind herself.

Except for the attention that everyone paid to Lily, it'd been as if Gail had never left. Used to early mornings, she'd risen with the rest of the family and helped her *mamm* and Hannah with breakfast. When Hannah left for her job at the quilt shop in town, Gail assisted her *mamm* with laundry. Her *brieder* had taken Lily to the barn with them for chores. It was hard to tell who was more excited for the adventure, her *dochder* or the new *onkels*. Taking pity on her as she apparently remembered Gail's love for the livestock, *Mamm* encouraged Gail to join them.

She'd relished all of it. The milking, the egg gathering, teasing her *brieder* during lunchtime, helping hitch up the Percherons to rake the mowed alfalfa and working with *Mamm* in the garden later in the afternoon with Lily hopping from plant to plant in wonder. Both she and Lily had flinched when their tender bare feet encountered rocks but being able to wiggle her toes in the tilled sun-warmed earth between the rows of vegetables had been worth it.

There were shadows over the visit, though. The first was why she and Lily were there.

After confirming her rig repair with the insurance company and the shop, Gail had turned her cell phone off, leaving it on the dresser of the bedroom she was sharing with Hannah and Lily. It saved the battery, as there was no way to charge it since the farm didn't have electricity. Shutting it down also severed, just briefly, her cares in the *Englisch* world. There was nothing she could do right now regarding finances with no transportation.

While she'd determined the woman's insurance did cover rentals, it had a dollar limit. The size of the truck she'd need to pull a trailer would be out of the allowance range. Before she'd shut the phone down, Gail had called her customers and told them she'd be unavailable for a while. She could only hope they'd still want her services when her rig was ready again. Following the last call, she'd sat on the bed in the quiet bedroom a moment until the nausea that churned in her stomach at her situation passed. Whether she lost some customers or not, and even with whatever part-time jobs she could pick up, she'd be late on another payment.

It took the reminder that *Gott* had taken care of her so far to get her off the bed. He said to be anxious for nothing and pray. He also said to consider the lilies that did not toil, but that Solomon in all his glory wasn't clothed, as well. Gail wasn't so much worried about clothing her own Lily. Keeping her fed and a roof over her head in the *Englisch* world and keeping custody of her *dochder* in the Amish one were what kept Gail up at night.

Which was the other shadow over their unanticipated stay.

Any buggy that went by or one that happened to turn into the lane was a risk that Ruby Weaver would find out Gail was back in the community. Back, unmarried and with a child of an age that could be connected to her involvement with the bishop's son. For the first few hours of the day, Gail had stiffened every time she'd heard a clip-clop of a horse going down the road.

But as the joy and comfort of having her family around her grew, her anxiety receded. Surely *Gott* wouldn't punish her that way for coming home? For this brief time with her family, Gail wanted to just... be. To recover some of the lighthearted girl she once was. To relax and enjoy what she and Lily might never have again. Surely *Gott* would allow that?

The silence in the gas-and lantern-lit room was broken when Dash, the male Border collie outside, barked. Woofing quietly, Socks got up from where she'd been curled at Hannah's feet and trotted over to the door. She woofed again, but her white-tipped tail wagged gently back and forth.

Gail glanced from the door to her *daed*, who was reading the Amish newspaper, *The Budget*, in his chair. She tensed; she couldn't help it. What if it was the bishop and his wife? Unclenching her fingers, she set a puzzle piece back on the table, glad that Lily, tired after an exciting day on the farm, was tucked up in a trundle bed upstairs.

Hannah calmly regarded her before selecting another flat-edged piece from those scattered in front of them. "Are you expecting company tonight, *Daed*?"

Zebulun Lapp looked toward the door over a drooping corner of his publication. *"Nee."*

With an unspoken glance at Gail, Hannah rose, crossed to the door and opened it.

When Samuel stepped through the door and bent to give Socks a pat, Gail exhaled softly in relief, her heartbeat accelerating. Firming her lips, she tried to keep a goofy smile off her face. After welcoming him in, Hannah returned to the table, leaving Samuel, hat in hand, to stand in the area between the kitchen and living room. His eyes widened when he saw Gail, making her realize this was the first time he'd seen her in Amish garb.

Zebulun let the paper sag a little farther as he regarded the new arrival. "I can only buy so many horses, Samuel Schrock."

To Gail's enchantment, Samuel flushed slightly. "I thought I might find out what Josiah was interested in. A young man wants his own rig when he comes into his *rumspringa.* I know Jonah already has one, but I've got a fast filly he might like to try."

"Jonah, Josiah and the two younger boys aren't here. They're at a baseball game."

Gail stifled a snort at the look her *daed* leveled over his reading glasses at Samuel. One that told their unexpected visitor that Samuel must've known very well there was a game and that was where most young men of the community would be.

Except, surprisingly, this one.

"*Ach*, I'm sorry I missed them. Perhaps I'll catch them at the barn-raising tomorrow."

"Perhaps you will. I'll tell them you stopped by." *Daed*'s gaze traveled from where Samuel stood to where Gail and Hannah were working on the puzzle at a side table. "In the meantime, I suppose, as you've traveled here for naught, one of my *dechder* could get you a glass of lemonade before you head back."

It was Gail's turn to flush, for when Samuel glanced toward the table, his eyes and smile settled only on her. "That would be much appreciated."

Gail bounced up, only because she couldn't sit still being the focus of his potent attention. "I'll get it. I'd like one, too," she chirped, conscious of Hannah's speculative smile. After retrieving two glasses from the cupboard, Gail pulled the pitcher of lemonade, ever present during the summer months, from the gas-powered refrigerator. She wasn't aware Hannah had moved from the table until she heard the slide of a chair on the linoleum behind her. Turning around, Gail found Hannah pulling a chair from the kitchen table over to the smaller one where they'd been working the puzzle.

"Have a seat." Nodding Samuel toward the third chair, Hannah settled back down in her own seat with a surprisingly sly look on her normally demure face.

Meeting his eyes, Gail handed the cool glass to Samuel. Her already rapid heartbeat escalated further when their fingers brushed in the exchange. Flustered, Gail scooted to the table, set down her own glass, slid into her chair and began sorting out all the pieces with flecks of red that she could find.

Samuel wandered over to the table and perused the thousand multicolored pieces scattered there. "What's it supposed to be?"

Hannah picked up the puzzle box cover propped against the wall beside her chair. The scene depicted a big red barn and milking shed with a stone foundation, ubiquitous to Wisconsin.

Samuel sat in the chair and eased it closer to the table. "You don't see enough of them in real life?"

"Not ones we get to put together."

"Anytime you want to crawl around on the rafters, let me know. I'll trade places with you."

Gail's hand jerked, knocking some puzzle pieces to

the floor at the reminder of how Atlee had died, in a fall during a barn-raising. By the time she'd heard of his fate, she'd long realized that she no longer loved him. In fact, she'd doubted that she ever had. Only that she'd been mesmerized by his attentive charm. Still, Atlee was Lily's *vadder* and his death was a tragic loss for his family and the community.

Leaning down, she collected herself and the scattered pieces. What'd happened to Atlee hadn't been her fault. Regardless of what Ruby Weaver might do should she find out about Lily, Gail wasn't going to allow that to dim what had been a *wunderbar* day back with her family. And what might turn out to be an interesting evening as well, with their unexpected guest. Returning to the table, she found herself the focus of its two other occupants. Dropping the pieces from her hand onto its surface, she rummaged through the bright-colored assortment until she found a potential match and checked the fit. Although close, they didn't work together.

"We can't do that."

Gail saw Samuel's smirk from the corner of her eye as she searched for another piece. She continued, "Because there's no way the men would be able to fix the beef, potatoes and enough shoofly and lemon drop pies to feed the hundred or so women working on the barn."

Rather than become upset, Samuel's smile blossomed into his signature full-fledged grin. "*Ach*, I suppose we could feed you fried or poached eggs. Gideon and I have been practicing the many, many ways there are to fix eggs. There are a few I can't recommend. But I doubt it would be necessary as a hundred women couldn't raise a barn."

Gail nodded as if in thought and frowned. "You're right. I'm sorry, I was wrong."

"Ja." Samuel's work-calloused fingers reached in to deftly pick up a piece and snap it in place. "I figured you'd discover that."

"It'd probably only take about eighty to get the job done."

Hannah's eyes were wide as she covered her mouth to smother a laugh. Gail's comeback had been a surprising statement for an Amish woman, but years making her own way in the *Englisch* world had made an impact on her. So had Samuel's presence. She felt lighthearted for the first time since she could remember. Lighthearted enough to flirt. Lighthearted enough to wonder if an attractive man's attention might be more than just a way of making conversation. She realized her world wouldn't topple over should she respond as an attracted young woman.

Because she was. Even if just for tonight it was safe to be so.

Samuel reached a hand over. For a moment Gail caught her breath, wondering if he was going to touch her. At the last second he dropped it to nudge a few puzzle pieces from the edge, back toward the center of the table. "Hmm. I might've had more luck playing baseball tonight."

"Do you play much?" From his physique, Gail figured he'd be very athletic on the ballfield.

"I'm usually very good at playing." Samuel took the puzzle piece she'd just set down and connected it with one of the stone foundation he was putting together before looking over at her. His expression told Gail he wasn't thinking of the same field she was.

A twinge reminded Gail that was what she feared with this man. He was exciting. He was attractive. But he was a much better player at this game than she was. And when she'd played before, she'd been the loser. Except for Lily. *But I'm wiser now.* Like the puzzle growing before them, she now knew the boundaries of where to stop the game. Didn't she? Gail looked into Samuel's smiling eyes. Suddenly dry-mouthed, she lifted her glass and took a hasty swallow of lemonade. Finding it much tarter than she'd expected, she started coughing.

"Are you all right, Abigail?" Hannah handed her a tissue for her watering eyes.

"*Ja*, Abigail. Are you all right?" Her given name on Samuel's lips sounded much different than when her *schweschder* said it.

Gail dabbed at her eyes. "*Ja, ja*. Too much, too fast." Like her attraction to Samuel. It was something she should take care to remember.

But that was difficult when sometime later he got up to leave. As twilight ran well into the evening and an Amish family's work began in the wee hours of the morning, Gail's *daed* had joined her *mamm* in retiring a while earlier. When Samuel stood, Hannah immediately got out of her chair, as well.

"Let me just clean up these glasses." She hurried them over to the sink.

Samuel looked at Gail. "Walk me out?"

Against her better judgment, Gail found herself nodding. A minute later she crossed the wide front porch and descended the steps, conscious of the man who walked a few inches from her. The hair on her forearm prickled. Crossing her arms in front of her to bring her senses back to good, predictable, unexcited behavior,

Gail winced when she poked the tender flesh under her arm on one of the straight pins that held the front of her dress together.

"You all right?" Samuel opened the white wooden gate for her to pass through.

"*Ja.* Just scratched myself on a pin. I'd forgotten about that aspect of Amish life." Gail tipped her head back to take in the uncountable stars cast over the dark sky above. "Wow," she murmured. "I'd forgotten this aspect, as well. With no yard light, streetlight or anything to dim their glow, the stars are just…" Her voice drifted off.

Samuel looked up, as well. "*Ja.* Hard to find the words to describe it in any of the languages we speak, isn't it? It's like a window into heaven."

It was an apt description. Side by side they silently looked up at the multitude of stars that streamed into infinity above them. Gail felt small with the beauty of *Gott*'s creation and the fact that she had a place in His world.

From the corner of her eye, she could see Samuel's chest rise in slow, steady breaths as he took in the vast spill of stars. What would it be like to have this man in her world?

Although the flirty Samuel was stimulating and fun, it was this sensitive Samuel that was drawing her in. She could guard herself against flirty Samuel, having been inoculated by Atlee's more clumsy charms.

Gail was very afraid she could fall in love with sensitive Samuel.

She studied his profile in the muted light of the starry night. The shadows couldn't disguise the strength of his jawline or obscure his equally powerful shoulders. This was a man with whom one could take shelter from life's storms. Or if not shelter, at least he would stand strong alongside, come what might.

But his world was not her world. Gail stepped back while she still could. Samuel's horse shook its head, the bridle jingling against a background chorus of cicadas, chirping crickets and frogs from the nearby pond. Needing to break the magic of this unsettling man in the quietly settling evening, Gail strolled over to the front of the hitching post where his mare was tied.

Reaching out a hand, she smoothed the horse's forelock over the bridle. The bay raised her head and twitched her ears back, but otherwise didn't react to the attention. "Why do you call her Belle?" He'd told her once the mare's official track name had been Sour Grapes.

Samuel followed Gail over and considered his horse before turning and leaning his elbows back on the hitching post. "All females deserve to be considered beautiful. Some are beautiful because of their disposition, some in spite of it."

"What's Belle?"

Hooking a corner of his lips in a wry smile, Samuel tipped his head toward the mare. "She's an *in spite of.*"

Gail smiled herself and mirrored his pose against the cross rail. A squeaking of leather heralded Belle's movement behind them.

"When did you go from Abigail to Gail?"

She sighed at the question. "When I left home, I guess. It was bad enough that I looked and acted like a lost and overwhelmed Amish girl. I couldn't change those factors right away, but I could change where my name shouted Amish, as well."

"I like your name. Both of them. But *Abigail* isn't a name made for shouting. It's more one made for whispering. Softly." When Samuel shifted to face her, it seemed like the space between them shrank more than the physical inches of his movement. "Abigail."

The whisper of her name on the quiet night sounded like a caress. But she recognized the transition to flirty Samuel. "Does this work on Rebecca, Lydia and Rachel?" She whispered back names of girls she'd grown up with, women who could still be single in the community, for all she knew.

"Pretty much. Although I've not tried it on Rachel, as I think she's walking out with Benjamin Raber's older *bruder*, Aaron." He didn't seem bothered that Gail had called him out on his flirtation. Samuel's grin faded to a smile as he straightened from the hitching post to stand in front of her. "I do like the name *Abigail*, though. May I call you that?"

Gail pondered his request through several heartbeats as she recalled the difficult transition from one name to the other. Studying his shadowed face, she hoarsely responded, "I'm not sure I'm her anymore. Abigail was more naive. Trusting. She thought she was smarter than she actually was. Braver, until she found out she wasn't."

"I think she was very brave. I have a lot of respect for Abigail. But I have a lot of admiration for Gail." His words drifted to her in a murmur as softly as he'd said Abigail.

She was confused. Was this the flirty Samuel or the sensitive one? Before she could decide, an abrupt shove between her shoulder blades, accompanied by the jangle of Belle's bridle, sent her sailing forward into his arms.

"Are you okay?" It was surprising how gentle Samuel's strong hands were when they circled her upper arms and eased her away from where she'd sprawled against his chest.

"*Ja.* I can see now, though, why Belle's name is in spite of her disposition."

"Oh, I don't know. I think she's pretty likable right now." His hands now tenderly eased her closer as his head lowered.

Years ago young Abigail thought she'd learned something about kissing while foolishly enjoying the embraces of the charming Amish man she assumed she would marry. Older and wiser Gail acknowledged she knew nothing about it when this man softly kissed her lips. She'd expected a practiced flirt like Samuel to kiss as a way of taking. What surprised her was what he gave instead. Tenderness. Patience. Hope?

Her eyes opened when he ended the kiss. Self-conscious, Gail avoided meeting his gaze and glanced over his shoulder to see a shadow of a person in the lamplight in front of a second-story window. Although she knew it probably wasn't, in her bemusement, it seemed like someone was looking out at them. "It's like I'm sixteen again. Maybe I needed someone to keep a better eye on me then."

Samuel followed her gaze. "They care for you." When his attention returned to her, Gail felt the weight of his pensive regard. "I think you're too hard on yourself. *Gott* is a forgiving *Gott*. Why are you so special that you don't think you can be forgiven for past mistakes?"

Was that why she'd left and stayed away? Running instead of returning? Because she couldn't forgive herself for her foolish mistake, and didn't think that *Gott* would, either? When did she become that person? Theirs was a community of forgiveness. Before she could wonder further, Samuel kissed her again and she could think no more.

A staccato sound drifted into her ears. Gail eased back, unsure if she was disappointed or relieved when Samuel let her go. She sagged against the rail. The clip-clop of hooves on blacktop carried through the cicadas' song that hummed through the farmyard.

"I better leave. That's probably your *brieder* coming home from the baseball game." Humor broke through the obvious reluctance in Samuel's voice. "As long as I don't actually talk with Josiah about a horse, I can come back to try again later." He leaned forward to kiss her on the forehead. His voice deepened. "Although we both know it's not him I'm coming to see."

Dazedly, Gail watched Samuel untie Belle and agilely spring into the buggy before backing the mare away from the hitching post. Her gaze followed them down the lane before she was able to straighten from the rail. Regardless of her resolve, either sensitive or flirty, Samuel Schrock was dangerous to her equilibrium.

Samuel gave the buggy full of Lapp *brieder* a two-finger salute, but didn't stop when the young men called out a greeting. He let the mare set her own pace, smiling when he realized his heart was pumping faster than the tempo of Belle's quick trot. His matchmaking horse deserved whatever she wanted to do tonight. In fact, he might buy some of the premium feed in Miller's

Creek and treat the mare. Watching the dark countryside sweep by, his smile expanded at the memory of Belle threatening the persistent Lydia with snapping teeth while nudging the reluctant Gail into his arms. Maybe he should let his Standardbred sort out the women for him.

Relaxing the reins in his lap, Samuel's smile faded. But he didn't want any other women. It was becoming more obvious to him every time he saw her that he just wanted Gail. Gail and Lily. They were a package deal.

The cadence of Belle's hooves on the road was generally soothing music to his ears. Tonight it wasn't having the same mellowing effect.

Was he ready for fatherhood? Samuel always knew he was going to get married. While he certainly planned to have *kinder* in the future, he hadn't thought much of being a father. Now he did. Of being Lily's father. Gail's husband. Samuel inhaled a lungful of the night air as he realized how much he wanted to watch the inquisitive little girl grow up to be a young woman. His breath held in wonder at the thought of Lily as the eldest girl of a growing family, one with Gail as their *mamm* and him as *Daed*. Belle flicked her ears back in question at his long exhalation.

Ja, he was ready to be a husband. But was Gail ready to be a wife? An Amish wife? Her time in the Plain world was only a temporary one until her truck and trailer were fixed. She insisted her and Lily's future were in the *Englisch* world. Was Gail overreacting in her concern for Lily in regard to the Weavers?

Could he convince her to stay? Would it make a difference to Gail's fear of remaining in the Amish community, or her desire to stay in the *Englisch* one, if she was staying as a wife—*his* wife—instead of as a single mother?

Chapter Fifteen

"He likes you." Hannah's comment was quiet, as an exhausted Lily snored softly on the trundle bed in the upstairs room they were sharing.

The possibility sent a thrill through Gail. She concentrated on removing the straight pins that held the top of her dress together. "*Ja*, well. I'm sure he likes a lot of girls." To distract her sister, she added, "Tell me again why we use these things instead of buttons?"

"Because buttons are considered ostentatious and we aren't to wear anything that would make us *hochmut*." Already in her nightgown, Hannah removed her *kapp* and began taking down her hair. "And while, *ja*, Samuel flirts a lot, I haven't seen him look at other girls the way he looks at you."

Gail poked her finger in the process of putting the pins in the cushion for the night. Frowning, she pressed the stinging pad against her teeth. *You deserve that for not paying attention. And it'll hurt much worse if you don't remain on guard against him.* Lifting her hands, she unpinned her *kapp*. Just for a moment she wanted to bask in the possibility that she could be special to him. *Bask quickly, though, because it won't last.*

She dropped the pincushion on the plain wooden dresser and glanced over at her sister. Gail couldn't help drawing a breath at the beautiful picture Hannah made with her golden hair streaming about her in the candlelight as she brushed it. Releasing a long sigh, she prepared for the inevitable. "What about you? Are you interested in him?"

Hannah's nimble fingers began the much-practiced task of braiding her hair for the night. "Samuel? *Ach, nee.* I'm cotton, plain and simple, where he's satin—smooth and probably a challenge to work with." She smiled at her quilting analogy. "He might have flashed his charm in my direction when he first arrived, but we both quickly realized we didn't suit. And since then, through Ruth, I'd like to think we've become good friends." Hannah cast a gently teasing glance at Gail. "But it wasn't a friend he was coming over to see to-night."

Nee. At least not according to what he'd said after he kissed her. Gail began taking down her own shorter hair, dropping pins to plink on the wooden floor as her shaking fingers fumbled in the task. Friends were all they could be. He was Amish. She was just wearing the trappings temporarily. She would be returning to the *Englisch* world as soon as her rig was fixed. Her only relationship with him would be a business one. Her stomach twisted at the thought that some morning she might pull into the yard to pick him up and a young wife would follow him out of the house to bid her new husband farewell for the day. Gail frowned. That was assuming her rig wasn't repossessed by that time, and she was still in business.

Needing to push the melancholy images from her mind, Gail sought a distraction. Hannah's comment reminded Gail of the many young men who'd flashed, if not their charms, then their attentions in her older sister's direction when Gail was around four years ago. After slipping out of her dress and into one of Hannah's nightgowns, Gail sat on the double bed next to her sister. "Why aren't you married? There were many that I remember who wanted to walk out with you. Surely there was someone who suited?"

Hannah's teasing smile faded. She looked down and secured the end of her braid. "There was one," she acknowledged softly. "But in the end, we didn't suit at all."

Gail probed for more information, but discovered that her gentle sister was more adept than even she was at deflecting questions about her past.

"I hope that you will rethink attending the barn-raising with us tomorrow. I think Lily would really enjoy it. The *kinder* have a *wunderbar* time playing together and the older girls do a *gut* job of watching over them while the adults are working." Hannah slipped under the cotton sheet, the only covering on the bed in the warm summer night. Tugging the edge from under Gail, she flipped it back, inviting her sister to do the same.

Gail froze at her sister's words. She couldn't go. Of course she couldn't. Ruby Weaver and the bishop would be there. The threat they posed to her *dochder* and their authority over those she loved in the community shouldn't be dismissed.

But Hannah was right on one thing. Lily would love

it. In a childhood that'd involved responsibilities and chores from a young age, some of Gail's favorite memories of her youth were ones of playing with friends at work and social frolics. Her and Lily's current life left few options for her daughter to have playmates. But how could they add more? Perhaps find an *Englisch* church to join? For some reason, Gail couldn't get excited about the prospect.

"You know why I can't go."

"The community has grown since you left. There are a number of new families. New faces. Ruby spends little if any time with the unmarried *youngies* and no time with *kinder*. Even if she recognizes you, she'd have no reason to recognize Lily. With no *boppeli* pictures like the *Englisch*, it's unlikely that she'll recognize her son in your daughter."

Gail's heart pounded at the prospect. Would it really be possible? To be part of the Plain community again, even for a while? Perhaps for a long while?

Could she return to her family and way of life? Reaching out, she gripped the wooden headboard to contain herself before she leaped up in excitement. "I'll think about it," she murmured.

The risk would be great. But so would be the reward. What if Hannah was right? With their similar clothing and hairstyles, and never having seen her before, why would Ruby believe that Lily was Atlee's child? Gail snorted softly. Besides, if she were truly the jezebel that the bishop's wife had accused her of being, Lily could be anyone's daughter.

Gail slid under the sheet beside Hannah, prospects for the morrow racing through her mind. She adjusted the feather pillow under her head. If tomorrow worked for her and Lily living Amish, what about the next day, and the next? And if they returned to the Amish community, it would change the possibilities of a friendship—or more—with a certain Amish man.

Gail listened to the sound of cicadas and crickets that drifted through the open window. It was a long time before she fell asleep.

Samuel fished a few nails from the carpenter's apron at his waist while he slanted a glance at the man working on the next rafter over. Although they'd visited about farming and livestock after church Sundays and at auctions, he didn't know Jethro Weaver well. A few years older and married, he didn't attend the Sunday night singings where Samuel had gotten to know most of the unmarried men of Miller's Creek.

Placing one nail between his lips as he set the other, Samuel studied Jethro's profile as he secured a purlin board to the rafter. He wondered if Atlee had looked like his older *bruder*. Furrowing his brow, Samuel supposed the man could be considered handsome. The first nail slid deep into the rafter under the force of his hammer.

He plucked the second nail from his mouth, tasting a bitterness that had more to do with the thought of the man's *bruder* with a young, innocent Gail than the metallic flavor of the galvanized nail.

A clatter of boards disrupted the organized symphony of hammer strikes that filled the morning. At the sound of a shout, Samuel jerked his head up to see a trio of purlins tumbling down the rafter. Samuel dodged the falling lumber, but the boards struck Jethro Weaver, knocking the man off his precarious perch.

With a startled gasp, he fell toward the empty space between the rafters.

Lunging forward, Samuel grabbed Jethro's scrabbling hand at the wrist. Both men grunted at the jerk and pull on their arms and shoulders when Jethro's dangling feet swung out over the unforgiving surface forty feet below. Samuel gritted his teeth against the strain on his healing back. His knees and feet scrambled for any anchor on the structure to keep from being pulled into the chasm.

A sharp-edged board gouged Samuel's chest as he skidded forward a few inches, pulled by the man's hanging weight. His hat tumbled down past a white-faced Jethro. The man's eyes were wide with fear.

"I won't let go." The vow was to both of them. Samuel would either get Jethro up, or the bishop's son would take him down when he fell.

A sun-browned hand was thrust into Samuel's peripheral vision. Reaching down, it grasped Jethro under his opposing arm. A quick glance revealed a grim-faced Benjamin. Between the two of them, they lifted Jethro enough so he could get an elbow, then an armpit, over a board. From there, they worked until all three were perched, panting, on a secured purlin.

At the rattle on wood, Samuel shifted cautiously to see Malachi and Gideon scrambling their way toward him over the barn roof's limited surface. He shook his head and waved them back. When he went to rub his sore chest, he was surprised to find he still had his hammer clutched in a white-knuckle grip. Inhaling deeply to control his residual shudders, Samuel looked up to see horrified expressions on the two teenagers working farther up the slant.

As they looked as shaken as he felt, Samuel decided they didn't need further chastisement. Not too much anyway. Tapping his bare head, he advised them with a crooked smile, "You owe me a hat." Because his heart was still thundering, he added, "You knock us all off, it might mean more food for you at dinner, but it also means more work to do by yourself afterward. Have a care." The boys' jerky nods ensured there wouldn't be any more clumsy fingers for the rest of the day.

At the squeeze on his shoulder, Samuel gave a nod to Benjamin as his former coworker maneuvered himself back to where he'd previously been working. Samuel glanced at Jethro Weaver. The man's face was still as white as his shirt.

To help him regain his composure, Samuel observed, "*Ach*, I hope I didn't swallow a nail. I'm surprised I didn't drop my hammer. Good thing, as the grip was only just getting comfortable in my hand." The man nodded solemnly, but some color began returning to his face.

"You all right?" Samuel asked quietly as the whacks of hammering, at first intermittently, then in chorus, began again around them.

With tight lips, Jethro gave a single nod and shifted back to the rafter he'd been working on. Samuel regarded his own rafter. Pulling a nail from his carpenter's apron, he positioned it against the raw lumber in front of him. He had to wait a moment for the tremors in his hand to stop before he could strike it with the hammer. Glancing over, Samuel found Jethro had set his hammer down and was just holding on to the board they sat on. It was a few moments before the man picked up his tool and continued his work.

Samuel blew out a breath between pursed lips. He knew he'd be shaken as well if he'd almost met the same fate as a deceased *bruder*. Setting the nail with a light tap, he frowned at the number of strikes it took him to bury it into the wood. Whatever he'd heard about the man's overbearing parents and dallying *bruder*, he'd gained respect for Jethro Weaver today.

Without turning his head, Samuel knew it was Gail's green sleeve that brushed his shoulder as she reached for his glass. Even after using homemade soap instead of whatever it was she generally used, he inhaled an essence of something that was just…her.

He'd wondered if she'd come. Knowing there wasn't any good way he could've asked Zebulun Lapp or his sons about Gail's plans, he'd kept watching for the Lapp women's arrival. A smile had lit his face when he saw Lily scramble from the buggy dressed in Amish clothing. While carpentry had been in the forefront of his mind, the back of it was wondering how Gail and Lily were doing. And why she'd decided to come. And if she was having any issues now that she was here.

Twisting slightly on the bench set up for mealtime, he watched her pour lemonade from a glass pitcher. *"Denki,"* he murmured and smiled. Nodding, Gail met his gaze from under her lashes, giving a private smile in return. Though the table where he sat with the other men was shaded by a huge oak, Samuel flushed. Swiveling back to his plate, he was conscious of Gail reaching on his other side for his neighbor's glass. He forked up a bite of food, but didn't identify the applesauce until his third chew.

Maybe the sun had affected him more since he'd lost

his hat. Otherwise, why would one woman's small smile affect him so? In his peripheral vision, he watched her green arm appear and disappear down the line of men. Only when she moved to another table did he lift his attention to find Malachi watching him from over the planks that made up the makeshift table.

"Remind me not to work below you this afternoon. You're so distracted, I'm afraid you'll drop a hammer on me." After some initial chuckles, the men around them were quiet a moment, possibly recalling the tragedy that nearly occurred that morning.

Samuel cleared his throat. "*Ach*, if I did that, you know it'd be intentional."

"If you drop a hammer like you pitch a baseball, it'd miss anyway," Gideon joined in. The surrounding laughter came a little easier this time. "But you know, he hasn't been playing much baseball lately."

Accustomed to his *brieder*'s teasing, Samuel was surprised to feel his flush, instead of dissipating, creep farther down his neck. He missed his hat, wishing it was on so he could tug it down to shade his face. "I haven't had time, what with establishing a new business and doing the majority of the work at both farms."

"I thought you said he's been gone some evenings." Malachi took a bite of potatoes.

"He has. But not to play baseball. Because his glove still remains on the bench in the porch. And I haven't seen him at the games. I think he's playing at something else," Gideon mused. "In my experience, Samuel plays the field no matter what the sport."

"Besides the barn-raising, that was what brought me here today." Malachi stabbed a pickled beet. "I was hoping to see the woman who Ruth said Samuel was making a fool of himself over."

Samuel wished his normally reserved older *bruder* would just stay that way. Forcing a flippant smile, he retorted, "That's going a bit too far. *Woman* and *fool* are never used in the same sentence with me."

Deciding he'd had enough of his *brieder*'s comments, Samuel shoveled a few more quick bites from his plate into his mouth before standing and stepping back over the bench where he'd been seated. Studiously meandering over to where the empty plates were returned, he spoke a few words to men he passed on the way before taking a moment to chat with the ladies when he handed in his glass.

Looking in both directions to ensure that no one, particularly either of his brothers, was directly watching him, Samuel casually strolled over toward where Gail was now bringing desserts to cover a table set out for that purpose. When the other woman there left to get more plates, he stopped in front of the table. And in front of where Gail was passing.

"Anything you can recommend?" The question was pitched to be heard by others. When she stopped beside him, he murmured one that was not. "I'm glad you came. Are you doing all right?"

Reaching out a hand, Gail straightened a row of shoofly pie slices. "*Ja.* Those who have recognized me have been pleasant, as if I've never left. I hardly recognized Lily myself with her little *kapp*." Gail looked over to where a group of children sat on the ground with their plates in their laps, supervised by a few older girls. She twisted her hands together. "I'm hoping others don't recognize her, as well. I spotted Ruby while we were setting up and have made sure that whatever she's doing, I'm doing something else. Hopefully she wouldn't even remember, much less recognize me, but just in case, I thought it wise to keep some space between us."

"Probably a *gut* idea."

Her gaze flicked past him to the rafters that stood out like a skeleton against the blue sky. "Be careful up there. I heard about this morning."

Samuel bit back the quip he would've used with anyone else. She had a reason to be worried. The thought that she might be worried about him warmed him. The possibility that she might be grieving for the father of her child, not so much. He wanted to ask which had prompted her, but saw Ruth coming with a tray of plated pieces of cake for the table. "I will be, don't worry."

He raised his voice. "As long as you're certain that Ruth didn't make the lemon drop pie, I'll take a slice of that, then."

"Samuel Schrock, you've made certain that you just 'drop by' at supper time so frequently that if my cooking hasn't sickened you by now, it's not going to." Ruth set the tray on the table and started unloading the plates of cake into empty spots. "Besides, I made a cake today. But I'm not going to tell you which one." Pivoting, she walked a few steps before saying over her shoulder, "I'll let you know when I'm out of range so you can start talking again."

Gail smiled, her gaze following the petite auburn-haired woman until she disappeared around a corner of the house. "I've always liked her."

"*Ach*, well, took me a bit, but she grows on you. Like mildew on a house."

Snorting, Gail lightly tapped him on his arm. "She's *wunderbar*, and you could've done a lot worse."

Samuel's thoughts weren't so much on his *wunderbar* sister-in-law, but on how much he'd like to catch Gail's retreating hand and enfold it in his. "*Ja*. I suppose. She does me good by keeping Malachi out of my hair as she has him so busy on other things."

"You don't want a wife who's a driver?"

His gaze on the woman he'd met transporting horses, Samuel responded, "*Ja*, I suppose I could handle a wife who's a driver, as long as she's the right one."

Her blush contrasted sharply with the *kapp* she wore.

Looking over her shoulder, Samuel saw men were beginning to drift back to the barn. Dinner for them was over. Now was time for the women to eat before they cleaned up from the meal. "How long are you planning to stay?"

"We came in a couple of buggies. *Daed* said I could take Lily home in one whenever I needed."

Samuel would've said more, but among the exodus toward the barn were his brothers, who were giving him significant looks. A man peeled off from the group and headed hesitantly in their direction.

"Jethro Weaver," Samuel called cordially as the man approached. Gail immediately dipped her head and focused her attention on arranging the dessert plates on the table.

"*D-Denki*, S-Samuel." Jethro stammered over Samuel's last name, closing his eyes in obvious concentration before he could get it out. "S-Schrock."

Samuel had forgotten the man had a stutter. Now

more aware of Jethro's overbearing parents, he wondered if that'd contributed to the impediment. The bishop's only son had a slight scar above his lip and furrowed lines in the brow above his guarded blue eyes. He reached out a hand, as calloused and work-scarred as Samuel's own.

Samuel took it and they shook. "*Schon gut.* You'd have done the same for me."

Jethro didn't say anything more. With a glance at Gail, he returned his attention to Samuel and nodded. When he left, Gail stopped shuffling the desserts and turned back to Samuel.

He sighed. "I suppose, much as I might hope, the barn won't build itself. I best be getting back to it." With a last smile for Gail, he reluctantly started toward the work site. His pace picked up after a few steps. The faster they got done, the sooner he could spend the evening not playing softball. As long as he kept his distance from Josiah Lapp today, he still had a reason to stop by their farm tonight on the premise of talking with the young man about a horse. Once there, maybe he could coax the man's sister out into the moonlight and ask if she'd like to spend her life with a horse trader.

Turning, he looked back to see if Gail was watching him, like he wanted to be watching her. His steps slowed when he saw the bishop and his wife standing in front of the table where he'd just been. Gail was nowhere in sight.

Chapter Sixteen

From his position up on the beam, Samuel could see a group of young children darting into the area between the construction and where the women were cleaning up from the meal. Knowing there were older children keeping charge of them, he wasn't worried. Amish *kinder* were accustomed to being at functions where men were working and knew to stay out of the way. He searched for Lily among them and smiled around the nail in his mouth when he spotted her dainty form. With her dress, miniature apron and blond hair under a diminutive *kapp*, she looked so Amish it was hard to envision her in the purple baseball cap and shorts she usually wore.

Setting the nail, he hammered it in. At a shriek from below, he glanced down to see an older Amish woman had waded into the group of children and grabbed Lily by the little girl's upper arm. Lily shrieked again and pulled back, but was no match for the woman.

The hammer was already on the beam and Samuel had begun his descent by the time the frightened wail "Mommy!" reached his ears. Splinters cut into his hands as he slid down the wood of the ladder, barely touching the rungs with his feet. Within scant heartbeats his boots thudded on the ground. A few ground-eating strides later, he swept Lily into his arms, breaking the black-clad woman's grip on the little girl's arm. With tears wetting his neck, Lily clung to him like a tickseed on socks.

Pivoting so he was between the girl and the rawboned, gray-haired woman who reached for her, Samuel stared into the face of Ruby Weaver. Although the color of her narrowed eyes was a faded blue, the look in them was pure steel as they matched his glare. Her lips pressed into a line as flat as the beams on the half-built barn.

"Who is that girl?" It was more of a growl than a question.

Samuel heard the percussion of running feet on grass before Gail skidded to a halt beside him, her face as pale as the cap on her head. Initially reaching for Lily, she seemed to think better of it when the little girl tightened her hold around Samuel's neck. Gail sidled closer to him, as well. Samuel longed to put his arm around her in dual protection and support, but knew that was impossible, even without the attention they were drawing from those nearby.

Her attention now focused on Gail, the older woman scrutinized her. "I remember you. You were the one provoking Atlee before he and Louisa were married. You were one of the Lapp girls. The one who left." Targeting Samuel again, Ruby tilted her head, trying to look around him to see Lily. Samuel adjusted his position so he blocked her view of the girl. Lily lifted her head and reached for her mother. Samuel tightened his grip. Without a murmur, Lily settled back in his arms.

"I asked you a question." The bishop's wife spoke again, in a tone that indicated she didn't usually have to repeat a request. "Who is that girl?"

Gail stiffened beside him. "That's my daughter."

Ruby shifted her penetrating gaze between Gail and the petite head pressed against Samuel's shoulder, darting him a suspicious look, as well.

"How old is she? And why is she blonde when you're dark?"

This time, when Lily reached for her mother, Samuel let her slide from his arms to Gail's eager ones. He figured both mother and daughter needed the contact.

"Ruby Weaver, if you know her, you know her sister. And her *mamm*. Both of whom are blonde."

"What do you have to do with this?"

Ach, she had him there. What did he really have to do with the pair beside him beyond realizing they were becoming more vital to his life than most anything else in it? Samuel crossed his arms in front of him. "I work with her in my horse-trading business."

The woman looked smug. From how easily the creases on her face fell into place, it was an expression she wore often. "Ah, *ja*, you took the business over from Elam Chupp. With my husband's support and approval."

Just in case Samuel forgot. And just in case he didn't know that Bishop Weaver discussed community things with his wife.

"*Ja*. It's been *wunderbar*. Thank you for asking. I don't suppose that you and the bishop would be in need of a new buggy horse? I've seen some fine ones. Ones

that'd get you to church so fast your head would spin."
The woman couldn't be charmed. Samuel didn't know
why he wanted to poke at her like a boy who'd found
a snake. Well, he did know. He wanted to take her attention from the two beside him. The two he wanted
to protect, but had no right to.

"We're more than capable of getting anything that
we might need." Ruby curled her lip.

"*Ja.* I heard that about you." Samuel felt the slight
elbow poke of Gail, still standing tensely beside him.
He knew he should back off, for as many reasons as
boards on the barn beyond them, but he found himself
rolling his weight forward on the soles of his work
boots. This woman had been a factor that'd forced Gail
from her home and into a four-year struggle by herself.
She wasn't by herself any longer.

Before he could say anything more, a flash of dark
purple materialized in his peripheral vision. Stiffly
looking over, he saw his bantam-sized sister-in-law
plant herself between Gail and Ruby Weaver.

"Abigail Lapp, I know you haven't done this for
a while, but we haven't finished cleaning up. If you
wanted a break, you should've said something. I know
it'd be easier if we'd just use paper plates when feeding
this many folks, but food always tastes better with real
utensils and plates. Leaves us a lot of dishes. Which
aren't done yet. So if you don't mind getting back to
work…" With a hand on Gail's back, Ruth Schrock directed her toward the crowd of women who were watching from the area set up for washing dishes.

"I wasn't done with her yet."

Ruth glanced back over her shoulder. "*Ach*, neither
am I, as the dishes won't wash themselves. Maybe you

can catch up some other time, but not when there's work to be done." Ruth shot a look at Samuel. "Speaking of which, haven't you got somewhere else to be?" She jerked her head toward the unfinished barn.

Without another word, she accompanied Gail back toward the women, who parted like the Red Sea as they passed. Samuel watched until they stopped in front of the farthest wash station and Gail, obviously reluctant, let Lily down from her arms. The girl didn't stay on the ground for long, as Willa Lapp swept her up and settled her on her own hip as she manned a dish towel while Hannah slid in next to her and began drying plates.

Satisfied that Gail and Lily were safely surrounded, Samuel turned back to a frowning Ruby Weaver. The smile that always came naturally to him was forced. "I've been given my orders. I've got things to do." Heading toward the barn, he could feel the bishop's wife's attention—hotter than the summer sun—burning down his back.

Her ominous words rumbled after him. "So have I."

At the bell for an afternoon drink break, the men scrambled down from the barn like ants on a hill. As soon as Gail saw Samuel's feet hit the ground, she moved toward him, trying to make her purposeful direction look as nonchalant as possible. She paused to pour lemonade from the pitcher into a few glasses before she reached him, nodding at the men she vaguely remembered as she went. Lily was under the diligent care of her family.

She'd almost left, but Hannah, Ruth, Willa and some of their friends had formed a border around Gail and her daughter since the confrontation with Ruby. They'd kept Lily entertained by having her help with various small tasks. Gail's heart, the part that wasn't frozen with fear, had swelled with gratitude. She'd looked up from dishes occasionally and caught a few stares aimed in her direction from Ruby and her few confederates, but no one came near.

By the time she'd worked her way to Samuel, he was in conversation with Malachi and Gideon. He smiled at her approach. Gail couldn't help feeling warmed by the look in his eyes. When she filled a glass for Malachi and Gideon first, their smiles of thanks were edging closer to smirks.

"*Denki*, Abigail Lapp." Gideon nodded his appreciation for the refreshment. "Malachi, I talk with Samuel enough at home. I doubt he'll listen to me here any more than he does there, so I might as well go speak with Reuben Hershberger. Now that we have a few more draft horses, we can handle some bigger pieces of equipment."

"Don't feel bad, *bruder*. He never listened to me, either." Malachi shot an uncharacteristic wink at Gail. "Probably depends on the speaker. Anyway, I see Ruth trying to catch my eye. I'll see if she needs anything carried to the buggy while I'm down from the barn."

Samuel called after his departing older *bruder*. "She caught your eye a long time ago. It just took your feet a while to catch up."

Gideon snickered as he left. Malachi waved away the comment without turning. Gail found herself alone, facing Samuel. The blush that crept up her cheeks surprised her. "Drink?" she offered awkwardly.

Her blush spread at his smile. *"Denki."*

Pouring lemonade into the glass he held, her eyes

widened at the smears of red on the damp surface. "What happened to your hand?"

When Samuel rolled his free hand palm up, she gasped. Samuel examined his hands as if he hadn't noticed the bloodstains and imbedded splinters there. "*Ach*, when I heard Lily's cry, I wanted to get to her as soon as possible. I guess the quickest route wasn't the friendliest."

"You're bleeding. Again." Gail set the now-empty pitcher on the grass beside them and reached for his hand. Holding it open, she gently touched one of the many splinters there. "I'm sorry you keep getting hurt protecting my daughter."

He shrugged. "She's worth it." He captured her gaze. "Are you all right?" The question was as soft as the look in his eyes.

Gail blew a stream of air through pursed lips. "*Ja.* I think so, at least." She lifted her free hand, which trembled slightly. "A bit shaken. I've been afraid of this for years. But you and Ruth deterred her. And now we have a human fortress surrounding us." Gail looked over her shoulder to find Lily assisting Hannah in providing drinks. "I'm amazed and humbled by how many friends I still have here, as if I'd never left. But Lily and I will go as soon as the drink break is over."

"It's *gut* having family close, *ja*?"

Gail turned back to find Samuel's gaze still on her. His look was intent enough that she knew it wasn't a simple question. Correction, the question was simple— the answer, not so much. But he was right. "It is. I only hope…" There was too much that she hoped for to say right here. The men were returning to their tasks. The exterior of the barn would be completed before nightfall. A few glances were thrown their way. Suddenly self-conscious, Gail let go of Samuel's hand. "If you can wait just a moment, I'll get something to clean your hands up a bit before you go back to work."

"I reckon I can do that."

Gail whirled toward where the women had been advised a first-aid kit was kept in the house.

"Gail." She turned back to see Samuel's hooked grin. He nodded to the pitcher at his feet. Returning with a grunt, Gail picked it up and hastened toward the makeshift table where she left the jug before rounding the corner of the house to enter the utility room door for the first-aid kit. Having located the white plastic box, she hurried out the door, directly into the path of Ruby Weaver and her husband, the bishop.

Her heart slammed in her chest as hard as the screen door that hit her in the back. After a stricken glance at their stern faces, Gail's gaze darted over the deserted area around her. A side yard with a few shade trees and a clothesline, it was on the opposite side of the house from where the day's activity was centered. She was alone. Ruby Weaver had chosen her ambush well.

"Abigail Lapp." Bishop Weaver's voice didn't invite any response. "I am told that you have a child. A child who is Amish."

Her eyes wide, Gail pressed her lips together, clutching the first-aid box against her churning stomach.

"An Amish child needs to be raised in the Amish community. Not an *Englisch* one. An Amish child needs to be raised by two parents, not by a woman without a husband," he admonished.

"She's *my* daughter." Gail could hardly get the words out.

"She is Amish and needs to live that way. An individual must be prepared to sacrifice for what is best for the community. We have a husband and wife in the community who are childless. They will be *gut* parents for the girl, raising her in the Amish way of life. I will speak with the ministers and deacons. You will be advised when the exchange is arranged." Matter obviously settled, he pivoted and left without a backward glance. Ruby Weaver gave Gail a smug smile before she spun and followed her husband.

Gail staggered to the base of an oak that shaded the side yard. Bracing a hand on its rough bark, she got sick. She'd forgotten the kit she grasped until she raised that hand to wipe her sweating face and the plastic grazed her cheek. Tossing it aside, she numbly heard it bounce across the grass.

"Gail, I need to get back up on the barn." Samuel came around the corner of the house. "My hands will be fine until…" He halted abruptly at the sight of her.

Sick with fear and guilt, Gail found a convenient target for her turbulent emotions that boiled over as anger like water out of an unwatched pot. He was responsible for this. Her attraction to him was what'd gotten her in this situation. Her penalty for wanting this man was losing her daughter.

"Stay away from me! If I lose her, it's your fault. I was just beginning to trust you! If you hadn't ambushed me by setting up a meeting with Hannah, this never would've happened! I should never have listened to… This is what I was afraid of all along. Why couldn't you just have left me alone? I might not have been happy, but at least I had my daughter." Gail panted, tears streaming down her cheeks.

"Gail, what are you talking about?" Samuel strode a few steps closer.

Pushing away from the oak, Gail held out a hand to ward him off. She staggered when her knees almost gave out. "Bishop Weaver is taking away my baby."

Samuel's face went as white as the house beside him. *"Nee."* He rushed nearer.

Gail sliced her hand between them in a chopping motion. "And it's all because of you."

"Gail, we can sort this out. Nobody's going to take Lily from you. I'll do whatever I can to stop them. Please listen to me. We can…"

"No. You've done enough." Each word was punctuated by a hitch in her breathing. "Stay away from me. Why didn't anyone listen to what I thought was best? It was hard, but we were fine. We were going to be fine." Through tear-blurred eyes, Gail caught a flash of dark color. Clearing her vision with a swipe of the back of her hand, she saw that Hannah had rounded the corner. Her sister shot a stunned look at Gail, before shifting it to Samuel in question. He shook his head.

Skirting Samuel in a wide circle, Gail stumbled to her sister. "We have to go. I have to find Lily and we have to go. Please help me find Lily."

"Lily's all right. She's with *Mamm*." Hannah draped her arm around Gail. Instead of leading her back around the house where crowds of people were gathered, she opened the door to the utility room and shepherded her sister inside.

Once there, Hannah released Gail to lean her against the washing machine. She opened the door to the kitchen and, just for a moment, Gail could hear the hum of women chatting while they worked before Hannah slipped through and closed it behind her. Moments later she returned with a glass of tea and wrapped Gail's shaking hands around it.

"Now, tell me what's going on."

The tea jostled in the glass, but Gail was gathering control of herself. Hannah's face grew increasingly pale as Gail relayed what Bishop Weaver had said. Knowing Gail's involvement with Atlee years before, she didn't ask any questions.

"I'll get Lily. You head to the buggy. I'll meet you there."

Gail nodded. "I'll stay at the farm until *Mamm* and *Daed* get home so I can say goodbye this time."

Hannah's blue eyes glistened with tears before she blinked them back. "I'll tell them we'll see you there. What are you going to do?"

Gail set the glass down on the washer and rubbed a hand across her mouth. Her lips were so numb from crying she didn't even feel them. "I don't know yet."

"I heard some of what you said before I came around the corner. I'm sure Samuel didn't mean for this to happen."

Just when she thought she was back under control, Gail had to draw in another shuddering breath before she could speak. "This wouldn't have happened if he hadn't interfered. I don't know what I'm going to do if I lose my daughter, Hannah. I have been trying so hard for so long just to keep her."

Hannah pulled Gail into her arms. "I know. We have to trust *Gott*. He knows your despair and your love for your daughter. He will not forsake you."

Gail nodded against her sister's shoulder and gave

her a last squeeze before stepping back. "I'll meet you at the buggy."

Hannah slipped out the door to the side yard. Gail watched her sister go before she, too, left the utility room. As she gently pulled the door closed behind her, she realized it was like her life. A door she'd been hopeful and yet afraid to open had been flung wide. The glimpse inside had been tantalizing, but now it was slammed shut. Now she just hoped they could get back to what they'd been living without it being irrevocably changed, as well.

It wasn't to be.

Even as she and Hannah hurriedly hitched the family's old mare to the buggy, Gail could see the bishop and his wife, dragging an obviously reluctant Louisa Weaver behind them, snaking their way through the checkerboard of parked buggies toward them.

Gail's fingers strangled the breeching strap in her hands. "Get Lily out of sight."

Hannah wasted no time hustling the tired little girl into the back of the buggy while Gail hastily finished hitching up the mare. Burned out of all other emotion, only fierce determination fueled Gail as she braced a hand on the horse and harness to work her way forward to face the approaching trio. She shot a glance behind them to the nearly roofed barn. *Oh, Samuel. I'm so sorry. I wish you were here. I need your strength and support.*

"Abigail Lapp." The bishop's voice rang out like he was addressing the congregation on Sunday. "You were going to run with the child. Back to the *Englisch*."

Gail pressed her lips together. She couldn't deny it.

"We brought Louisa to take the girl, as we feared

you would do so. Louisa and her husband will give the child a *gut* home. Bring the girl out now."

"No." Gail crossed her arms tightly over her chest to hold herself together. A quick glance at Louisa revealed the frail woman was shaking almost as much as Gail was.

"You," Ruby spit, joining the fray. "You lured my son into sin. I'll not have my *kinskind* raised by such a jezebel." She tried to look inside the shadowed buggy. Not seeing Lily, she stepped around Gail to stride closer.

Gail shifted to block her. "I was wrong to do what I did with Atlee, but you will not take my child."

"It's what is for the best of the community."

"It's what is for the best for you." Gail's heart was pounding as she stared the woman down.

"N-nee!" Both women jerked at a nearby shout. Jethro Weaver was winding his way through the buggies at a jog. Gail initially thought his stammer was due to exertion until she recalled his stammer earlier with Samuel. "S-s-stop this now!" He jolted to a halt between his mother and father. "You w-will not t-take someone else's ch-child."

Ruby narrowed her eyes at her only son. "You stay out of this. The girl is Atlee's. You and Louisa will raise her."

"N-nee. I w-will decide what h-happens in my own household." Jethro strode over to grasp his wife's limp hand. "Louisa is w-with ch-child." Both of them were red-faced. Gail was too stunned to care if it was due to embarrassment at the announcement or the situation.

A change came over Ruby at the disclosure. For a moment a wistful look was evident in her pale blue eyes. But it was for just a moment. Quickly her face tightened again. "But Atlee's child…"

"You w-will be glad about m-my ch-child." Jethro's throat worked as he swallowed. Briefly breaking his mother's stare, he glanced at Gail. "Go."

Gail didn't need to be told twice. She hurriedly climbed into the buggy.

"We will talk further of this." Ruby marched over to stand next to her husband, confronting the younger couple.

"*Ja*, we w-will, but n-not n-now." Jethro loosely put his arm around his wife's shoulders and turned her in the direction of the distant barn. After a look back at Gail, the bishop followed after them.

Ruby stood immobile, staring into the depths of the buggy as Gail released the brake. "That is Atlee's child. She'll not be raised by a single jezebel in this community." Her glare returned to pin Gail in place. "Your… friend is still somewhat new in this community. His horse business depends on my husband's goodwill. Goodwill that would quickly fade should he be associated with such a hussy." The curl of Ruby's thin lips warned Gail that, should she remain, the bishop's wife would find a way to punish them for it. She, Lily and Samuel would all pay the price.

Shaking so violently she was surprised she was able to stay on the seat, Gail maneuvered the horse around the other buggies and headed toward the farm as fast as the mare could go.

Chapter Seventeen

The reins were slick in Samuel's sweaty hands as he guided Belle up the lane to his *bruder*'s farm. It was Thursday. He was hoping Malachi was at home instead of in town at his furniture business. As Samuel stepped down from the buggy, Ruth poked her head out the kitchen door and pointed toward the woodworking shop he'd helped Malachi convert for Ruth from one of the unused outbuildings on their farm.

When Samuel nodded and waved back, she disappeared again. Hands on hips, he took in the neat farmyard, although his thoughts were far from there. It'd been almost a week since Gail left the barn-raising and, from what he understood from Hannah, the community. When he thought they'd both had time to calm down, he'd called her. She hadn't answered and hadn't called back. After what she'd said…

Their last conversation had replayed in his mind over and over again. She'd been right. It'd been obvious from the start that she'd wanted to keep her distance. From him. From Amish. But he'd taken it as a challenge to his much-touted charms and pursued her anyway. And then… And then he'd fallen in love with her. With them both.

Picking up a small rock from the gravel under his feet, Samuel threw it. Belle jerked her head up as it clattered against the barn. Yes, he'd manipulated Gail. He'd set up the intentional meeting between her and Hannah originally because he was growing interested in his *Englisch* driver and he wanted any excuse to see her more. It'd also been an initial attempt to see if he could begin to crumble the Amish-to-*Englisch* barrier between them. Because of what he wanted. Not paying any mind to what Gail wanted. And look where it got her.

He certainly couldn't do what he really wanted anymore, which was to marry her. So if he couldn't do that, well, at least he could do this.

Ducking his head in the doorway, Samuel blinked a few times to adjust to the dimmer room after the glare of the summer midday sun. Inhaling the familiar scent of cut lumber and whiff of stain, Samuel glanced up to see dust motes floating in the sunlight that streamed through the skylights and high windows at the end of the building. A quick scan of the neatly ordered room found Malachi sitting on a stool at the workbench along a wall. His older brother looked up from where he deftly worked a sanding block on the flat side of an oak board.

Samuel sighed in resolve as he strolled toward where Malachi was working. "Smells better than when it was a hog house. Looks better than the last time I was in here, as well."

Malachi grunted, but didn't stop his practiced strokes over the board as he watched his brother's approach. Samuel's gaze drifted over other pieces of oak neatly stacked on the bench. "A cradle?"

Malachi hesitated before nodding with a sheepish smile. Samuel hid his own grin at the flush of red that edged up his *bruder*'s neck. He was thrilled for his older brother.

"As particular as she is, I'm surprised she didn't make her own." Ruth was an exceptional woodworker. Samuel respected her standards, but not the few times early in their relationship that she'd called him out when he hadn't matched them.

Malachi's smile expanded. "*Ja.* I had to convince her that I like doing things for her." His gaze dropped to the shaped oak in his hands. "And the *boppeli.*"

"*Ja.*" Samuel agreed faintly, but his hand clenched into a fist. He wanted to do things for the woman he loved.

But for him, the doing of things would be far easier than any convincing. After their last conversation, he didn't think convincing was at all possible. Reaching out a hand, he stroked it over the top piece of oak in the stack. It was smooth as glass under his fingers.

"I imagine a *boppeli* will change a few things in your life." Samuel strove to act disinterested as he lifted and examined some of the cradle components. "Will Ruth finally stop working when the *boppeli* arrives?"

Malachi tipped his head as he considered the possibility with his always busy wife. "I'm thinking it will slow her down some."

"*Ja.* I figured you might be busier, as well." Samuel closed his eyes as his pulse accelerated. This was what he came for. Might as well get it out there. As soon as he could swallow past the lump in his throat.

"Busy enough to need another worker at the shop?" Attention fixed on the oak in his hand, Samuel heard the rhythmic strokes of the sand block abruptly halt. He felt Malachi's sharp gaze on him. He waited until he heard the block slide again across the wooden surface before he turned to his *bruder*.

Although his hands had resumed their task, Malachi's eyes were still on Samuel.

"Part-time?"

The lump wouldn't go away. Samuel swallowed again. "Full-time."

Malachi's brow furrowed between his thoughtful eyes. "Even when you were a *kind*, you always talked about having a horse business. I thought it was what you always wanted."

Samuel twisted his lips at the brief realization and abrupt loss of his dream. "Now I want something else."

"Something? Or some*one*?"

Inhaling sharply, Samuel conceded, "I don't think I'll get the someone, but the something is helping her get what she wants."

"And you think this is it?"

"She needs money. More than she can earn. *Ja*, I love horse-trading, but it doesn't make much money. Sure, it's enough for me to live on here, but not enough for what she needs to keep Lily in the *Englisch* world."

"You think she'll accept it from you?"

"What's with all the questions? Are you willing to give me a job or not?" This was hard enough as it was without the soul-searching grilling from his brother. It wasn't as if he hadn't asked himself the same questions. And hadn't liked the answers.

"I think I'd be surprised if the woman who I observed would be willing to take money from anyone."

Samuel shifted to stare blindly at the woodworking
equipment in the compact room. "I'd figure out a way
to make sure she gets it."

"You already quit the horse-trading business?"

"I put out word at the track that I wouldn't be coming anymore and was looking for someone else to do
it." Samuel faced Malachi again and spoke through
clenched teeth. "So do you have a place for me at
Schrock Brothers' or not?"

Setting his work on the bench, Malachi rubbed a
hand across the back of his neck. "I'm already getting
one new mouth to feed. If you don't find work, you'll
be at my door making another."

Samuel knew his brother was teasing, but he wasn't
in the mood to joke back. "You don't have to worry
about that. Somehow, I'll make my own way."

"*Ach*, that's not what I mean and you know it. Of
course there's always work for you in the business."
Shaking his head, Malachi stood from the stool and
clapped a hand on Samuel's shoulder. "What happened?
I remember a time when you told me that when you
found the woman you wanted to marry, you were going
to make it less complicated than my courting of Ruth."

For some reason the warm grip of his *bruder*'s hand
allowed Samuel to relax for what felt like the first time
since Gail told him that she never wanted to see him
again. "If that's what you called courting, you needed
some advice." Samuel put his hand up to rest it on Malachi's calloused one a moment before dropping it back
to his side. "At the time it looked a little easier from my

angle. Had I known then what I know now, I might've been a little more sympathetic to your plight."

"*Bruder*, I know you, and I have more confidence than you that *Gott* will help you through this. You've skated through your relationships with women, relying on your charm. Mayhap this time you need to rely more on Him." Malachi tightened his grip on Samuel's shoulder briefly before letting go. "But you're not getting out of doing most of the farmwork."

Samuel nodded, recognizing his *bruder*'s comment as an effort to make him feel better. With a halfhearted retort, "Only because I do it better than you or Gideon," he headed for the door, his heart aching with equal parts relief and regret. He might not be able to be with Gail and Lily, but at least he could help them stay together and survive in the *Englisch* world.

Ducking out the low doorway, Samuel lowered his eyelids against the bright glare of the afternoon after the dimmer interior of the converted workshop. Hand on the rough boards of the doorjamb, he kept them down as he mouthed a prayer. *If she could find a way to forgive me,* Gott. He squeezed his eyes shut. He had no right to ask, but he added the words anyway. *And if You could help them find their way back home.*

Gail pushed the bank's recent letter and the calculator aside. She could punch all the numbers on it she wanted, but they wouldn't change the outcome. Even if all her customers returned after her absence, with or without Samuel's—her hand clenched on the pen she held—business, she'd lose the truck and trailer.

She'd made frantic calculations with numbers that were more wishes than realities—more part-time jobs, a full-time one, what she could get with her education and experience anyway—and came up with the same results. She loved her daughter, but love alone couldn't put a roof over Lily's head or feed her, something Gail could barely do now, much less pay any kind of childcare. There'd be no time or money to treat her daughter to any kind of life. And they'd always be only one step from disaster.

The pen rolled across the table's chipped Formica surface as Gail put her head in her hands. According to what the repair shop had said on the day of the accident, her rig would be ready tomorrow. With no way to do business, she hadn't needed the phone. Since she paid by the minute used, she'd kept it off. Numbly, she reached over to power it up.

Although it twisted her heart to consider it, maybe Lily would be better off in the Amish community with a two-parent family. In contrast to the bishop and his wife, Jethro Weaver seemed a decent man. Food and housing for her daughter would be no issue. She'd also have friends to play with. Community. And now a younger sibling. One parent would always be around, as an Amish wife's primary role was to run the home and family.

Gail's eyes welled with tears when she realized her parents could then see Lily. Maybe from a distance, at church and frolics. Maybe closer, depending on what could be worked out with the family Lily lived with. But at least they would see her.

But Gail would not. She couldn't stay in the Amish community and not be with her daughter.

Rasping in a breath, Gail's shoulders shook with

suppressed sobs. She started at the touch of a hand on her arm.

"What's wrong, Mommy?"

Gail slowly sat up to find Lily watching her somberly. Snagging a tissue from a box on the table, Gail wiped her eyes and nose before opening her arms to draw her daughter into her lap. "Sometimes mommies get sad."

"Do you miss your Amiss family?"

Gail reached for another tissue. "I do, sweetie." After dabbing her eyes again and taking a few shaky breaths, she cuddled Lily against her chest. "What would you think about living with the Amish?"

"Would we have horses? And ride in a buggy again?"

Gail almost smiled at her daughter's first thoughts of a changed world. "Yes, but it would mean giving up TV and cartoons."

Lily was quiet a moment. "Would I see my *gr-gross-mammi* and *daadi*? And Hannah and my *onkels*?" She stumbled only barely over the unfamiliar words.

Gail pressed a fist against her lips to quell their trembling before she kissed the blond head nestled under her chin. "You might see them, but you wouldn't be staying with them."

"Would I see my Amiss man?"

Gail's hand tightened, wadding the tissues in it into a tight ball. Oh, how she longed to see Samuel. To apologize for how out of control she'd been that day. Yes, he'd arranged things without asking, but the fault for Saturday's situation wasn't his. She was the one who'd ultimately decided to meet with her family. And she was the one who'd decided to go that awful day. The fault had been all hers. A tear ran a hot track down her nose to drop onto Lily's hair. "You might. I don't know."

Lily's little chest rose on a sigh. "I miss my Amiss man."

Gail's voice wobbled as she responded. "I know, sweetie. I do, too."

The perfect situation would've been to marry Samuel. Ruby could hardly argue against a biological mother in a two-parent family, no matter what she tried to stir up. Gail and Lily could return.

And Gail could be with the man she now knew she loved with all her heart.

She'd tumbled the rest of the way for him that day. Before that last, awful confrontation. It'd been a hard fall. Maybe that'd contributed to her overemotional reaction. Sensitive Samuel had pulled her in, charming Samuel had tightened the knot and protective Samuel had sealed the deal. For a while, when she'd thought there was a chance things could work out, that she and Lily could stay in the community, Gail had been counting the minutes until that evening, hoping Samuel would stop by the farm and she could give him a hint of how she'd felt.

Instead, she'd shrilled at him like a banshee and told him to leave them alone. Samuel probably never wanted to see her again. Gail couldn't blame him. *If this is the way you treat someone you love, he's better off without you.* With the wadded tissues in her hand, she dabbed at a fresh trickle of tears.

At the harsh vibration of the phone on the table, both Gail and Lily jumped. Gail reached over to turn the device toward her and saw a number she didn't recognize. Surely the bank wouldn't be calling so soon after sending the letter? Or was it the number of the communal Amish phone hut? Were the Weavers calling about Lily? Was it Hannah with news of her family? Hesitantly, Gail picked up the phone.

"Hello?" she answered dubiously. She cleared her throat. "Yes, this is Abigail Lapp." As Gail listened to the masculine voice on the phone, her tear-swollen eyes widened. Clutching Lily to her, she stood.

Chapter Eighteen

As the weight of financial worries had always hung over her during the time she'd worked at the track, Gail was surprised at the melancholy that washed through her as she pulled into the back parking lot Saturday for probably the last time. Turning off the key, she sat for a moment, listening to the transition from the rumble of the motor to the ticking of the cooling engine. The track and the truck had been good to her, in their own ways. Without them, she'd never have had this new opportunity.

You never know where *Gott's* path will lead.

Without the wreck, a situation that had prompted despair, she'd never have connected with the owner of the freight company. The owner who was so grateful and impressed Gail had avoided a collision with his wife and children that he'd been trying to contact her for a week to offer her a job driving for his outfit. He was providing the vehicle and a salary that she and Lily could easily live on.

But they would be moving to another state.

She still hadn't heard from the Weavers. Maybe Jethro had been successful in his intercession? For his sake and hers, she hoped so. She prayed so. At least, that might keep Ruby's malice from being directed at Samuel.

The truck's door creaked as she pushed it open and climbed out. Upon locking it, Gail paused a moment to gently pat Bonnie's bug-splattered external mirror. Determinedly dry-eyed, she headed to the stables to find George Hayes. This new job and move should be the answers to her prayers. Her financial worries were over. But if that was the case, why wasn't she happier about it? Gail forced a semblance of a smile when she finally found George leaning against the fence as he watched his equine charges in time trials on the track.

His weathered face creased in a pleased greeting as she approached. "Gail! It's good to see you again. I'm assuming your rig is fixed and ready to go?"

Nodding weakly, Gail drew a breath to tell her friend and supporter about her new job and plans to leave. She would miss others at the track, but George most of all.

He spoke again before she could get a word out. "Sorry to hear that Samuel Schrock is stepping away from the Amish horse-trading business. He was a likable guy."

Gail froze. Samuel was more than likable. So much, much more. "What do you mean?"

"He came by earlier this week. Said he appreciated working with me, but he was going to leave the business. Something about going back to work with his brother making furniture."

She blinked. Samuel didn't want the furniture business. He'd hate working all day inside. His passions were horses and farming. Had Ruby made good on her threat even though Gail was staying out of the community? The words were hoarse when she finally got them out. "Did he say why he was quitting?"

George frowned. "Not exactly. Something about different priorities. I'm surprised he didn't talk with you about it."

Blood drained from Gail's face, leaving her light-headed. Was that why Samuel had called her? Sometime after reeling with emotion from her new employer's call, she listened to voice mails that'd accumulated while the phone had been off. One of them had been from Samuel, left the Monday after the barn-raising.

She'd cried when she'd heard his unusually grave voice asking her to call him. Already several days old, Gail hadn't responded to his message. She didn't know how. Too vivid was the memory of the shock and hurt on his face when she'd railed at him. She'd wanted to blame him when all he'd done was what Gail had wanted all along reunite her with her family.

Surely he wouldn't leave everything he'd ever wanted because of her? Was that what the call had been about? Telling her he didn't want to work with her anymore? She should explain that was no longer a factor as she was leaving. She would help him find another driver. He could keep his business.

Pulling out her phone, Gail keyed up Samuel's number.

George glanced over from the notes he was making on his trotter's performance. "Hope you can catch him on that. He said he was shutting off his phone. Something about baptism."

Baptism? That ended *rumspringa*, which usually concluded when a man found a woman he wanted to marry. But who? Gail's breath caught as she thought about their time together. What if Hannah had been right? Had there been more to Samuel's attention to Gail than just his flirtatious nature?

"Oh, and I gave him my address. He didn't know yours and he said he wanted to send you something." George's voice tapered off as he focused on the track when the sound of a motor indicated another group of trotters were preparing for a trial.

Gail furrowed her brow. Samuel didn't have anything of hers to return.

Except, perhaps, her heart.

Did he even know it was his?

Why would Samuel quit the job he obviously loved? Unless…he loved something more?

She stared down at the name on her display. Samuel Schrock. The name seemed so flat on the device compared to the vitality of the man. Her trembling fingers bumped the keyboard and a question popped up. Did she want to delete the contact? Her hand hovered over the display. Did she? Was it already too late? Gail lifted her hand to her cheek to ensure it didn't accidentally touch the phone. Her memory lingered over the precious days spent with her family. The unquestioning support they'd given her. The support he'd given her.

Although she'd dishonored them in the community by leaving, no one in her family had let her down. She'd let herself down by running away and not trusting them. Yes, Samuel had done the wrong thing for the right reasons. But he'd given her back her family.

Gail drifted several yards down the fence from George before resting her arms on the rail and staring numbly at the racing Standardbreds as they thundered by behind the moving starting gate. The horses' black legs were churning so fast, they were a blur. Churning like her thoughts.

Wasn't that like her? Always running? She'd started running because of shame and fear. And she'd been running ever since.

This new job would be continuing that unhappy path. Certainly, it would be easier financially, but they'd still be running. How long was she going to continue? What was she teaching Lily in the process?

Ja, the job opportunity was an answer to prayers. But was it the only one? Gail's fingers tightened on the slickly painted rail. Or even the right one? Without the wreck, she wouldn't have had contact with the freight business owner. She'd also not have had the precious days at home, embracing how much she'd loved the Amish life. And she wouldn't have faced Ruby and her biggest fears.

Or recognize how she felt about Samuel.

She'd been running for years. Years, filled with struggles. What would've happened if she'd walked back up the lane that day instead of leaving?

Whatever would've happened, *Gott* would've seen her through it.

Oh, the time she and Lily had missed with family! What possibilities might she be missing with Samuel if she ran again, instead of taking a chance with him?

The horses swept into the backstretch. A few lagged behind the pack. They likely wouldn't make the time trials. But what if their purpose wasn't on the track, but somewhere else? What if *Gott* wanted her purpose to be somewhere else, as well? If only she'd trust Him and stop running. Was she courageous enough to take the chance? To trust the man He'd put before her?

Samuel. Oh, Samuel.

The beating of hooves and heavy breathing indicated the horses were pounding up the homestretch and nearing the finish line. Gail's breath was racing, as well. Was it possible that *Gott* wanted her to go home? The horses flew across the finish and began slackening their pace. Gail blindly watched them, her fingers clenched on the top board. Her breath slowed at the wave of peace that swept over her at the prospect. Home…

When Gail was certain her knees would hold her, she hurriedly retraced her steps down the rail to where the trainer was again making notes.

"George, do you have a minute?"

Four Belgian draft horses lifted their huge heads and watched from the pasture as Gail drove up the lane. Her arrival was quieter with just the truck and not the rattle of the horse trailer, but Samuel must have heard it anyway. He came to the door of the barn and watched from there as she parked the truck and got out.

Fair enough. After what she'd said the last time she'd seen him, Gail wasn't surprised he didn't want to come any closer. She'd have to be the one to close the distance between them. Gail just hoped Samuel would listen when she did. She hoped she wasn't wrong this time, with this man. Chest tightening with each step, she walked over until she faced him in the afternoon shade of the big barn.

"I'm making a goodbye trip."

Samuel winced before slowly nodding, his blue

eyes uncharacteristically somber under the brim of his straw hat.

Oh, she loved those eyes. Try as she might to avoid it, Gail knew she'd started to fall that first morning in this very farmyard.

"Since you've shared some adventures, I thought you might like to say goodbye, as well."

Glancing over to the truck, Samuel inhaled deeply and nodded again. "Is she in the truck?"

"She is the truck."

Samuel looked back at her in confusion.

"I'm selling Bonnie."

"What?"

"I'm selling Bonnie. And the trailer."

"But…what are you going to do?"

From his concerned bewilderment, Gail allowed herself to hope. She smiled crookedly. "I'll still drive horses. But they'll just be in front of me instead of behind."

Samuel's brow furrowed, then his beautiful blue eyes widened. The look in them gave her courage. Stepping closer, he lifted his arms like he was going to wrap them around her, before halting a foot away with clenched fists. "But what about the Weavers and Lily?"

"They were right. It is best for an Amish child to be raised in a two-parent home. But you were right about Bishop Weaver, as well."

Samuel shook his head in puzzlement.

"When you said he was something of a matchmaker. They had a part in bringing us together. If I hadn't confronted them, I'd never have had the courage to be your wife." Samuel didn't say anything. Gail's mouth grew dry. "If you ever get around to asking me," she added hoarsely. When he remained mute, Gail shifted her feet and slid her hands down the front of her jeans. They were as sweaty as the first time she'd met him.

"I'm hoping you were thinking about asking me. I'm hoping the way you acted and made me feel wasn't because I was just one of the many girls you've flirted with. That there was something more between us." Gail struggled to read his face, but for once, his attractive features were expressionless. What if she'd misread his actions? Her heart was hammering. "I've been wrong before when I thought a man cared for me. Oh, please don't let me be wrong this time, because what I felt for him is nothing compared to what I feel for you."

When Gail couldn't stand his stillness anymore, when she almost turned back to the truck to run again, Samuel lunged forward. She lost her breath when he swept her into his arms.

"Oh, Gail. There's more. There's so much more. From the moment I met you and you admitted you gave a name to a piece of metal, it's been you. You and Lily. Why do you think I worked so hard to get you back into my world? Maybe my methods weren't good, but my intentions were. I thought that was what you wanted, too. Until what you said…"

Gail lifted a hand to rest it gently at his mouth, stopping his words. "Samuel, you gave me back my family. I could love you for that alone, but my heart became yours for countless other reasons. I'm so sorry I lashed out that day. I was scared. I felt guilty."

Samuel tenderly kissed her fingers. "*Nee*, I thought about what you'd said. Thought about it a lot. You were right. I called you but when I didn't hear back, I figured that you didn't want anything to do with me. So I determined I'd find a way to help you support Lily, or at least be able to keep the Weavers from her. I couldn't stand the thought of you two struggling on your own. I was going to send you money."

"I wouldn't have let you. Just like I can't let you give up your job as the Amish horse trader."

He raised his eyebrows as he lowered her to her feet. "Why?"

"Because you love it. And I love you, so I want you to be happy." Gail didn't know if she could stand without his support. She curled her free hand behind his neck. Flicking the back brim of his hat, she smiled when it slid farther down his forehead. "Besides, I'll be in the market for a horse."

Samuel dipped his head, giving her a quick kiss on the lips. When he leaned back, Gail got lost in his dazzling grin. "You know what would really make me happy?"

"What?"

"You becoming my wife. And Lily, my daughter."

Gail's heart drummed so loudly, she was surprised he didn't ask what the racket was. "By all means, let's make us both happy." She kissed his clean-shaven chin. As a married man, it wouldn't stay clean-shaven for long.

"I'm glad you realize one thing." Samuel's eyes were suddenly serious. Gail's breath caught for a moment before she noticed the glint in them. "You'll need a horse. *Gut* thing you know a *gut* horse trader."

Gail closed her eyes, relaxed in his strong arms and thanked *Gott*. "*Ja.* Very *gut* for me."

Epilogue

Gail started for the window to again look out on the snowy landscape before she caught herself, heading instead toward the stove to make more coffee. It shouldn't be too long now. As was tradition, she didn't attend church the day of publication. Hannah had offered to stay with her, but Gail had sent her sister on, leaving Gail alone at her folks' farm with Lily. As soon as the deacon announced their intention to marry, just before the last hymn, Samuel would leave church and come straight here to tell her that they'd been "published."

Gail concentrated on keeping her hand steady so she wouldn't scatter a dusting of coffee grounds all over the counter. This time, instead of that marriage announcement four years ago, her jitters were due to excitement, not shock and dismay.

As she'd left before being baptized, Gail could return to the community, but she did need to make a freewill confession to one of the district church leaders. Although it would've been easier choosing one other than the bishop, she'd talked with Ezekiel Weaver. As it was freewill, with a set face, he'd solemnly offered counsel and determined to close the issue in private, probably to protect Atlee's reputation. Gail didn't care. To the Amish, a sin confessed was a sin forgiven. Gail was finally free of her burden of guilt and shame. Free to stop running and return home. Free to love Samuel. With her pending marriage to him, free to keep Lily.

Ruby Weaver hadn't acted on her threat against Samuel. Based on the way Samuel's business had grown and the respect he obviously held in the community, if she tried now, she'd have a difficult time turning people away from him.

After several weeks of classes, Gail and Samuel had both been baptized into the church. At the end of the ceremony, as was customary, she'd received the holy kiss from the bishop's wife. Ruby's eyes had been narrowed during the awkward encounter, but with the rounding under Louisa's apron visible where Jethro's wife sat on a backless pew nearby, nothing was said.

Maybe over time, they'd see about the Weavers' interactions with Lily. Gail knew, as she was forgiven, she needed to forgive, as well. Besides, she'd learned to trust her and Lily's future to *Gott*. He did a far better job with it than she had done.

A flash of brown and black went by the window. Samuel was coming up the lane. When Gail set the coffee can on the counter with a thud, Lily, Amish outfit complete down to apron and *kapp*, skipped over to her. Gail lifted her daughter to her hip so she could see out.

"Is our Amiss man coming?"

"*Ja*, Lily." She'd been teaching Lily the language of the Amish. "Our Amish man is coming." Gail slid a hand over her forearm, smoothing down the goose bumps that rose there at the privilege of claiming Samuel. Of being claimed by him.

"I'm glad he's ours."

Gail was surprised to hear her daughter voice her own thoughts. "Why, sweetie?"

"Because he's making our family bigger. And families are important."

Gail watched Samuel draw Belle to a halt. Breath pluming in the cold November air, he swung lithely out of the buggy, secured the horse and hurried toward the house. When he saw them looking out the window, he waved, wearing the biggest smile she'd ever seen on his face. And that was saying something for him. Heart full, Gail smiled and waved in return.

"They are indeed, Lily. They are indeed."

* * * * *

On Wednesday after work, Hannah drove toward home, the
twins in the back seat, and tried not to be nervous that Luke
was in the front seat beside her.

"I really appreciate this," he said. His car hadn't started this
morning, and he'd walked the three miles to Rescue Haven.

Of course, Hannah had insisted on driving him home. What
else could she do? It was cold outside, spitting snow, and he
was her next-door neighbor.

"I hate to ask another favor," he said, "but could you stop by
Pasquale's Pizza on the way?"

"No problem." She took a left and drove the two blocks to
the only nonchain pizza place in Bethlehem Springs.

He jumped out, and she turned back to check on the twins,
trying not to watch Luke as he headed into the shop. He was
good-looking, of course. Kind, appreciative and strong. And he
had the slightest swagger in his walk that was masculine and
appealing.

But he was also about to go visit his brother, Bobby, if he kept his promise to his ailing father. And when she'd heard about that visit, it had been a wake-up call: she shouldn't get too close with him. The fewer chances she had to spill the beans about Bobby being the twins' father, the better.

He came out of the pizza shop quickly—he must have called ahead—carrying a big flat box and a white bag. What would it be like if this was a family scenario, if they were Mom and Dad and kids, stopping for takeout on the way home from work?

She couldn't help it. Her chest filled with longing.

He climbed into her small car, juggling the large flat box to make it fit without encroaching on the gearshift.

She had to laugh at the size of his meal. "Hungry?"

"Are you?" He opened the box a little, and the rich, garlicky fragrance of Pasquale's special sauce filled the car.

Her stomach growled, loudly.

"Pee-zah!" Addie shouted from the back seat.

"Peez!" Emmy added, almost as loud.

"That's just cruel," she said as she pulled the car back onto the road and steered toward Luke's place. "You're tempting us. I may have to order some when I get these girls home."

"No, you won't," he said. "This is for all of us. The least I can do is feed you, after you drove me around."

Her stomach gave a little leap, and not just about the prospect of pizza. Why was he inviting her to have dinner with him? Was there an ulterior motive? And if there was, would she mind?

Don't miss
Finding a Christmas Home *by Lee Tobin McClain,*
available October 2021 wherever
Love Inspired books and ebooks are sold.

LoveInspired.com

LOVE INSPIRED
INSPIRATIONAL ROMANCE

UPLIFTING STORIES OF FAITH, FORGIVENESS AND HOPE.

Join our social communities to connect with other readers who share your love!

Sign up for the Love Inspired newsletter at **LoveInspired.com** to be the first to find out about upcoming titles, special promotions and exclusive content.

CONNECT WITH US AT:

Facebook.com/LoveInspiredBooks

Twitter.com/LoveInspiredBks

Facebook.com/groups/HarlequinConnection

HARLEQUIN

Heartfelt or thrilling, passionate or uplifting—Harlequin is more than just happily-ever-after.

With twelve different series to choose from and new books available every month, you are sure to find stories that will move you, uplift you, inspire and delight you.

Get 4 FREE REWARDS!

We'll send you 2 FREE Books <u>plus</u> 2 FREE Mystery Gifts.

Love Inspired books feature uplifting stories where faith helps guide you through life's challenges and discover the promise of a new beginning.

FREE Value Over **$20**